Praise for *The Restoration of Celia Fairchild*

"Celia F_____ _____olution for every problem except _____ _____tranged family before it's too late _____ _____armth, heart, and hilarity, Marie Bostwick dazzles with a story about taking risks and letting go of the past to make way for the future of her dreams."

—Adriana Trigiani, *New York Times*
bestselling author of *Tony's Wife*

"Perennial fan favorite Marie Bostwick has done something special. This new novel has all the hallmarks readers have come to love about her books—and then some. This bighearted tale of redemption, family ties, secrets, tough choices, and happy endings is filled with her trademark warmth and wisdom that will leave readers deeply satisfied."

—Susan Wiggs, *New York Times* bestselling author

"With gorgeous writing, Marie Bostwick has hit new heights with this surprising story of one woman's redemption. *The Restoration of Celia Fairchild* is wise, witty, and utterly compelling."

—Jane Green, *New York Times* bestselling
author of *The Friends We Keep*

The
Restoration of
Celia Fairchild

Also by Marie Bostwick

The Promise Girls
Just in Time
Hope on the Inside
The Second Sister

COBBLED COURT QUILT SERIES

Apart at the Seams
Ties That Bind
Threading the Needle
A Thread So Thin
A Thread of Truth
A Single Thread

TOO MUCH, TEXAS SERIES

From Here to Home
Between Heaven and Texas

HISTORICAL NOVELS

On Wings of the Morning
Fields of Gold
River's Edge

NOVELLAS

Secret Santa (with Fern Michaels)
Snow Angels (with Fern Michaels)
Comfort and Joy (with Fern Michaels)

The Restoration of Celia Fairchild

A Novel

MARIE BOSTWICK

WILLIAM MORROW
An Imprint of HarperCollins*Publishers*

P.S.™ is a trademark of HarperCollins Publishers.

HarperCollins books may be purchased for educational, business, or sales promotional use. For information, please email the Special Markets Department at SPsales@harpercollins.com.

FIRST EDITION

Designed by Diahann Sturge

Paint roller art on chapter openers © Pico Studio / Adobe Stock
Text bubbles on page 128 © Chief Design / Shutterstock, Inc.
Line art on page 146 © Dn Br / Shutterstock, Inc.
Ball of yarn on page 146 © Viktorija Reuta / Shutterstock, Inc.

Library of Congress Cataloging-in-Publication Data has been applied for.

ISBN 978-0-06-299730-2

21 22 23 24 25 LSC 10 9 8 7 6 5 4 3

For Mark Lipinski,
my best friend forever.
And ever.
And ever.

The
Restoration of
Celia Fairchild

Chapter One

The stage lights were blinding, not in a metaphorical way.

When the emcee introduced me and the audience began applauding, I exited from the wings, teeth bared in what was meant to be a smile but felt more like a grimace, squinting and blinking like a groundhog emerging from hibernation. I couldn't see a thing, including the black electrical cord that snaked from the front of the stage to the podium.

When I tripped and tumbled forward, I flailed frantically, like a cat who'd misjudged the distance from the balcony to the ground. If the quick-thinking emcee hadn't caught me under the arms, I'd have ended up doing a face-plant in front of seven hundred people who'd paid sixty dollars a head to eat chicken marsala and hear me talk.

Well . . . they didn't come to hear *me*. They came to hear Calpurnia, which isn't quite the same thing.

Against my better judgment, I'd worn a pair of five-inch heels to the fundraiser, hoping to stave off the inevitable comments of "Somehow I thought you'd be taller" that always followed fan meet-and-greets during my infrequent personal appearances. As many times as it's happened, I still never know what to say to that. I mean, what *can* you say? Sorry to disappoint you? I'll try harder? I drank coffee as a child and it stunted my growth?

I stand five foot four in my bare feet: not tall but not short either. In fact, it's the average height for American women. But that's not enough for Calpurnia's readers. They expect her to be above average in every way. And that (as well as the fact that I'm not really that famous and therefore not that deeply in demand) is why I almost never make personal appearances; after meeting me, people are bound to leave disappointed.

But how can you say no to a really good but sorely underfunded after-school program serving at-risk kids of single parents? You can't. Besides, my therapist said it was time for me to get out there again and she was probably right. So I squeezed into my only pair of Spanx and the glittery red evening dress that wasn't quite so tight only a few weeks ago, strapped on a pair of stupidly tall stilettos, and got out there.

Somewhere between tripping and tumbling, one of the heels broke off. After the emcee set me back on my feet, I hobbled toward the podium like Quasimodo.

A murmur of laughter rippled through the crowd. When my prayer for the floor to open and swallow me up went unanswered, I did what Calpurnia would have done: I brazened it out.

Gripping both sides of the podium, I leaned forward so my mouth hovered just in front of the microphone, and drawled, "Well. What can I say? I always *did* like making an entrance."

The crowd laughed again but this time they laughed *with* me instead of at me. I smiled. "Guess I don't need these anymore, do I?" I reached down, slipped off one shoe, then the next, and tossed them to a fifty-something man in the front row who, thanks to the sparkly green vest he wore under his tux, was the only person I could actually see. "Here you go, sugar. They're just your size."

The crowd went crazy, howling with laughter and applauding for at least a full minute. Honestly, I think that a lot of them thought I'd planned the whole thing, that this was just part of the show. And I guess it was, in a way.

But that's why I hate these things, because it's all a show. That's also why—only sometimes and only a little bit—I kind of hate my fans too. Because they aren't really mine, are they? They don't want me; they want the show. They want Calpurnia.

After I'd made brief remarks about the important mission of the program and how the money raised today would impact the lives of kids all over the city, somebody finally lowered the stage lights so I could see the audience and take questions. The man in the sparkly vest, still clutching my broken stiletto, was first to the microphone.

"This is really more of a comment than a question," he said. "But I'm a big fan. I feel like I know you and I wanted to say, well . . . I just love you."

See what I mean?

How can he love me? He doesn't even know me. And I've had enough of that!

Sorry. Deep breath.

Look, I get it that we are dealing with hyperbole here and that *love* is maybe the most overused word in the English language, the second most overused being *hate*. Sparkly Vest Man doesn't love me. He likes me or, more accurately, he likes what I write. It's a compliment. I get it. Sparkly Vest Man doesn't love me and I don't hate him. But I do find him irritating, more now than I would have even a few months ago.

It only took five thousand dollars and four months of counseling with a slightly cruel therapist for me to understand that the reason I keep getting my heart broken is that I am desperate, too desperate, to regain what was taken from me so many years ago. Desperation will make you do dumb things, like ignoring red flags and the warnings of too-frank friends.

But none of that was Sparkly Vest Man's fault, so I smiled and said the only thing I could say, "Well, I love you too, sugar," then took the next question, and the next, and the next.

They asked me about finances and fiancés, former wives, wished-for careers, and thwarted dreams. But really, they were all looking for the same thing, hope and a way forward. As they came up to the microphone to tell their stories, irritation gave way to tenderness, and then to admiration. Their vulnerability was touching and, as I thought about it, really kind of brave.

If I were as brave as they were, maybe I would have lifted up my hand, stopped them mid-question, and told them what a mess my life is, what a mess *I* am. But I'm not that brave. Even if I were, how does knowing that help them?

I did my best. I listened to what they were saying—and what they weren't saying—and tried to be the Calpurnia they were counting on, pointing them in the right direction. It's crazy that talking should be so exhausting but it is. I was grateful when the emcee said that we'd run out of time. The audience started to applaud once more. I smiled, and waved, and walked into the wings in my bare feet with the hem of my glittery red evening dress dragging behind me, carving a dusty trail on the black stage floor.

Backstage, the executive director of the program found me a pair of flip-flops, the thin, flimsy kind you wear for pedicures, then put me into a cab for the ride back to my apartment. The driver was kind of chatty but I deflected his questions and closed my eyes, making it clear I wasn't up for conversation. The only thing I wanted to do was get home, take off the glittery gown with the dirty hem, extricate myself from the boa constrictor death-grip of the Spanx, and go to bed.

I was tired, so tired that I thought about letting the call go to voicemail. But no matter how hard I try, even when the screen says "Number Unknown" or even "Possible Spam," I cannot ignore a ringing phone. There's this part of me that always thinks, or maybe just hopes, it'll be good news. Or bad?

Either way, I can't stop myself from wanting to know.

Months would pass before the verdict was in on Good vs. Bad. But from the moment I answered that call and a voice said, "Ms. Fairchild? This is Anne Dowling. I'm an adoption attorney," my life would never be the same.

Chapter Two

The almond croissants looked tempting. So did the chocolate. But I'd made up my mind. Today I would order a *plain* croissant. Why? Because Anne Dowling had called and it was a new day, with heretofore unimagined possibilities. And because, as my slightly cruel therapist kept pointing out, enough was enough.

When it comes to food and grief, there are generally two types of people: those who are so emotionally ragged that they can hardly force a morsel between their lips, and those who go in the entirely opposite direction.

I am the second type.

In the three months since my divorce, I'd gained nine pounds. Well, eight and a half after I stepped on the scale a second time, minus my socks and underwear, on the morning after the fundraiser. But half a pound didn't alter the fact that I had to change into yoga tights before leaving the house because I couldn't button my regular pants.

It's not that I'd been grieving the end of my marriage per se. In my long history of spectacularly bad relationships, Steve represented a new low—five affairs in three years of marriage, the first with the justice of the peace who performed our wedding ceremony.

Seriously, who *does* that?

Steve Beckley, that's who. My husband. Now my ex-husband.

If I'd been advising me instead of *being* me, I'd have seen it coming a mile away. My whirlwind courtship with Steve was a parade of red flags, all flapping like crazy. But "do as I say and not as I do" is kind of a theme with me, the irony of which is not lost on anyone who knows me. Marrying Steve felt like my last chance for the life I wanted desperately. Too desperately.

Look, I understand that the events of my childhood definitely played a role in my less-than-wise decisions about Steve. But no matter what my therapist says, not *everything* about my longing for motherhood is tangled up with my family issues; there's this little thing called biology, you know? The desire to procreate is a normal, natural, and powerful urge. I mean, it's not like I'm the only mid-thirties single woman in New York who wants to get married and have kids, right? We can't *all* be neurotic, can we?

The point is, I've done the career thing. I've even done the celebrity thing, albeit in a small way—I'm a D-list celeb at best, maybe even E-list—and it's fine. I'm grateful for the opportunities that have come my way. But . . . it's not enough. Being well-known to a lot of people who admire the person they think you are, the role you play, isn't the same as being important to a few people who truly know you and love you anyway, even if you're not perfect, or don't have all the answers, or do as you do instead of as you say. That's what family is: the people who love you anyway. That's what I long for. Is that so terrible?

But when Steve left, he took my last chance at that life with him. Or so I thought, until Anne Dowling called.

I quit writing "Dear Birth Mother" letters almost a year ago. By then, it was obvious the marriage wasn't going to last, and even I knew that bringing a baby into a family that was on the verge of falling apart wasn't a good idea. I also knew that trying to adopt as a single parent would be even tougher, so I gave up on motherhood altogether.

But a few of those letters must have still been floating around, because after reading through a pile of "Dear Birth Mother" missives, Anne Dowling's client, an unwed mother from Pennsylvania, narrowed the pool of potential parents who might adopt her baby down to three couples. Steve and I were at the top of the list.

A baby! After all these years, after the disappointments and dashed hopes, someone was actually thinking about letting me adopt a baby! At that moment, all the things that my therapist and I had agreed upon, the stuff about my desire for a child stemming from a deep-seated and probably unhealthy compulsion to re-create the family I'd lost, went right out the window. There was a baby and I wanted it. The therapist could just go pound sand.

But when I explained the change in my marital status, Ms. Dowling said, "Ah, I see. I'm sorry, Ms. Fairchild, but my client prefers to place the baby in a two-parent home," and my heart plummeted back to earth and crashed onto the rocks. I was desperate, *really* desperate. To have the thing I wanted most in the entire world just inches from my grasp, only to see it snatched away because Steve was a pathologically adulterous, card-carrying asshat was unendurable. And so I did what I'd promised myself I wouldn't: I played the Calpurnia card.

"You're kidding," Ms. Dowling said, laughing. "You're Calpurnia? My mother loves you. She sends me clippings from your column at least once a month."

This wasn't the first time I'd heard this. I say the kinds of things people want to tell their adult children but can't.

"Really? I hope you won't hold it against me."

Ms. Dowling laughed again, sounding almost giddy, which didn't surprise me. Unexpected celebrity encounters, even when the celebrity in question is as minor as I am, fill people with a strange delight. I was counting on that response, hoping it would help tip the scales in my direction.

"It doesn't seem fair to exclude you just because your husband walked out," she said once the laughter subsided. "After reading your columns, I know you'd be a great parent, single or not. Let me talk to my client and get back to you."

The next morning, she did. Even without Steve, I was still in the running. There were no guarantees, Ms. Dowling explained; there were two other families under consideration, as well as background checks to pass and hoops to jump through, the biggest being the home visit in the middle of August.

Still, I had a one-in-three chance, and a little over three months to get my act together. And that is why, even though the chocolate croissant was calling my name, I would order plain. A small step, perhaps, but an important one.

Starting tomorrow, I would forgo croissants entirely. I would go shopping for vegetables and join a gym. I would lose those nine pounds and six more besides. I would eat clean, possibly do a juice cleanse. I would start taking my own advice. I would become self-actualized. I would avoid cruel, selfish men and take note of flapping red flags. I would love myself, and live in the moment, and smell the roses, and seize the day.

I would wear smaller jeans and find a bigger apartment. They say it takes a village to raise a child. I needed to find one of those, and quickly. So I would join a church and the PTA and a book club. I would buy a crib and a stroller and those plastic things that you stick in wall sockets so kids can't electrocute themselves. I would purchase life insurance and make the maximum contribution to my 401(k).

I would do *all* of this. And more! In the next three and a half months I would transform myself into ideal parenting material and a completely different person.

But to make it happen, I needed more money.

As if my world hadn't been rocked enough already, Steve had been awarded significant alimony payments in the divorce settlement. I had to move out of our Upper West Side apartment with the doorman and peek-a-boo view of the park, and into a studio in Washington Heights with a shared laundry and view of the alley. It's fine just for me, but I couldn't raise a child there. I had to find a nice two-bedroom apartment in a safe neighborhood with good schools, preferably near a subway stop, and definitely within walking distance of the park. Apartments like that don't come cheap in New York, and so today I would ask for a raise.

That is why I was going to order a croissant, albeit a plain one. Because, in spite of all the things I've written about knowing your worth and not settling for less, I was dreading the conversation. (Do as I say, not as I do.) Anxiety consumes even more calories than grief and so I needed a croissant, badly. And a latte, with whole milk.

Ramona, who works at The Good Drop, a bakery and coffee shop four blocks from my office, spotted me examining the pastry.

"Hey, Celia. What can I get for you?"

"Large latte and a plain croissant."

"Plain? You sure?" She picked up a pair of tongs but made no move to retrieve my selection. "Guillermo tried a new filling today, pistachio with a touch of cardamom. Everybody who's had one says they're real good."

"No thank you, ma'am. I've got—"

Ramona laughed and I rolled my eyes. Why do people find this so hilarious?

"Celia, how long have you been in New York? Fifteen years? You don't have a Southern accent anymore, but after all this time, you're still ma'aming people?"

"It's a habit. It's how I was raised."

Ramona picked up the tongs again. My eyes drifted toward a tray of flaky, buttery pastry dusted with powdered sugar and sprinkled with pale-green pistachios, chopped fine as sand. I thought about my upcoming encounter with my boss, pictured myself sitting across from him in that desk chair, the one that always wobbles, and saying, "Dan, I want a raise."

My palms began to sweat.

"On second thought . . . I'll take the pistachio. And a chocolate." I paused, thinking about pants that wouldn't button and the fat content of pistachios. "Make the latte nonfat."

"How you holding up?" Ramona asked after shouting my order to the girl who was running the espresso machine. "Calvin told me about Steve. He left you for the lady who did your wedding ceremony? What a tool."

"No. He left me for his orthodontist."

Somehow I thought that having my husband leave me for his orthodontist (whose bill for Steve's invisible braces I was still paying) instead of a justice of the peace sounded less pathetic, but as soon as the words left my mouth, I realized that it didn't.

"Hey, before I forget," Ramona said, her face lighting up with the kind of anticipation people get when preparing to share a juicy bit of gossip, "that letter you got from the guy who ran up all that credit card debt and then had his car repossessed, Poorhouse Paul?" She clucked her tongue and slipped the croissants into a bag. "That guy was a hot mess. Loved your answer to him."

"Oh. Thanks."

Though I should be used to it by now, I always feel uncomfortable with this type of praise. I think of my column as a private correspondence between me and the person writing to me. Sometimes I forget that thousands of other people, more like tens of thousands, are eavesdropping on our conversation, poring over the letters to and from Dear Calpurnia for entertainment, or affirmation. Sure, their lives might be a train wreck but at least not as big a train wreck as Poorhouse Paul's.

"No, really, Celia. I'm serious. How can you be so young and so wise?"

I hate it when people say things like this. Calpurnia is the one with all the answers. Sometimes it feels like I'm just her scribe. Also . . .

"I'm thirty-seven. About to turn thirty-eight. I feel ancient."

"You're a spring chicken," Ramona said, flapping her hand. "But a smart one. If Poorhouse Paul had been writing to me for advice, I'd just have told him to quit whining and find a second job."

"Well, that's kind of what I did say. That and to find himself a good credit counseling company. I just said it more sympathetically."

Ramona shook her head. She wasn't really listening.

"I've worked hard all my life. Never took nothing from nobody. But these millennials? They're all like that Poorhouse Paul, expecting everything to be handed to them. Think they should get a trophy just for showing up. Won't take responsibility for their own bad choices." Ramona turned toward the twenty-something woman who was running the espresso machine. "You got that latte ready? Then come over here and watch the register for a while. I need a smoke."

The Good Drop was packed. I craned my neck, trying to find Calvin. Just when I decided that he hadn't shown up, I heard a familiar whistle, turned around, and spotted Calvin LaGuardia.

Calvin and I had met in this very spot about six years before. After taking a seat at the counter, I'd struck up a conversation with the very tall and large but impeccably dressed man on the next stool. When I asked about the origins of his unusual name he said, "I just made it up one day, along with my entire persona."

I loved that. It's such a New York story. Half the people in the city moved here in hopes of becoming somebody else, including me. The moment he said it, I knew in my bones that Calvin La-Guardia and I were destined to become friends. And we were, for close to three years. But things changed after I married Steve. It wasn't that I ghosted Calvin or anything; we still talked but not as often, and our conversation was more guarded. There were things I felt I couldn't tell him, mostly having to do with Steve. To start with, Steve was jealous of Calvin, which was stupid.

"How can you possibly be jealous of Calvin? He's the gayest man in Manhattan. If I climbed into bed with him stark naked, all he'd do is ask me to turn out the light. Which is a lot more than I can say for your friends. During our last party Joey backed me into a corner and tried to shove his tongue down my throat."

"He was drunk," Steve said dismissively, missing the point. As usual.

"Your friends are always drunk. Seriously, how can you be jealous of Calvin?"

"Because you spend *hours* on the phone with him! What do you talk about?"

"Stuff." I shrugged. "Recipes. Politics. Life. Work. Who wore what to the Oscars. What happened on *Real Housewives*. That's why I like Calvin; *he* talks to me."

Steve upped the volume on the basketball game.

"Yeah, I know. For hours."

Apart from having done it in the first place, the thing I regret most about my marriage was letting my friendship with Calvin lapse. When Steve left, one of the first things I did was call Calvin to apologize.

"I don't know what to say. I was an idiot. You always knew it couldn't work."

"Everybody knew," Calvin replied. "It wasn't just me."

"Yeah, and a bunch of them had no qualms about saying so right to my face. Just about everybody except you. Why? Because you knew I wouldn't listen?"

"Because I hoped I was wrong. I just want you to be happy, cupcake."

"Me too."

"Hey, do you want to come over? I just made a big batch of perogies. We can eat them and binge-watch old episodes of *Dance Moms*."

"Okay. But can we watch *It's a Wonderful Life* after?"

"*Again?*"

"Christmas movies renew my faith in humanity."

"They renew your *fantasy* about humanity. Cupcake, Bedford Falls is not the real world."

"And *The Bachelor* is?"

"Fine," he said, groaning the groan of the defeated. "Bring on George Bailey."

Honestly, it was almost worth losing Steve just to get Calvin back. What am I saying? It was completely worth it. Calvin is my best friend.

I plopped down into the chair opposite his, broke the pistachio croissant in two, and offered him half. Calvin held his hand up flat.

"I've already had a brioche, a tall mocha, and three madeleines."

"I thought you were starting your diet this week."

"Shut up," he said in a chirpy voice that made me smile, then reached across the table and took a piece of my croissant anyway, as I'd known he would. "Oh my," he groaned. "*That* is beautiful. Guillermo has outdone himself."

Calvin trained as a chef and worked at some of the best restaurants in the city but gave it up when he married Simon, who is something of a saint. Simon travels all over the world as a physician with Doctors Beyond Borders. He can be called off to work in some disaster zone at a moment's notice and be gone for weeks. The long hours of restaurant work made it hard for them to spend time together when Simon was home, so Calvin turned in his chef's whites and became a cookbook editor. He says he doesn't miss the frenetic grind of the restaurant at all, but I'm not so sure.

I wish I liked Simon more. I mean, of course, I *like* him. It's just that I don't *like* him. He's priggish and has a tendency to pontificate. Maybe he's entitled to that. I mean, the man spends his life literally saving humanity. But I feel like he looks down on those involved in less meaningful lines of work, which, let's face it, is pretty much everybody. Plus, he has this habit of pulling on his own nose that really skeeves me out. Shouldn't a doctor know that's unsanitary? Fortunately, I don't see him very often because he's usually off saving the world. When I do, I avoid shaking hands with him, so it's all good. He makes Calvin happy and that's what counts.

"So, cupcake," Calvin said after taking the last bite, "what are you up to today? I mean, apart from going into the office to write letters to a bunch of sad, self-absorbed—"

"They are *not* sad and self-absorbed." Calvin stared at me.

"Okay, fine," I admitted. "Some are. But most are just confused.

Or lonely. They just need somebody to talk to. Is that so bad? *Somebody* has to care about the losers."

Calvin didn't actually call them losers but I felt like he wanted to. I feel like a lot of people do that and it always upsets me. Because even though I've never met most of the people who write to me, and have a tangled love/hate relationship with a lot of them, I also feel very protective of them. I can't help it.

"Hey, I was just joking. I'm the last person on the planet who can cast aspersions on someone else's profession. Know what I'll be doing today? Same thing I've been doing for the last six weeks," he said. "Testing recipes for the project that never ends, *The Ultimate Encyclopedia of Baking*.

"Celia, I swear this book will be the end of me. Look at me." He pushed himself back from the table and spread his hands wide, displaying the full breadth of his custom-made, 3XLT oxford shirt, coral-striped with a blue monogram, perfectly pressed as always. "I'm enormous. I'm a zip code."

"Oh, you are not."

"Yes, I am. I'm the *Hindenburg*. The next cookbook I edit is going to be something healthy, and slimming. *The Complete Lettuce Cookbook. Winning Ways with Kale*. Something like that."

"You hate kale."

"Everybody hates kale," he said. "They just won't admit it."

"So you've gained a little weight," I said with a shrug. "So what? You'll lose it again, just as soon as you finish this project. How much more do you have to do?"

"I'm only up to the *m*'s. This week I'm testing macarons. Hey," he said brightly, "can I bring them by your apartment? Otherwise I'll end up eating them."

"No. Absolutely not. Why can't you just take a bite out of one to make sure it's good and then throw the rest away?"

"Because I can't," he moaned. "You know I can't. Because my grandparents lived through the Depression and never let me forget it. You loved the linzer torte I brought over last week. Come on, Celia. Help me out. Please?"

"Nope," I said firmly. "Sorry, but I can't."

Calvin leaned closer and dropped his wheedling tone, his expression slightly flat but also more open and honest. Calvin's a born performer. I mean that almost literally: he feels obligated to entertain almost everyone he meets. But with me, he knows he doesn't have to. That's what makes us friends.

"I've gained thirty-two pounds since Christmas," he said. I winced, feeling his pain. I knew he'd bulked up a bit while editing the baking book, how could he not? But he's such a big guy to begin with, towering over me by at least a foot, that I hadn't realized it was that much. "Well," he said, leaning back after completing his confession. "That's my hostage. What about yours?"

For years now, Calvin and I have played a game he calls "trading hostages." The first person tells the second person something about themselves that they wouldn't want everybody to know, then the second person returns the favor. I wasn't sure about this at first, but Calvin said it was a good way to get to know someone very well, very quickly, and he was right. At this point, Calvin knew everything about me. Well, almost everything. Some things about my childhood are too complicated to explain even to myself, let alone Calvin. Normally, the "hostage" exchange involves sharing information that's bad, even embarrassing. But today, for the first time in a long time, I had *good* news to report.

"I've made up my mind, Calvin. I am transforming myself into a new person, a better person."

Calvin's forehead creased with confusion. "Why? What's wrong with the person you are now?"

I grinned, took a deep breath, and blurted out the news.

"A baby? Really? Oh, honey! A baby! I'm so happy for you!" Calvin jumped from his chair, scooped me out of mine, and wrapped me in his big arms, lifting me off the ground and into his embrace.

"Hang on," I said, laughing. "Nothing is sure yet. The birth mother is considering two other families."

"She'll pick you," Calvin said. "I know she will. Who better to raise a baby than Dear Calpurnia?"

"Well, let's not jump the gun. I don't want to get my hopes up," I said, though it was way too late for that. "I've got to find a new apartment before the home visit."

"Move into our building! There's a two-bedroom coming available at the end of the month. You'd have on-site babysitters— Uncle Calvin and Uncle Simon!"

"I can't afford your building, not unless I can get a raise. I'm asking Dan today." Remembering my mission made my throat go dry. I took a drink of coffee and wiped my damp palms on the paper napkin.

"He'll give it to you," Calvin said confidently. "How can he not? You're the most popular advice columnist since Dear Abby."

"Yeah. Well. We'll see." I pulled the chocolate croissant out of the bag and took a big bite.

"I thought it was a new day," he said. "I thought you were being transformed."

"Shut up," I chirped.

Calvin laughed.

Chapter Three

After finishing my latte and getting a pep talk from Calvin, I marched over to the lion's den to demand a raise—the den being the offices of McKee Media, the lion being Dan McKee, the owner of the company and my boss.

Dan started his online newspaper, The Daily McKee, with a handful of amateur journalists who were willing to work for donuts and a byline and built it into one of the most successful online publications in the country, not far behind HuffPost and BuzzFeed. He "discovered" me twelve years ago.

I studied journalism in college and wrote several groundbreaking articles for my college paper. Perhaps you remember my exposé on the actual number of working hours clocked by tenured faculty? Or my series about Rush Week hazing practices that resulted in the suspension of the Kappa Sigs for a whole year?

No? Neither did any of the managing editors in New York.

I started waiting tables to make rent and blogging to help process my transition to life in the big city. As a title, *Georgia Peach in the Big Apple* was a little misleading but I figured that my attending the University of Georgia made it true enough. Besides, it wasn't like I thought anybody was actually going to read it.

But for some reason, they did. *Georgia Peach* wasn't as popular as a lot of blogs; I never got a TV show or movie or book deal out of it, but I did develop a sort of cult following, mostly because of the comments.

If you're raised in the South, certain things are baked into you from birth. You say, "Yes, sir" and "Yes, ma'am." You respect your elders. Back then when someone wrote to you, you wrote back, on proper stationery and in your very nicest handwriting, unless you were Calpurnia, who had shockingly poor penmanship for a woman of her era and got away with tapping out her correspondence on her trusty Olivetti typewriter with the wonky *y*, always sending some sugar when she signed off. The rest of us were supposed to pen our thanks by hand; this and many other rules of etiquette were pounded into me from an early age. I received my first set of monogrammed stationery for my fourth birthday, long before I actually *could* write. So, of course, I read and answered all those comments personally and at length. It would have been rude not to, especially for a blogger who was tapping into her southern sensibility.

Before long, people started posting questions as well as comments, often asking for my advice. Why they thought I'd have any special insights to offer still baffles me but I always wrote back. That's when I started using the pen name Calpurnia and developed my signature sign-off, "Sending you some sugar." Doesn't get a lot more southern than that.

By the time Dan McKee found me, the blog was making a little money, so I turned down his initial "donuts and a byline" proposal. I was surprised when he came back with an offer of thirty-five thousand a year. It seemed an enormous sum at the time. I've gotten a few raises since, all hard fought. Last time, I threatened to take the column to another publication. It was a bluff that paid off. Dan made me sign a three-year contract that included a noncompete and a substantial raise.

That was a tough negotiation. I wasn't looking forward to repeating the experience. So when I got to the office and found that Dan wasn't in, I was disappointed but also a little relieved.

After settling down at my desk, I opened my email. Dozens of messages for Dear Calpurnia popped up. It seems like writing an advice column should be the easiest job in journalism but it's not, and when you've been doing it for as long as I have, avoiding repetition is hard. Lately, I feel like I've been recycling myself a lot. After twelve years as Calpurnia, what fresh insights do I really have to offer?

Though only a couple of the emails that come in will appear in Daily McKee, I respond to everybody who writes to me. This isn't a job requirement, only a personal one. Like I said, somebody has to care about these people. Most of my responses boil down to three vital nuggets of advice. Nobody is perfect, even you, so don't be so hard on other people. Nobody is perfect, and that's okay, so don't be so hard on yourself. And nobody is perfect, especially you, so why don't you look in the mirror and quit being such a jerk.

But I say it more sympathetically.

Reading between the lines, figuring out the stuff that people *aren't* saying and might not know about themselves is the tricky part of my job. But you've got to be gentle. People can't hear you if they're feeling attacked or judged. That's part of the reason I sprinkle my letters with little endearments—baby girl, buttercup, and the like. It helps people know that I still like them, even when I'm delivering a much-needed lecture. Also, it's just my style.

After reading through the day's batch of mail, I decided to

publish a letter from a widow who had moved in with her son, daughter-in-law, and three teenage grandchildren, and was very, *very* unhappy. She came off as a cranky old bag, the kind of person who spends the day peeping through a crack in the living room curtains so that she can run out onto the porch to scream at any damn kids that dare to step on her lawn. But when I read her letter, I could tell those were just symptoms of a deeper and more universal problem.

Those letters are kind of my specialty.

Dear Grammy in Miami,

When I was twenty-two years old, I left home and moved to New York City, one of the most crowded pieces of real estate on the planet. Every place I went, I was surrounded by other people, yet I'd never felt so alone.

That's the worst kind of loneliness, isn't it? The kind that comes from feeling unknown and unrecognized even when you're standing in a crowd. Everybody feels that way at some point— invisible, irrelevant, obsolete, alone, and terribly, terribly afraid.

Sound familiar?

It's not just you, Grammy in Miami. It's everybody. I've got proof.

A couple of weeks ago I took a cab ride with a driver who had the radio tuned to a Christian station and liked his music loud. I could have asked him to turn it down, but though she has lived in the big city for many years, Calpurnia has never cottoned to confrontation, especially when it is raining out and she might be unable to find another ride should an angry driver eject her from his cab. This being the case, I held my tongue.

But before the passage of many blocks, the words to one of the songs caught my attention. The singer voiced a prayer for deliverance from the things that made her feel most afraid and alone . . . the need to be understood, the need to be accepted, the fear of being neither and being humbled in the process, the fear of death, and trial, and having nothing, and being nothing.

The needs and fears that woman sang about are the same needs and fears that once made me feel like the lone castaway on an island with a population of a million and a half. They are the same needs and fears that are making you feel so lonely and unhappy now, the ones everybody faces at some point in their lives, when all that was familiar has been stripped away and we're thrust, willingly or unwillingly, into the next phase of life. It's not just you. It's everybody.

How do I know this?

Because somebody wrote a song about it. Because somebody else recorded it. Because my cab driver cranked up the volume when it came on the radio. Because my eyes welled up when I heard it, and because, even after all this time, I remember how it feels to be so alone and so afraid. Sometimes I still feel that way.

If you had been in the cab and heard that song, you'd have felt the same, like you wanted to cry. But you wouldn't, would you? Somewhere along the way, you learned that it wasn't acceptable to cry. Or maybe it wasn't safe? Instead of crying, you'd swallow your tears and shout at the cab driver to turn down the damn radio, then maybe stiff him on his tip. I'm not sure about the details but somehow or other, you'd react. Because admitting you're scared is just too scary. It makes you feel vulnerable and more alone than ever. I get it.

It isn't just you, Grammy. It isn't just me. It's everybody.

It's your son, and your daughter-in-law too. It's definitely your grandson. You said he's off to college in a few months, to a school *that was far from his first choice that is also far from his friends and family. Small wonder he's snappish and sarcastic and even rude. Like you, he's afraid of the unknown, and so afraid of being lonely that he's already isolating himself. Like you, he's reacting.*

Exactly like you.

(Those pippins don't fall too far from the family tree, do they, Grammy Smith?)

Talk to him, buttercup. Start a conversation. An exchange, not a lecture. Let him know that you understand what it feels like to be scared and lonely and lost. Be real with him.

If you are, chances are good that he'll return the favor. When he does, listen. Listen as hard as you can. Then repeat the process with the rest of your family. And the neighbors. And the guy who rings up your grocery order. And the lady who checks in your books at the library.

I think you'll be amazed at how much you have in common but even more amazed at how quickly bitterness and isolation are replaced by acceptance and even love, love for your family, love for your friends, love for your new life.

Loneliness is hard, Grammy. Really hard. But the antidote is easy: connect with the people who are already all around you. They need you as much as you need them, maybe even more.

Sending you some sugar,
Calpurnia

"Celia?"

I gasped. Dan McKee was standing in front of my desk. This was unusual. When Dan wants to talk to somebody, he stands at his office door and shouts, "Get in here! Now!" (Though he never adds a name to this command, the person who is about to get chewed out always knows who he means.) Even stranger than Dan's making a personal appearance at my desk was the look on his face.

He was *smiling*. It made me nervous.

"Sorry. You were really focused there, weren't you?" He chuckled.

What was going on? Dan McKee chuckled? Out loud? And apologized?

"Is this a good time?" he asked. "Jerome said you were looking for me."

"Uh . . . yeah. Now's good."

"Great. I wanted to talk to you too. Why don't we head over to my office?"

DAN OFFERED ME a seat in the dreaded wobbly chair. When he closed the door, I took a deep breath and catapulted into my pitch.

"Dan, apart from the big news stories, my column gets more traffic than any other Daily McKee feature. Page views for Dear Calpurnia are up seventeen percent, which means the advertising revenue I'm generating—"

"Is a big contributor to our bottom line," Dan said, finishing my sentence for me.

I stopped and tried to regain my bearings. Calvin and I hadn't role-played a scenario where Dan agreed with me. The way it was supposed to work was that he'd argue with me, downplaying my value to the paper, and I would come back at him, saying my effort added a lot of the bottom line and that I should be fairly compensated for that contribution. Then I was supposed to de- mand a raise.

Having Dan agree with my main point was throwing me. I felt like a performer in a two-person play when the other actor inexplicably skips a few pages of dialogue. I was confused to the point of stammering, trying to figure out my next line.

Dan took a blue box with a white ribbon out of a drawer and handed it to me.

"What's this?"

"A present. To let you know how much I appreciate you. Open it." When I hesitated he said, "It's a bracelet. Or a bangle. That's what the lady called it. Rose gold with two diamonds. Small ones." He smiled. "I bought it at Tiffany's."

"Wow." I sat there. "I really don't know what to say. Thank you."

"You're welcome. Listen. Celia. I wasn't going to say anything to anybody until tomorrow but . . ." He leaned forward in his chair, eyes glittering with the secret he was dying to tell.

"I sold the company today."

"Wait. What? You mean *this* company? You sold Daily McKee?"

Dan nodded.

"Oh. Wow. Well . . . congratulations."

Was it cause for congratulations? His grin indicated it was, at least for him. I wasn't so sure about the rest of us worker bees.

"Who bought us? I mean it . . . the company. Who bought it?"

"Tate Universal."

My mouth went dry. As the name indicated, Tate Universal was a media behemoth, an empire composed of newspapers, a cable network, hundreds of small- and mid-market television stations, a movie studio, and a theme park. Like any good empire, they made their money by gobbling up the smaller provinces and wresting every bit of profit, productivity, and life's blood from the unfortunate conquered noncombatants, pawns to the ambitions of more powerful and more ruthless people.

The worker bees were *not* to be congratulated.

Dan started to laugh, not chuckle, but really *laugh* and in a voice that was strangely high-pitched. He sounded almost giddy, like an anxious schoolgirl who had finally nabbed a date the day before the prom.

"I did it," he said, getting up from his chair and pressing his palms to his temples as if to prevent his head from exploding. "I actually did it. When I started Daily McKee, I told myself I was going to make enough to retire by the time I was forty. Now I can. And with six weeks to spare."

"How much did they pay you?"

The figure he named almost made *my* head explode. For that kind of money, my entire apartment building could have retired, in luxury.

"*Finally*. After all these years, I can have a life! I can travel, get a girlfriend. Sleep in! Do you know the last time I got more than five hours' sleep? Fourteen years ago, the day before I started the paper." He leaned against the edge of his desk, shoulders drooping as he exhaled an enormous, relieved sigh.

"You've worked hard. And I'm happy. For you. But . . . what happens now?"

"I'm not one hundred percent sure." He laughed again. "I've been so busy pulling the deal together that I haven't thought it out entirely. But a week from tomorrow, I take delivery on a new sailboat. Three berths, four sun decks, sixty-two feet long."

"I meant what happens to us? And to Daily McKee?"

"Oh. Well. It'll go on like it always has," Dan said, "just under the Tate Universal umbrella. I doubt readers will even notice. Tate wants to keep the name."

"And the staff? Does Tate want to keep them? Or are there going to be cuts?"

"A few, I imagine." He shrugged. "But that's not really my problem anymore."

No, indeed. It's ours. And mine.

"What about my column? Are they keeping it?"

"They are." He got up and walked around to the front of the desk. "Tate wants to syndicate it to all their publications. Without Dear Calpurnia, I'm not sure I'd have been able to pull off the deal. Thus the present," he said, nodding toward the still-unopened box in my lap as he resumed his seat.

My stomach unclenched a little. I still was concerned for my coworkers but it was a relief to know that my job was safe. And even, possibly, my hopes for a raise? And a baby? If Tate wanted to publish my column in their many publications, they'd have to increase my salary, wouldn't they? Maybe I should get an agent. Negotiating with a big corporation would be different from dealing with Dan. But could I make a deal quickly enough to get a bigger apartment before the home visit? Doubtful. Maybe Dan would intercede on my behalf? After all, the deal might never have happened without me. He said so himself.

"Listen, Dan. Something has happened, something great. And I need a —"

But Dan wasn't listening.

"Tate is keeping Dear Calpurnia," he said, cutting me off. "But they're not keeping you."

"Excuse me?"

I blinked, certain he must be joking. But he wasn't smiling anymore.

"That's crazy. They can't publish the column without me. I *am* Calpurnia."

"You're Celia Fairchild. Calpurnia is a persona, a pen name. Somebody else can assume it and write her just as well as you did, but for less money."

He pulled a sheet of paper out of the same drawer where he'd stowed the Tiffany's box and laid it on the desk in front of me.

"What's this?"

"It's a letter of termination and separation, with a one-year severance attached. Sign it and you'll get a check today."

"What!"

"Don't look at me like that, Celia. Do you know how hard I had to battle with Tate to get this for you? I went to the mat for you. The others won't get even half as much. A whole year. You're going to come out money-ahead. It won't take you nearly that long to find another job."

"Not one that pays anything close to what I make writing the column," I snapped, knowing it was true. "And I don't want another job. Calpurnia might be a persona but she's *my* persona. If Tate isn't willing to pay for her, someone else will."

"You can't do that."

"Our contract was for three years, which means my noncompete will be up at the end of next month. After that, I can write for anyone I want. I don't care how much money Tate throws at me, I'm not signing away the rights to Calpurnia."

"Celia. You already did."

Dan stared at me. I stared back.

"Your last contract says that the name Dear Calpurnia in all its forms belongs to McKee Media and that in the event of the company's being sold during the duration of the contract, the rights transfer to the new owner."

"No." I shook my head. "No. I would never have agreed to that."

"But you did. It's all there—clause sixteen, paragraph nine B."

He opened his desk drawer again, this time to extract a copy of my employment contract, which just happened to be turned to clause sixteen, paragraph 9B and highlighted in yellow marker. Clearly, Dan had spent a lot of time preparing for this meeting, I guessed about three years, starting on the day he'd watched me sign a contract that he knew I didn't completely understand.

For a moment I was struck dumb, overwhelmed by the realization of my own stupidity and the depth of Dan's deceit. How could he have done something so . . . so evil? Then I thought about the adoption attorney and the bigger apartment I needed to convince her that my home would be a fit place to raise a child and that I would be a fit parent. But was I? With no husband, no job, no visible future in front of me? How was I going to support a baby if I couldn't even support myself?

Maybe I should sign the letter. The severance wouldn't get me into a better apartment—every building in town would want confirmation of employment—but a year's salary wasn't exactly chump change. Could I walk away from that? On the other hand, how could I walk away from Calpurnia? If not for her, I wouldn't even be in the running for this baby. Without Calpurnia, I was nothing and nobody.

I considered my options, which were precisely none. Dan held all the cards. Maybe if I told him about the baby? Appealed to his sense of decency?

Then I remembered: he had none.

How could I ever have trusted him? And why, oh why, after advising so many of my readers to have an attorney look over any contracts before signing, hadn't I done so myself? Because I *had* trusted him, that's why.

Which was stupid. Really, really stupid.

I dropped my head and saw the Tiffany's box sitting in my lap. So he'd bought me jewelry because he appreciated me? And he'd fought to get me a year's severance because I'd been with him from the first?

Bull. I wasn't the one who should be embarrassed here.

I stood up and dropped the blue box onto Dan's desk. It landed with a thud.

"You can't fight this, Celia. It's already done," he said as I crossed the room. "Don't be an idiot. Sign the letter and take the money."

I opened the door.

"Hey, Dan. About your boat? I hope it sinks."

Twenty minutes later, escorted by a security guard who had watched me pack the contents of my desk into a box, I exited the offices of McKee Media. I'd started the day resolved to transform myself entirely. Now it had happened.

I walked in the door as Dear Calpurnia.

I walked out as Celia Fairchild, a woman I used to know but had lost touch with a long, long time ago.

Chapter Four

Lawyers in Manhattan must all use the same decorator.

In the six days since I'd been unceremoniously escorted out of the offices of McKee Media, I'd had meetings at eight different law firms. Every one of them had glass coffee tables and painted portraits of the founding partners in the lobby, glassed-in conference rooms lined with floor-to-ceiling shelves of hardbound law books that I'm sure were just for show (Seriously, isn't all the research done on computers by underpaid, overworked associates these days?), and plush, expensive, red Oriental rugs with fringed edges. I'm not making that up: it was almost the exact same rug! And the lawyers appeared to be just as generic, even Carlotta Avilla.

I had hoped that a female attorney would be a bit more sympathetic to my cause, or somewhat more willing to take a chance. But I guess you don't pay for ten-thousand-dollar rugs, walls of books that nobody ever reads, or office suites on high floors by taking on cases that are anything less than a slam dunk, especially when the client is an out-of-work advice columnist who has big alimony payments and next to nothing in savings.

But at least the coffee was good. Apparently, really great coffee is something else you can afford to buy when you only bet on sure things.

"The thing is," Ms. Avilla said, putting a blue demitasse cup of espresso down on the glass conference table after I finished my story, "you *did* sign the contract. No one made you do it."

I nodded. I'd heard this before. "But I never would have done it if I'd seen the part about them getting the rights to my pen name. Dan never mentioned anything about that during our negotiations, and the first draft of the contract didn't include that clause." I'd confirmed this. In the original contract Dan had emailed for me to look over, clause sixteen didn't have a paragraph 9B. "He added it later on purpose, knowing I wouldn't read the whole thing before signing."

"But you should have read it." Ms. Avilla looked almost apologetic, as if she was genuinely sorry to be the bearer of bad news. She definitely was more sympathetic than the male attorneys I'd spoken to but no more helpful. "You should have hired a lawyer to look it over before you signed."

"I know, I know. But . . . better late than never?"

I smiled, hoping to win her over. For a moment, I thought I might have. She chuckled a little, then made a church with her hands and tapped the steeple against her lips. She was thinking about it. That was more than the others had done. I clenched my fists tight but said nothing, waiting for the verdict.

"Miss Fairchild, it's obvious you've been taken advantage of. But McKee Media is a big company with deep pockets. Now that it's been acquired by Tate Universal, those deep pockets are basically an abyss. These huge corporations have teams of lawyers on staff and they *hate* to lose. They'll do everything they can, spend any amount of money, fighting this. Even if I took on the case, the firm would require a one-hundred-thousand-dollar retainer.

I'm serious," she said, obviously noticing the way the color had drained from my face.

The other attorneys had dismissed me so quickly that we'd never even talked about the money part. But . . . one hundred thousand dollars?

"And that's just to get started," she said. "Believe me, when you're up against a company like Tate Universal, we'd burn through the entire retainer and a lot more before we ever got to court. And the chances of your winning are slim at best.

"I'm sorry, Miss Fairchild. I wish I could take your case. But if I did, I'd only be taking your money. I know that a year's severance doesn't come close to compensating you for all you've lost, but the smartest thing you can do is take it and use it to start a new career, a new life."

All the other lawyers had blown me off like some kind of pesky, too-dumb-to-read-a-contract fly. That had made me mad and even more determined. Carlotta Avilla's pity made me feel defeated. I unclenched my fists and looked down at my hands and the chipped polish on my fingernails.

"Of course, I'm not the only attorney in New York," she said, smiling in a way I knew was meant to give me hope. "Would you like me to recommend some other firms?"

I lifted my head. "Is there any point?"

Her smile melted away. "Not really."

I COULD HAVE gone to Calvin's. He'd have made me dinner, opened a bottle of wine, and tried to convince me that there was still hope. But there wasn't. Besides, he was on a deadline for his book. I couldn't bother him. And while talking to him might have made me feel marginally less miserable, it wasn't going to change anything.

I could have called my therapist but I really didn't like her. She was so earnest and yet so distant, not to mention really vague. People can write to me for advice and get an answer for free. I might not always be right but at least I'm definite. My therapist gets two hundred and eighty dollars an hour to nod and murmur and say, "And how did that make you feel?" I didn't need to know how I felt, I needed to know what to *do*.

I could have gone home but suspected this would end with my climbing into bed with a pint of Ben & Jerry's and a spoon, playing the Smiths' "I Know It's Over" on a continuous loop while contemplating the fact that the best years of my life were behind me and that they hadn't been that great to begin with. Not an appealing prospect, and on so many levels.

So I went to the park.

Maybe if I walked around the reservoir, I'd come up with an idea about what to do next. But who was I kidding? Carlotta Avilla was right; the only real option left was to take the severance and try to start over.

Funny thing, just a week ago I'd been on a stage in a beam of blinding bright lights, feeling annoyed with Sparkly Vest Man and everybody else who'd ostensibly come to see me but really wanted Calpurnia. I resented them for demanding I put on the show and play the part. Now I realized that the part was all I had.

I was nobody's wife or daughter or mother. And now I wasn't even Calpurnia. What happens after the thing you based your life and identity on gets taken away? What do you do? Where do you go?

The Okefenokee Swamp? Key West?

I picked up a pebble from the path, plopped it into the lake, and watched the ripples spread. I thought about tossing french fries off the Daytona Pier and watching seagulls swoop down to gobble them in mid-air, and remembered that some problems are just too big to run from.

Once I read an article that said you have to clear your mind of questions to make room for answers, so I walked around the lake twice, three miles in total, trying to keep my brain as blank as possible, and got nothing for my trouble but a blister where the seam of my shoe rubbed my little toe. So much for enlightenment. Rounding a corner, I heard happy shrieks and squeals.

I go through phases when it comes to playgrounds. There have been seasons when I haunted them on a regular basis, admiring the sturdy, bandy-legged toddlers busily digging in the sandbox and the pink-cheeked infants slumbering in strollers, and dreamed of the day when I'd have one of my own. And there have been other seasons when I've avoided playgrounds at all costs, depressed because it felt like the dream was dead.

But with the blister getting worse and the pain becoming so intense that I was limping, I didn't have a choice. I had to sit down, and the only place to sit was at the playground, on the empty end of a bench that was occupied by a twenty-something woman with messy blond curls, dark circles under her eyes, and an infant in her arms. I took a seat and bent down to slip off my shoe. The woman with the baby, who must have been watching, gasped and sucked air in through her teeth when I did, as if she could tell how painful it was just by looking. It *did* hurt, a lot.

"Ow," she said, wincing at the sight of blood. "Hang on a second, I'm sure I've got a Band-Aid in here somewhere."

I told her it was okay, that I'd be fine, but she paid no attention and plopped the baby, who was sound asleep, down in the bed of a big stroller that had seen better days, then started digging through a diaper bag, pulling out pacifiers, nursing pads, bags filled with cereal, plastic action figures, miniature boxes of raisins, and finally a bandage from its depths.

"Here we go," she said, handing it over to me. "I hope you don't mind Minions. My twins are crazy about them."

"Thanks," I said, then pulled off the backing and wrapped the bandage around my ravaged toe. Blood seeped out the side, making the cheery yellow Minions look ruthless and diabolical. "You've got twins?" I asked. "And a baby?"

"Boys," she said, bobbing her head. "Marcus and Miles are five, Geoffrey is four, and Walt will be three next month." She tilted her chin toward the slide and waved to a towheaded toddler who was laboriously climbing the ladder. "And *this* is Julia," she said, reaching down into the stroller and scooping the sleeping infant up in her arms.

My jaw dropped. "You have five children?"

Five? How was that possible? In spite of the dark circles under her eyes, which she clearly had earned, she didn't look to be more than twenty-four or twenty-five years old, twenty-six at the most.

"Yeah," she said wearily. "I can use my husband's toothbrush and get pregnant. But we really wanted a girl. Now we've got one. Finally." She smiled down at the baby, whose soft snoring made a little bubble of snot in her nostril inflate and deflate with every breath.

"I don't know what I'd have done if we'd had another boy," she said, looking up at me with earnest eyes. "Boys are holy terrors. Well, at least *mine* are."

At that moment, as if to prove her point the twins—Marcus and Miles—came hurtling across the playground, leaping over a see-saw, emitting a war cry, like a band of savage, marauding Celts storming the castle, heading straight for our bench. The surprise attack came out of nowhere, a true "shock and awe" operation. Before we knew what was happening, the two little terrors grabbed the handle of the battered stroller and ran it off in the opposite direction with their prize, howling in triumph as they careened across the bumpy, pitted, uneven ground, probably destroying what was left of the stroller's overworked springs. The young mom jumped to her feet, baby still in her arms.

"Marcus! Miles! Come back here right now!"

They ignored her, let out another battle cry, and took a sharp left, heading straight for a brown-haired little boy who was wearing the same kind of rubber boots as they were, green with googly frog eyes on the toes. Seeing the maniacal marauders coming after him, the smaller boy shrieked in terror and ran.

"Marcus! Miles! You two leave Geoffrey alone! I am *not* kidding!"

They still ignored her. The terrorized Geoffrey ran toward the lake and around a clump of bushes with the Evil Twins in hot pursuit. Before I really knew what was happening, the Mother of Dragons thrust the baby into my arms.

"Hold her for a second, will you? And keep an eye on Walt. I'll be right back."

And just like that, without even giving me a chance to respond or asking if I might be a felon or had any communicable diseases, she dashed off and left me, a perfect stranger, in charge of two of her five children.

She was gone for about ten minutes, the most wonderful, most heartbreaking ten minutes of my life.

I spent probably five of them just looking at that baby, admiring her perfect little lashes, smiling at the snot bubble and the way her rosebud mouth quivered and worked when I stroked my finger across the impossibly soft skin of her porcelain pink cheek.

She was a beautiful baby and a perfect fit; it was as if she'd been custom-sized for my arms. It was heaven; I could have held her forever.

I heard a sound of shuffling feet and looked up to see Walt, the towheaded boy who'd waved from the slide, also clad in green frog boots, standing in front of me.

"I'm hungry," he said, blinking at me with blue eyes.

"Oh. Well . . . how about some raisins?"

He didn't say anything, just climbed up on the bench and sat down next to me. I took this as a yes and started digging through the diaper bag—if she hadn't minded leaving me with her kids, I didn't suppose she'd mind me looking through her bag—until I located a small, slightly crushed red box.

"Here you go."

Walt opened the box, fished out three raisins with his chubby fingers and put them in his mouth.

"Are they good?"

He chewed and nodded and wiggled his little torso back and forth in a bench-bound happy dance.

"Wanna play I Spy?" he asked after digging a few more raisins from the box.

"Sure," I said. "You start."

Walt frowned and chewed and twisted his towhead from left to right, searching for a subject. "I spy . . . something green."

"Something green. Hmm . . . Is it a tree?"

"Yes!" Walt exclaimed, swiveling his head in my direction and dropping his jaw in amazement, as if I had just performed some sort of magic trick. "How did you know?"

We played a couple more rounds. Walt spied only green things—a bush, a bench, his boots, maybe it was the only color he knew—continuing to be astounded every time I guessed right.

He was the cutest little boy, sweet enough to spread on toast, as Calpurnia used to say. And for those ten minutes, I got to live my fantasy. I was just a mom in the park, charged with the care of two lovely, perfect little humans. Nobody walking by would have guessed they weren't mine. My heart was happy and completely full. That was the wonderful part.

Did she know, that weary and worn-out Mother of Dragons, how incredibly lucky she was? To have such abundance? A husband and home, more children than one set of arms could hold? Did she have any idea what other women, those who'd spent time, money, and anguish on fertility treatments that didn't work, penned desperate "Dear Birth Mother" letters that went unanswered, felt when she told them that, for her, conception was as easy as using her husband's toothbrush?

Jealousy, yes. But much more than that. Jealousy and longing and the fear that somehow they themselves must be undeserving or unfit, angry to be denied something so simple and natural, a gift that others opened again and again without effort or thought. I'd have given anything to trade places with her.

Those ten minutes were precious but, of course, they didn't last. The young mother returned before long, the beleaguered Geoffrey sitting cross-legged in the middle of the battered stroller, triumphantly licking a sucker, while the disgraced marauders trailed behind, scuffing their feet on the ground with their frog boots and glowering, clearly plotting revenge. God help poor Geoffrey. He should have just let them run him over.

She smiled and thanked me and said they should be going. I swallowed hard and said it was my pleasure and handed the baby back. It wasn't easy but I did. But when they walked away, trailing their overworked mother like a line of green-footed ducklings, and little Walt spun around as they reached the sidewalk, grinning and waving his arm over his head . . . that's when I lost it.

When I got on the subway, I sat with my face turned toward the window and let the tears flow all the way from West 86th to West 168th Street, wiping my nose on my sleeve as I emerged from the station. I was so upset that when a call came in from an unknown number with a somewhat familiar area code, I actually ignored it. The way my life was going, it would only be bad news. And when I listened to the voicemail left by the man with the deep voice and slow drawl the next day, I found out my instincts were right. It was bad news, terrible news that made my tears fall anew.

But when I calmed down enough to listen to the message again, all the way through this time, and return the call of the man with the drawl, Trey Holcomb, I learned there was more to it than just bad news. By the time I hung up, I was feeling sad, guilty, hopeful, and confused. One phone call had turned my life upside down.

Twenty-four hours later, I was standing in a place I had never planned, or wanted, to see again.

Chapter Five

Fifteen years had passed since I'd last stood on that particular patch of ground. Everything was eerily familiar but in a way that was oddly comforting. The time-at-a-standstill nature of the surroundings gave rise to hope that maybe, just maybe, there's something eternal after all.

Maybe that's the purpose of cemeteries.

Charleston natives have always been deeply concerned with geography. Not on a wide scale, mind you, but only as it relates to their beloved city. Tell another Charlestonian that you live south of Broad, or in the French Quarter, or in Harleston Village or Radcliffeborough, and you're halfway to relating your life story. The same holds true for cemeteries. To a Charlestonian, where one is buried in death says as much about a person as his or her street address did in life, supplying clues about family history, religious preference, and social status. When it comes to cemeteries, St. Philip's Church is as desirable an address as can be found, at least that's what Sterling had always told me.

"It's an interesting graveyard," my father would say whenever we came to put flowers on the graves. "With character. Why would anyone buy a plot in one of those awful 'memorial gardens,' where every slab looks like every other slab, when for the same money, you can pass the time among these beautiful green trees and in the company of all the best people?"

When Calvin saw me smiling, I told him about my dad and "the best people."

"The best people? And they are?"

"Members of St. Philip's and native Charlestonians. Not necessarily in that order."

Calvin laughed, loudly. Considering the setting, it seemed slightly inappropriate. But that's one of the things I love about Calvin. Yes, he may have invented himself but now that he knows who he is, he's one hundred percent Calvin, one hundred percent of the time, no matter the setting.

I squatted down in front of my parents' headstone, a low and wide granite marker engraved with a Grecian-style cross. It had rained recently and my kitten heels made two divots on the damp sod. Grandma Beebee's marker, located only a few feet away, was engraved with a death date just four days later than my mother's.

"You okay?" Calvin asked.

"Whenever Sterling and I would come here to put flowers on my mother's grave, he'd point to that spot, right in front of where you're standing, and remind me that he'd be there someday, buried next to her. It seemed creepy to me as a kid but I think I get it now. It must be comforting to know where you'll end up and that you'll be lying next to somebody you love."

Calvin read the inscription on the headstone. "'Until the times of restoration of all things, whereof God spake . . .'"

"Acts 3:21. My father's favorite verse, probably because it was obscure. Sterling lived in fear of being thought ordinary."

"Well, I think it's nice. A nice sentiment anyway. Do you think it'll ever happen?"

"Like you said, a nice sentiment." I placed a hand on the headstone and pushed myself to my feet. "Ready to go?"

"You don't want to see your aunt's grave?"

I should have but I didn't. Maybe in a couple of days, I told myself, before we flew back to New York. But it was too much just then.

I'd tried so hard to forget this place. Maybe that was a mistake. After seeing their graves, shaded by the spreading branches of venerable live oaks and crape myrtles festooned with Spanish moss, sequestered behind the brick walls carpeted with ivy that softened the noise of traffic and clop of horse-drawn carriages loaded with camera-clicking tourists, I could just about believe they truly were resting in peace.

It would be different to stand at Aunt Calpurnia's grave. There would be no headstone, not yet. The sod wouldn't have taken hold yet and the ground, so recently disturbed, would be unsettled. It was too soon. I was too raw.

"Maybe later. I'm kind of tired."

"Do you want to go to the house?"

"Let's just go back to the hotel."

"Okay. But remember, we've got a seven o'clock reservation at Fig."

We were only going to be here for four days, just long enough for me to settle things with the attorney and put the house on the market. I was not here to sightsee. But Calvin had a list of twenty-seven restaurants he wanted to try before we left.

"Can I beg off? I'm not very hungry."

Calvin blinked twice, staring at me like I was speaking a foreign language.

"You understand I'm talking about Fig, right? Buckskin pumpkin soup with crème fraiche? Fish stew Provençal with shrimp, squid, mussels, and butterbeans? Fig is on top of every single Charleston ten-best list. It was a *very* tough reservation to get. I dropped names, Celia. I called in favors."

"There's no reason you can't go without me," I said. "It's just that . . . I'm sorry, Calvin. Just for tonight, I think I need to be on my own."

He worked his lips for a moment, as if he was thinking about arguing, then exhaled loudly through his nose.

"Fine. I get that. I guess."

"Starting tomorrow, I'm all in. Promise."

"I'm bringing you back a dessert," he said, making it clear that this was nonnegotiable. "Do you want Asian pear tarte tatin or butterscotch pot de crème?"

CALVIN HAD USED his old restaurant connections to get us a deal at Zero George, one of the best boutique hotels in Charleston. My room was spacious and elegant, the bed made up with crisp, ironed sheets and a pile of fluffy, cloud-soft pillows. If this had been a vacation rather than a confrontation, an assault by the memories I'd worked so hard to wall up, I might have enjoyed it.

I guess this is the part in the story where the heroine normally reveals her traumatic childhood. But mine wasn't, not as it started out. We were happy.

Or maybe just I was.

We were three generations in one house. Grandma Beebee was a kindly and benign presence, fat and pillowy as a mound of bread dough, who knitted sweaters that were too hot to wear and played languid hymns on the piano every morning, never seeming to care that the Charleston humidity kept the instrument permanently out of tune. Her daughter-in-law, my mother, Genevieve, called Jenna by everyone but my father, was likewise benign but for different reasons. She suffered from lupus, a debilitating autoimmune disease. With all her medical problems, she just didn't have the energy to be a mother, and what little she did have was spent almost exclusively on my father. She worshipped him. We all did, in our way.

After the birth of one daughter, followed by a decade of almost annual miscarriages, Beebee birthed a son at the age of forty-three and the family rejoiced. Sadly, my grandfather didn't live long enough to see his only son's greatest achievement.

At the tender age of twenty-two, Sterling penned *Fragrance of Wisteria*, a beautifully written and tragically resonant, if not quite groundbreaking morality play about an interracial Romeo and Juliet during the Vietnam era. It ran off-Broadway for three months in 1981, earning a little money and more than respectable reviews, one of which referred to Sterling as "a rising star among Southern playwrights, a young DuBose Heyward in the making." It was a prophecy Sterling spent the rest of his life trying to fulfill.

Teaching English at the college paid the bills, but everyone in the family understood that my father's true mission in life was to write another, even more insightful and successful play. The mission for the rest of us was to support him in this endeavor. It sounds grim on the surface, I know, but we were so proud of him. Back then, Sterling was such a joyous, outsized personality.

Even in the summer, he wore waistcoats under a wrinkled linen jacket with the chain of his father's gold watch draped from the pocket. His voice boomed, "God bless all here!" whenever he came home from the college and smacked kisses onto the lips of his adoring, waiting women before disappearing into his office to work until dinner. He ate heartily, laughed easily, made big sweeping gestures with his hands, and basked in the glow of small-town brilliance, a glow that I didn't realize extended no farther than the state line until I went to New York and discovered that no one, apart from a few moldy academics and aging theater junkies, remembered *Fragrance of Wisteria* or my father.

But when I was growing up, Sterling was the sun and the rest of us proud planets in his orbit. But it was Aunt Calpurnia who made the planets spin. She made sure the house ran smoothly and the meals were served on time, that Beebee took her blood pressure medicine and Momma got to her doctor appointments, that Sterling wasn't disturbed, and that everyone was happy and had everything they needed to stay that way, including me.

Calpurnia was my mother in every way but biologically. Blessed with boundless energy and the world's loudest and most easily triggered laugh, Calpurnia was always ready to listen, never dismissive of my problems or discounting of my feelings. But she was also very practical and consistently steered me toward solving problems instead of wallowing in them.

"That's terrible. Really, sugar, simply awful. You've got every reason to be upset," she would say with sincerity and a satisfyingly shocked tsk of her tongue whenever I came to her with a problem. "Now what are you going to do?"

Now what are you going to do?

It's not a complicated philosophy, but a lot of the time, it works. I'm not always good at spotting holes before falling into them, but thanks to Calpurnia, I can usually find a way to climb out. When people first started writing to me for advice, I tried to think of what Calpurnia would have said and how she would have said it, back in those days when she was still herself and we were still a family, before the accident.

I was twelve years old and away at summer camp when it

happened. Aunt Calpurnia was driving my mother to one of her many doctor's appointments when a driver coming from the opposite direction crossed the yellow line and hit them head on. My mother was killed instantly and Calpurnia ended up in the hospital with internal bleeding and a skull fracture. It was too much for Beebee; she had a massive heart attack at my mother's funeral and died the next day.

It would be years before the casualties reached their full count. Calpurnia survived but was never the same. Neither was Sterling. Before the accident, everything revolved around his work. After the accident, everything revolved around his grief. The moment the other driver had decided to unwrap a cheeseburger instead of watching the road had forced the survivors onto a different path, a southbound highway that led to the end of the continent and the end of my family. I wasn't an orphan yet, but I might as well have been.

It was terrible. It was awful. It was tragic. But more than anything else, it just *was* and no amount of wallowing would change that, so now what was I going to do? The only thing I could: get on with life as best I could. Calpurnia's teachings were hardwired into me even after she forgot them herself. Even after she forgot me.

I hadn't talked to her since I was twelve, hadn't even seen her face since I was twenty-one. But she was always there in the back of my mind, like a book on a shelf that you're looking forward to reading someday, when life calms down.

When I returned the voicemail from the stranger with the slow drawl who said he had news of Aunt Calpurnia, and I learned she had suffered a massive stroke and died two weeks before, I didn't just cry, I sobbed. In spite of everything, a part of me always thought I'd see her again. Now I never would.

The lawyer, Mr. Holcomb, didn't tell me to calm down or say it might be better if we talked later. He just stayed on the line, waiting, letting me do what I had to do. It was kind of weird, looking back on it. But it made me feel a little less alone.

When I finally pulled myself together, he told me the rest of the story.

Aunt Calpurnia had died intestate, without a will. According to the laws of South Carolina, when that happened, the estate went to the closest living relative, in this case the only living relative, so the house and its contents now belonged to me.

It was hard to wrap my head around that. But then I remembered Calpurnia, who could see wisdom in even the most tired clichés, saying, "There's always a silver lining, sugar. Always."

Was there?

The real estate market in downtown Charleston was booming. Would selling Calpurnia's house give me enough to buy an apartment of my own, or even a house? Maybe in New Jersey? A kid really should have a yard. When I was growing up, Calpurnia's garden, cool and shady and colorful, had been my favorite spot, the center of my imaginary world.

It was a Hail Mary pass, I knew that. Or maybe Hail Calpurnia. There were so many things that could go wrong. To start with, who knew if the birth mother would pick me? Three families were hoping for this baby, and being the only single mother in the pool certainly didn't help my chances. But supposing the birth mother *did* pick me? Even without the column, if I owned a home outright, no mortgage, surely I could find a job that would support us, couldn't I? Still . . . To sell a house, buy another, and move in within two and a half months would take a miracle.

But considering the timing, you can't blame me for wondering if she might not be up there somewhere, arranging for one.

After hours of tossing and turning, I finally fell asleep only to wake three times during the night, with the cobwebs of a dream clinging to me. The third time was the most vivid.

There was a man with a beard, stationed a pace or two beyond Aunt Calpurnia's right shoulder. It struck me as odd because I didn't know anybody with a beard, and even though he was standing so close, his face was in shadow so I couldn't make out his features or see what he looked like. The man didn't say anything but neither did Calpurnia. She stood directly in front of me, holding a swaddled infant in her arms. She gazed into the face of the baby and then at me with an expression that radiated love, and then held the child out, inviting me to take it in my arms. That was all.

Of course, it could have been wishful thinking, the nocturnal emergence of my subconscious desire. But . . . what if it wasn't?

When I woke up the third time, the first fingers of dawn were shining through the slats of the wooden shutters. I sat up in bed and hugged my knees to my chest, convinced I had Calpurnia's blessing.

Chapter Six

*I*t was early in the morning and only the middle of May but already the air felt thick and juicy and full of history, mine especially. Calvin was my closest friend; I trusted him with almost all my secrets. But I'd never told him much about my early life in Charleston; it just felt like ancient history, a different world, because it was.

"I'm sorry?" Calvin asked as we passed a storefront that had once housed a stationery shop, the scene of my first conscious transgression. When I was five years old, I pocketed a handful of pink erasers and ran out the door. I knew exactly what I was doing but that doesn't mean it made sense.

"Who steals erasers?" he asked. "Were these particularly cute erasers? Covered with glitter or shaped like animals?"

"Nope. Just the plain, ugly pink ones you put on top of pencils. I've always had a thing for office supplies; untouched notebooks and new pencils have always made my heart go pitter-pat. As a kid, erasers were my particular favorite. When I saw a bin near the shop door, I stuffed a bunch into my pocket and ran."

"Hmm . . . ," Calvin murmured. "Doubtless you'd had a pre-monition about your future career as a journalist and the need for making massive numbers of corrections."

"Failed journalist," I reminded him.

I paused to shove the last exquisite bite of a sausage, egg, and pimento cheese biscuit into my mouth. I didn't buy Calvin's justifi-cation that the walk from Upper King Street to our appointment in Harleston Village would burn off the calories, but the biscuits were irresistible, as was the city I had left so long ago.

Downtown Charleston is compact and parking is scarce, so resi-dents tend to walk everywhere, just like they do in New York. But there's a different vibe here. For one thing, you don't see a whole lot of palm trees in Manhattan. But Charleston is far enough south to allow nearly every tree, shrub, or flower known to man to flourish. Charleston prides itself on its gardens as well as its architecture. The buildings are older and shorter, the scale more human, and the styles more interesting than in most of Manhattan—at least to my way of thinking. Having practically invented the historic pres-ervation movement, Charleston remains at its forefront, ensuring that the unique character of the city remains intact. Maybe that's why people walk more slowly here, because there's so much to look at? Though I suppose humidity also plays a part.

"Everybody in Charleston knew everybody else back then," I said, licking the last traces of pimento cheese from my fingers before going on with my story, "and the shop owner phoned Cal-purnia to rat me out the second I bolted. She was standing on the steps, waiting for me when I got home, and marched me right back to the store to return the loot and apologize. So humiliating. That was the last time I took something that didn't belong to me.

"Well," I confessed as we reached a corner, "except that USB drive with copies of all my old columns. I slipped it into my pocket when the security guard was looking the other way. But I feel like that really was my property."

"Nice to know you haven't lost your touch," Calvin said. "So Calpurnia saved you from a life of crime?"

"Among other things," I said. "If a kid has at least one person who they know is crazy about them, they usually turn out okay. Calpurnia was my one person. She was the only grown-up I knew who still remembered what it was like to be a child.

"Once, my science teacher assigned me a project to find a hundred different bugs, and Calpurnia was so excited about helping me. I'll never forget her, crawling around the garden on all fours in the dark after a rain, shining a flashlight into the bushes and searching for centipedes." I smiled, remembering the grass stains on the knees of her slacks. "She didn't just make me feel loved, she made me feel important."

"Do you look like her?" Calvin asked.

I shook my head. "Oh, no. She was beautiful. Really beautiful. Especially when she was young. Long, light-brown hair with a just a little bit of wave, amazing cheekbones, full lips, blue eyes with the longest lashes you've ever seen, and *incredible* eyebrows. Everybody used to say she looked like a young Lauren Bacall."

"Well, you're beautiful."

I am not beautiful.

Don't get me wrong, apart from my pointy chin, I mostly like how I look. My hair is medium brown, thick, and straight. I wear it in a blunt cut to my jawline, an attempt to draw attention away from the too-pointy chin. My eyes are brown too. My skin is fair and, so far, devoid of major wrinkles. My nose has a sprinkling of freckles, which I like. Overall, I would say that I am attractive enough for all normal purposes. Possibly even kind of cute. But I'm not beautiful and never was, so I let Calvin's comment pass.

"When's the last time you saw Calpurnia?" he asked.

"Not long after my father died—liver failure," I explained. "Sterling was a high-functioning alcoholic, able to hold it together during the day, enough so he could teach classes, but on nights and weekends . . ." I sighed. "He was just so bitter, blamed Calpurnia for everything."

"But I thought it was the other driver's fault, that he drifted into the other lane while he was unwrapping a cheeseburger."

"It was, but Sterling didn't care. And that wasn't the only thing. When I was twelve, Sterling decided that we should move out. Calpurnia was devastated. She lost her mind a little bit and . . ."

I stopped. The odyssey was too terrible, too wonderful, too complicated to explain to Calvin, and sometimes even to myself. I skipped ahead.

"Anyway, it's a long story. After Sterling died, I thought things would be different, so I went to the house and rang the bell. I knew Aunt Calpurnia was there because I saw the curtains move. I stood on the porch for a good twenty minutes, ringing the bell over and over, but she wouldn't answer. That was the day I decided to go to New York."

Calvin stopped in his tracks and looked at me. "That is really sad."

It was.

We walked in silence for a while. I tried not to think about that day, the way the curtain had moved, just an inch, the time I'd spent standing there, the hollow, hopeless sound my footsteps made as I dismounted the steps and walked away. Instead, I looked at the palms and the people, the storefronts I remembered from the past, now with different names and stocks of goods, formerly familiar houses that had been updated, or painted a different color, or left absolutely untouched. When we walked past the college and a brick building with a fourth-story window of the room that had once been Sterling's office, the memories clung so close that it was all I could do not to lift my hand to my face and brush them away.

We took a left onto Coming Street, past the overgrown ramshackle line of fraternities and sororities, separating into single file to avoid running into clutches of coeds, then crossed the street and headed into the heart of Harleston Village, the last and only place I'd ever really called home.

Harleston Village is a good neighborhood in a convenient location, close to the King Street shops and restaurants, with an energy that's lacking in the stately mansions and staid streets south of Broad. Even when I was growing up, it was something of a mixed bag architecturally. You could find row houses, cottages, mansions, and classic Charleston singles from just about every era, even a few twentieth-century ramblers, often within the same block. But it was very much a neighborhood back then, a place where people knew each other.

We were early, so I took a detour to show Calvin the Queen Street Grocery, a corner store that's been in business since 1922, once a full-fledged market, now more a café selling crepes, craft beer, and a few convenience goods. I told Calvin about buying ice pops there as a child and coming home with my fingers stained orange whenever the heat melted the syrup faster than I could eat, which was almost always.

We headed north on Queen Street, taking a couple of turns and arriving on time. But when we rounded the final corner, I stopped in my tracks. Calvin kept right on going, walking a good ten feet before realizing he was alone.

"Cel?" He turned to face me and frowned. "Are you okay?"

I looked right past him.

When I was growing up, Calpurnia's house was one of the

biggest, prettiest, best-kept residences on the block. Now it was *my* house. And it was a disaster.

The paint was peeling and the shutters were hanging at precarious angles. Three were missing entirely. The porch steps were completely stripped of paint, with treads that curled up at the ends, as if engaged in a battle to free themselves from the grip of the nails, a battle they appeared to be winning. If I'd had to guess, I'd say that a number of shingles were missing from the roof. When it came to the condition of the chimney, no guessing was required. The half-dozen broken bricks lying on the ground attested to its neglect.

An image of what the house once had been flashed in my mind then faded and melted into the shocking scene I saw before me now, like the clumsy special effect some talentless film student might use in his self-written, self-edited, postapocalyptic indie movie. It was awful and the garden was even worse.

Bordered by a decorative wrought iron fence and once Calpurnia's pride, the tidy, trimmed courtyard I remembered from childhood was overgrown with brambles and weeds and littered with a junkyard of broken and rusting objects.

I spotted four bicycles that were minus wheels, a water fountain with a crack as wide as my thumb, several rakes with missing teeth, a claw-foot bathtub with a gaping hole in the side, a child's Flexible Flyer wagon without a handle, and towering stacks of chipped terra-cotta pots. The only cheerful note in this otherwise dismal scene was the pink toilet that sat at the foot of the steps. The bowl had been turned into a planter. Inside it, red geraniums bloomed in shameless profusion.

"*This* is Calpurnia's house?" Calvin asked, blinking. "Are you sure?"

I'd told him all about it: the stately house, the decorative brick arches on the ground floor, the three stories that towered above, the two piazzas—*piazza* is Charleston-speak for "porch"—that ran the full length of the house supported by tall white columns, the painted front door with beveled glass sidelights, the beautiful gardens, the corner lot with an outbuilding where my great-grandfather had once sold haberdashery. But the place where we now stood looked nothing like the house I'd described to Calvin. Hope fled from my body like air from a punctured bicycle tire; I could practically hear the hiss.

"It used to be," I said.

The man standing in front of the house was tall, lanky, and oddly dressed. A good two inches of wrist was visible above the cuff of his ill-fitting suit of rusty black, too short in the arms and too wide for his waist. As we approached, he turned around and extended his hand.

"Miss Fairchild? I'm Trey Holcomb."

I recognized his voice and slow drawl from our phone conversation, but in that cheap suit he didn't look like a lawyer. Not a successful one, anyway. Still, I wasn't really paying attention to that. I was focused on his face, specifically his chin.

Trey Holcomb had a beard.

Reinflated by a small puff of hope, I returned his greeting and introduced Calvin. Then, like the New Yorker I have become, I cut to the chase.

"*What* happened here?" I asked, spreading my arms.

"It wasn't always like this?" Holcomb asked.

"No! Why didn't you warn me?"

At this point, I was practically shouting and a little over-wrought. I couldn't blame Mr. Holcomb for scowling.

"Miss Fairchild, I run a one-man firm that's about fifty percent focused on elder law and the rest on whatever comes through the door. Now and then, when a resident dies intestate, the state of South Carolina contracts me to locate the next of kin and dispose of the estate. Normally, I would come see visit the property beforehand. But I've been in court all week suing a nursing home for neglect and I wasn't able to come by until yesterday. So, I'm sorry if—"

He stopped in mid-sentence, took a breath, and modulated his tone.

"I'm sorry. Especially for your loss. I know your aunt meant a lot to you."

Trey Holcomb didn't exactly radiate warmth, but there was something in his eyes and the set of his brows that made me believe he'd meant what he said. I'd been gone a long time but not so long that I couldn't tell the difference between the thin veneer of good southern manners and sincere regret.

"Please, call me Celia. And I'm sorry. I just . . . I wasn't expecting this." I took a breath and pasted on a smile. It wasn't sincere but it was the best I could do under the circumstances. "So. We're just waiting for the Realtor?"

"Dana Alton," Trey replied. "She called to say she might be late but will get here as quick as she can. I have the keys. Do you want to go inside and have a look around?"

"Sure. That would be great."

"I'd better warn you; the inside is even worse."

"You're kidding." I said.

"Worse than *this*?" Calvin laughed.

His expression practically glittered with prurient fascination. It was the same look that came into his eyes while engaged in one of his favorite obsessions, watching some of the less reputable brands of reality television, programs that were the modern equivalent to circus sideshows.

"Come on, cupcake," he said, grabbing my wrist and pulling me toward the gate. "This whole trip just got a *lot* more interesting."

Chapter Seven

Interesting was not a word I would have used to describe the interior of Aunt Calpurnia's house. *Filthy, disgusting, crammed, stuffed, bursting*—any and all of these adjectives would have applied. *Overwhelming* was another possible descriptor, and probably the most apt.

When people return to a childhood home, they're often surprised that it seems so small. There's a logic to that, I guess. When you're little, everyone and everything around you seems big. But Calpurnia's house really was as huge as I remembered. It was just a lot more crowded.

We entered on the ground floor, passing under the brick arches and through a warped and sticky wooden door into a large, open space with rough brick walls and a ceiling so low that both Calvin and Trey barely cleared the wooden beams. Flooding isn't uncommon in Charleston—there's a reason they call it the Low Country—and some houses were constructed on what amounted to above-ground basements, to provide not only storage but a buffer zone in case of flood. That was how my family had always used it, as an unfurnished, unoccupied space to store stuff. But not *this* much stuff. There were boxes and bins, cartons and crates, and piles of junk everywhere I looked.

And though I wouldn't have believed it possible until we climbed the rickety wooden steps, the upper floors were even worse.

My great-grandfather bought a lot in Harleston Village in 1918. He built a haberdashery shop on the corner and lived above the store. After the business moved to more commodious premises on King Street, he built the biggest house on the block, a structure designed to impress.

The first floor was home to a big kitchen and butler's pantry, cavernous dining room, living room, the enormous entry hall that had been home to Grandma Beebee's out-of-tune piano, a powder room, and a library. The wide staircase split into two staircases at the landing, leading to an open, wrap around hallway on the second floor, with four bedrooms, two baths, and two dressing rooms. The larger of these had once been my father's office, the smaller turned into a linen and storage closet. The effect was imposing but somewhat impractical. The open stairwell allowed sound to travel throughout the house, from one floor to the next, and ate up a lot of square footage. The third floor was enclosed and really more of an attic, gabled and tucked into the roofline, with storage, two smaller bedrooms, and a small bath with a tiny pedestal sink and a shower the size of a phone booth.

Though the attic was small in comparison to the rest of the house, you could have fit my studio apartment up there twice, eight times more if you took the whole house into consideration. But there still wasn't room for all of Aunt Calpurnia's stuff.

Every room was filled to bursting, so much so that we could barely open some of the doors. The stairs to the third floor were completely impassable. I kept looking for some of the pieces that I remembered from my childhood—the long, inlaid mahogany dining table, Beebee's piano, the sideboard filled with her china and sterling. If they were there, they were buried under an avalanche of stuff. Every flat surface was covered with boxes, bins, stacks, and piles. In many instances, the piles had grown into towers and created canyons with walls of stuff on two sides from floor nearly to ceiling, leaving only a narrow walkway to allow passage from one room to another. Trey called them "goat trails."

We followed him through one of the canyons into a relatively open area in the living room, a space about eight feet square. Sitting in the corner was an aunt-size armchair, a television set topped with an old-fashioned rabbit ears antenna, and a TV tray that held rubber-banded stacks of grocery coupons and a flowered teacup with an imprint of pale-pink lipstick still visible on the edge.

I felt so sad and so ashamed. Sad that Calpurnia had ended her days in this room. Shamed that it had come to this. Shame on me.

"Can you *believe* this?" Calvin said, clearly impressed. "Bet you anything that there's a dead cat in here somewhere, probably a few."

"Calvin!"

"What?" He turned out his hands, attempting to look innocent. "I'm not being mean. I've seen every single episode of *Hoarders* and there's always a dead cat. Always. Oh, don't look at me like that. And don't cry. You know I hate that. Please? Oh, cupcake."

I couldn't help myself. I was gutted.

Seeing our family history, strange though it was, disappear under a pile of garbage felt like losing them all over again. When Calvin crossed the room and wrapped me in a bear hug, I only cried harder. By the time I got a grip on myself, the whole front of his shirt was wet.

It was embarrassing to fall apart like that, especially in front someone I'd just met. And this was the second time I'd lost it in front of Trey Holcomb. He probably thought I was an emotional basket case.

"Sorry," I sniffled.

"That's okay. You had to get it out sometime," Calvin said. "And don't worry, I'll send you a bill for the dry cleaning."

"It's a polo," I pointed out. "Wash and wear."

"I know," he said, and patted my shoulder. "I'm sending you a bill anyway."

Even at the lowest moments of my life, Calvin always finds a way to make me smile.

"Sorry," I said again, looking at Trey. "I haven't seen my aunt in so many years. If I'd known . . ." I pressed my lips together. I was *not* going to cry again. "I should have stayed put and hammered her door until hell froze over if I had to. I should have *made* her let me in."

At that point I was talking to Calvin, but it was Trey who answered.

"Even if you'd known what was happening, I doubt you'd have been able to stop it or get your aunt to change. Hoarders are hard to treat."

I didn't like hearing the word *hoarder* applied to Calpurnia, lumping her in with a whole sector of humanity she had nothing in common with apart from this strange malady. It made her seem smaller somehow.

"Sorry," Trey said, hesitating a moment before going on. "Of course, I never met your aunt. But several of my clients have been through court-enforced clean outs. It was traumatic for them and fairly pointless. Most filled the place back up within a few months.

The only time I've seen it work is when the clean out is very grad-ual and overseen by therapists who specialize in hoarding, and sometimes not even then.

"Unless your aunt understood she had a problem and was will-ing to cooperate, there probably wasn't anything you could do. Most hoarders think that other people are the problem. That might explain why your aunt shut you out. Maybe she thought that if she opened the door, you'd try to take away her things."

"But how could she not know? Why would she choose to live like this?"

"I don't know," Trey said, sounding as if he wished he did.

Calvin had been moving about the room while Trey and I were talking, quietly shuffling through stacks of papers, deliberately but cautiously lifting the lids off boxes and examining the contents, probably searching for dead cats. Now he walked to the window and peeled back a sheet of newspaper that had been pasted to the pane.

"Maybe they can tell you," he said, peering through the grimy glass.

I joined him at the window. It was hard to see but I could make out a clump of people standing on the sidewalk, just outside the gate, looking toward the house.

Calvin squinted. "Looks like the neighbors have come calling."

Chapter Eight

Felicia Pickney threw her arms out wide when I opened the door, beaming a smile. "Celia, sugar! You're home!"

Felicia belonged to that particular subset of older southern women I have always admired, the gracious, upbeat, energetic, well-spoken, well-traveled, intellectually curious set who give the impression of finding everyone they meet hugely interesting and somehow make you believe they might be right. Never devoid of pearls, lipstick, a sweater set, and a smile, they all tend to look like retired high school Latin teachers. In Felicia's case, it was true.

She'd taught an entire generation of Charleston's youth to conjugate the verb tenses for love in a Low-Country drawl. But the oversized red eyeglasses she always wore emphasized the spark of delight in her eyes and hinted that the woman who wore them might be a lot more fun than her impeccable manners and otherwise conservative wardrobe suggested. And she was. Felicia might have been the only teacher of dead languages in the country whose classes always had a waitlist. The annual toga/garden party she threw for graduating seniors and Latin alums was considered a very hot ticket.

With Trey and Calvin following in my wake, I wended my way through the totally trashed courtyard. Felicia opened the gate and climbed over the tangle of rusted bikes and broken pots to meet me halfway.

"It is *so* good to see you," she said, giving me a good hard squeeze before placing her hands on my shoulders and looking me in the face. "But dear Calpurnia . . . such a loss. She was a lovely lady. God rest her soul."

"Thank you. It's good to see you too. And Beau."

If Felicia's red glasses offered a subtle hint of her fun-loving nature, Beau Pickney's sartorial choices were more along the lines of a flashing neon sign reading, "Let the good times roll!" He was famous for his wild bow ties and rainbow of brightly colored pants. Back in the day, before Felicia threatened to leave him, Beau's other favorite accessory had been a highball glass filled with bourbon. He cut his consumption back to birthdays, holidays, and one drink on Saturday nights, and surprised everyone by being fun when he was sober too. No matter his age, Beau was kind of a frat boy at heart, always ready for a good time.

His fingers were bony and his hands trembled as he took hold of mine, but he looked as dapper as ever, sporting a bow tie fashioned from brilliant blue, green, black, and bright-orange feathers, a light-blue linen sport jacket, and a pair of lime-green pants. Nobody else could have pulled off that outfit, but on Beau, it worked.

He grinned and patted me on the shoulder. "I was starting to think we might never see you again. Thought you'd gotten too famous to remember all us old coots back home."

"Trust me, I'm not that famous. But look at you!" I said. "Still the best-dressed man in Charleston. Love the tie."

Beau straightened his stooping shoulders and preened a bit, obviously pleased that I'd noticed.

"Just got it. Peacock, pheasant, and guinea feathers. Cost an arm and a leg but what the heck. Might as well spend it while I have a chance. I'm going to turn eighty next month."

"Well, you couldn't tell by looking at you," I said, stretching the truth a little.

"And the tie is very snazzy. Maybe you can give some fashion tips to my friends here," I said, leaning closer and whispering in Beau's ear.

"Maybe," he whispered back, shaking his head. "The one in the suit could use some help."

I introduced Trey and Calvin to both Pickneys. The men shook hands and then stood back to observe the proceedings, Trey with an appearance of patient disinterest, Calvin with the expression of someone who can't wait for the next episode of the soap opera. I returned to the problem at hand.

"Mrs. Pickney, what happened?" I asked, gesturing toward the ruined house.

"I think you're old enough to call me Felicia now, don't you?" She shifted her shoulders and sighed. "Sugar, I wish I could tell you. Calpurnia wasn't ever the same after the accident, but you already knew that. I've always thought it had something to do with the crack she took on her head, when she slammed into the windshield. But it got worse after your daddy died. That's when things started to pile up in the yard. It didn't happen all at once, it took a few years for things to get this bad, but I'd say it's been like this for . . ." She narrowed her eyes, thinking. "Oh, at least six or seven years."

"Why didn't you get hold of me? I'd have come down if I'd known how bad she was."

"Well, I tried getting in touch about four years ago but you'd moved and I couldn't find you. I wrote you a letter."

"I never got it," I said, feeling even guiltier.

"I know. The envelope came back marked 'address unknown' twice. I thought about sending an email to you at the newspaper but, you know, we don't have a computer and—"

"You don't know *anyone* with a computer?" I asked incredulously.

Felicia cringed a little, looking guilty. "No, you're right, Celia. I'm making excuses. I could have gotten hold of you if I'd tried harder; maybe I should have. I did try to call you at the newspaper, just last week, to tell you that your aunt Cal had passed, but they said you weren't working there anymore. But after those first two letters came back . . . Well, the more I thought about it, the more I felt it might be better if you *didn't* know." She put her arm over my shoulder. "Please don't be upset with me, Celia. There wasn't a thing you could have done. You know how stubborn Cal was."

"Well, someone ought to have done *something*." The well-dressed, fifty-something woman had been hanging back, but now she elbowed her way forward and locked eyes. Clearly, I was the someone she had in mind. "I sent complaint after complaint in to the city and got nowhere. This eyesore is bringing down home values on the whole block."

Felicia, who had that particularly southern gift for ignoring any unpleasantness, smiled sweetly. "Celia, allow me to introduce you to Happy Browder. Happy moved here from Atlanta a couple of years ago and bought the Drakes' old house."

Felicia gestured next door, toward a 1950s-era home constructed in a French colonial style, clad with green stucco and sporting a mansard roof and black shutters. As I said, Harleston Village can be a mixed bag, architecturally speaking, but it was a pretty house and much better kept than it once had been, with perfectly trimmed hedges and a newly laid brick driveway in which no blade of grass would dare to sprout.

"Of course, the Drakes haven't lived there for years," Felicia continued. "They sold it to the Edelmans, who sold it to the Walshes, who sold it to . . ." She wrinkled her brow, trying to summon the name. "Well, I can't remember anymore. There have been so many changes in the neighborhood. I read somewhere that twenty-nine people move to Charleston every day. Can you imagine?"

Happy Browder was one of those people whose name absolutely didn't fit. Grumpy Browder, Cranky Browder, Disapproving Browder—any of these would have been perfect for her. But Happy? It just didn't work. I wondered if she'd always been like this or if something had happened to create a personality so much at odds with her name. Happy let out an impatient cough before I could give it much thought, prodding Felicia to move things along.

"But Happy lives here now. And we're so pleased," Felicia trilled, beaming a smile that looked absolutely sincere. "She's an interior designer; turned that old carriage house into a showroom for her business. Wasn't that clever? If you need decorating advice when you move in, you'll know just who to ask."

Move in? Felicia clearly misunderstood my intentions. "Oh, but I—"

Before I could say anything more, Felicia gripped my elbow and steered me toward the next neighbor. "And of course, you remember Mr. Laurens."

I did remember Mr. Laurens. He was famous for two things, being a descendant of the Mr. Laurens who had signed the

Declaration of Independence for South Carolina, and being the snobbiest, crankiest old man in Charleston, a man who despised children, Yankees, and anyone who worked for the government. Mr. Laurens did not, however, appear to remember me.

"You're the new owner?" His voice was gravelly and his drawl as thick as sorghum. He fixed me with his beady eyes; I thought about *Jurassic Park* and the piercing gaze of the raptors just before they bit the heads off whatever sad, unfortunate human had crossed their path.

"Yes, sir. I suppose I am." It was still hard to believe, let alone say out loud.

The old man scowled. "Just what we need. 'Nother damn Yankee moving into the neighborhood."

Felicia put her hand on my forearm. "Now, Charles, Celia is not a Yankee. She's Calpurnia's niece. She was born here, a native Charlestonian. Remember?"

He shook his head so hard I thought his glasses were going to fly off.

"Not anymore. She left. Moved to New York City." He said each word separately, spitting them out like expletives. "No true Charlestonian would *ever* leave Charleston. And if they did? Well, they'd just be a damn Yankee. And we've already got *too many* of those," he said, shoving his glasses back up onto his nose and beaming out the raptor stare, first at me, then at the petite woman who was standing next to him.

She appeared to be in her early thirties, was thin to the point of being delicate, with freckles across her nose, pixie-short auburn hair, and the most amazing legs I've ever seen on anyone who wasn't a professional gymnast. I know that seems weird. I'm not generally in the habit of noticing other women's legs, but the two stems that extended beneath the pleats of her breezy blue cotton skirt were shapely and muscled and basically spectacular. *Was* she a professional gymnast? Or had she simply won the genetic leg lottery? I was dying to know but this isn't the kind of thing you can ask a stranger and I had other matters to deal with just then, like cutting Mr. Laurens off at the knees.

"I'm sorry," I said, raising my hand like a sixth grader requesting a hall pass, "but did you just say that anybody who was born here and then leaves is automatically voted off the island, is that right?"

The old man shot me the raptor stare and I shot it right back.

"That's interesting. Does a moving van have to be involved, an actual change of address, or can your citizenship be rescinded for a temporary leave? Say if you go on vacation for a couple of weeks. I'm just trying to clarify the terms here."

I smiled sweetly and tilted my head to one side, waiting for an answer. Mr. Laurens said, "Harumph."

Really. I'm not making this up; he said, "Harumph," like it was an actual spelled out word, not just some indeterminate noise of contempt, then stomped off across the street.

Felicia laughed and squeezed my shoulder. "Well, my goodness, Celia! You have been gone a long time, haven't you?"

The delicate woman with the great legs put out her hand. "I'm Caroline Fuller," she said. "And I think that was mostly for me. My husband and I bought the house next door to Mr. Laurens."

She turned and pointed across the street to a small Charleston single house, so named because when seen from the street they're just one room wide, with a two-story wooden piazza running on the long side of the house.

"The Taylors used to live there," Felicia whispered in my ear. "But after Clarice died, Valentine moved to Memphis to live with his daughter. The Fullers seem like the sweetest young couple, but what with her coming from up north and her husband being black, Mr. Laurens hasn't exactly welcomed them with open arms. Ignorant old coot."

Felicia's whisper was soft but not so soft that her words would have been impossible to overhear. But if Caroline had heard Felicia's commentary, she must have chosen to pretend otherwise because when she turned toward us again, she seemed not the least bit perturbed or annoyed.

"Heath, that's my husband," Caroline explained, "is from Charleston but we met in Dayton. We worked at the same museum. He was a curator, I was in marketing. But then he got a job offer from the Historic Charleston Foundation, so we packed up our stuff and here we are. He's the museums coordinator and I'm consulting from home. It's kind of been an adjustment but I sure don't miss the Ohio winters. Anyway . . . I just thought I'd come over and say hi."

Mr. Laurens, who had hobbled back across the street, chose that moment to signal his disgust by slamming his front door closed. The noise was so loud that everybody's heads swiveled north, toward the sound. When Caroline turned back toward me, her cheeks were pink but there was a look of determination in her eyes. She took a big breath.

"Look. The bottom line is it's been kind of a rough transition and I'm in the market for a new best friend. I don't suppose you're a runner, are you? I've been hoping to find somebody to train with in the mornings."

Ah. So Caroline Fuller hadn't won the Leg Lottery; she had to work at it. This and her frankness made me like her more. All my friends were in New York, but if I had been looking for more, Caroline definitely would have made the short list.

"Sorry, but the only time I run is if something's chasing me."

"What about dancing?" she asked hopefully. "Heath and I are into salsa and tango. We found a great little studio over in West Ashley."

"Afraid not. And, anyway, I won't be—"

"Well. It was worth a shot." She glanced at her watch. "Uh-oh. I'm late for a conference call. Sorry. But I'm sure I'll see you around, right?" She trotted off before I had a chance to explain that no, she wouldn't be seeing me around because I wasn't staying.

A car pulled up and a blond woman with bright-blue eyes and a harried expression jumped out of it, said she was Dana Alton, the Realtor, and started apologizing, over and over again, for being late.

"I am so, so, *so* sorry! My youngest forgot her permission slip for the field trip so I had to run to the school and— Never mind." She flapped her hand dismissively. "You don't care about all that. Sorry again. Hey," she said, addressing Trey, who had been listening politely this whole time. "Did I miss anything?"

"Yes, you did." Happy Browder's voice was scowling but her face was smooth as a piece of wax and weirdly frozen, one of those faces that could have passed for mid-forties in the dim light but which you realized was probably a decade older once you saw it in daylight. Happy was clearly a regular at one of the local medi-spas. "You missed the part where she explains what she's going to do to clean up this monstrosity. It's a mess! It has rats! I saw one crawl out from under that dead oleander bush two weeks ago. It was big as a cat!"

Calvin's eyes glittered. Felicia squeezed my hand.

"I have never seen so much as a mouse in Calpurnia's garden," she said evenly. "Maybe it was a cat."

"Well," Happy sputtered, "all I know is that this house is destroying property values for the entire block."

"Funny, you didn't seem to mind that when you bought your place," Beau said, jerking his chin toward Happy's house.

"Beau," Felicia said gently.

"What? She knew the condition of the Fairchild house when she decided to move here; it's not like she could have missed it," Beau said, throwing out one of his hands. "So I don't see where she's got a lot of business griping about it dragging down prices now that she's here."

"Beau," Felicia said again, this time in a slightly firmer tone.

Beau wasn't taking the hint. "If anyone's to blame, it's her! Everybody knows what she paid for her place. She got it for a song!"

"And did a *wonderful* job with the renovation," Felicia enthused, deftly changing the subject. "I've been meaning to tell you how much I like those new entry sconces. Do you carry those in your shop?"

Happy shot Beau a look before answering. "They were a special order. I can see about finding another pair if you're interested."

"I might just do that. My goodness but it's warm standing out here in the sun!" Felicia said, fanning herself with her hand and then gesturing toward the pink Italianate house with the black shutters near the end of the block that she and Beau had lived in since before I was born. "Would y'all like to come over to our house for a glass of tea? It'll be so much cooler on the piazza."

Happy begged off, saying she needed to get to work, which is what I suspect Felicia was hoping would happen. Keeping Happy and Beau in close quarters didn't seem like a very good idea. When Felicia shooed Beau off home, saying he looked like he needed to sit down, which was true, I made my apologies, explaining that I had paperwork to deal with.

"That's all right," Felicia said with a smile. "We'll have plenty of time to catch up and drink tea now that you're back home. Mr.

Holcomb, I can't thank you enough for tracking Celia down. It would have been a shame to see the house turned over to the state and then passed into other hands. Times change, of course. There are so many new people moving into the neighborhood," she said, her gaze drifting down the street. "But I can't remember a time when there weren't Fairchilds living here. No one in Charleston can."

Before I could respond, Felicia draped her arm over my shoulder again, giving me a farewell squeeze before tottering off after Beau. As she walked away, she looked at me over her shoulder, beaming.

"Celia, sugar, I'm just so thrilled that you're home. I'm *so* happy we're going to be neighbors again!

Chapter Nine

A waiter appeared carrying a tray loaded with sweet tea, deviled eggs, miniature lobster rolls, and a cheese platter.

"I thought we needed a snack," Calvin explained. "Aren't you hungry?"

Of course, I was. Emotional upheaval always brings on an appetite.

Trey had given Calvin and me a lift back to the hotel. Trey and I had some paperwork to fill out, so the three of us found a table in the palm tree–shaded courtyard where guests could enjoy lunch, dinner, or drinks when the weather was fine. Dana Alton came in her own car, arriving shortly after the food. I caught sight of her walking down a brick path toward the courtyard and waved for her to join us.

She smiled and started toward us but was waylaid by an absurdly tall man with wavy black hair, a jaw chiseled enough to slice cheese, and shoulders so broad they looked like they were about to burst the seams of his blue linen sport coat. He and Dana seemed to know each other; they talked for a few minutes, Dana nodding now and again and casting glances toward our table. I was too occupied with the paperwork to pay much attention, but I glanced in that direction just as they appeared to be wrapping up. The man with the iron jaw looked at me, flashed a big, friendly grin, and lifted his hand in a wave. If I'd been in New York I'd have ignored him, but in Charleston waves are returned, even waves to gigantic strangers with teeth too white to be real.

The giant walked off. Dana sat down, asked the waiter to bring her an unsweet iced tea, and proceeded to tell me a lot of what I already knew.

"It's a lovely property, of course. So much potential. But if you're hoping to attract a residential buyer, there's a whole lot of work that would need to be done before you put the house on the market."

"I was hoping for a quick sale."

"Well, you'd need to find a buyer who would be willing to purchase it as is, with no inspections and no contingencies. Those buyers are out there but they're generally investors, people who are looking to buy cheaply, fix it up as quickly as possible, and flip it to a new buyer to reap maximum profits. But the sheer size of your house limits the pool of potential buyers. More square footage means more time and money in the renovation.

"I don't know if you noticed, but that man I was talking to?" Dana's eyes shifted toward the spot where the man had intercepted her. "His name is Cabot James and he's a real estate developer. He buys large properties and divides them up into smaller units that he can rent or sell for a profit, mostly duplexes. Cabot's been looking to do a bigger project for some time now, but it's hard to find lots big enough downtown and he's had his eye on your aunt's house ever since she passed away.

"I know that sounds kind of creepy," she said, responding to the discomfort on my face, "but believe me, he wasn't the only one. The competition for land and property downtown is fierce. If ownership of your aunt's house had reverted to the state, he would have tried to pick it up at auction. Since that didn't happen, he'd like to make you an offer, a cash deal, as-is, with no inspections."

Considering the condition of the house, the figure she named wasn't insulting or predatory. But it was far below what I'd need to buy a home anyplace near New York, including New Jersey. Still, I can't say I wasn't tempted by the thought of some ready cash; being jobless will do that to a person.

"What would he want to do with it?"

"Hard to say at this point," Dana said. "He could do what he's done with other properties, divide it up into apartments, but on a bigger scale. Six units? Maybe eight?"

"Eight? That's crazy. Where would people park?"

"My guess is he'd pave over the garden."

What? Cabot James wanted to rip up Calpurnia's oleanders and palms and magnolias and crape myrtles? Tear out the brick planters and the pergola and replace them with asphalt? The garden was a mess, utterly overgrown and neglected, but the idea of paving it over seemed almost sacrilegious.

Dana paused just long enough to nibble a piece of cheese before going on. "But rather than apartments, I suspect he'd prefer to tear the place down, build about four or five brand-new condos, and sell them."

I gasped. "Just bulldoze down a beautiful historic house? The city would never let him do that, would they?"

"Hard to say," Dana replied. "But the house was built in the 1920s, which isn't all that old by Charleston standards. He'd have to get a zoning exemption, but the city is under a lot of pressure to provide more affordable housing, and Cabot has a lot of connections."

I looked toward Calvin to see what he thought of all this, but he was uncharacteristically quiet and deeply involved with the lobster sliders. Trey Holcomb was just sitting there with no expression on his face, listening but not talking, basically being Switzerland.

"Of course, fixing it up yourself is still an option," Dana said cheerfully. "You wouldn't get the kind of return you'd see if the house was located south of Broad, but Harleston Village is still a desirable area. A lot of young families prefer a mixed-use neighborhood and having their favorite shops and restaurants nearby. If your house was move-in ready, I'm sure it would sell quickly and for a good price."

Dana must have mistaken my silence for hesitation because when I frowned, she shot Trey a quick look, perhaps wondering if he knew something she didn't.

"Of course, I understand completely if you've changed your mind about selling. It's one thing to say you're going to do it when you're a thousand miles away and something else after you've actually walked through it. All those memories. But it is an awfully *big* house," she said. "For one person, I mean. Still, if you'd like to live there yourself . . ."

My head was starting to hurt. I rubbed my forehead with my hand.

"No. It's not that. I mean—of course, I have memories of the house, some good ones," I said truthfully.

Though the house was squalid and the image of what it once had been was buried beneath piles of rubble, the memories it carried were still intact. But it *was* a big house—too big for one person. And my life was in New York. Everyone I knew, everything I had, was in Manhattan.

"Celia? Are you all right?"

Dana touched my hand. I looked up and found them all staring at me. Even Calvin had stopped eating to look at me. "Sorry. I'm fine," I said with an embarrassed laugh. "I've got a lot on my mind, I guess. Everything has been so crazy for the last couple of weeks."

Dana bobbed her head sympathetically. "I'm sure. Losing your aunt must have been a shock."

"Yes. But it's not just that. So much more has happened," I said.

And then, for some insane reason, I told them exactly what.

All of it. In detail.

It took a while.

"Wow," Dana said when I finally finished. "And I thought my life was stressful. You've really been through the wringer—the divorce, and the baby thing, and then losing your job and rights to your pen name. I didn't know they could do that. *Can* they do that?" she asked, shooting Trey an indignant look but going on without waiting for an answer. "And I had no idea that you were Dear Calpurnia! For some reason, I always thought she was older."

"Yeah. I get that a lot."

"Didn't *you* think Dear Calpurnia was older?" Dana said, shooting a look toward Trey.

"Until this moment, I never knew there was a Dear Calpurnia."

Dana's jaw went slack. "Seriously? Who hasn't heard of Dear Calpurnia?"

I've never really been crazy about beards—they always make me wonder if the guy has a weak chin or something—but Trey had really nice brown eyes. If he shaved off the beard and got rid of the awful suit, maybe he'd look a little younger and less serious. Not that I cared one way or the other, but when he spread and flipped over his hands and made a sort of sorry-but-I-live-under-a-rock face, he was actually kind of cute. And the way Dana rolled her eyes in response made me feel bad for him. I mean, it wasn't like never having heard of my column meant he was a cave dweller or anything.

Truthfully, it's always kind of a relief when I meet someone who doesn't look at me and see Dear Calpurnia. Trey Holcomb didn't think of me as younger, or shorter, or lesser than he'd thought I would be because he'd had no preconceived notions about me. I doubted we'd meet again after today, but still, it felt refreshing to start out with a clean slate, to be known just as myself.

"Well," Dana puffed. "I just don't understand how that paper can claim to own your name. It's so unfair! I am *never* going to read Daily McKee— Excuse me." Dana interrupted herself when her purse started to buzz, then pulled out her phone, looked at a text, and groaned. "Oh, no. I'm late picking my daughter up from kindergarten again. Forgive me, but I really have to run."

She picked up her purse and got to her feet.

"Celia, if you want to sell the house to Cabot, then I'll help make that happen. But you'll make a whole lot more if you can put the time and money into cleaning it out and fixing it up. I know that approach doesn't help you with your immediate problem but . . ." She shrugged helplessly. "Give it some thought. I'll do anything I can to help you."

Dana left. I took a sip of tea and looked at Trey, who had gone back to looking serious. I was feeling kind of dumb. "Well, I guess you know my entire life story now. Sorry. I don't know what got into me."

"Listen," Trey said, stroking his beard for a moment before going on. "I don't know if you'd be interested, but if you want, I'll take your case."

I glanced at Calvin, who lifted his eyebrows in a well-isn't-this-interesting kind of expression.

"Why? Every lawyer I've talked to says it's a lost cause."

"Yeah, well." Trey shifted his shoulders. "I kind of specialize in those. I'm not saying we'd win. I've never taken on a huge corporation, so you'd probably be better off with someone who has more experience. But if nobody else will represent you, I will."

"Wow. That's . . . That's incredibly nice of you." I bit my lip, feeling awkward about asking the next question. "Can I ask how much you'd want for a retainer?"

"How much have you got?" I swallowed hard and Trey grinned. "Just kidding. If we win, I'll take thirty percent of any damages. If we lose, I'll only charge you for out-of-pocket expenses—mailing, copying, filing fees, and stuff like that."

"But why would you do that? You'd basically be volunteering your time. I mean, you know I've got almost no chance of winning, right?"

"I know," he said simply. "But I'm just dumb enough to believe that everybody deserves their day in court. In all honesty, it might be smarter to take the severance. I'll understand if you do. But if you decide to fight, I'm willing to help."

He got to his feet and said his good-byes, saying again how sorry he was about Aunt Calpurnia. Calvin's eyes followed him as he walked away.

"There goes the nicest and worst-dressed lawyer in Charleston."

I couldn't argue with that. But he *did* have nice eyes.

Chapter Ten

*Y*ou can't think on an empty stomach," Calvin had argued. "I am not letting you skip dinner two nights in a row."

"Honestly, Calvin, I'm not hungry."

"You will be by the time we get to the restaurant. Trust me."

He knew me so well. When the server put the appetizers down on the table between us, I realized I was starving.

"So much for dieting. Guess I'll start my transformation next week. *So* good," I said, groaning after taking a bite of fried tomato, topped with a sprinkle of tangy goat cheese and savory-sweet candied pecans.

Poogan's Porch, known for taking classic southern dishes and kicking them up a notch, is one of the oldest restaurants in downtown Charleston. The two-story Victorian was painted a sunny yellow and had wide piazzas on each floor where diners can people-watch and catch a breeze. But Calvin and I were seated inside, in a dining room with beamed ceilings and wide-planked wooden floors.

"*This* is amazing," I said, pointing at the plate with my fork.

"New York chefs have no idea how to fry a tomato. I wonder why that is."

"Not enough lard?" Calvin asked, tipping his head to one side.

"Shut up." I laughed and took another bite.

Our entrees arrived just as the door of the restaurant opened to admit two women, one older and one younger. Happy Browder was dressed to the nines in a blue St. John knit suit with a white silk scarf at the neck, her attire very much at odds with that of her companion. The younger woman, who couldn't have been more than twenty, was wearing faded denim shorts, black tennis shoes and black stockings that hit her above the knee, a green-and-black flannel shirt over a black T-shirt adorned with an image of a handprint that said "Talk To The Palm," and a green knitted beanie on her head, with two long brown braids hanging down. It wasn't a look that I could have pulled off but I thought she looked darling. Happy didn't appear to share my opinion.

The girl removed her flannel shirt, revealing a large, colorful tattoo of a dragonfly flitting near a lily that covered most of her forearm. Happy turned toward her. The stormy look in her eyes and twisting of her lips made it clear she was about to snarl an instruction to *put that back on right now!* But before Happy could speak, she caught sight of me watching the scene. Though it obviously required an effort, she smiled at me and waved. I waved back.

"Don't look now but we're about to have company."

Calvin glanced over his shoulder and saw Happy crossing the room. "Who's that with her? And why are they coming over here?"

"I'm pretty sure it's her daughter. And they have to come over. She saw me looking at her and so now they have to come and say hello."

Calvin gave me a quizzical look.

"It's the South," I explained. "There are rules."

"Well!" Happy said brightly when she reached our table. "So nice to see the two of you again so soon. This is my daughter, Priscilla. I just picked her up at the airport. She's home from college for the summer, so I'm taking her out to celebrate."

"Nice to meet you," Calvin said, looking her up and down as he shook her hand. "*Love* your outfit."

Priscilla's face lit up at the compliment. "Thanks! I'm a fashion blogger."

"She's a *student*," Happy corrected. "She's studying business at Florida State."

"What's the name of your blog?" Calvin asked, ignoring Happy.

"*Heck Yes, Hipster*. I just started it in January."

"You know, Celia used to be a blogger," he said, nodding toward me.

"Really? What was your blog?"

"*Georgia Peach in the Big Apple*. But that was a long time ago."

The girl's eyes went wide and she clapped her hand over her mouth. "No way!" she exclaimed after removing it. "You're Dear Calpurnia? I love your column. And your blog. I'm taking a class on the History of the Internet of Things; my professor used your blog as a case study on the early successes in online commerce. Oh, my gosh. I *cannot* believe I'm actually standing here talking to you!"

Calvin grinned. "Did you hear that, Cel? You've made history. Ancient history. Future generations are learning from your example."

"It's always nice to meet another writer," I said, after shooting Calvin a look.

Priscilla's cheeks colored. "Oh. I'm not really a writer. I've only got eight hundred Instagram followers. Well, eight hundred and twenty-six as of today."

"And you only started blogging a few months ago? That's impressive," I said. I wasn't just being nice. It's a lot harder to attract an audience than it was when I started out. "You must be doing something right."

"Well. We really should let you two get back to your dinner." Happy was still smiling but there was ice in her eyes. I don't think she appreciated my encouraging Priscilla's interest in blogging. "I'm sure we'll be seeing you around the neighborhood. When do you plan to start cleaning out your aunt's house? *Soon*, I hope."

Ah, yes. There it was. So much for the veneer of good manners.

"Wait. You're Miss Fairchild's niece?" Priscilla shook her head and laughed. "Of course, you are. Dear Calpurnia. I should have figured that out. It's so great we're going to be neighbors!"

"Well, I don't think—"

"Hey, could I come over and talk to you about my blog sometime? Just for a few minutes." She raised her hand flat, like she was taking an oath. "An hour, tops. I'd just really appreciate any tips you could give me."

She was so earnest and very sweet and her eyes had the pleading, hopeful look of a puppy begging to be picked up. How could I say no? "Sure. I'd love that. Come over anytime."

"Thanks!"

"Pris," Happy said, turning the end of the syllable into a hiss and taking a firm hold on her daughter's elbow. "Their food is getting cold and we're going to miss our reservation."

Priscilla blushed again. "Right. Sorry to interrupt your dinner. It was nice to meet you. See y'all later," she said, grinning before heading off with her mother.

Calvin watched them walk away. "Those two are going to have a *very* long summer."

"I know, right? Do you think her parents named her Happy as a joke?"

My shrimp and grits had cooled off a bit but were still delicious. Calvin said the fried chicken served with collard greens and hot honey was fabulous and totally worth the required upping of his cholesterol medication.

After delivering his verdict on the food, Calvin observed how completely adorable that little Priscilla Browder looked in her beanie, braids, and denim shorts. I had to agree. She definitely had her finger on the pulse of hipster fashion. This observation brought up the topic of fashion in general and a discussion of the current trend toward rompers and jumpsuits, something we both agreed should die a rapid and ignominious death, which led to some commentary about Melanie, who had tried to pull off the jumpsuit look on a recent episode of *Real Housewives of New Jersey* and failed, which led to a discussion of the relationship between Honey Boo Boo and Mama June, which led to some observations about complicated mother-daughter relationships in general, which led us back to Happy and Priscilla, then just to Priscilla, whom we both agreed we liked.

It was a nice evening, all considered. The food was great and the conversation was as fluffy and inconsequential as a mouthful of cotton candy, which was exactly what I needed. If Calvin had pushed away his plate, looked me squarely in the eye, and said, "So. How *are* you?" I would have burst into tears. Again. Cotton candy conversation about jumpsuits and Honey Boo Boo came as a relief.

But that didn't mean he wasn't thinking. Calvin is always thinking.

AROUND ONE IN the morning, there was a knock on my door. It was soft, more a tap than a knock. If I'd been sleeping, I probably wouldn't have heard it. But I hadn't been sleeping. My brain was too busy thinking about everything that had happened, trying to sort through my options, none of them attractive, and getting nowhere. Calvin, apparently, had been doing the same thing. But unlike me, he'd actually reached some conclusions.

"Are you okay?" I asked after opening the door and finding him standing in the hallway, dressed in blue striped pajamas and a white bathrobe with a monogram—CLG—in the same shade of blue as the pajamas.

"You travel with your own bathrobe?"

"Shut up. The hotel robes are never big enough to go around." He walked in without waiting for an invitation and took a seat on the edge of the bed. "Listen, I've been thinking it over." He took a deep breath. "You should stay in Charleston."

"What?" My mouth dropped open, shocked that he'd even suggest such a thing. "Why would I do that? My whole life is New York."

"Wrong. Your job was in New York. So was your marriage. But those are over. So what's keeping you?"

"My friends, for one thing." I paused for a moment, considering how many people I knew in New York that I truly cared about. "Well, you, anyway. What's going on? Are you trying to get rid of me or something?"

He shook his head. "Celia, what's the one thing you want more than anything in the world? A baby, right? A family. You've been talking about it for as long as I've known you. Now, after all this time, you've got a chance. You can't walk away from that.

"First thing tomorrow, you should hire a crew to clean out Calpurnia's house and fix it up into a real home. It'd be a great place to raise a kid—plenty of room, nice garden, nice neighbors. Well, except for Happy." He shuddered. "When the lawyer comes for the home visit, steer her clear of the charming Mrs. Browder."

"Calvin, I—"

He shook his head, harder, and held up his hand to cut me off. "Think about it, Celia. The birth mother won't care where you live as long as the house is nice. The place is a wreck right now but it *could* be gorgeous. Unless you win the lottery, you'd never be able to afford anything that nice in the city."

"Well, okay, but right now it's a wreck. Where am I supposed to get the money to fix it up? We're not talking about a little paint, some new throw pillows, and a trip to IKEA. This is going to involve lumber and electricians, possibly a backhoe. All that takes money. I'm out of a job, remember?"

Calvin looked at me square on. His expression was uncharacteristically serious and, I thought, a little sad.

"Take the money, Celia. Sign the stupid separation letter and take the severance. It'll be enough for you to remodel the house and then some."

I gasped. "And let Dan McKee get away with it? You heard Trey Holcomb, he said he'd help me go after McKee and won't charge me anything unless we win!"

"Yeah, but you're not *going* to win. Cupcake," he said in a flat, get-real tone, "I understand McKee was sneaky and underhanded, but you should have read the damned contract before you signed it."

I set my jaw, irritated that he was throwing that up at me. It wasn't like I hadn't told myself the same thing about two zillion times but wasn't he supposed to be on my side? Whatever happened to loyalty?

"So, you just expect me to give up on making him have to face up to what he did? Give up on—"

"On Calpurnia. Yes," Calvin said, nodding. "Honey. You don't *need* to be her anymore. You're so good at being yourself. Or you would be, if you'd just give it a chance. Don't you see? This is the only way. You don't get to be Calpurnia, Celia, and a mother all at the same time. You have to choose."

He was right, I knew that. But why did I have to choose? Plenty of other women got to have kids and careers. Why was I the only one who had to choose? And what if I chose wrong?

"What if doesn't work?" I asked. "What if I do all that—walk away from the column, take the money, fix up the house—and the birth mother picks a different family? I'd have given up everything, and for what?"

"For a chance to be happy," Calvin said. "That's the most anybody ever gets, Cel. A chance. But you already know that. Just like you know that the only way we get that chance is to take a chance, on ourselves, on other people. That's why I married Simon. That's why you married Steve."

"Yeah. Look how that worked out," I muttered.

Calvin is never short on banter or snappy retorts. But for the first time in my memory, twice in one conversation, he had nothing to say. Or nothing he was willing to say. Maybe, like me, he was afraid that talking would end in tears.

Calvin was my best friend and I was his. Nothing was ever going to change that. But if I left New York, it would leave a hole in both our lives. Yes, we'd talk on the phone. We'd Skype and text and leave hearts and emojis and comments on each other's Instagram stories. But that's no substitute for spending time together, face to face and side by side. If I left New York, I would miss Calvin so much, and he would miss me. Even so, he was telling me to go, because he wanted me to be happy.

Would I be happy? Would anything work out the way I hoped it would? Maybe. Maybe not. Like Calvin said, a chance is the best that anybody gets.

I took a deep breath.

"Okay, then. I guess . . . I'll stay." Calvin bobbed his head and I paused for a moment, trying to let the finality of my decision sink in. "I guess tomorrow we should go over to the house and—"

"Cel," he said, shaking his head and cutting me off, "I've got to go back in the morning. Simon called. The warlords have shut down the clinic and they're being thrown out of the country. He'll land at JFK late tomorrow night and I'm going to meet him at the airport. I'm sorry. I hate leaving you in a lurch but . . ."

He didn't need to apologize. Simon was Calvin's chance for happiness, just like the baby might be mine. I wouldn't stand in the way of that.

"It's okay," I said, and tried to smile so he'd know it really was. "I've got this. Tell you what, we'll have breakfast in the morning and then I'll take you to the airport. Want to go to the biscuit place again?"

He shook his head. "I'm on a six o'clock flight. I'm going to sleep a couple of hours, then pack and grab a cab. You should go back to bed. You've got a big day tomorrow."

He got to his feet and gave me a hug. I hugged him back, holding on tight, willing myself not to cry because if I started, I knew he would too. I've lost count of how many times we've watched *Miracle on 34th Street*. But whenever Susie jumps out of the car and into the house that's her Christmas wish come true, Calvin always tears up. He uses humor to hide it, but the truth is, Calvin is even more sentimental than I am.

"I'm really going to miss you," I said.

"Me too, cupcake. Like a front tooth," he said, giving me a squeeze. "I love you, Cel. I'd never, *ever* want to sleep with you, not in a million years, but I love you."

I laughed and swiped at my eyes and let go.

"Same here."

Chapter Eleven

When I woke up it was Sunday. Calvin was gone and, for the first time in my life, I wished I had a dog.

Don't get me wrong; it's not that I'm anti-dog. Dogs are cute, from a distance. And I can understand why some people might want one. I've just never been one of those people. Dogs are slobbery and invasive and a little rude, sticking their noses into places they have no business being. They're also super needy. I once heard a comedian say that getting a dog is like having someone move in with you who's been through a lot lately and needs to talk about it. That about sums it up.

But you're never out of place when you're walking a dog. A dog gives you purpose, a reason for being wherever you're at. I'd have handed over twenty bucks for a rental dog that day. Everybody but me seemed to be traveling in a pack.

South of Broad, gaggles of tourists posed in front of mansions and took each other's pictures. At White Point Gardens, a park at the southern tip of the downtown peninsula, a dozen or so women wearing silk dresses and pearls, accompanied by men wearing sport coats and shined shoes, stood at the foot of the gazebo to watch a bride and groom exchange vows. Two little boys in blue suits and a girl with a wreath in her hair, having apparently lost interest in the proceedings, played a game of tag around the massive trunks of the ancient oaks. At the battery, a group of twenty-somethings in shorts and backpacks stood at the railing and gazed across the harbor to Fort Sumter as a tour guide in cargo shorts and a broad-brimmed straw hat gave a CliffsNotes version of the history of Charleston. On East Bay Street, couples held hands as they strolled past the ice cream–colored town houses of Rainbow Row.

I passed at least a dozen churches of Charleston's four hundred houses of worship on my walk, and all of them seemed to be doing a bang-up business. Charleston isn't called the Holy City for nothing. When the double doors opened at St. Philip's, a Bach organ sonata spilled out onto the street along with streams of worshippers in their Sunday best, chatting and smiling and pausing to shake the hand of a priest wearing a white robe and green chasuble.

There were one or two faces I thought I recognized in that crowd, but it was unlikely: I hadn't gone to a service at St. Philip's since before I'd left for college, more than twenty years ago. Though she was standing with her back to me, when I glimpsed a tall, willowy figure with a tangle of red curls, I thought it might be someone I'd known once, a long time ago. But she looked different from the front, too old to be my onetime friend. Our eyes locked for an instant, then she looked away quickly and I felt sort of silly. I don't know why I'd thought it might be her; she'd left Charleston years before and never even gone to St. Philip's, or any church as far as I knew. Wishful thinking, I suppose.

I walked away, feeling empty and invisible, averting my eyes from the cemetery across the street, taking a roundabout route so I wouldn't have to walk past that far corner of the churchyard where Calpurnia was resting beneath uneven ground and new sod. It was too soon. I wasn't ready. Maybe I never would be.

Feeling like the only untethered person in town resurrected that sole-castaway-on-an-overpopulated-island sensation I'd experienced during my first months in New York. But this was worse. It's one thing to feel all alone when you're in a new city and another to feel that way in the place where you grew up. Every building, monument, bush, and tree was as familiar as my own reflection, but the city had forgotten me. I felt almost spectral, like a ghost who could see others but couldn't be seen herself.

"Eat something sweet and the feeling will pass" was my Grandma Beebee's advice in regards to basically everything. Knitting and eating pralines were her primary occupations, which probably went a long way toward explaining her size and health problems. On the other hand, she always seemed to be pretty happy. When I walked through the open sheds at the Old City Market, past the vendors selling trinkets and candles and sweetgrass baskets and muslin bags of Carolina Gold rice, then exited onto Market Street and spotted River Street Sweets, it seemed like an omen.

The pralines were fresh and buttery and ridiculously sweet. The momentary pleasure of eating them dulled my mood but didn't lift it. I thought about going back to the hotel, but the mental image of me sitting alone in my room as the sound of laughter and tinkling glassware floated up from the courtyard where families and lovers and friends would be enjoying brunch was too pathetic to contemplate. Calvin was right; the life I'd led in New York was over. But so was the life I'd once led in Charleston. Which seemed to leave only one option, to find a new life.

Easier said than done. Suppose, just suppose, that everything went according to plan. Suppose the remodeling went smoothly, and the home visit went great, and the birth mother picked me, and the baby became mine.

Then what?

If there was one thing I'd learned from years of reading and writing Dear Calpurnia letters, it's that there are about ten gazillion ways for parents to screw up a kid. Love went a long way, but there had to be more to raising a child than that. I'd told Calvin that as long as a child had one person who loved and believed in them, they generally turned out okay. But was that really true? Even if it was, I didn't want my child to turn out just okay. I wanted her—assuming it was a girl, something told me it was—to feel happy, successful, loved, and spectacularly comfortable in her own skin.

How was I supposed to make that happen? How would I guide her, protect her, show her the right path? How would I keep her from repeating my mistakes?

And on a more practical note, how was I going to provide for her? I still wasn't one hundred percent convinced about taking the severance, but if I did, the money would only last so long. How would we live after that? The only thing I actually knew how to do was write, and that, as my current circumstances illustrated, was a far from sure and somewhat ridiculous way to try and make a living.

If you're a writer, you really can't *not* write; it was too late for me to save myself. But I should try to guide her toward steadier, more lucrative lines of work, if possible. I definitely needed to make sure she took a lot of math and science classes and steered clear of student debt, as well as men who had too many ex-girlfriends, or whose eyes drifted toward other women when they went out to dinner with you, or who didn't put up at least *some* kind of fight when you suggested splitting the check on a first date.

There were so many ways to go wrong in life, I thought to myself as I crossed the street and approached the shop with the red door and the black awning. The chances of everything working out the way I hoped were slim: I understood that. But suppose, just suppose, that everything *did* work out and the birth mother picked me. I didn't want to leave everything until the last minute, did I? There were so many things I needed to tell her, all important. Maybe I ought to start writing them down?

At almost the exact moment these thoughts were circling my brain, I saw it—the bookstore display of exquisite leather-bound journals. They were beautiful. And they were calling to me.

Given the precarious state of my finances, I had no business going into a bookstore, even if I told myself I was only going to browse. And really, who was I kidding? Experience has proven that I am preternaturally incapable of leaving a bookstore without buying something. Buying a gorgeous, fifty-nine-dollar, chocolate-brown journal with hundreds of pages of thick, sturdy, cream-colored pages and end papers decorated with delicious red-and-gold hand marbling would be irresponsible bordering on crazy. The only books I'd ever spent sixty dollars on were college textbooks; this one didn't even come with words.

I bought it anyway and, an hour later, took a seat at the too-small-for-real-writing desk in my hotel room, opened the journal, lowered my nose to the first pages, and sniffed.

The paper smelled like dust, leather, and beginnings. But several minutes passed before I was able to pick up my pen and start. How should I begin? What did I want to tell her? The answer of course was everything.

But if there was one thing I'd picked up during my career as a pseudo journalist, it's never to bury the lede, which basically means you should get to the point, and quickly.

Dear Peaches,

My name is Celia Fairchild and, if everything works out like I hope it will, I'm going to be your mother.

If hearing that makes you nervous, I won't hold it against you. I'm pretty nervous about it myself. Excited but nervous. But that's normal, isn't it? I mean, does anybody ever feel totally prepared for motherhood?

According to the Internet, at approximately twelve weeks' gestation, you're about two inches long, weigh half an ounce, and have all your major organs in place. (Way to go, Peaches! Keep up the good work!) You are also the size of a plum.

I considered calling you "Plummy" but only briefly. It sounded too British, a name for some not particularly popular school chum who wears tweed and rides to hounds. Next week, you'll be lemon-sized, but that didn't bode well as a name either. At week fourteen, you'll be the size of a peach, a sweeter and far more adorable fruit, so I decided to go with that. But Peaches is just a nickname, something I'll use for now. I don't think it's fair for parents to pick out names before they've even laid eyes on the baby. How many times do you meet someone whose name just doesn't fit them?

That's a rhetorical question; you haven't met anybody yet but, trust me, it happens. I had a friend in college named Tiffany who was studying astrophysics. She was absolutely brilliant but nobody would take her seriously. And I once met a Rupert who belonged to a biker gang and cooked meth in his garage. Names matter, Peaches, so I don't want to choose yours until we've had a chance to get to know each other.

Speaking of getting to know each other, you're probably wondering why I'm writing to you. Though you might suppose it was a professional hazard, I'm not actually in the habit of handing out unsolicited advice. I prefer to wait until asked. But when it comes to you, Peaches, things are different. I can't stop thinking about what I might say to warn you or guide you. It's weird, Peaches, and not really like me.

It makes me wonder; am I already becoming a mother?

Will I trade thongs and leggings for granny panties and high-waisted jeans? Will I begin pulling to the side of the road to read historical markers aloud? When the car comes to a sudden and screeching halt, will I start flinging my arm across the person in the adjoining seat? Will I start saying "tee-tee" and "poopy" without feeling skeeved out? Will I give up reasoned argument in favor of "Because I said so" and "Don't make me come up there!" Is my downward spiral into utter uncoolness inevitable?

Maybe. But I don't care.

I keep thinking about things I want to tell you in hopes of saving you from making the same mistakes I've made. How many times in my life have I thought, "If I only knew then what I know now . . ."?

But if someone had told me then what I know now, would I have listened? Will you? Are you the sort of kid who will be willing to read the book and absorb the lesson? Or are you the type who has to take the field trip to find out for herself? Most people fall into the second category. I know I do. You probably will too.

Even though I haven't met you and there's only a thirty-something percent chance I ever will, I already love you. I want to protect you but I also want to know you, good and bad, strengths and weaknesses, inside and out. I want you to know me too. Because at the end of the day, that's what love truly is: knowing and

*being known. That's what we long for more than anything, to be
known and loved for who we truly are.*

If we . . .

My pen stopped in mid-sentence, interrupted by the image of
myself standing in front of St. Philip's, longing and afraid of being
recognized, then walking away quickly, hurrying past the churchyard with downcast eyes.

I crossed out the two words of the paragraph I'd started and
began again, more honestly.

*Advice and counsel aren't the only reason that I want to write,
perhaps that I need to write, this journal. Yes, it's about you,
Peaches. But I think it's about me too.*

*For fifteen years, I've been playing a part, avoiding the past,
averting my eyes, refusing to dig through the garbage or ask the
hard questions. Only a child believes that covering her eyes makes
the thing she's afraid to see disappear.*

*How can I ever hope to be known by you, by anyone, if I don't
know myself?*

Chapter Twelve

The desk clerk, a handsome, twenty-fiveish man wearing the ubiquitous blue blazer favored by desk clerks everywhere, smiled when I gave my name and room number.

"Good morning, Miss Fairchild. I see you're checking out this morning. I hope you enjoyed your stay."

"I did. Very much. But my plans have changed." I glanced at his name tag. "Josh, could I possibly extend for a few more days?"

His cheery expression turned regretful. "We've been completely booked up for weeks, every hotel in the city is. There are several big conventions in town."

He paused, waiting for me to draw the obvious conclusion. I said nothing and blinked my eyes. Sometimes silence is the best persuasion. "But . . . let me see if there's anything I can do."

Josh looked at his computer, typed and tapped through several screens, frowning and taking his sweet time. I slipped my phone from my purse and surreptitiously checked Expedia. Josh was right: there were no rooms at the inns within a fifty-mile radius. Nothing on Vrbo either, at least nothing I could afford. There was a four-bedroom South of Broad town house with a private courtyard, on-call concierge, and stunning view of the harbor, but one night was equal to a month's rent on my apartment. Things were not looking good. But then, miracle of miracles, Josh's handsome face lit up.

"Good news. We've just had a cancellation."

"Great!"

"But it is a smaller room," he said.

"That's all right. As long as it's got a bed and bathroom, I'll be fine."

"Very good."

He printed out some papers and pushed them across the desk for me to sign. I read them and felt the blood drain from my face.

"Is everything all right?"

"Oh . . . yes. I didn't realize it would be so much. It's double what I was paying."

Josh pulled an apologetic face. "Yes, I think you and Mr. La-Guardia were offered a special rate, professional courtesy. But now, with the conventions in town and the hotels all being full, I'm afraid that I can't . . ."

I pulled out my phone again and refreshed Expedia. Still no rooms, so I signed my name, handed Josh a credit card, and moved on. What choice did I have? It was Monday, exactly twelve weeks and five days before the home visit, and I had a million things to do.

My FIRST CALL was to Anne Dowling.

I told her the truth about what was going on. Well, mostly. She didn't need to know the details of why I wasn't going to be Calpurnia anymore, only that I was retiring from the column and had inherited a lovely home in Charleston which I intended to make my permanent residence. It was a historic house in need of restoration, I explained without spelling out the full extent of the project, and would be a perfect family home once the work was completed.

Anne accepted all this without too many questions. We had a brief discussion about finances; I told her I'd be sending information about my net worth soon. Owning a home outright, with no mortgage, would be a big plus. And having a year's salary in the bank, once the severance came in, would display my financial stability, at least on paper. She wanted to know if the renovations would be completed in time for the home visit. I assured her they would, which, while not an outright lie, was a wildly optimistic guess. I hadn't even talked to a contractor yet.

Anne said that living in a smaller city and in a house instead of an apartment might be a mark in my favor, so that was encouraging. But she did pose one question I wasn't quite prepared to answer.

"I think the birth mother will be happy that you're planning to take time off to focus on the baby, but what are you planning to do after that? I imagine you'll want to keep writing," she said. "But are you planning to do another column? Or maybe a book?"

"Well. Uh . . . yes. I *have* started working on something recently." The journal qualified as "something," didn't it? After all, it had pages and a cover so, technically, it was a book. And I *was* writing in it.

"Really? That's great," Anne said, sounding genuinely impressed. "What sort of book? Self-help? Novel? Nonfiction?"

"Umm . . . I really can't talk about it right now."

"Sure, sure," she said quickly. "I understand. I have a cousin who writes mysteries. She won't discuss a book before it's finished, says that talking about it saps her creative juices. Or maybe . . ." She paused as another possibility occurred to her. "Maybe you really *can't* talk about it yet? Maybe your publisher wants you to keep it under wraps?"

My publisher? I started to say something but was so caught by surprise that it just came out as a garbled squeak, like someone was strangling a chipmunk.

"Sorry!" Anne said. "You're right. I shouldn't be so nosy. Just promise me that you'll let me know when it comes out. And if you'd be willing to sign a copy, my mom would be over the moon. She's so impressed that I know you. She's told everybody in her mah-jongg group about it. I don't suppose you'd consider signing books for the whole group, would you?" She laughed and apologized again. "Forget it. It's too much to ask. And you already said you didn't want to talk about it. But when the time comes, a signed book for Mom would be amazing."

"Anne," I said honestly, "if I ever have a book published, I'd be thrilled to sign a copy for your mom."

Except for the part about the nonexistent book deal, I thought the conversation with Anne went really well. My exchange with Dan McKee went about like I thought it would. In short, he was a serious jerk.

According to Dan, it was a one-time offer, extended from the kindness of his heart and a sense of loyalty to me, which had been rescinded when I walked out the door, blah, blah, blah. Then he hung up on me.

I was kicking myself. Why hadn't I taken the money when I had the chance? I should have taken the bracelet too. Stupid on both counts. Now he was mad and I stood basically zero chance of convincing him to give me that money.

I took Trey Holcomb's business card from my wallet and dialed the number.

"Remember the part where you said you'd help me fight? Well, put on your boxing gloves."

"Okay," he said, after I finished explaining my plans and how Dan McKee had brought them to a grinding, and possibly permanent, halt. "I'll take care of it."

"How?"

He sounded so confident. Too confident.

"I'll call him up and have a conversation. That's what lawyers do."

A conversation? As in, a reasonable and measured discourse between adults. *That* was his plan? He obviously didn't know Dan McKee. Dan didn't converse. He hunted and killed and crushed his opponents without mercy.

"Celia, I've got this," he said. "You start working on finding a contractor and I'll take care of McKee. I'll call you in a couple of hours."

"A couple of hours? But how are you going to—"

"Good-bye, Celia."

Twice in one day, a man hung up on me. With Dan I expected it. But Trey was from Charleston which meant he was *supposed* to be a gentleman. I put down my phone and buried my head in my hands. Trey was going to call Dan and be all calm and Atticus Finch on him. That would never, ever work. Not in a million years. I might as well pack my bags and catch the next flight back to New York. Instead, I did an online search for "Best Charleston remodeling contractors" and started making calls. It didn't go well.

When the housing market is hot, builders are in demand. Most were backed up for the rest of the year and wouldn't even talk to me. The few who were willing to consider taking on the job said it would be between two and three months before they could even give me a bid. I spent four hours on the phone and made over thirty calls. No one was willing to take on the job of remodeling the house within my very abbreviated time frame.

It really was hopeless.

Then Trey called.

"Okay," he said, "everything is set with McKee. All you have to do is sign the separation letter. The money will be deposited into your account tomorrow."

My jaw dropped. Either he was kidding me or Trey Holcomb was a way tougher customer than I'd taken him for.

"Are you serious? How'd you get Dan to cave? He wouldn't budge an inch when I talked to him."

"Easy," Trey said, "I just played Bad Cop to your Good Cop, made him think that you were going to sign the letter against my advice and hinted that I would have preferred a long, drawn-out court battle, and that I had recommended you sue him person-ally."

"That's all? And he bought it?"

"Well . . ." He drew out the word, then paused and sniffed be-fore going on. "It's just possible he thought I was a senior partner in a firm that is much larger and more powerful than is actually the case." He sniffed again. The tone of his voice told me he was very pleased with himself.

"There's a lady who cleans my office every Monday morning, Velma. I asked her to stick around for a couple of hours to answer the phone. When Dan called back, she said, 'Holcomb, Holcomb, Hanley, Witherspoon, and White. May I help you? Mr. Holcomb is on a call with the governor, but let me see if he's about to wrap up. Please hold.' Velma left him there a good three minutes; gave him time to think.

"Dan did a pretty good job making sure you'd lose if you brought a legal challenge, but he's no dummy. Even if you lost eventually, he knew that paying you a year's salary would be cheaper than going to court. That's why he offered it to you in the first place. All I did was remind him of that and let him make his own assumptions about your legal team. Piece of cake."

I was stunned. Trey Holcomb turned out to have a sneaky streak. And a sense of humor. Who'd have guessed?

Almost from the first minute, I'd pegged Trey as a Crusader, a particular kind of guy I'd often encountered and sometimes dated back in New York. Crusaders usually worked for nonprofits, were into social justice and radical recycling. Often they were vegan. It was impossible not to admire Crusaders but equally impossible to really like them. They're so tuned in to all the terrible things happening in the world that joking seems to be against their religion.

Look, I worry about the world too, all the time. I have low-flow showerheads in my bathrooms. I only drink fair trade coffee. I planted pots with lavender and echinacea and put them on the balcony because I'm worried about the future of pollinators. I care. I do.

But being outraged every minute of every day is exhausting. I admire Crusaders but being around them makes me feel guilty. Trey was definitely a Crusader, no doubt about that. But he's a funny Crusader, and I've always given out bonus points for humor. The trick Trey played on Dan, along with his delivery, earned him three points. He was a long way from hilarious, but I appreciated the attempt. Plus, he got me the money. I threw in seven more points for that.

"Thanks, Trey. And forgive me for doubting you. But it looks like it might all have been for nothing; I can't find a contractor."

After explaining the situation and making me endure his questions and suggestions regarding my failed attempts, Trey informed me that he had an idea.

"But it might not be a good one."

"Well, it has to be better than nothing. That's all I've got at the moment."

"I don't know, Celia. I'm not sure I'd be doing you any favors here."

"Would you quit being so mysterious? Just give me the name. I'm desperate. If I can't find somebody to take on this job in the next few days, I'm finished."

"Lorne Holcomb.

"Relative of yours?"

"My little brother. He used to work in construction."

"Used to? What happened?"

I don't know a whole lot about the construction business, but I know it's not uncommon for contractors to overextend themselves financially during a housing boom, only to go under when the boom suddenly turns to bust. If Trey's brother had gone through a bankruptcy, he'd be no different than any number of other people in the construction industry, decent guys with a good work ethic and bad timing. It can happen to anybody.

But this was not that.

"Lorne was a subcontractor for a home builder. He got caught substituting lower-grade materials on a job, charging the company for premium material, and pocketing the money. By the time he got caught, he'd overcharged them by almost a hundred and sixty thousand dollars. My brother did thirty-two months for fraud and drug use. He was released four months ago and hasn't been able to find work since."

"Oh. Wow. Well . . ."

A cheat *and* an addict? I was desperate to find a contractor. But was I that desperate? If there was one thing I had learned from my marriage, it's that acts of desperation generally result in regrets. But the problem with being desperate is that . . . well, you're desperate. When you've got to do *something*, you usually do. Even if it's the wrong something.

If somebody had written to ask for my advice on what to do in this situation, I'd have told them to walk away and search for another solution. I'd tell them that there was so much that could go wrong here that it just wasn't worth the risk.

My problem, of course, was that it *was* worth the risk. There was a baby at stake and the only chance I had of making it mine was to gamble on a recently released ex-con.

"Forget about it," Trey said. "It's a bad idea. We'll find someone else."

But we wouldn't. I'd already called every contractor within a hundred miles and they'd all said no.

"Is he clean?"

"As far as I know. He checks in with his probation officer every week and has to undergo random drug testing." Trey paused. "Celia, are you sure about this?"

I wasn't.

"What's your brother's phone number?"

Do as I say, not as I do.

Chapter Thirteen

Apart from Rupert, the meth-dealing biker whom I interviewed during my brief and ill-fated career as a serious journalist, I've never knowingly had coffee with a felon. So I was a little anxious about meeting Lorne Holcomb. I was also desperate.

Lorne was my Plan A. There was no Plan B. Assuming he didn't pull a knife on me or show up to the meeting high and with a swastika tattooed on his face, I was absolutely going to offer him the job. But after we sat down and started to talk, I began to think that this might be the one time in my life when an act of desperation turned out to be a good idea.

He looked enough like Trey that if I'd seen them walking down the street together, I'd have known at a glance that they were brothers. The eyes were different; Trey's were a darker brown and more serious, his gaze more direct. But they had the same color hair, wavy and black, and even the same way of walking, their long arms and long legs swinging opposite in a steady, unhurried gait of a metronome set to *largo*. But Lorne was clean-shaven instead of bearded, downright clean-cut, and gave every indication of being a nice guy.

We met at Bitty and Beau's Coffee in the French Quarter. Like every other city, Charleston has fancy coffee spots on practically every corner, most all of them good, so it wasn't surprising that I'd never heard of this one. But Bitty and Beau's has something special going for it: most of the employees are people with intellectual disabilities. Lorne seemed to be a regular. He exchanged high fives with a tall, portly man with a ready smile and close-trimmed beard whom Lorne introduced as Teddy. After shaking my hand and welcoming me to Bitty and Beau's yet again, Teddy took our orders and handed Lorne a nine of diamonds playing card. A few minutes later, when a woman with short blond hair called out, "Nine of diamonds!" and handed our coffee and muffins across the counter, Lorne asked how her dad was doing after his hip replacement.

Definitely a nice guy. And surprisingly honest.

In his former life, Lorne Holcomb had been a liar, cheat, and thief. He'd also injected numerous illegal substances into his body. There was no miscarriage of justice here, no mishandled evidence or overeager prosecutors. I know this because he told me so himself.

"Guilty as charged. On all counts," Lorne said when we sat down to talk. "Everything that happened to me was my own fault. But I'll tell you something true: getting caught probably saved my life. It was only a matter of time until I ODed. Going to prison gave me lots of time to dry out and take a long look at my life. Wasn't pretty," he said, before taking a sip of coffee.

"Look, Miss Fairchild, I'm not kidding myself. If you hire me, I know you'll only be doing it as a last resort; Trey told me what you're up against. But I can do the job. I'll work hard. I'll stay sober. I'll do everything I can to bring the project in on time and under budget. Not to blow my own horn, but I'm one helluva carpenter," he said in a drawl that was thicker and mellower than Trey's, a voice like amber sap seeping from a tree trunk. "When I'm not high as a kite, that is."

He let out a laugh and I mentally gave him five points—two for humor and three for self-awareness. Then his grin faded away and he looked at me with eyes that were, if not quite as nice as his elder brother's, every bit as serious.

"I'll do a good job, Miss Fairchild. I have to. You're my last resort too."

Of course, I hired him. How could I not? I haven't met many men who were willing to own their mistakes and be vulnerable. Also, I didn't have another option. But even if I had, I felt sure that hiring Lorne was the right decision. Looks aside, he seemed very different from his brother.

Trey had a searchingly serious expression, especially in his eyes, as if he were steeling himself for the next bad thing that could happen. But Lorne seemed always to be laughing, at himself and everything around him. I guess it makes sense: happy-go-lucky types don't usually gravitate toward the law as a career.

Without Trey, I'd have no money and no contractor. But if I had to pick which brother I would have preferred to come into contact with on a daily basis for the next two months, Lorne would win hands down. He just seemed like more fun. Trey was just so careful and lawyerly. For example, he insisted there be a signed contract between Lorne and me and that Lorne send him copies of all the invoices. I understood about Lorne's checkered past and all, but it just seemed kind of weird, like he didn't quite trust his own brother.

"Don't worry about it," Lorne said when I handed him the contract. "Trey's just doing his job, watching out for you. Let's see what we've got here," he mused, eyes shifting left to right as he scanned the documents. "Scope of work. Timelines. Budget and estimates. Oh, and will you look at that? A clause that says I don't get paid if I'm arrested. Very nice. Gotta hand it to my brother; he's nothing if not thorough."

The display of brotherly tension was awkward. For a moment, I thought he might say thanks but no thanks. Instead, he looked up and said, "Can we go see the house? Might be a good idea to get inside and see what I'm dealing with before I sign anything."

LORNE TURNED SIDEWAYS and squeezed through the canyon of refuse that was the only path through what once had been the dining room. I turned as well to follow, skittering sideways like a crab crossing a sandy beach.

Lorne let out a low whistle. "Damn. When you said the place was a wreck, you weren't kidding, were you?"

My cheeks flushed. The mess wasn't of my making but it was embarrassing just the same. We exited the canyon to the somewhat more open area in the center hallway. Lorne stood at the bottom of the nearly impassable stairway and stared toward the upper floors.

"It's terrible, I know. Really awful. But if you—"

He waved his hand to cut me off but didn't lower his eyes from the dim, cavernous stairwell. "It's okay. I'm just trying to figure out where to begin."

His eyes narrowed and he made three popping sounds with his lips. Apparently, this was his thinking noise.

"Exterior first," he said after a long moment. "We're going to need a dumpster asap. I'll go through the junk in the courtyard, toss everything that's not worth saving—"

"So basically everything."

"Well, that's up to you but . . ." He popped his lips again. "Yeah. Pretty much. That'll keep us busy until we've got the permits."

"How long will that take?" I asked.

"Hard to say. Trey knows a couple of people at City Hall. Hopefully that will speed the process, but I'll let you work that out with him. In case you haven't already picked up on it, we don't talk."

I had noticed and was dying to find out why. Sure, there was the whole prison thing, but aren't lawyers used to dealing with criminals? Reformed and otherwise? And Trey didn't seem like the kind of person who would cut someone out of his life because of that. There had to be more to the story.

"Once the paperwork is approved," Lorne said, "I'd rebuild the porch, fix the chimney, replace the roof, the rotted casement windows, rehang the shutters, all the stuff that's listed in the contract. But the problem with buildings this old is that you never really know what you're dealing with until you start opening up walls."

"But that's why we added that extra fifteen percent on the budget, right? For contingencies? Should be enough, don't you think?"

I flashed a hopeful smile, waiting for him to confirm this. Instead, he murmured noncommittally, craned his neck backward to gaze at the ceiling, then popped his lips again.

"I've got an idea for some guys who can do the painting. Do you mind hiring a couple of ex-cons?"

"Uh . . . sure. If you're willing to vouch for them. The more the merrier, right?"

"Glad you feel that way. Because these are the only guys you can afford."

My stomach clenched. "Oh. You don't think the budget is big enough?"

The figure had seemed pretty generous to me, but what did I know about remodeling? The most ambitious home repair job

I'd ever tackled was when Steve and I moved into our new apartment. We'd painted an accent wall in the living room, added some wooden trim to a set of IKEA bookcases so they'd look like built-ins, and installed a new light fixture and some dimmer switches. That little project took nearly six weeks to complete, went three hundred dollars over budget, and came close to ending our marriage before it got started, which, in retrospect, wouldn't have been such a bad thing.

"Well, it's tight," Lorne said, shifting his shoulders. "But it's . . . doable. I think."

"Gee. That's reassuring," I said.

"I just meant that we need to save where we can."

"By, for example, hiring felonious housepainters."

"Red and Slip do good work."

"Red and Slip? Seriously? Am I hiring the cast of *The Shawshank Redemption*?" I laughed and threw out my hands. "Okay, sure. Bring on Red and Slip. But is there any chance you could start work on the inside first? I need to move in as soon as possible."

Lorne turned toward me and frowned. "You're planning to live here during the remodeling? That always complicates things. Wouldn't you be more comfortable in your hotel?"

"Definitely," I replied. "There's nothing not to love about Zero George, except that I can't afford to stay there, or anyplace else. The remodeling budget isn't the only one that's tight."

Lorne's frown deepened, furrowing his forehead. He shook his head slightly, then walked down the goat trail that led toward the front door, peering as best he could into the rooms that adjoined the center hall, each packed floor to ceiling with Calpurnia's hoard. He hooked his thumbs into his belt, stared into the middle distance, and popped his lips again. I felt pretty sure he was having second thoughts.

"You understand that I'm not talking about cleaning out the whole interior right off," I said. "Maybe just the first floor?"

He sniffed and shuffled down the goat path in the opposite direction. I followed behind, negotiating. "Or a couple of rooms? Or even one. I just need someplace to camp out while the work is being done. In fact, I can clean out a room for myself."

He kept pacing and popping his lips, saying nothing, ignoring me. My anxiety fizzed and bubbled over into irritation. I was done negotiating.

"Here's the bottom line: I can't afford to stay in a hotel so I'm staying here. That's the deal. Period. End of discussion. If you can't live with that, then I'll just find myself another contractor."

"That so? Who?"

He turned toward me and grinned, calling my bluff. I spread my feet and planted my hands on my hips.

"Somebody who *wants* the job. Somebody who *doesn't* have a record."

That was kind of a low blow, I'll admit. But his patronizing attitude pushed me over the edge. Lorne's grin disappeared.

"Sounds like you've been up north so long you don't remember that you'll catch more flies with honey than vinegar. At least in Charleston."

"I didn't forget," I said. "I just never believed it in the first place. Now do you want this job for not?"

I took the contract out of my bag and held it out. Lorne considered me for a moment, then took a pen from his shirt pocket and the contract from my hand, set it down on a waist-high stack of yellowing newspapers, and signed his name and initials in all the right places. His smile reemerged.

"Here you go, boss."

I didn't smile but I let my face relax. "When would you like to start?"

"Tomorrow morning okay with you?"

"Sounds good."

"And when would you like to move in?"

"Same time," I said.

He bobbed his head. "Sounds good."

Dear Peaches,

If I am lucky enough to be your mother and if you're lucky enough to grow up in Charleston, someday somebody who is trying to get you to give up or back down, or to make you feel bad about having an opinion contrary to theirs, is going to tell you that "you'll catch more flies with honey than vinegar" and urge you to "be sweet."

This is bad advice, and for a couple of reasons.

First, who wants to catch flies? They should be deflected or eradicated, not attracted. Second, anybody, male or female, who insists that you smother your personality, desires, or opinions under a sticky veneer of false gentility is a fly that's not worth catching.

If I get to be your mom, I'll never ask you to be sweet. I will urge you to be kind. And strong. Though it's not always easy to do both at once, the two are not mutually exclusive. The times I've backed off from either are the times I've been most disappointed in myself.

If you're kind and strong, people will respect you for it. Maybe not everybody, but most people, the people whose respect is truly worth having, including your own.

Chapter Fourteen

Only hours after moving into Calpurnia's house, my body felt exactly like it had on January fourth of 2018, the day after I'd given up on a short-lived, ill-conceived resolution to join a gym. Every single muscle in my body was aching, sore, and screaming for rest, and it was barely past noon.

The morning after my meeting with Lorne, I checked out of the hotel, took a Lyft to the house, and unloaded my luggage onto the sidewalk. Besides my suitcase, I had a box with books, shoes, my favorite saucepan, and a few other essentials that Calvin had retrieved from my apartment and shipped to me, and four Target shopping bags containing sheets, pillows, towels, soap, toothpaste, shampoo, work gloves, and the biggest box of garbage bags I could find, as well as flavored seltzers, granola bars, cheese sticks, three apples, pretzel crisps, and a mug that said, "This Coffee Is Making Me Awesome."

I have no idea why I bought that mug; it wasn't even on sale. Maybe I hoped that drinking out of it would make it true? But since I'd neglected to purchase either coffee or something to make it in, that probably wasn't going to happen.

It was hard to figure out what I needed to get by for the next few weeks. Calpurnia's house was bursting with stuff, but was any of it usable? Or sanitary? God only knew what I might find once I started digging through the piles. That was why, in addition to the bedding, snacks, and other essentials, I'd also purchased four spray cans of roach killer.

A pickup truck that I assumed belonged to Lorne was parked near the gate and a dumpster was parked in front of the impassable driveway. It was already mounded with junk, but the courtyard and garden looked exactly the same to my eyes. Carting my suitcase and bags to the door was tricky. As I dodged and weaved through the detritus, I thought about a documentary I'd once seen about the wreck of the *Titanic* and the mile-long debris field that trailed the ship when it split apart before crashing into the ocean floor. But the walkway was nothing in comparison to what awaited me inside.

For the fiftieth time since arriving in Charleston, I tried to imagine what could have driven my aunt, who had once been as tidy, hospitable, and house-proud as any woman in Charleston, to live like this. For the fiftieth time, I came up with nothing. It was sad and awful and didn't make sense.

I stood in the foyer, surrounded by garbage and a ponderous silence that pressed in from all sides, and felt my throat thicken. Then I felt . . . I don't know what to call it . . . a presence? That makes it sound more spectral and eerie than was actually the case, but I definitely felt something and remembered what Auntie Cal would have said if she'd been there.

Yes, it's awful. So sad. Now what are you going to do about it?
What could I do? I found a trash bag and got to work.

FOUR HOURS AND fifty-something trips to the dumpster later, I could walk from the front door to the bottom of the stairs without turning sideways. I'd also cleaned off the left half of the bottom two steps of the staircase. It wasn't much, but at least it gave me a place to rest my aching body while I considered my next move.

Obviously, there was no way I was going to be able to get to the top of the stairs and clear out a bedroom before day's end. Plus, I was running low on garbage bags. Just as I was about to call Josh at the hotel and beg him to give me my room back, the doorbell rang.

Caroline Fuller was standing there, wearing a smile and another cute pleated cotton skirt, this one a blue-and-pink plaid, that showed off her amazing legs. A tall man with mocha-colored skin, black-rimmed glasses, and one of those shiny, close-shaved heads that actually makes being bald look sexy, stood next to her.

"Hey! We saw the truck out front so we thought we'd pop over and welcome you to the neighborhood," Caroline said, then thrust a plate of cookies into my hands.

I stared at the plate for a moment.

"Oh. Gosh. That's so sweet of you. Do you have time to come in?"

Hopefully not. Caroline was nice and obviously still in the market for a best friend, but now was not a good time. If clearing mountains of junk out of Calpurnia's house wasn't enough, *now* I had to buy monogrammed stationery and write a note thanking Caroline for the cookies. I didn't have time to make friends!

I smiled anyway. Caroline smiled back.

"Well. Maybe just for a minute. We know you're busy, but Heath was hoping he might have a chance to talk with you. Oh, gosh!" Caroline giggled, momentarily putting her hand in front of her mouth. "I forgot the introductions! This is my husband, Heath Fuller." She gestured toward the man with the glasses.

"Nice to meet you," I said, and opened the door wider so they could come inside. Even after all my work, the foyer was a tight fit for three people, so I left the door ajar, hoping it might feel slightly less claustrophobic.

Heath nodded and shook my hand. "I think Caroline mentioned that I work for the Historic Charleston Foundation, so I was just wondering—"

"Don't worry," I said, anticipating his concerns. "This project is a restoration, not a renovation. We're not making any structural changes or additions to the footprint of the house. Even if I wanted to, there isn't time. I have three months to clean this place out and make it habitable."

"Three months?" Heath's eyebrows popped. "How are you going to manage that?"

"Funny, I was just asking myself the same thing." I sighed and tried to smile. "Guess I'll just keep doing what I've been doing, hauling out the junk and throwing it in the dumpster as quick as I can. The rest will be up to Lorne. He's my contractor," I explained.

Heath frowned. "Throwing everything out without sorting through it first is a mistake. Some of these things may have historic significance."

Historic significance? Was he serious?

"What? You mean like this?" I reached for the closest pile and closed my fingers around the first thing they touched, a plastic bag containing hundreds of individual packets of synthetic coffee creamer. I fished a packet out of the bag and held it up so Heath could see.

"These are three years beyond the sell-by date, which, considering the shelf life of this stuff, probably does qualify them as historic, but are you seriously suggesting I hold on to them?"

Caroline giggled nervously and I realized that my tone had been a little strident, bordering on rude, and definitely not kind.

The fact that she was probably rethinking the whole shopping for a best friend thing didn't really bother me, but we were going to be neighbors and I didn't want to hurt her feelings.

"Sorry," I said. "I'm just a little stressed. Look, Heath, I get what you're saying. But I don't have the time, energy, or money to sort through every piece of trash my aunt squirreled away in here. I'm only one person!"

"What if I helped?"

I spun around. Pris Browder stood in the open doorway, dressed in a pair of black-and-brown houndstooth trousers with black suspenders over a white cotton shirt and a broad-brimmed black felt hat. Once again, she looked adorable.

"Hey, y'all!" Pris raised a hand to acknowledge the group. "Sorry, Celia. I didn't mean to eavesdrop. But I saw the truck and figured I'd come over. Look! I brought kombucha!"

She thrust a six-pack of the fermented tea/vinegar beverage hipsters can't seem to get enough of into my hands. This brand was flavored with ginger and turmeric, a combination that promised to be simultaneously healthful and vile.

"Pris." I sighed. "I know I said we'd get together and discuss your blog, but this really isn't a good time."

"That's okay. I was just coming over to say hey and welcome you to the neighborhood. But if you need help sorting through things, I can give you a hand."

"Maybe we can too," Heath said, looking to Caroline. "It's my day off and we don't have any plans this afternoon, do we?"

"Nope," Caroline said, shaking her head. "I've got a couple of emails to write but those can wait. If everybody pitches in, we ought to be able to clear out at least one bedroom and a bathroom. You won't need more than that for now, will you?"

"No, but I—"

"Great!" Pris said, and bounded toward the stairs. "Where should we start? Did you pick a room yet?"

"Hang on." I set the kombucha six-pack down on the floor and held up my hands. "Look, I appreciate the offer, really. But I can't let you do this."

Caroline squinched up her eyes and looked in Heath's direction, as if requesting a translation. "Why not? Who else is going to help you?"

WITH FOUR SETS of hands instead of one, things should have gone more quickly.

They didn't. Not at first.

Heath insisted on surveying the entire house and coming up with a plan to separate trash from potential treasure, disposing of the former and cataloging and preserving the latter, approaching the task like the academic he was. But where Heath saw an archaeological dig, I saw a pile of garbage.

"Did you know that some of the most valuable historical finds were discovered in ancient garbage piles?" he asked, grinning in response to my observation. "One of the best ways an ancient culture—how people lived, what they valued, practiced, or believed—can be understood is by digging through the trash they left behind."

I rolled my eyes. "Fascinating," I said wearily. "But I just want to clear out enough of the crap so I'll have someplace to sleep tonight."

"We will," he said, lifting a hand to seal the promise. "But first we've got to get organized. I've got an idea. Pris, come with me. You two stay here. We'll be back in a minute."

Heath bounded down the front steps. Pris followed him.

"Don't worry," Caroline said. "If Heath says you'll have a place to sleep tonight, you will."

Would I? Not at this rate. Heath and Caroline were a cute couple and it was sweet of them to want to help, Pris too, but I was so tired and discouraged. The only thing I had to show for aching muscles and hours of work was two stairsteps. If I couldn't even clean out a room for myself, how would I ever turn this wreck into a home for Peaches? I sat down on the stairs and propped my chin in my hands. In another second, I might have started to tear up. Then Caroline reached down, squeezed my shoulder, and said, "Hey."

It doesn't make sense if you're not from here, but in the South, "hey" doesn't just mean "hey." It means "I see you and I know you. You're not in this alone. I got you, girl."

Caroline hadn't been in Charleston for long, but she had already picked up some of the important nuances of southern culture. It made me feel better.

"Thanks," I said.

"Anytime," Caroline replied, then smiled and squeezed my shoulder again before walking to the front door and looking outside. "Looks like Heath's brought reinforcements. Friends of yours?"

I got up and joined Caroline at the door. Heath and Pris were coming up the walk. Two scruffy, tattooed men in torn blue jeans and ratty T-shirts trailed them.

"More like employees," I said. "Red and Slip."

"Oh." Caroline said. "Good guys?"

"I guess. Just don't leave your purse out anywhere."

"Okay, let's huddle up," Heath said once everybody was inside, clapping his hands together like a coach getting ready to deliver a locker room speech. "Our goal is to clear this first flight of stairs, the first bedroom at the top of those stairs, and an adjacent bathroom. It's a lot to accomplish in one afternoon, but if we work together, we can make it happen. Here's my plan."

Heath's plan involved dividing up into teams, handing items off from one team to the next, like a bucket brigade. Heath and Caroline would remove items from the upper part of the house and bring them down to me and Pris. We would sort through the items, deciding what should be kept or donated to charity and what should be thrown away. Items in the first two categories would be stowed into marked boxes, the rest would be handed off to Red, Slip, and Lorne, who would carry the trash to the dumpster.

Heath was a little bossy but, I had to admit, things moved more quickly after that. We cleared the whole bottom flight of stairs in less than two hours. As long as the junk I had to sort through really was junk, stuff I could banish to the dumpster with barely a thought, it was easy. But when we got to the second floor, things got trickier.

A box filled with fairly nice picture frames had to be sorted through one by one so I could put aside those that contained family photos before putting the others into the box earmarked for charity donations. Several other boxes contained china dishes, mostly mismatched and none that I recognized as belonging to the family, but still perfectly usable. These went into the charity collection as well.

"Maybe you should have a tag sale," Caroline said.

"No. Put them on eBay," Priscilla suggested. She picked up a salad plate decorated with a delicate garland of pink roses and turned it over. "Right now, somebody is on the Internet looking for this exact pattern to replace a plate in the set their great-grandmother left them. You'll get money if you can reach an audience of people who are already searching for what you've got."

"Maybe. But all that takes time," I said. "I mean, look how long it took me just to sort through this one box."

"Well . . . ," Pris said slowly, as if the idea had just come to her. "Why not hire me? I could help you sort through the stuff, throw out the trash, and put the treasure up online."

Hiring a helper would definitely make things go more quickly, but . . .

"I thought you were going to work for your mom this summer."

Priscilla wrinkled her nose and shook her head. "I don't really see that working out, do you? Besides, she was only going to pay me minimum wage."

"I see. And what would I be paying you?"

"Minimum wage plus a forty percent cut of the eBay profits."

Hmm. Obviously, this idea had not just come to her. Pris responded so quickly and with such definite ideas about her rates that I knew she'd thought everything through beforehand.

"It's a better deal for both of us," she said. "You'll cover what you pay me and still make money."

Would I? It was hard to imagine people would be willing to pay much for a bunch of old dishes. But Pris was right about one thing: I definitely needed help.

"Fine," I said. "Minimum wage plus forty percent of any eBay profits."

"And one more thing," Pris said. "Ten hours of professional consultation on my blog. Deal?"

Pris stuck out her hand. With chutzpah like that, I doubted she needed business advice from me, but Pris was easy to like and it would be nice to have an extra pair of hands.

"You're hired."

"Really? That's great!" Pris exclaimed, her face lighting up like a kid with a new puppy. She started toward me and for a second I thought she might hug me. But before she could, Heath's head appeared over the banister.

"Celia? You'd better come up here."

In my experience, "You'd better come up here" almost never precedes good news. I frowned and felt my stomach clench again.

"Why? What's wrong?"

"Just come," Heath said, beckoning me with a hand. "You're not going to believe this."

Chapter Fifteen

So? What was it?

A thinking emoji appeared next to Calvin's text, the one where the little happy face guy is kind of gazing sideways and holding the fingers of his white-gloved hand to his cheek and chin.

OMG! It was a DEAD CAT, wasn't it?!

I started tapping in my response but another panicked text came in before I could finish.

Or a ROOM FULL OF DEAD CATS!!!

See? I told you! There's always a dead cat. Always!

Stop! NO. Don't be ridiculous. No dead cats!

Calvin's imagination was getting the best of me. Thanks to him, my heart pounded with the discovery of each new box or bag, and I leaned backward as if preparing for something to jump out, turning my head sideways and looking out of one squinty eye, the way I did whenever I watched horror movies. I started texting again but the phone rang before I could hit send.

"So? If it wasn't a dead cat, what was it?"

"I was just getting to that part."

Calvin groaned. "I can't wait that long. The suspense is killing me and you are the slowest texter on the *planet*. Besides, I haven't talked to you in two whole days. I was beginning to think you'd lost my number."

"You haven't seen Simon in so long, I didn't want to bug you."

"Well, you can bug me all you want to now," Calvin said. "Simon's off saving the world again. There was a mudslide in some remote little village in Central America." He sighed. "It's not easy being married to a saint. In fact, sometimes it's kind of annoying. That's *my* hostage for the day; I am a terrible person who sometimes resents the fact that he has to share his husband the saint with the poor and downtrodden. What's yours?" he asked. "I was really hoping it'd be something about the dead cat."

"Calvin. For the fiftieth time, there was no dead cat."

"Fine," he grumped. "If it wasn't a dead cat, what was it?" Calvin gasped as another possibility occurred to him. "Wait. Was it a dead *body*?" He gasped again. "Don't tell me! A pile of newspapers fell on somebody and suffocated them. And when you dug them out, there was nothing left but a skeleton!"

"No!" I snapped, shuddering at the image, which would now haunt my dreams. As if dead cats weren't enough, now he had to do this to me? "Ick. Seriously, Calvin, where do you get this stuff?"

"Simon says I watch too much trash, so I switched from Bravo to PBS. Now I'm binge-watching *Midsomer Murders*," he said casually, as if this explained everything. "So tell me: what was the big discovery?"

"Yarn!"

"Yarn."

Hmm. Clearly, he didn't find this as exciting as I had.

"Well, not *just* yarn, Calvin. A whole *room* of it!" I said excitedly, still getting chills as I remembered trudging up the stairs and then walking through the door. Heath was right: if I hadn't seen it myself, I would never have believed it. "Every wall is lined floor to ceiling with white cubbyhole shelving and every cubby is stuffed with skeins of beautiful yarn. It must have been Beebee's, but I had no idea she had so much!

"And it's all organized by color," I continued. "The bottom cubbies on the left side of the door are filled with white yarn, then it goes to cream farther up, then yellow at the top of that stack. The next row starts with gold, then peach, then orange. It goes on like that all the way around the room, like a continuous rainbow, to the shelves on the right side of the door, which are filled with browns and blacks."

"Okay," he said grudgingly. "That actually does sound kind of cool. Not as cool as finding a missing murder victim, but still."

"But here's the really interesting part," I said, feeling those chills again. "Apart from the yarn, a floor lamp, and a single wingback chair and side table with a basket of knitting needles and notions, the room was *completely* empty. The whole house is a wreck, so stuffed with boxes filled with old clothes and shoes and junk jewelry that it took four people all day just to get to the door, but the room behind that door was pristine, not so much as a piece of newsprint on the floor. Isn't that crazy?"

"Huh. You think Calpurnia just closed it up after your grand-mother died?"

"Could be," I said. "But I don't remember that room ever being used to store yarn. I remember the chair; Beebee always sat there when she was knitting. It was exactly the same—pink velveteen with channel-back upholstery."

"Very nineteen fifties," Calvin replied. "Everybody's grandma had a chair like that."

"But Beebee's chair used to be downstairs," I said. "So weird. The entire house is a disaster zone except for this one perfectly arranged and organized room, hidden away for who knows how long?"

"That is weird. But lucky for you, right? It's a little island of order in the sea of chaos."

"More like a cocoon," I said, sitting down in Beebee's chair and pulling my knees up to my chest as I gazed at the fluffy, colorful rainbow walls that surrounded me on all sides. "I decided to make it my bedroom, at least for now. But who knows? Maybe I'll stay in here for the duration. It's cozy."

Cozy and comforting and safe. Outside this room, the task before me was overwhelming. But when I closed the door, it was possible to remember this house as it once had been—peaceful, pretty, and orderly, a place of refuge and welcome.

"What are you going to sleep on?" Calvin asked.

"I borrowed a sleeping bag from Heath and Caroline. I'll buy a new mattress tomorrow."

"Good. I was worried that you just dragged in a mattress from some other room. They're probably all riddled with bedbugs. Or worse!"

"So much for the cocoon of safety. Thank you, Calvin."

"Well, it's not my fault. I was just trying to warn you. Did you know that bedbugs can lay up to five eggs in a day? And as many as five *hundred* in a lifetime? Since I switched to PBS, I've been watching these nature programs too. They're fascinating! And kind of creepy. Did you know that . . ."

I had seen more than one roach during the course of the day, skittering away as their hiding places were revealed and disturbed. Here in the South we call them "palmetto bugs," but a cockroach by any other name, no matter how cute and colloquial, is still icky. And though I hadn't personally met any mice, they'd left enough evidence to suggest that I was not the lone mammal in residence. After going next door to borrow Felicia's vacuum, I had banished every bit of dirt and dust from the bedroom, so I knew it was clean. But now, while Calvin continued on about bugs, his voice quivering with excited disgust as he vividly described some of the more horrific infestations he'd seen on television, I noticed a sizable gap between the floor and the lower edge of the door.

I put down the phone, rolled one of the two new bath towels I'd bought into a tube, and shoved it into the crack under the door, taking my time and making sure that the gap was totally blocked. Calvin was on a roll and so I figured he wouldn't know the difference, but when I picked up the phone, I was greeted by silence.

"Calvin?"

"You just walked off and left me talking to myself, didn't you?"

"Sorry. I was putting a towel under the door. There was a draft."

And a crack big enough for a Central Park rat to crawl through.

"It's okay," he sighed. "I'm getting used to being ignored. Simon's eyes glaze over every time I open my mouth."

I frowned and tucked the phone in closer to my ear. "Everything okay between you two?"

"Yes," he said. "I wish we'd had more time together before he had to go off on his next crusade, but what can you do? You can't schedule a mudslide."

"Maybe you should talk to him about taking some time off."

"We're fine," he assured me. "It's you I'm worried about. The yarn cave does sounds kind of fabulous, and it's great that the neighbors pitched in to help, but you sound tired."

"I am," I admitted. "And maybe a little discouraged. How am I going to get it all done in only three months?"

"You will. You're tough."

"Sometimes I get tired of being tough."

"I know," he replied, the tone in his voice telling me that he really did know. "Maybe it will help to think about it as, well . . . kind of like labor. Nothing about this is going to be easy. You're going to have to push, and push, and push yourself, maybe to the breaking point. But it's going to be worth it because, in the end, you'll get a whole baby out of the deal."

"Eyes on the prize?"

"Exactly. Focus on where you're going, not where you are. Do you want me to fly back down there? Simon will probably be gone for weeks. There's no reason I couldn't come and help."

"None except the cookbook you have to edit," I said. "What are you up to so far? Pies?"

"Pastry."

"Only pastry?" I tsked my tongue. "You can't come down here, Calvin. You're on deadline. And I'll be okay. Like you said, I'm tough. Also highly motivated. I'm going to get a whole baby out of the deal, right?"

"Have you thought about names yet? Because I have. Calvin is really an awfully nice name for a boy. Or a girl."

"Shut up." I laughed and took a cookie from the plate Caroline had left.

"But if you really *did* need me," he said, dropping his teasing tone, "you know I'd come down there, right? Deadline or no deadline, I'd be there."

He would, it was true. Which was why I couldn't ask him.

"I'm good," I said, forcing a smile. "Things will look better in the morning."

"They usually do. Sleep tight, dumpling. Don't let the bedbugs bite."

He made a noise with his teeth that sounded like the skittering of insects.

"Gee. Thanks a lot, Calvin. I'm hanging up now."

"Uh-uh. *I'm* hanging up now. Night, cupcake."

"Night."

I GOT OUT my computer and tried to watch *Miracle on 34th Street* but turned it off after a few minutes. Maybe it was just because I was used to living in smaller spaces, but even tucked up in my yarn cave with the door closed and a movie playing, the house felt too big and too quiet. Funny, I'd never thought of it that way when I was growing up.

Of course, there'd been more of us back then, a lot more.

What must it have been like for Calpurnia, rattling around here all by herself? Had she thought the house was too big, too quiet, too lonely? Was that why she'd started hoarding this junk, because she was trying to fill the empty space? Maybe. But the more stuff she brought in, the more isolated she'd become. You can't have a relationship with a box of old Sears catalogs or a bag stuffed with out-of-date packets of coffee creamer.

I got up from Beebee's chair and paced the edges of the room like a cat in a cage, stretching out my arm and letting my fingers bump against the wooden edges of the white cubbies, then brush the soft skeins of silky, or woolly, or nubbly yarn. Tired as I was, I was also restless and bored and, more than anything else, lonely. After I'd circled the room a fourth time, my eyes fell on the empty cookie plate I'd left sitting on the little table next to Beebee's chair. I hugged it to my chest, opened the door to my cave, and trotted down the partially cleared staircase, tucking my elbows in tight so I wouldn't bump on piles of junk during the descent.

Out on the piazza, it wasn't dark but nearly. After I tripped over the handle of a rusted wheelbarrow and almost dropped the plate, I was more careful. I took my time picking my way down the walkway to the gate, which emitted an embarrassingly loud squeal when I pushed it open, and stepped onto the sidewalk.

The Pickneys' house was dark, the only light from an upstairs bedroom. Happy Browder's house was dark as well, but I could smell the fragrance of her freshly cut boxwood hedges as I walked past and saw a constellation of tiny, blinking blue lights from a swarm of fireflies that flittered and hovered above her lawn. I heard the buzz of cicadas too.

I smiled to myself, remembering what I'd almost forgotten: the soundtrack of summers in the South and how good it felt when shadows fell at the close of a hot and humid day and the twilight breezes caressed and cooled your skin.

Every light was on at Caroline and Heath's; the house looked like the party boats that cruised the dark waters of the harbor after sunset, loaded with tourists and lovers and conventioneers. The windows were open to catch the breeze, and music poured from them, but it wasn't the type that a hip early-thirties couple generally listens to. I heard violins, a steady but not quite driving beat, and the lilting hum of what I thought was an accordion. It was hard to know for sure because of the background noise, a scratching and fuzzy underlayment, but I smiled because they were most definitely home.

I crossed the street, mentally rehearsing what I would say after explaining that I'd just dropped by to bring back the plate and they insisted I come inside. I didn't want to seem too eager.

Just as my foot made contact with the curb, two shadows appeared in the first window, one taller and darker, one smaller and more delicate. They clung closely, turning and floating and moving as one, then disappeared from sight, only to reappear, golden and lovely, framed by lamplight in the next window.

They danced so beautifully and in such perfect sympathy, as if they were born to do this but only with each other. I couldn't take my eyes off them. Caroline twisted left and then right, tapping tiny steps with her tiny feet. Heath held her as if he could not and would not ever let her go.

The music swelled theatrically and Caroline twisted away so her back was to her husband, then slid down the length of his body. He swept his hand over his head before sweeping it down again, placing his palm flat against her stomach. Caroline rose slowly and turned to face him, as if drawn by the force of desire. The current of passion that passed between them was so strong that I felt my cheeks go hot.

The music ended but they stood there still, breathless, looking into each other's eyes. I turned away and hugged the plate to my chest, crossed the street, opened the creaking gate, and went inside to trudge up the close-crowded stairway to my room, feeling claustrophobic and incredibly alone.

Writing my letter to Peaches that night, I admitted to her, and myself, that I'd been feeling that way for a long, long time.

Chapter Sixteen

The antidote to chaos is routine, and I fell into mine almost immediately.

The alarm went off at six thirty every morning. I went downstairs, poured orange juice into my newly acquired Target "This Coffee Is Making Me Awesome" mug, then brought it back to my room and drank it in bed while surfing headlines on my phone. Next, though I always promised myself I wouldn't, I'd end up on The Daily McKee, reading the Dear Calpurnia column and becoming incensed because the quality of the writing had taken a nosedive and my readers—faithless ingrates—hadn't even noticed.

Then, because fury is weirdly energizing and an appetite stimulant, I would jump out of bed, shower, dress, and walk down to Bitty and Beau's for an extra-hot, extra-shot, extra-foam, nonfat latte and a breakfast burrito. The food would quell my hunger, and the baristas, who greeted every customer with a wide and sincere smile, would remind me that the world was still filled with good people.

After breakfast, I would take a long, circuitous walk back home, a different route each day, getting some exercise and refamiliar-izing myself with Charleston. Upon my return, I'd check in with Lorne, who would already be hard at work. Pris arrived around nine and we'd spend the rest of the day, all day, sorting through Calpurnia's leavings. At five, Pris would go home and I would keep working until I couldn't. Then I'd eat something, call Calvin, watch a Christmas movie on my laptop, write in my journal, then turn out the light and dream about Calpurnia and the bearded man in the shadows and the baby. This last part had become a nightly thing. Frankly, it was starting to bug me.

The next day, I'd do it all again. And the next. And the next. And the next.

Routine *is* the antidote to chaos. But it's pretty boring. And when you're working as hard as you can but seeing only minimal progress, it's also pretty frustrating.

After a week and a half, it already was starting to get to me. Even a smile from Teddy, the aptly named big bear of a barista who usually worked the morning shift and never failed to say, "Welcome to Bitty and Beau's," even after he got to know me by name, couldn't shake my mood. Teddy noticed.

"You're not happy," he said, when I handed my eight of hearts card to him in exchange for my latte and burrito. Teddy always spoke frankly, calling it like he saw it. This was a little awkward initially—the first day we met he told me I had my shirt on inside out—but it was also refreshing and kind of sweet.

"Not today," I admitted.

"Why not? What's wrong?"

He frowned, looking genuinely concerned, so I assured him that it was just a temporary situation. "I've been working very hard on a big project. I know I'm making progress, but right now, I can't really see that. I'll be fine. I'm just tired."

"Maybe you should take a break," he said.

"I can't. It's kind of a rush job."

"Then maybe you should take a little break. Like here at work, we take fifteen-minute breaks every few hours. We take coffee breaks from making coffee." Pleased by his joke, he grinned momentarily. "You can't do a good job if you get too tired."

"No, I suppose you're right."

"Take some breaks," he advised. "Little ones."

"I'll think about it."

He nodded earnestly. "You should."

But before I had a chance to think about little breaks or anything else, even before I had a chance to take a badly needed sip of coffee, someone tapped me on the shoulder.

"Miss Fairchild?" The well-dressed man with the huge shoulders looked familiar but I couldn't place him. "Cabot James," he said. "I made an offer to buy your house."

"Oh, yes. The developer. I remember now. Nice to run into you."

He grinned, showing his too-big, too-straight, too-white teeth. He could have been a stand-in on *Shark Week*.

"Well, it's not really a coincidence," he said. "I dropped by your house but missed you. Your contractor said you might be here. Do you have a couple of minutes?"

He motioned to a table by the window. I took a seat.

"I see you've already started the renovation," he said.

"As best we can," I said. "The building permits finally came through, so things should go more quickly now."

He nodded, deeply, as if he found this terribly interesting. "Well. It's quite a project you're undertaking. I've been in the business a long time; started out doing historical restorations but I gave it up a few years ago," he said, flapping his hand and shaking his head.

"Something always goes wrong with these big old houses. They always end up being more trouble and costing more money than they're worth. But"—he shrugged—"you're probably starting to realize that."

I sipped my coffee and said nothing. Subtlety wasn't exactly Cabot's strong suit, and I knew where he was trying to steer the conversation. I also knew there wasn't much point in trying to explain to him that it's impossible to put a price tag on history, especially when it's yours. Cabot sniffed and cleared his throat.

"So. Miss Fairchild, now that you've realized what you've gotten yourself into, I'd like you to reconsider my offer. In consideration for the work that's already been done," he said, flashing his shark teeth, "I'm willing to add another four thousand to my original offer."

"Thank you, but no."

"All right, six thousand." The shark smile hardened into a grimace. "You drive a hard bargain, Miss Fairchild."

"No, thank you, Mr. James. I'm going to finish the restoration and live in the house."

"Why?" he asked, scowling. His scowl was so much more genuine than his smile. "Why would you want to live in a big house all alone?"

That really wasn't any of his business. But I'd met men like Cabot James before, men who hated anybody or anything that got in the way of their plans and profits. And so, because I wanted him to understand that I wasn't being coy or trying to negotiate for better terms, I explained why I was undertaking the restoration. Not all the details, mind you, just that I was hoping to adopt a child and that the restoration of the house, which needed to be completed before the home visit, was integral to making that happen.

His expression seemed to soften and he actually seemed to be listening to what I had to say. I reconsidered my initial opinion of him, thinking he might not be as bad as I'd first thought. He was bobbing his head in agreement as I neared the end of my story and sat in silence for a moment when I was finished, head still bobbing but more slowly, apparently mulling things over.

"Okay," he said, looking down at his big hands. "But . . . what if there was a way we could both get what we wanted? Some way that I could build my project and you could have a home for your kid." He lifted his head, giving me an expectant look.

"I already had some initial meetings with an architect," he said when I didn't respond. "He figures we can build six condos on the property, two baths, two or three bedrooms each, fourteen hundred to sixteen hundred square feet with one off-street parking space for each unit. Here, let me show you."

He pulled a black-and-white rendering from his pocket and laid it on the table. The sketches were simple but gave a good idea what the project would look like when it was finished. The condos were modern-looking with clean lines and plenty of windows.

"What do you think?" he asked. "Pretty nice, huh?"

"They are," I said truthfully. "But they don't really fit in with the rest of the neighborhood, do they? Do you really think the city would approve your design?"

"You just let me worry about that," he said, and folded the drawing in half. "The approvals won't be a problem. All I need is the land.

"Here's what I'm thinking," he said, clasping his hands and rubbing them together. "You sell me the property at the price I offered originally. I'll let you move into one of my other properties rent-free while the condos are under construction. When they're done, I'll sell you one of the two-bedroom units at my cost, which should run about . . ."

He took out a pen and wrote a figure on the back of the drawing. I'd been back in Charleston long enough to know that it was far below market value.

"I'm even willing to protect you against cost overruns," he said. "You'll know exactly what you'd be paying before we break ground." He chuckled. "Can't say that about your restoration project, can you?"

No, I couldn't. Only the day before, Lorne had informed me that the damage to the chimney was worse than we'd thought and repairing it would cost an extra thirteen hundred dollars.

"But how can you afford this?" I asked. "You'll be losing out on a whole year's rent, plus the chance to make a profit on one of the condos."

"I'll make my profits, don't you worry," he said, leaning back in his chair and crossing his arms over his chest. "People will be willing to pay whatever I ask for the chance to live downtown. And it'll be worth it. I've been waiting years to do a project like this, to move away from renovations and rentals into high-end new construction. Cabot Court will put me on the map.

"Think of it," he continued, leaning forward once again, placing both of his big hands on the table. "You'll have a brand-new, modern condo with no headaches and no upkeep in a great neighborhood, a wonderful place to raise a baby, *and* a big chunk of change in the bank. So? What do you say?"

A brand-new, fourteen-hundred-square-foot condo? Two bedrooms and two baths? With parking?

Back in New York, that was the kind of place I dreamed about but knew I could never afford. To have such a thing with no mortgage and money in the bank besides was beyond the boundaries of any dream I could have conjured. A few weeks ago, I'd have jumped at his offer.

Now I was hesitating. Because this wasn't just about me.

How would Felicia and Beau, and even cranky old Mr. Laurens, feel about having six new, ultramodern condominiums built on the street they'd spent their lives on? And what about Caroline and Heath? They'd shown up on my doorstep with cookies and concern and helping hands. We were connected now, all of us. Yes, it was my house but it was *our* neighborhood. If Cabot James had his way, it would never be the same. And how would Calpurnia and Beebee have felt about seeing the place where generations of Fairchilds had lived bulldozed to make room for Cabot Court? Taking his offer would mean erasing my family's history.

And yet . . . A home. A baby. A means to provide for her. A family.

It was everything I'd always wanted and incredibly tempting. The look on Cabot's face told me that he understood exactly *how* tempting.

I'd seen that look before. It was the same look that Dan McKee had on his face when he dropped the box with the bracelet into my lap, the look of a man who is one hundred percent certain that, for the right price, everything and everyone is for sale.

Chapter Seventeen

So you really turned him down?"

"Uh-huh."

"Wow. How very George Bailey of you."

Calvin knew me so well, maybe too well.

It was true: the scene where George turns down the job, and the money, and the cigar, and then takes Mr. Potter to school, telling him that money *can't* buy everything, before storming out of the odious old man's office, had indeed flashed through my mind when I told Cabot James, once and for all, that my house was *not* for sale, not at any price.

The shock and disbelief that registered on his face when he realized he hadn't gotten his way had been extremely satisfying. He sputtered and blustered and all but shook his fist at me, telling me I was making a big mistake, that I had no idea what I was getting myself into or who I was up against. It bothered me not at all. The house was mine, free and clear, and there was nothing he could do about it.

(Take that Mr. Potter, you scurvy little spider! And you too, Dan McKee!)

I lobbed my paper cup into the trash on my way out the door and gave Teddy a cheery wave.

"You look happier now," Teddy said. "Break's over?"

"Yep. Break's over."

I walked out the door, strode down the sidewalk with the swagger of a prizefighter who's just scored a knockout, then pulled my cell phone out of my bag and called Calvin, certain that he would not only approve of my decision but award me style points for delivery. But now . . .

"You think I made a mistake?"

Calvin sucked in his breath and held it for what seemed like a very long time, then let it out in a whoosh. "No," he said at last. "No, you did the right thing."

"You sure?"

"I'm sure," he echoed. "It's your house, your history. You have every right and reason to want to hold on to it. It was the right call. And it's not like anything changed. You made a choice, that's all."

"A harder choice," I admitted. "This restoration is going to be so much work, even more than I'd thought."

"But it'll be worth it," he said, sounding more convinced than he had a moment before, as if he were warming up to his own rhetoric. "He offered you a house but it could never be a home, not in the way Calpurnia's house will be, once you've finished the work. The harder choice is always worth it, you'll see."

"You think?"

"Absolutely," he said. "And speaking of hard choices, cupcake, I must now make the hard choice between continuing to talk with you or taking my rugelach out of the oven."

"Me or burned rugelach? There's no choice. Go."

"Call me tonight," he said. "Love you."

"Love you."

I ended the call and kept walking. Calvin sounded sure of my decision by the end of our call but . . . was he really? What if it was my engagement to Steve all over again? What if Calvin had doubts but only got on board with my choice because he hoped I'd be happy. Was this like that? Was he just trying to be supportive?

Calvin was a good friend. But he was there and I was here and the rugelach was about to burn.

Just minutes before, I'd been feeling pretty good. Now I sighed, dreading the day to come, dreading the mess and the chaos and the possibility of discovering a dead cat or something worse in the mountain of garbage Calpurnia had left behind, dreading a day of endless work that would end with little discernible progress and knowing that more days just like it loomed ahead.

I trudged along, farther up King than I'd ever walked before, disappointed to discover that Jeni's Splendid Ice Cream wouldn't be open for another two hours. Teddy was right. I needed something to break up the drudgery, something I could look forward to doing in the evening. Christmas movies just weren't doing it for me anymore. I needed something productive and a little more creative.

That's when I saw the sign.

Sheepish

A SHOP FOR KNITTERS AND CRAFTERS

I've never put a ton of faith in the whole "setting your intentions" thing. If that stuff actually worked, I'd have a wildly successful career, a husband who adored me, a house in the Hamptons, and three kids by now. But I do believe in signs. Given the timing, it was hard to think that my stumbling on this yarn store at that particular moment was just a coincidence.

The shop was tiny, narrow, and a little claustrophobic, stuffed to bursting with yarn, needles, notions, racks of pattern books, and displays of every kind. It reminded me of Calpurnia's hoard, not in a good way. Part of me wanted to turn around and leave but what could I do? A sign is a sign.

I wended my way through the shelves and tables that blocked my path to the counter near the back of the shop. There weren't any other customers, only a tall woman with red hair who was standing behind the counter. She was bent over with her back toward me. It looked like she might be writing something but I couldn't tell for sure.

"Excuse me, I was wondering if you offered any beginner's knitting classes?"

I wasn't exactly tiptoeing when I approached, and a little cluster of bells on the doorknob had jingled when I entered the shop, but the woman behind the counter yelped at the sound of my voice and clutched her hand to her heart.

After taking a breath, she laid down the Magic Marker she'd been using to make a sign that said, "40% Off Sale! Storewide!!"

"Sorry, ma'am. I didn't hear you come in." She turned toward me.

My heart jumped and my hand flew up to cover my mouth.

"Polly? Polly Schermerhorn?"

Polly had always been tall, willowy, and thin but now she was even thinner, almost gaunt. Her hair was still the same vibrant red but the tangle of curls was gone, cut short and gelled into a crown of soft spikes that framed her face. When she moved her head, the diamond stud that pierced her nostril sparkled in the light but the eyes were the same, so deep blue that when she blinked, as she did now, they were almost purple.

"Are you kidding me? Celia Fairchild?" She laughed when I nodded. "Wow! After all these years? I can't believe it. Wow. So . . . what brings you to Charleston? Visiting family?"

I shook my head. "Nope, I moved back a couple weeks ago. My aunt passed away and left her house to me."

Polly's violet eyes went wide. "Your aunt Calpurnia? The one who—"

"Yes. That one," I said quickly, cutting Polly off before she could fill in the blank. I didn't like talking about what had happened back then, especially with the friend whose friendship I'd lost in the aftermath. "The house is a wreck but I'm fixing it up."

"Great. That's great." Polly bobbed her head but her voice was distracted and I could tell she was thinking about something else. "You know, it's the funniest thing, but I could have sworn I saw you a couple weeks back, standing on the sidewalk across from St. Philip's."

"Wait. On Sunday? Right after church let out?" She nodded and I gasped, my face split into a grin. "I thought I saw you too but then you turned around and I thought, no, it couldn't be. That was you? But . . . what happened to your hair?"

"Oh. I cut it. Just a few days ago." Polly lifted her hand and touched the red spikes, as if checking to make sure they were still there. "I felt like I needed a change. The nose piercing is new too. But . . . I don't know." She wrinkled her nose. "I'm still not sure if I like them."

"No, it looks good," I said, even though I wasn't quite sure either. She just looked so different. But maybe I'd get used to it. "You look good."

"I don't," she said. "I'm skinny, I've got bags the size of steamer trunks under my eyes, and more wrinkles than a shar-pei pup. I finally gave up smoking—and drinking—four years ago. But," she sighed, "the damage has been done."

She did have wrinkles, especially around her lips, as if she'd spent the last twenty years sipping soda through a straw. They weren't awful but they did make her look older. Maybe that was why I hadn't recognized her that day outside St. Philip's. Well, that and the fact that Polly was just about the last person I ever expected to see hanging around outside a church, any church. The attitude hadn't changed; she was still sassy and cut to the chase as ever. But the lines on Polly's face and the sadness lurking behind her eyes said she'd been through a lot. I guess we both had. It was strange though . . .

Once upon a *very* long time ago, Polly and I had been best friends, practically joined at the hip. Now I not only barely recognized her, I knew nothing about her. Who was she now? What had she been up to for the last twenty years? Of course, I hadn't been invited to the wedding, but I remember hearing she'd married Jimmy Mercer after he joined the navy and that they'd moved away. When had she come back to Charleston? And why? Was she still married?

I had so many questions but kept them to myself. It had just been a coincidence, running into her like this, a chance encounter. It would probably be another twenty years before our paths crossed again, if they ever did at all.

"Celia Fairchild," Polly murmured, moving her head slowly from side to side. "When was the last time we saw each other? Do you remember?"

I did remember.

"The graduation beach bonfire on Sullivan's Island."

"That's right! The bonfire!" Polly laughed. "Although, the last time I recall seeing you, from the little I *can* recall about that night, I was seeing two of you. Way too much vodka," she said, her expression regretful but not entirely so. "Wow. Celia Fairchild. What are the chances? I can't believe it's you."

And I couldn't believe it was Polly. But there wasn't a whole lot more to say about that, so I craned my neck, taking in the surroundings, and changed the subject.

"So. This is your shop? It's really something," I said, which was definitely more diplomatic than asking why everything was such a crowded mess. "You've got a lot of inventory."

"Too much," she said. "And not enough space to display it in. And no real room to teach either. But this is the only retail space I could afford so . . ."

"But it's been going all right? The shop, I mean?"

Polly choked out a laugh. "Well. You don't have a forty-percent-off sale if customers are streaming through the door. But . . . you know. I've only been open for five months and it takes time to build a customer base. Things will turn around."

The way she said it, like repeating a mantra, made me think this was something she told herself on a regular basis but didn't quite believe.

"So," she said, clapping her hands together, "what can I help you with? We've got good deals on yarn."

"I was thinking about signing up for a beginner knitting class."

Polly's face fell. "Sorry. I just wrapped up my spring class and won't start a new one for a couple of months. But maybe I can help you. Have you ever knit anything before?"

"Only a pot holder. Back in college. But I never finished it," I admitted.

"Okay, so you're not a *total* beginner. Why don't I set you up with some needles, yarn, and a simple scarf pattern? I'll help you cast on and show you the knit and purl stitches. You'll be able to take it from there."

"Are you sure?" I asked. "I don't want to interrupt your work."

"No worries," Polly said. "Like I said, I'm not exactly over-whelmed with business. The way things have been going, you might be my only customer today. Let me get you a pattern."

She started toward the file cabinet behind the counter and pointed to a glass fishbowl sitting next to a basket filled with yarn, knitting and crochet needles, and other supplies.

"Oh, and be sure to write down your name and phone number for the drawing. I pick a winner at the end of every month, a gift to my loyal customers."

I smiled. "But I haven't even bought anything yet. Are you sure I qualify?"

"Celia," Polly said as she started riffling through the pattern files, "if you buy so much as one skein of really cheap yarn, you'll be one of the most loyal customers I have. At this point, the thresh-old is very low."

Chapter Eighteen

Pris showed up to work sneezing and hacking, so I sent her home. Around two o'clock, while sorting through a box of ugly, moth-eaten draperies that probably dated back to Reconstruction, my hand brushed against something that felt weird. I looked down and . . .

"Ahhhh! Ahhh! Ick! Ick! Ick!"

Yes, indeed, the day I had been dreading was living up to my most horrific expectations. My hand had touched a dead, disgusting, desiccated mouse. I had probably contracted bubonic plague.

My screams were followed by the sound of doors slamming open and big feet pounding up the stairs. Seconds later, Lorne appeared in the doorway. Red and Slip were right behind him. All three were panting and appeared surprised to see I was still alive and not bleeding from every pore. Lorne made a fist and looked frantically around the room, alert for intruders.

"What happened? Are you all right?"

"Yes, I just . . . I stubbed my toe." He rolled his eyes. "It *really* hurt," I said indignantly. "It might be broken!"

Lorne unclenched his fist. "Come on, guys. Let's get back to work," he said, then mumbled something about wimpy women as they made their exit.

It was embarrassing. But being thought a wimp wasn't as bad as having him tease me about being afraid of mice until hell froze over. By this time, Lorne and I had settled into our roles. He thought I was a bossy female who probably voted the straight Democratic ticket and had no actual life skills or appreciation for country music. I thought he was a misogynistic redneck who hadn't cracked a book since high school. But I respected his skills and determination to turn his life around, and he respected the fact that I signed his paycheck. Plus, each of us thought the other one was kind of funny, so it all worked. I didn't want to mess with that.

Once the whine of a Skilsaw told me that Lorne and the crew were back at work, I got a broom and dustpan and disposed of the mouse carcass. Then I went into the bathroom and unswallowed my lunch.

Just another day in beautiful Charleston.

Oh, and I forgot to mention that all of this happened after we got a new building inspector. The one we'd had before, Carl, wasn't exactly a pushover but he was reasonable. The new guy, Brett Fitzwaller, was younger and brand-new on the job and nitpicked every little thing. Earlier that morning, he'd apparently told Lorne that the grade at the back of the house was wrong.

"What does that mean?" I asked. "Is it going to cost me more money?"

"No," Lorne said. "All I'll have to do is shovel off about two inches of dirt near the foundation. This guy acts like the building code is holy scripture and he's God himself. He gave me a list of twelve things to fix before he'll sign the approval—including replacing the bottom step to the piazza. According to Brett, it's three-eighths of an inch too high."

"Is it?"

"I *know* how to use a tape measure," Lorne said, sounding offended. "But when it comes to construction, inspectors have the last word. Only thing to do is suck it up and try to get on his good side. Piddly stuff like this just ends up costing us time. I miss Carl."

"Maybe he'll be back?"

"Doesn't sound like it," Lorne said. "Well, ma'am, if you'll excuse me, I've got to go rebuild a step I already built and shovel some dirt that doesn't need shoveling."

It was that kind of day.

At the end of it, I settled myself into Beebee's old pink chair and took out my knitting. By the time I'd left Polly's shop, I felt like I had the knit stitch down pat. But somehow, in the course of about nine hours, I'd managed to forget everything she taught me. When I paid my bill, Polly had thrown in an instruction book for free.

"I insist," she'd said when I objected; it didn't look to me like Polly could afford to be giving stuff away. "The world has enough unfinished pot holders."

But the book didn't help. If anything, it made things worse. When I got to the end of the row, I somehow ended up with ninety-seven stitches instead of eighty-four. Then, when I tried to go back and fix my mistake, I ended up dropping a bunch of stitches and unraveling half of what I'd done. Finally, I got so frustrated that I ripped out the whole thing and shoved the yarn back into the bag and stuffed it into one of the cubbies with all the other useless yarn.

"Thirty-eight bucks down the drain."

Clearly, stumbling upon Polly's craft shop was not the sign I'd thought it was. I had no plans to return, which was probably just as well. Though it was good to see her face, and to know she was still alive and more or less well, seeing her reminded me of things I'd just as soon forget. Until I'd come home, until I'd started writing letters to Peaches, and found bits and hints about the past making their way into what was supposed to be a life guide penned for a Maybe Baby, letters that now seemed to be turning into something closer to a memoir, I'd been pretty successful at forgetting, or at least at choosing not to remember. But it was harder than it had been before. Running into Polly had made it harder still.

I pulled out my computer and booted up a Christmas movie, but even George Bailey failed to cheer me up. When I got to the scene with Mr. Potter, it occurred to me that maybe George was a chump to turn down all that money and an easier life. Maybe I was too. I closed my computer.

After almost two weeks, nothing had changed. The house was still too quiet and too big. If it hadn't been so late, I'd have phoned Calvin. Instead, I got out my journal. If I tried to go to sleep, I already knew what would happen. I'd wake up an hour later, dreaming the same dream, still wondering what it meant. Maybe writing to Peaches would help me figure it out.

Besides, it wasn't like I had anyone else to talk to.

Dear Peaches,

Beebee used to go to the City Market every Thursday morning to see Sallie Mae, a proud old Gullah woman who sold sweetgrass baskets and honey and would tell Beebee what her dreams meant.

I wish Sallie Mae was still around. Maybe she could tell me why I keep having the dream. The first time, I took it as a good omen and Calpurnia's blessing. But if the dream meant I was on the right path, why is she making me watch a rerun every night? I feel like there's something more I'm supposed to do. But what?

Sallie Mae wasn't a fortune-teller. Beebee never paid for her interpretations. However, Beebee did amass a large collection of sweetgrass baskets. Pris and I found boxes and boxes of them hidden under decades' worth of Sears catalogs and Southern Living magazines. Sweetgrass baskets of that age and quality can be valuable, and Beebee had a good eye. The baskets were our most valuable find so far. Heath used his connections at the Historic Charleston Foundation and found a buyer who bought almost all of them. That will help cover the cost overruns to repair the roof.

I've been clear-eyed about what stays and goes, almost brutally so. A couple of days ago, I came close to selling Calpurnia's vintage Olivetti manual typewriter with the wonky y's that look like slashes, the one she used for every piece of correspondence, including all those letters she wrote to me and ended with "Sending you some sugar."

Yes. That typewriter.

Heath talked me out of it.

"Think of this house as a museum," he said, "and you as the curator. If a stranger walked through the door, what would you want them to know about your family before they left? Keep only the objects that tell your story and tell it well."

It always seemed strange to me that Beebee put so much faith in Sallie Mae's interpretations when she was wrong as often as she was right. But I'm starting to think it had nothing to do with dreams. At that time, in this part of the world, it wasn't possible for a white woman and a black woman to simply be friends. There had to be some sort of transaction involved, something to explain why two women from two different worlds would choose to spend so much time together, talking and listening and being heard. It wasn't about the dreams; it was about loneliness.

If this house is a museum, then I think a whole gallery could be devoted to isolation and what it does to people.

Chapter Nineteen

*C*oncern about the ravages of isolation led me to accept the invitation to Beau Pickney's surprise eightieth birthday party. That and guilt.

I've never liked parties, but Felicia was so excited about Beau's party, she would have been heartbroken if I'd begged off. And Charleston wasn't New York. I couldn't just invent some excuse about a work deadline or a sick relative and then disappear behind the door to my apartment to spend the night eating pistachio ice cream in my underwear while binge-watching back-to-back episodes of *The Blacklist*, indulging my recent, inexplicable, and probably unhealthy attraction to James Spader without people finding out. Harleston Village was a lot like a college dorm; everybody knew everybody else's business and got up into it on a regular basis.

Pris volunteered to be my stylist for the evening. She brought in a silk shirtwaist dress she'd rescued from one of the thirty gazillion garbage bags she'd found stuffed in the first-floor powder room. A lot of the things she'd rescued had already been shipped off to eBay bidders, but this one had failed to sell. I thought I knew why.

"You can't be serious," I said after looking in the mirror. The dress screamed 1983—white daisies with blue centers on a pink background, shoulder pads that made me look like I was playing defense for the Carolina Panthers, and a floppy pussy bow at the neck. "I look like an aging version of Princess Diana before she got money, and taste, and a crown."

"Hang on," Pris said. "I'm not done yet." She took some scissors out of Beebee's old sewing basket, an heirloom that I had decided was worth saving. "Untie it," she said, gesturing with the scissors. "And unbutton the top." She walked across the room, scissor blades pointing toward me, which, as everybody knows, is something you should never do. I clutched the bow tighter around my neck.

"Why?"

"So I can cut out the shoulder pads." She rolled her eyes. "Celia, you have *got* to quit watching *The Blacklist*. It's making you jumpy. And suspicious."

"The world is a dark and dangerous place," I muttered as I undid the buttons. "Full of dark and dangerous characters."

"*None* of whom live around here. I'd give a pair of vintage Doc Martens to run into a good bad boy this summer. A Post Malone type." She sighed. "But maybe with a few less tats."

"Why?"

"I don't know. Same reason you're crushed on James Spader, I guess. There's something irresistible about a guy who's all wrong for you."

"Stick to the celebrity bad boys," I advised. "The real ones will break your heart into a million pieces and then demand alimony for the privilege." Pris wasn't listening and probably wouldn't have believed me if she had been. When it comes to romance and the misery it creates, we *all* insist on taking the field trip.

Pris reached inside my dress and snipped away, then extracted the shoulder pads. The shoulder seams drooped to my biceps.

"Just wait a minute," she said after I shot her a look. "I'm not finished yet." She reached into the big shoulder bag she'd brought from home and pulled out a pair of old-school, white canvas tennis shoes and a gray sweatshirt with three-quarter-length sleeves. "Trust me," she said.

I slipped my feet into the sneakers and the sweatshirt over my head. Pris fussed with the sleeves and the bow, retying it so it looked a little less limp, then stepped away so I could see my reflection.

"What do you think?"

"It works." I blinked a couple of times. "I don't know why but it does."

"Because it's fun," Pris replied. "And original. You don't have to worry about anybody else showing up wearing the same outfit."

"True. Not unless Felicia decides to clean out the back of her closet." I twisted my body from side to side, trying to see how it looked from a different angle. "I like it. But I feel like something's missing."

I rummaged in the top drawer of a taupe-and-white dresser with leaves and vines on the drawer fronts, stenciled by Aunt Calpurnia when I was about ten. I remembered helping her paint it, watching her spray aerosol glue to the back of the stencils, coating the brush carefully with paint and handing it to her, hearing her mutter under her breath when she pulled off a stencil and saw the paint had bled a little. I'd discovered it a couple of days before, fortressed behind three walls of boxes and a lumpy, button-tied mattress, and decided to keep it, another carefully curated piece for my collection, along with some of what I'd found inside.

"What do you think?" I held the pearls together at the back of my neck with my hand, the strand falling halfway between the bow and my breast. Pris grinned.

"Perfect."

"IT'LL JUST BE a small get-together," Felicia had said when she had first invited me to the surprise party. "Beau doesn't like a lot of fuss at birthdays."

I wasn't sure if she'd lied about Beau or simply decided to ignore his wishes, but the crush of bodies crammed into the Pickneys' cavernous home was the furthest thing from a "small" get-together.

"Hubert and Sissy Lee are coming," Felicia said, as she escorted me down the hallway toward the bedroom. "You might remember them; he was a deacon at St. Philip's and she painted watercolors. I asked Mr. Laurens but, of course, he said no. But Mrs. Aiken is here—"

"Sonya Aiken?" Mrs. Aiken had been ancient when I was a little girl. If she was still alive, she had to be a centenarian.

"No, no," Felicia said. "Deborah Jean Aiken, her daughter. Let's see . . . who else? The Wrights will be here. The Mazlows. Oh, just lots of nice people. I'm sure you'll have a lovely time. Just leave your wrap in the guest room," she said. "But hurry! I told Foster to bring Beau back to the house right at seven. They'll be here any minute."

I tossed my shawl onto a bed in the guest room and hesitated, thinking about just picking it back up and slipping out a side door. Felicia had already seen me, so my presence had been counted. If I left early, she'd probably never know.

"Thinking about bailing?"

I turned around. Trey Holcomb was standing in the doorway. He was wearing his usual awful suit but had paired it with a royal-blue shirt. It was an improvement over his usual white and made

+++

his brandy-brown eyes look even browner. Though I'd noticed Trey's eyes from the first, I'd always thought of Lorne as the handsome one. But when Trey was smiling, like he was now, it really was hard to decide which brother was better looking.

"Celia? Did you hear me?" Trey's smile twisted into a question, and he tipped his head to one side.

"Hmm? Sorry. What did you say?"

"I asked if you were thinking about bailing."

"Maybe," I admitted. "I don't really like parties. Or small talk."

Trey shoved his hands in his pockets. "Yeah. I get that. But word on the street says Felicia's crab puffs are pretty spectacular."

"They are," I said. "She used to bring them to neighborhood things when I was little."

"Sounds worth hanging around for." Trey smiled. "Tell you what, I'll keep you from being a wallflower if you keep me from having to talk to my brother."

"Lorne's here?"

"Everybody's here," Trey said. "I think she even invited Red and Slip but the terms of their parole don't allow them to attend gatherings where intoxicating beverages will be served." I looked at him blankly. He shook his head. "It was a joke."

Okay. If he said so. But I hadn't been thinking about Red and Slip.

"Why don't you like talking to your brother?"

"We don't get along."

"Yes. I figured that out. But why?"

"It's a long story."

"I love long stories. How about I buy you a drink and you tell it to me?"

"Uh-uh. We don't have enough time or liquor for that."

Felicia's head popped through the doorway. She had on new red glasses, even bigger than the others, with one sparkly rhinestone at each corner. They must have been her party glasses.

"Hurry up and find a place to hide, you two. It's nearly seven." We watched as she tottered down the hall, kitten heels beating like castanets on the wood floor as she called out, "Hush, y'all! Find someplace to hide. They'll be here any minute!"

Trey turned to face me. "If we hurry, we can probably score a couple of crab puffs before they're all gone." When he offered me his arm, the sleeve of his jacket inched halfway up his forearm.

"Why do you always wear the same suit?" I asked.

"Because a couple of years back, I had a client who sold mens-wear. He was going bankrupt and didn't have any money, so he paid me with the last of his stock. I've got five more just like it."

"Hmm. Too bad he didn't have any suits that came in other colors."

Or a thirty-eight long.

He shrugged. "It's all the same to me. I've never really cared about clothes."

Yes, this much I had figured out. I took his arm and we walked down the hall toward the din created by eighty people telling each other to be quiet.

"Besides," he continued, "this way I never have to think about what I'm going to wear. But that is a nice dress."

I spread the skirt out with my free hand, pleased that he'd no-ticed. "Pris found it for me. You like it?"

"I do. My mother used to have one exactly like it."

WALKING INTO FELICIA and Beau's living room was like stepping through a time portal to my childhood. With the exception of the dark-blue velvet curtains that had replaced the brocade drapes in the exact same shade of blue, everything looked just like it had twenty-five years before. Which is not to say that the room looked dated or the least bit tired. That's the thing about antiques, I guess. Once a good piece of furniture has endured beyond a certain age, it never really goes out of style. It occurred to me that this was a pretty good metaphor for Felicia herself.

I waved to Heath and Caroline, just before they ducked down behind a fainting couch. The scrolled back curved upward, so it was perfect for them. The top of Heath's head was barely visible at the higher end of the sofa back and Caroline, who was wearing a robin's-egg-blue dress almost the same color as the couch's silk upholstery, was well camouflaged.

Lorne and Pris were plainly visible, standing on opposite sides of a mahogany tall-case clock, but didn't seem to care. Lorne, who had spruced up for the occasion, topping his usual jeans with a crisp white shirt and light-gray sport coat, kept popping his head around his side of the clock, saying things that Pris apparently found pretty funny. I liked Lorne, I really did, but flirting was kind of a default setting with him and I was a little worried about Pris, especially after her comments about wanting to find a bad boy. Lorne wasn't bad, not really, but he was too old for her. However, everybody gets to choose their own brand of heartbreak, so I looked away and kept searching for a place to hide. There wasn't much left to pick from.

Five people I didn't know were already crouched down behind the camelback sofa. Happy Browder, Deborah Jean Aiken, and the Mazlows were hiding behind a baby grand piano near the front window, their legs clearly visible under the ebony piano case. There wasn't any place big enough to hide two people, so I squatted down next to a slim little writing desk and Trey stood behind a potted palm.

Trey's head was plainly visible above the fronds, but he made a great show of flattening himself against the wall, then snapped his head toward me and froze, like a deer who has been discovered in the headlights and can't figure out which direction to run. I shook my head and grinned, trying to keep from laughing. It wasn't that Trey was exactly hilarious, but there's something kind of cute and endearing about a guy who's trying to show off for a girl.

I'd have been less amused if it was Lorne; he really did seem to flirt with anything in a skirt, almost like an involuntary reflex. But Trey didn't seem like that kind of guy. And he really did have the *nicest* eyes. Were they brandy-colored? Or were they more like toffee? Either way, they were delicious.

Felicia peered through a tiny crack in the almost-closed curtains and let out a little gasp of excitement. "Somebody's coming up the walk! Turn off the lamp! Quiet now!"

Happy flipped a switch on a Tiffany lamp that sat atop the piano. The room went completely dark and, apart from the wheezing sound coming from behind the piano when Mr. Mazlow breathed, completely silent. We waited. And waited. And waited. Nobody moved a muscle. Finally, the front door opened and two people entered the house.

"Hello? Is anybody home?"

Sissy Lee flipped a light switch and everybody groaned.

"Sissy, darling," Felicia said, "it's a surprise party. You were supposed to come in the *back* door."

"Is it?" Sissy blinked twice. "Hubert didn't tell me."

"*I* told you when I saw you in the bakery last week. Never mind," Felicia said. "Come on in and find a place to hide. Beau and Foster will be here any second."

Things went on like that for a while. Somebody would come up the walk and everybody would hide, only to realize that the somebody was another latecomer. After the third failed drill, people got tired of hiding and went to the bar.

I looked around for Trey, hoping to continue our conversation. We'd never really talked before, except about the legal stuff, but he seemed more relaxed tonight, more open. Though he seemed pretty adamant that the subject was off limits, I'd have liked to pry out more about what had happened between him and Lorne. But I was also curious about him individually. Trey was obviously smart and probably could have gone to work for a big firm and made all kinds of money. Instead, he ran a one-man show and took on clients who paid their bills in old menswear. What was that about? And well . . . It would have been nice to know if there was more to his showing off than *just* showing off.

Not that I had time for more, or the inclination; Steve had had nice eyes too, and look how that had turned out. Probably Trey was just goofing around, or maybe he'd pregamed and had a drink before the party. Either way, I'd kind of enjoyed it. It had been such a long time since any man, sober or otherwise, had showed off for me. And I liked Trey. Bad suits notwithstanding, he seemed like a good guy.

But the room was crowded, and before I had a chance to locate Trey, I was cornered by Sissy Lee. Though I'd known Sissy since childhood, not only did she not remember me, she seemed to be under the impression that I was a cellist and had played a sonata during the Spoleto Festival. There was no polite way to escape, so while Sissy jabbered on about Bach, I looked past her shoulder and thought about how all cocktail parties mostly look and sound the same, filled with well-dressed people who laughed too hard and tried too hard and drank too much.

When I went to parties in New York and people found out I was Dear Calpurnia, they immediately started telling me all about their problems. By comparison, this party was a piece of cake. Memory lapses notwithstanding, Sissy was still a talker, so I didn't have to do much besides nod my head and murmur occasionally. But as my eyes wandered the room, I couldn't help but wonder about my new neighbors.

Why was Caroline standing off by herself, not talking to anybody? How much had Happy spent on her outfit? And Botox? Did it make her feel safer? More confident? Why was Pris still talking to Lorne? Didn't she realize he was all wrong for her? And why did Felicia's smile fade the minute she thought no one was looking? I'd known Felicia since I was a little girl, but did I really *know* her? If Felicia, if any of the women in the room, had written a letter to Dear Calpurnia, what would they have asked her? What advice would I have offered?

I couldn't help but wonder, but maybe it was easier not to know. It's one thing to worry about a stranger, and another to become emotionally invested in someone you see on a daily basis. That kind of caring takes energy I wasn't sure I had, and a brand of vulnerability I wasn't sure I wanted to expose myself to.

When Foster and Beau finally did arrive, the party was in full swing. Foster's idea for getting his father out of the house had been to take him to the Champagne Bar at the Peninsula Grill for three old-fashioneds. By the time they showed up, both men were well lubricated, and Felicia was furious with her son. I overheard her chewing him out when I went to get a glass of wine.

"All I wanted you to do was get him out from underfoot for half an hour. Was that so much to ask? I was counting on you."

"Well, Mother, that was your first mistake," Foster slurred. "You should know by now that, where I am concerned, the only thing you can count on is that you can't." He paused and lifted a glass of dark amber liquor to his lips. "Me, I mean. You can't count on me."

Before Felicia could continue her scolding, Beau tripped on the fringe of a thick Persian rug and fell into the arms of Bradley Baudoin, starting a chain reaction of whoops, laughter, and breaking glass. Felicia thrust a tray of bacon-wrapped dates she'd been carrying into Foster's hands.

"Take these and pass them around. I'll deal with you later," she hissed, then hurried away to rescue her husband and sweep up the broken glass before anyone stepped in it. "Beau, darling, that is *enough* bourbon. Save some room for cake."

"Do you think she's going to ground me?"

Foster turned toward me, plucked a date from the tray, and popped it into his mouth. I assumed this was a rhetorical question and didn't respond. But Foster had a point; Felicia should have known better.

Foster was shiftless, unreliable, and spoiled and everybody knew it. Once upon a time, he had been something approaching handsome. I'd had a brief crush on him when I was about eleven but that was almost twenty-six years ago. Now he reminded me of an overfed, sunburned toddler.

"Date?" Foster mumbled, his mouth full.

"No, thanks. I already ate too many crab puffs."

Foster shook his head and swallowed. "I was asking if you'd like to go out on a date." I looked at him blankly and he clarified his terms. "With me."

"Oh."

He took another drink. "What are you doing on Friday? There's an Italian restaurant on Spring Street, Kink Practice—"

Before I could say thanks but no thanks, Foster started coughing.

His already florid face turned scarlet. I pounded his back and scanned the room, searching for help. Was he choking? Or having a heart attack? Or was this just a usual thing with him? Whatever it was, it sounded bad, and scarlet was turning to vermilion.

Trey was standing near the buffet table. I made my eyes go wide in a silent but desperate call for rescue. He immediately put down his plate and started wending his way through the crush of inebriates, forced to take a circuitous route to reach my side of the room. But then, just as abruptly as he'd started, Foster stopped coughing and lifted his bourbon to his lips as if nothing had happened.

"Kink Practice," he slurred after swallowing, and blinked several times in succession, as if trying to force the room into focus. "Friday. Around seven?"

I felt a hand on my elbow. Lorne had appeared out of nowhere and was standing very close to me, possessively close.

"Pink *Cactus*," Lorne said. "And it's Mexican, not Italian. But I'm afraid she can't make it, Foster. She's already got a date on Friday night, with me." Lorne winked at me and smiled, then draped his arm over my shoulders. I smiled back, grateful for the intervention. Lorne glanced down at my wineglass.

"Looks like somebody needs a refill," he said, even though it was still half full. "Excuse us, Foster."

When Lorne squeezed my shoulder and steered me toward the bar, I turned just in time to glimpse the back of a too-tight black suit and see Trey walk out the door.

Chapter Twenty

*W*hoa."

I sucked in a breath and blew it out then looked over the figures again, hoping my addition was off. It was. My initial calculation was off by almost a thousand dollars, but *not* in my favor. The sensation in my stomach went from sinking to plummeting.

"This is even worse that I thought it would be."

"I know," Lorne said. "There's some trade war thing going on and the price of lumber has gone up fifteen percent in the last two weeks. And the roof . . ." He shrugged and sipped his Coke; he wasn't saying anything I didn't already know. "The thing that's really killing us is the electrical. There's not a thing wrong with the electrical panel. But Inspector Brett—"

"Says we have to replace it with a new one. I remember. I really hate that guy. What's his problem anyway?" When it came to our new building inspector, Lorne and I were absolutely on the same page.

"I don't know." Lorne shrugged. "Power trip."

"Can't we buy him off or something? Or maybe just . . . make sure he has a terrible accident of some kind? You're an ex-con, you must know people, right?"

Lorne laughed. "Sorry. I was only in for white-collar stuff. Now, Slip," Lorne said thoughtfully, before taking another drink, "he's been in and out of the joint a couple of times. He might be able to help you."

"Hmm. Okay, remind me never to get on Slip's bad side."

Our server returned and put a bowl of olives and a pizza down on the bar. I reached for a slice and took a bite. It was really good but I had other things on my mind besides food, like unanticipated bills and overrun budgets.

"Well," I sighed. "It is what it is, right? Sorry, but I can't pay you right now. I don't have my checkbook with me."

"No worries," Lorne said. "Monday is fine. But, listen . . . Could you do me a favor and not mention this to Trey?"

I hadn't planned on doing so and Trey probably wouldn't take my call anyway—he'd been either incredibly busy or avoiding me since Beau's birthday party—but Lorne's question made me wonder if I should.

"Every dime is accounted for," Lorne assured me, apparently reading my expression. "I added it up four times, just to make sure of the math. And I've got receipts and estimates for every single item, right down to the three-penny nails, which, by the way, now cost four forty-five a pound."

I smiled, my concerns quelled. I felt like I'd gotten to know Lorne even better in the last weeks. He was a little too aware of his own good looks for his or anybody else's good, and he insisted on playing country music at high volume while he worked, singing along to every single Rascal Flatts song, but he worked as hard as anybody I'd ever met. He was also smart, too smart to risk going back to prison a second time for the same crime.

"I'd just rather Trey didn't know about cost overruns. He doesn't trust me. And I get it," Lorne said, lifting his hands before I had a chance to point out the obvious. "He's got good reason not to. But you know, Trey has defended some pretty shady characters over the years, and made less money than any lawyer in Charleston doing it."

"He defended you," I reminded him, not that I really needed to. Something told me that debt was never far from Lorne's mind.

"Yes," Lorne said evenly, "and I'm grateful. Trey thinks everybody deserves their day in court. He's an idealist and the world could use a lot more of those. Funny thing about my brother, though." Lorne dipped his head down and took another drink of soda. "He thinks everybody in the world deserves a second chance, except me."

I didn't know what to say to that, so I took a sip of my ginger ale. I would have preferred a beer. But Lorne was, as he called it, "a recovering everything," so I stuck to nonalcoholic beverages when I was with him, even though he'd told me it wasn't necessary. "Seriously, Celia. Don't worry about it. It'd take a whole lot more than you to knock me off the wagon. Or a whole lot less," he would say with a grin. "Depends on the day."

I do give points for humor. But I felt bad for Lorne. I suspected his humor was insulating a whole lot of pain, just like everybody else's.

"What's happened between you and Trey?"

Lorne chewed his pizza and gave me a pointed look.

"No, I mean besides your conviction. I feel like there's more to it than that."

"We're brothers," he said, as if this explained everything.

"Come on. I asked Trey but he said there wasn't enough liquor in Charleston to get it out of him."

"See? And with me it'd only take half a bourbon. Which is another reason I don't drink. Miss?" Lorne waved his hand, trying to catch the eye of our server, then mimed a signing motion.

He'd told me before we sat down that he was in a hurry because he had an AA meeting later. His momentary distraction gave me an opportunity to take a good look at him. His jaw was sharp and as angled as a cleaver, his eyes deep brown and fringed with a bristle of thick lashes, a feature that all the mascara in the world cannot buy, as I am all too aware.

Handsome. An ex-con. A recovering everything. A million red flags, all waving madly. No wonder I was suddenly finding myself attracted to him. Until a few months ago, he'd have been just my type, a man who presented yet another opportunity to make myself absolutely miserable. Now there was Peaches.

When the server brought the check, I grabbed it first. Lorne protested, said he was the one who'd invited me, so he should pay the bill.

"You didn't invite me. You rescued me from Foster Pickney, remember?"

"Well, I *wanted* to invite you. Doesn't that count?"

"This was a meeting, Lorne. I'm the boss, so I should pay."

"You're the *client*," he said, his tone making it clear that he had no boss, "so I should pay. Besides, it's not that much. Half-price pizza during happy hour. Don't take this the wrong way, Celia, but you're a cheap date."

I smiled. How could I not? Lorne grinned, looking pretty pleased with himself, then leaned closer, and waited. If I had moved my head forward an inch and a half, two at the most, our lips would have met. I won't say it wasn't tempting. But then what? Whatever happened next, I knew it wouldn't end well.

I turned my head to one side and dabbed my lips with my napkin, pretending I hadn't noticed him. Lorne narrowed his eyes as if he was trying to size me up and see if I was worth the trouble. Finally, he shrugged and picked up another olive.

"Okay. I get it. Probably the last thing you need right now is a man."

Probably.

"So? Did you go out with him?" Calvin asked when I talked to him over the weekend and told him about what had happened at the Pickneys' party.

"No. Yes. But not like *that*," I said when Calvin gasped and started to sputter. "What I mean is, we got together after he wrapped for the day but just to go over budgets and the punch lists. It wasn't a date. We shared a pizza—"

"Where'd you go?"

"Someplace on King Street, I can't remember the name. But the pizza was fabulous. It had shaved brussels sprouts, thin slices of apple, pancetta, and some kind of cheese."

I've known Calvin long enough to accept that the conversation could not continue until I related the particulars of the meal. However, I didn't tell him anything about dodging Lorne's kiss because there was honestly nothing to tell.

"Ricotta," Calvin said authoritatively. "And did they drizzle a little honey on it? I bet it was Indaco."

"Calvin, do you spend all your spare time memorizing the menus of every restaurant in America?"

"Only the good ones." He sniffed. "So, how was it? Besides the food, I mean. Did you have fun?"

"I wasn't there to have fun. I was there to crunch numbers and check things off lists. Honestly, Calvin, the only thing I am thinking about right now is getting the house ready in time for the home visit."

"No room for romance?"

"None. And if there was, you can bet it wouldn't be with a thrice-divorced felon and recovering addict."

"Wouldn't have stopped you before."

"Yeah, well. The prospect of impending motherhood changes a person. No more bad boys for me," I said.

"What about good men? Trey Holcomb seems like a solid citizen."

Yes, he was. And I liked Trey, or might have, if the circumstances had been different. But they weren't. Honestly, it was just as well. I had plenty on my plate as it was. Plus, he wasn't speaking to me.

"No boys *or* men," I said. "Period. End of sentence. Trey's a nice guy. A little earnest maybe. And a terrible dresser. But I'm not in the market for a guy. Also, he seems to have a jealous streak. I called him the morning after the party and he still hasn't called back."

Yep. Just as well.

"Besides, the whole estranged brother, Cain versus Abel thing is a major red flag. I've plenty of family baggage of my own, thank you very much."

"Uh-huh," Calvin said. "You seem to have spent an awful lot of time thinking about this man you have no interest in."

"No, I'm just being clear. And focused. I'm serious, Calvin. I know it sounds weird but I feel like I'm on some kind of mission."

"You're still having the dream."

It wasn't a question. Calvin knew me so well.

"Every single night," I said. "It's got to mean something, don't you think? I'm not just talking about me or even the baby. It's all mixed up with my family and this house. I feel like I'm meant to bring it back to what it was. Or maybe what it never was but should have been. Does that sound crazy?"

"Yes. A little," Calvin admitted. "But hey. Just because something sounds crazy doesn't necessarily mean it is. We're all here for some reason, aren't we? There has to be some purpose to all this, don't you think?"

Only a few months before, I'd have said no. Now, I wasn't so sure.

Dear Peaches,

I keep thinking about the inscription on my parents' grave, "Until the times of restoration of all things, whereof God spake . . ."

Maybe this is my time. Maybe that's why I'm here, to find what is lost and restore what was.

Maybe that's why we're all here.

Chapter Twenty-One

*I*t's quarter after five," I reminded Pris. "Shouldn't you be heading out?"

The day after Beau and Felicia's party, Pris had gotten her wish and met her bad boy. Larson Benning was a twenty-three-year-old, bedroom-eyed tattoo artist with an attitude and huge gauges in his ears. He sounded creepy to me but Pris was head over heels. She'd gone out with him every night of the following week and spent a big chunk of every day talking about him. That was why I'd decided to work on the dining room by myself that day. Listening to her sigh over Larson was exhausting.

"We broke up," Pris said, angrily slapping packing tape onto a box. "Turns out he already has a girlfriend, they live together. She spotted us at the club, poured a beer over his head, and stormed off. Lars followed her and left me with the tab."

"Ouch. You okay?"

She bobbed her head. "I knew it wasn't going to last."

"Very convincing. I almost believed you."

Pris laughed and then sniffled. I patted her on the shoulder.

I couldn't say I was sorry that the interlude with Lars had come to an end, but I remembered what it felt like to be twenty and have a guy you thought might be the one tell you lies and make you look stupid. I remembered what it felt like at thirty too. And thirty-five. And thirty-seven . . . Everything I'd said to Calvin was true. The last thing I needed right now, and possibly ever again, was to get involved with a man. It wasn't worth the heartache and it never worked out, at least not for me.

"I'm sorry, Pris. Men suck."

"I'll get over him." She shrugged. "Those gauges were kind of gross."

That wasn't what she'd said a week ago, but whatever.

"You should knock off early," I said. "Go out and do something fun, maybe with your mom. Bet you haven't spent much time with her lately."

"Yeah, well . . . Fun and my mom aren't words I generally use in the same sentence. What about you? I thought you were trying to take breaks at night."

"I know. But I'm kind of over Christmas movies at the moment. I'm kind of over *The Blacklist* too. The story never really goes anywhere and James Spader isn't really as cute as I thought. Besides, I want to finish the dining room. Being able to see the table is highly motivating. I've only got a few more boxes to go."

"Of books," Pris reminded me, tossing me a pointed look. "You know it'll go a lot quicker if you quit stopping to read them, right? I found the box of novels we'd agreed should be donated to the library that you tried to sneak back into the house."

Before I could protest, or tell Pris that the rescued box included a copy of Mary McCarthy's *The Group* and that this might be the perfect time for her to read it, my phone rang. I didn't recognize the number but when has that ever stopped me?

"Hey, Celia. It's Polly Mercer. I'm just calling to tell you that you won the drawing."

"Excuse me?"

"The drawing," she prodded, "for the basket of yarn and knitting supplies? Congratulations! You're the winner!"

More yarn? Just what I needed.

"Oh. Well . . . that's great, Polly. Thanks. But I thought you picked the winner at the end of the month?" My question was met by extended silence. "Polly? Are you there?"

"Okay, you're right," she said, her tone less cheery. "I haven't drawn a winner yet. But your chances are still good. I've had maybe twenty entries, and customers, since you came in."

Only twenty? No wonder she sounded so discouraged.

"I just thought . . . Argh! This is so embarrassing. I sound like a stalker. And a big loser." She took a deep breath and started talking fast, like she'd just decided to rip off the Band-Aid and get on with it.

"Look, I won't blame you if you never want to see me again. But it's been so long and we're grown-ups now. When you came into the shop, I just thought . . . Well, I don't know what I thought; I'd always figured I'd never see you again. But then, all of a sudden, there you were. I've been thinking about you ever since, and I keep wondering if it meant something, like maybe we were supposed to start over?"

Start over? I honestly didn't know what to say to that. Fortunately, I didn't have to because Polly didn't give me a chance to respond, she just kept talking.

"The truth is, it's been lonely since I came back to Charleston. Everything's different, you know? All my old high school girl-friends have married stockbrokers and joined the country club and turned into their mothers. We don't have anything in common anymore. Well, except for Josie. She's farming medical marijuana in Colorado now. But Denver is so far away and, with me being me, it's probably just as well. Lead us not into temptation and all that.

"Anyway," Polly sighed, "I've been feeling kind of down. And I was wondering if, you know, maybe we could hang out sometime? It seemed kind of weird to call up and say that, so I decided to say you'd won the drawing and then ask if we could meet up so I could hand it off to you."

"Wow," she said, finally pausing long enough to take a breath. "That sounds even more pathetic when you say it out loud, doesn't it?"

Pathetic? No. So much of what she'd said about everything changing and feeling lonely rang true to me. But *lonely* was a word I never thought I'd hear coming from Polly's lips.

We were always so different. I think that's what made it work for as long as it did. I also think that's why our teacher, Mrs. Florsheim, decided Polly and I should sit together from the second month of first grade on, because she knew that each of us had something the other one lacked. Our peculiar strengths and extremes balanced out each other's weaknesses and gaps.

Polly helped me be more outgoing, practical, and adventurous. I helped her to be more studious and imaginative, and a little less impulsive. She knew how to stand up for herself to the point of being combative. I knew peacekeeping to the point of becoming a doormat. I taught Polly to read. She taught me to stand up for myself and, if I couldn't, she did it for me. Polly was fun to be with, easy to like, and had lots of friends. But the two of us had a special bond. Once upon a time, we were best friends.

Until we weren't.

I wanted to tell her what had happened and why I'd disappeared.

But how could I explain it to her when I still couldn't explain it to myself? I was so confused and so ashamed. Besides, Sterling had told me not to tell anyone because it would only make things worse. Since my telling had already caused the final disintegration of the ravaged remnants of my family, I couldn't take the chance. To this day, I've never shared the whole story, not with Polly or anyone else.

I couldn't explain that I didn't invite her over anymore because I didn't want her to see where and how we were living, in a sterile gray box on the fifth floor, the wastepaper baskets filled with Sterling's empty bourbon bottles. All Polly knew was that I'd disappeared, come back a different person, and refused to talk about it no matter how many times she asked. After a while, she quit asking and started ignoring me, which came as a sad relief. We ignored each other and I ignored everyone: it was safer that way. I retreated into books and studied hard, and I got used to being on my own.

And Polly had so many friends, I figured she didn't miss me that much. But she was the first one who called me Daria, a reference to the sarcastic cartoon character with the deadpan delivery who thinks she's smarter than everybody else (because she is). It might have been retribution, an attempt to hurt me for hurting her. If it was, it worked. But I found a cold comfort in her cruelty: better to be despised than forgotten entirely. Whatever her reasoning, once Polly signed off on my nickname, everybody else fell in line. All through high school, kids called me Daria.

There were some similarities. I was bookish and standoffish, but not because I felt superior. While other girls were worrying about cheerleader tryouts, I was guarding the secret of a father who was trying to drink himself to death and would eventually succeed.

If I was Daria, then Polly was Brooke Davis from *One Tree Hill*.

Unlike Brooke, Polly never evolved out of her party-girl persona. Whenever we would pass in the hall, Polly was always surrounded by her posse, other popular party girls who gave the impression of being happy, confident, and carefree. Even then, I wondered if she really was. Happy, carefree people don't drink as much alcohol or smoke as much weed as Polly did. We never talked but I worried about her. Though I had problems of my own, a part of me wished there was some way we could connect. At the time, it seemed impossible. Things were different now.

"I'd love to get together, Polly. Does Saturday work for you?"

"Really?" Years of cigarette smoke had given Polly's voice a gravelly edge, but in spite of that, she sounded more vulnerable than she'd ever allowed herself to be at seventeen. "Yeah! That'd be great!"

"Who was that?" Pris asked after I hung up.

"A friend," I said. "A long-lost friend."

Chapter Twenty-Two

*P*olly and I decided to meet at Miller's All Day, a hipster-chic diner on King Street that served southern-style brunch at all hours. It was a popular spot, especially on Saturdays, so the wait for a table was long, and really awkward.

Our encounter in Polly's shop, being unexpected, had been less fraught. We hadn't spent the hours leading up to it trying to think about what we were going to say to each other. The problem now was that there was so *much* to say. When you haven't seen each other for twenty years, and had painfully and purposely chosen not to talk for so many years before that, where do you start?

So instead of really talking, we shuffled our feet and checked our phones, and took turns asking the hostess to see where we were on the list, and occasionally made comments about how good everything smelled. Polly even joked about how her chances for attracting a boyfriend would increase exponentially if somebody would just invent perfume that smelled like bacon, but it was still awkward, and I'm sure I wasn't the only one who was beginning to think that getting together was a bad idea.

Eventually, we were shown to a table—the booths were all

taken—and given menus. I ordered the daily grits bowl with collards, cauliflower, and cheese. Polly ordered a caramel waffle and some banana bread with chocolate-hazelnut cream cheese for us to share.

"What?" she said, blinking in confusion when she saw me staring at her after the server left. "No, really. What?"

"Caramel waffles?" I laughed. "And you're even skinnier than you were in high school. How do you get away with it? Do you even know what vegetables are?"

Polly clicked her tongue and pretended to look offended. "'Course I do," she said. "Vegetables: that green stuff you cook in bacon grease to cover up the taste."

I reached for my water glass. "You haven't changed a bit."

Polly's teasing expression faded. She looked me square in the eye.

"Oh, yes. I have. So have you."

That's all we needed, one sharp, honest answer to chip through the ancient ice. Apologies tumbled out so quickly that we were talking over each other, so anxious to be heard that we barely bothered to listen, but that was all right. We knew what we meant. We *had* changed. We were older, hopefully wiser, and tired of feeling so alone. If and when we were ready, there would be time for explanations, but only one thing mattered just then.

"I'm so happy to see you again, Celia. Really." Polly dabbed her eye with her napkin. "When I saw you in the shop that day, it was everything I could do not to jump over the counter and hug your neck."

"And when I stood outside of St. Philip's and saw a tall redhead that I thought might be you, then decided it wasn't possible, I was so disappointed."

"That's *just* how I felt when you walked away," Polly said, clamping her hands on the table edge and leaning in. "For a second

I thought it was you, but then you walked away and I thought, 'No, couldn't be.' But then, just few days later, after I'd finished adding up all the red in my account books and was feeling very sorry for myself—bam! You walked right through my front door! I mean, what are the chances?"

"A zillion to one," I said. "It was supposed to happen."

"It was!" Polly exclaimed. "It absolutely was."

The server plopped a plate down between us and Polly's eyes lit up. She snatched the hot bread from the plate and broke it in two, releasing a puff of steam and strong scents of cinnamon and banana, and held half out toward me. "You have got to try this," she said. "Put some of the cream cheese stuff on top. It's heaven."

"Oh, my. Wow," I said, rolling my eyes rapturously toward the ceiling after popping a piece in my mouth, then fanning my hand in front of what was left. It was still too hot to eat but that wasn't going to stop me. "I've got to bring Calvin here when he comes to visit."

"Who's Calvin?" Polly asked.

I told her all about him, and Steve, and the various iterations of Steve who had come before, and my life in New York, and the broad outline of all that had happened since I'd left Charleston, and the events that had brought me back.

"You're adopting a baby? No kidding?"

"*Trying* to adopt a baby," I corrected. "It's a long shot, especially as a single woman, but I really want a family. I want it more than anything. Even if I lose, I had to take the chance."

Polly nodded slowly and deeply as I talked, dipping and lifting her long neck and red head like one of those weighted desk toys with the rocking red bird that dips its beak into a glass of water when you give it a shove.

"I get that," she said when I finished. "Well, not about the baby.

Don't get me wrong, I like kids, but I just never wanted any myself. I wouldn't mind getting married again someday, if I could find a guy who's fun *and* nice. The fun guys I meet always turn out to be jerks and the nice guys always turn out to be as boring as a dry weekend." She took a bite of her waffle and grinned. "'Course, all my weekends are dry now, so maybe it wouldn't make any difference. Maybe I would settle down with a nice guy, if I could find one."

She shrugged and shoved another piece of waffle in her mouth, then reached over for the pitcher and poured a lake of syrup onto her plate. I'd never seen a grown-up eat like that. It was actually kind of impressive.

"But a baby?" she said, chewing and shaking her head. "Not for me. But I understand about taking a chance on something you want so much. The craft shop, that's my dream. I've put everything I have in it."

"That's great." I took a bite of my grits. They were good but part me wished I'd ordered a waffle. "But Polly . . . did I miss something? I don't remember you being all that crafty."

"Oh, I wasn't. I flunked art in my sophomore year, among other things. Mind-altering substances are bad for your GPA," she said, rolling her eyes at the memory of her younger self. "It's a miracle that I graduated at all; I damn near didn't. The geometry teacher took pity and let me take the final again, but I didn't know if I was going to be allowed to walk until the day before graduation. That's why I got so drunk at the bonfire. That was a new low, even for me, but I wasn't celebrating, I was trying to drink down the terror. At that moment, every college I'd applied to had turned me down and I had no idea what I was going to do with my life. I was terrified. Eventually, my mother called a cousin from Decatur who somehow got me into Agnes Scott, but I think we could have predicted how that was going to turn out." Polly took another big bite and rolled her eyes. "Me at an all-women's college? Please. My grades were so bad that I doubted they'd invite me back for a second year, even with an influential cousin. When I came home for spring break and Jimmy proposed, it seemed like the answer to everything, for both of us.

"He joined the navy because he thought it might give him some direction. I hoped marrying him would do the same for me. I was determined to grow up and be a good wife. But Jimmy was deployed on a submarine for months at a stretch, and I was stuck on base in Groton, Connecticut, with nothing to do.

"Well"—she tipped her head to the side, flashing a retired party-girl grin—"nothing that wouldn't have gotten back to Jimmy's commander. Gossip spreads fast on a naval base. I didn't really clean up my act for years, but instead of going out drinking and partying, I stayed home drinking and knitting—and crocheting and quilting and embroidering and hooking rugs. If it involved fiber, I was into it. That's why I ended up carrying some of everything in my shop; I love it all, couldn't pick just one.

"Anyway, after a while I realized I liked crafting a whole lot more than I liked Jimmy, so I got a divorce and moved to Atlanta. Kept his name, though: Mercer is a lot easier to spell than Schermerhorn."

"How long were you in Atlanta?" I asked.

"Almost nine years. I got a job working in a big chain craft shop and teaching on the side. The pay was lousy but my manager was nice: recovering alcoholic." Polly raised her brows meaningfully, as if to say I could guess what happened next. "Dorothy had me pegged in the first month. The company insurance policy included rehab, but the program didn't take the first couple of times. I'd be okay for a few months and then something would happen and I'd fall off the wagon. One day, Dorothy sat me down and said, 'If you could do anything you wanted with your life, anything at all, what would it be?' I was thirty years old but I'd never once asked myself that question." Polly blinked a couple of times and stared sightlessly past my shoulder for a moment, as if still amazed by her own lack of imagination.

"Dorothy drove me to the rehab herself. On the way, we stopped at a bank and I put fifty dollars in a savings account for my craft shop. Took me seven years and a lot of overtime to save enough to make it happen."

"That's amazing," I said, and meant it. When we were kids, Polly had been long on enthusiasm but short on follow-through. In the course of one year, she'd enrolled in ballet, gymnastics, karate, and Brownies, only to give each one up within a month or two. I remember her mother complaining about it once to Aunt Calpurnia: "Polly's interest in a new hobby only lasts until the credit card payment for the uniform comes due."

Seven years of saving to fulfill her dream and open her shop? I was looking at a different and more determined Polly. But would determination be enough? Not if she'd been serious when she said she'd only seen twenty customers in the days since I'd been in the shop. But maybe she was exaggerating? Business couldn't be that bad, could it?

"Thanks," Polly said. "But it really started with Dorothy. I don't know what would have happened if she hadn't come along when she did. That's the amazing part, don't you think? How the people you need most show up at the moment they're most needed?"

I sipped my water, thinking about Trey, Lorne, Pris, and even Caroline and Heath. "It is," I agreed. "But Polly, I really admire the way you pulled yourself together. That can't have been easy."

"No," she said. "But I didn't do it alone. Rehab dried me out but joining AA finally helped me stay that way; changed my whole life, the way I looked at everything—myself, other people, even God."

"I wondered how you ended up at St. Philip's. So AA is the reason you joined the church?" I was really just teasing, but Polly bobbed her head in response.

"Step two: Put your faith in a higher power. And the other steps are mostly about where faith leads you. But I haven't joined St. Philip's, at least not yet. I'm still shopping around, trying to see where I fit. Hopefully, I won't have to visit all four hundred Charleston churches before I decide, but it might take a while." She grinned and dragged the last bite of waffle through the pool of syrup, making sure it was sopping before putting it in her mouth.

"Well, if my father were here, he'd *definitely* urge you to join St. Philip's"—I laughed—"so you could start hanging out with all the best people."

Polly used her napkin to wipe the syrup from her lips.

"Maybe I already am."

That might have been the nicest thing anybody ever said to me. I'd missed her so much but I hadn't realized how much until that moment. I thought about what Heath had told me when I started cleaning out Calpurnia's hoard, when my first inclination had been to toss out everything and start from scratch. Heath had advised me to curate my collection carefully, to preserve and protect the truly special artifacts that could illuminate and celebrate the family history that was also *my* history. Sorting the worthless from what was worth keeping was a lot more work than throwing it all out would have been. Now I was so glad I'd heeded Heath's advice.

I treasured Calpurnia's typewriter, pearls, and hand-stenciled dresser, Beebee's yarn, piano, and sweetgrass baskets. I cherished my mother's Chantilly sterling silver service, wedding veil, and the worn, much underlined Bible that made me wish we'd talked more and known each other better, as well as my father's gold watch and books, including a perfectly preserved copy of his play and the hardbound, beautifully illustrated edition of *Winnie the Pooh* that my grandfather had read to Sterling and Sterling had read to me, something that I'd forgotten until I'd found the book.

When I'd spotted that red cover in the bottom of a crushed and battered box, my mind was flooded by vivid memory. I saw myself sitting on Sterling's ample lap, and slats of sunlight pouring through the shutters of his office window, casting sharp, angled shadows onto my father's big, capable hands when he turned the pages, relived the contentment and sense of safety that enveloped me as I laid my head on his chest to hear and feel rumbling and vibrations within as he dropped into a lower register and gave voice to the complaints of Eeyore or observations of Owl.

That book was an artifact worth finding, a memory worth keeping, a piece of my history. So were the other pieces I'd preserved, the relics that told our story. Not every memory that I'd excavated was happy, but all were true and real and helped me grab hold of who I was and where I'd come from. I hadn't found everything I'd hoped to. Some memories, pieces of the puzzle that had mattered most to me, were missing, possibly even intentionally discarded, and that hurt. But so much of what I had found had given me a clearer picture of the past and a vision of how to shape the future.

The same principles apply to people, don't they? Old friends remind us of who we were and what we've become. New friends hint at who we could be and inspire us to move forward. We need both, the new and old, the grounding of the past and hope for the future, because life is terrible and wonderful all at once, and too hard to face alone.

I put down my fork and tossed my napkin onto the table. "Polly? I know it's short notice, but I was just wondering, are you busy Monday night?"

Chapter Twenty-Three

On Saturday afternoon, after my meeting with Polly, my effort to finish cleaning the dining room took on new urgency. While sorting through some drawers in the sideboard, I found still another treasure, a framed photograph of me and my parents taken on my eighth birthday.

Though I was still in the fries-and-chicken-fingers stage, Sterling said it was high time I learned to eat oysters and drove us out to a seafood shack near Folly Beach. Having the waitress put a platter piled high with bumpy, crustaceous, unshucked oysters down in front of me was fairly alarming. But I wanted to please my father, so I dug in. Turns out that anything tastes good with lots of mignonette sauce on it.

Sterling praised my "sophisticated palate" and put his arm around me. The waitress snapped the picture. I was sitting behind a pile of empty oyster shells with a lobster bib around my neck and a grin on my face. It was a good day. It was nice to remember that some days with my father truly had been good.

I'd unearthed many similarly evocative artifacts—Calpurnia's typewriter and pearls, Beebee's sewing basket and collection of cameos, handwritten copies of a couple of Sterling's poems, which were really very good, several abandoned drafts of his never-completed second play, which was not. I found my mother's old college yearbook too, with a snapshot of her and some girlfriends dressed up as the cast of *The Wizard of Oz*. But I still hadn't found any photos of me and Calpurnia together. That bothered me.

She'd saved practically everything on the planet but not one picture of us together, not one artifact of our adventures. Why? Was thinking about all we'd lost too painful to bear? Or maybe she blamed it all on me? Some questions can never be answered, but that didn't stop me from asking them.

I hauled off mountains of junk, including a couple hundred nearly empty egg cartons. I say nearly empty because after I'd accidentally cracked two undetected eggs, the stink made my eyes water. But when the smell faded, the dining room was clean at last, empty of everything but Beebee's table and chairs and a walnut sideboard in remarkably good condition that had been passed down from my great-great-grandmother.

I limped up the stairs to my bedroom feeling tired but pleased with my progress, then popped two ibuprofen and climbed into bed, telling myself that physical exhaustion had its upside and at least I'd sleep soundly that night.

That was the theory.

The dream came back, same as always—Calpurnia, the baby, the bearded man in the shadows—but this time it played on a continuous loop. I'd dream the dream, wake up blinking and restless in the dark, shake it off and go back to sleep, only to find myself dreaming and disturbed again fifteen minutes later.

Shampoo, rinse, repeat.

All. Night. Long.

Finally, a little before four, I bolted upright in my bed, angry as well as groggy, and shouted to the empty room.

"Calpurnia! Knock it off! If there's something you've got to say to me, then say it already. If not, shut up and let me get some sleep!"

Just at that moment, the moon emerged from a bank of clouds. It beamed a shaft of blue-tinged light through the narrow opening of the curtains and onto the scarred heart-pine floorboards, illuminating a crack I'd never noticed before, perhaps half an inch wide and partially hidden by the fringe of the rug.

I crawled out of bed, knelt down on the floor, and folded back the corner of the rug. The floorboard beneath was shorter than those surrounding it, only about two feet in length. The crack wasn't quite wide enough for my fingers to get into, so I grabbed one of the box cutters I'd been using earlier that day and pried up the board with the end of the blade.

A metal box was hidden between the floor joists, the kind merchants use to store cash and sort bills, flat green in color and coated with dust. There was a cheap lock on the side with a key already inserted and a thin chrome handle on the flip-top lid. It was the handle that got caught in the moonlight, glinting like a beacon to demand my notice. If the moon had been a little less bright, in a slightly different phase, if the slit in the curtains had been wider or if I had closed them completely, like I normally did, or if I hadn't been awake at just the right moment, I might never have noticed it.

Maybe it was a coincidence. But you'll never get me to believe it.

I twisted the key in the lock, lifted the lid, and reached inside. The box was filled with pictures, nearly all of them of me. There were clippings too. I found announcements of my high school and college graduations, another of the dean's list in the fall of my sophomore year with my name circled in blue pen, three stories

I'd written for the college paper, and a copy of the headshot that always appeared next to my Dear Calpurnia column, glued onto heavy cardstock, neatly framed with a length of navy-blue gros-grain ribbon trimming the edge.

The moment I opened the box and saw that first clipping, my eyes started to fill. But it was the discovery of a lined notebook with a story I'd written when I was twelve inside, "Letticia Phoe-nicia: Jungle Guide," and a picture of me at the same age, bent over with my head stuck into the gaping mouth of an enormous taxi-dermied alligator and Calpurnia standing by with her eyes gaping and a hand pressed against each cheek, pretending to scream, that finally did me in.

Sitting cross-legged on the floor in my sleep shirt, I cried so hard that the room went out of focus. And when I had no more tears, that's when I saw it—a small, separate packet of pictures, some of Calpurnia alone, some of Calpurnia and someone else. She'd tied them together with a blue ribbon, so the images must have been related somehow, and the edges were worn from much handling, so she must have looked at them often. They'd been im-portant to her.

Who was the man in the pictures? I didn't recognize him. Maybe someone else would.

FELICIA SHUFFLED THROUGH the photos; there were five in all. Her brow furrowed and she paused briefly to look at each one before moving on to the next, as if she were organizing a hand of bridge.

"Have you seen these before? Do you know the man who's with her?"

"I've never seen the pictures but I do recognize the boy. He was one of the cadets at the Citadel. But of course, you knew that from his uniform. I remember that he'd asked her to a formal and Cal came over to introduce him and show me her dress before they left for the dance. Seemed like a nice young man. And very handsome in his dress uniform."

"Do you remember his name?"

Felicia shook her head. "Calpurnia had so many boys running after her when she was young; seemed like she had a new beau every other month. There didn't seem to be much point in learning their names.

"She was a beauty," Felicia said softly as she shuffled through the pictures again, her gaze focused on a Calpurnia who was smiling, laughing, and who seemed impossibly young. "One of the prettiest girls in Charleston. It always surprised me that she didn't marry. Seemed like something happened to her after your grandpa died, like a light went out inside her. I tried to talk to Beebee about it once, told her that Calpurnia was too young and too pretty to spend the rest of her life taking care of her momma."

"And what did Beebee say?"

"That I should mind my own business," Felicia said, flashing a smile. "You know how she was. Stubborn. There wasn't a poor, invalid widow in all of Charleston with a spine like Beebee's. Straight as a ramrod and just about as flexible."

"And selfish?" I asked.

"Sometimes," Felicia admitted. "But when it came to Calpurnia, I honestly think she was just trying to protect her."

"From what?"

"Oh, honey, I have no idea. Knowing Beebee, it could have been anything. Grief, heartbreak, black cats. She was so superstitious. Remember that Gullah woman she was always telling her dreams to? What was her name?"

"Sallie Mae," I said.

"Sallie Mae! That's right!"

Felicia flipped to the final photo in the stack, a Polaroid snapshot. Calpurnia was standing in front a redbrick building with an arched doorway, wearing a heavy wool coat. She was smiling, but not as broadly as she had been in the other pictures.

The image was a little blurry, but in some sense I found this Calpurnia to be more recognizable. There was a familiar sadness in her eyes that I remembered well. It wasn't always present but I would sometimes catch a glimpse of it when she was gazing out a window and didn't know I was watching her. When I would ask what she was thinking about, she would jump a little, as if I'd touched her after walking across a thick carpet in my socks, then flash a smile and say, "Well, you, sugar! Who else could I be thinking about?"

At the time, this made perfect sense. I was a child and, as far as I knew, the center of Calpurnia's universe. Who else *could* she be thinking about?

"What about this one?" I asked. "Do you know where it was taken?"

Felicia shook her head. "No. But not around here. Nobody in Charleston would wear a coat that heavy, not even in January. I'm sorry not to be more help. I guess the only one who could tell you for sure is Calpurnia."

Felicia handed the photographs back to me. "I sure miss her."

"So do I."

Chapter Twenty-Four

There were no more Beard-Baby-Calpurnia dreams that night, or ever again. I slept soundly that night and the next and ever after. Monday was going to be even busier than usual, but I woke with the sun, got my usual latte from Bitty and Beau's, and then walked to St. Philip's to do what I couldn't before.

The grass covering Calpurnia's grave was tufted and uneven, still trying to take hold. Her marker was simple, a plain white cross with nothing more than her name, birth date, and death date. The sight of it made me sad in a way that was hard to pin down. It seemed disproportionate in relation to the impact she'd had on my life. How could someone who had meant so much to me come to so little?

In the end, it comes to that for everyone, I suppose. Still.

The sun beamed leaf-shaped shadows onto the earth. Across the street, in the sanctuary of St. Philip's, people had gathered for Morning Prayer. The murmur of their voices seeped through the open windows and permeated the air like a fine mist. I slipped the pictures from the pocket before taking off my jacket, then spread it out next to Calpurnia's grave and sat down, taking care not to crush the newly sprung tufts of grass, and sat staring at Calpurnia's name, engraved in white marble, waiting. I wasn't sure exactly what for. Some kind of sign? Another dream?

Instead, I felt a flutter of wind brush my face and ruffle my hair. It rustled the leaves and blew a murmur of voices in toward me, swirling fragments of prayers into the air and my ears.

> *We have erred, and strayed . . .*
> *followed too much the devices and desires . . . .*
> *left undone those things which we ought to have done . . .*
> *have mercy upon us . . .*
> *Spare them . . .*
> *Restore thou them . . .*
> *according to thy promises . . .*

The wind calmed, and the leaves stilled, and the voices muffled into a murmur once again. There was no answer, only stillness. Yet I felt heard. And strangely at peace.

"I'm sorry, Auntie Cal. For both of us."

I fanned the photos out in my hand, wondering about the story behind them and what, if anything, I was supposed to do with them now that I'd found them. If I'd had more time, I might have lingered longer, but there was so much to do. I needed to go to the market but hadn't even decided on a menu. Maybe Calvin would have some ideas.

I got to my feet, slipped the pictures back into my pocket, and told Calpurnia good-bye. As I turned to go, the doors of the church opened and a small stream of worshippers trickled out. I spotted a lanky man in a rusty-black suit and lifted my arm to wave a greeting, but Trey didn't see me. He was hunched over to support the slow, shuffling, and painfully laborious progress of the wizened old man who clung to his arm. Maybe a relative? But Trey practiced a lot of elder law, so the old man could have been a client too. Whoever it was, the time didn't seem right for greetings.

I lowered my arm and left the churchyard from a different entrance. When I turned the corner, somebody coming from the other side ran right into me, hitting me so forcefully that I stumbled and was knocked to my knees.

"Uh-oh! I'm sorry!" A beefy arm reached down, grabbed my elbow, pulled me to my feet. "Are you okay? I'm sorry, Miss Celia. I didn't see you coming."

I brushed dirt from my hands and looked up at the big man who towered over me. Teddy, my favorite barista from Bitty and Beau's, looked so alarmed that, for a second, I thought he might cry.

"I'm okay, Teddy. Really." My left knee was hurting but I gave him a wide and reassuring smile anyway. "But I told you before, you don't need to call me Miss. Celia is just fine."

"Can't do it," Teddy said. "Momma said you always call a lady miss, unless she's family or a friend. It's just how I was raised."

I understood that. Some habits die hard.

"Are you sure you're all right?" Teddy asked, dipping his head lower and looking into my eyes.

"I'm sure. No worries. Where were you off to in such a hurry?"

"Running to catch my bus," he said, sounding disappointed.

"That's all right. There'll be another one in about half an hour."

"Do you have a long ride home?"

He bobbed his head. "I used to live in Wagener Terrace. Only had to take one bus to get to work then, right down King Street. I could even walk if I wanted to. I never did *want* to," he said, grinning. "But Momma said I needed the exercise, so sometimes she made me. But then she died and I had to move into a group home out in West Ashley, so now I've got to transfer."

Teddy was dressed in one of Bitty and Beau's signature #notbroken T-shirts. That hashtag was fitting. From everything I'd seen, Teddy was the furthest thing from broken. He was a kind, conscientious, and capable man. Obviously, he had some intellectual challenges, but he was a hard worker and clearly took pride in doing his job well. Losing his mom must have been hard. Losing the autonomy to decide where he wanted to live and with whom must have made things even harder. I felt bad for him.

"Sorry I made you miss your bus," I said. "Let me buy you an ice cream to make up for it."

"Oh, I can't let you do that," he said. "You probably need to be someplace. Besides, I'm the one who ran into you."

Teddy wasn't wrong; I had a lot to do. But twenty minutes one way or the other wasn't going to make any difference and I really did feel like I owed him.

"Well, we kind of ran into each other," I reasoned. "So how about this: you buy me an ice cream and I'll buy one for you. Then we'll be even."

Teddy frowned. "That doesn't make any sense. We could just buy one for ourselves."

"You're right," I said. "I'm just looking for an excuse. There's a new ice cream shop a couple blocks away that I've been dying to try. They've got some really weird flavors, like goat cheese and fig."

"Goat cheese and fig?" Teddy made a face. "Cheese does *not* belong in ice cream. I like mint chocolate chip."

"Okay, mint chocolate chip it is. We've got just enough time for a cone before the next bus. You in?"

Teddy dipped his head down, thinking for a moment before answering. "Okay, Miss Celia. I'm in."

"Good. But maybe now you can drop the Miss? We're going to have ice cream together. That makes us friends, doesn't it?"

Teddy dipped his head again and came up smiling.

"Yes, ma'am. I guess it does."

Chapter Twenty-Five

When Pris knocked on the back door fifty minutes before the appointed hour, my hands were sticky and purple, stained with the juice of pomegranate arils I planned to put in the salad. I hollered for her to come on in.

"Hey! I know I'm early but I thought you might want some—"

She crossed the kitchen threshold. Her jaw dropped. "Celia. *What* are you doing in here?"

"Cooking dinner. What does it look like I'm doing?"

"Demolition? Destruction? Slaughtering animals for some sort of ritual sacrifice?" Pris shook her head as her eyes moved across the kitchen carnage: cabinets and drawers left open; sink overflowing with dishes; food, bowls, and utensils obscuring every square inch of the previously pristine countertops. "What happened? Did you have another dream? Did Calpurnia tell you to put it back the way it was?"

"Funny."

"Please tell me that's not dinner," she said, eyes bugging out as she pointed to a bowl filled with glistening red chicken livers. I couldn't blame her. They looked pretty gross. I whisked the bowl from the countertop and dumped the contents down the disposal.

"I was going to make pâté. But there's not enough time now."

"So? What are we having?"

"Duck."

"Duck?" Pris's forehead wrinkled in doubt. "Isn't that kind of hard to make?"

"As it turns out, yes," I said grimly.

I split another pomegranate in half. One of the seeds popped out and hit my glasses. I squealed in surprise, then smacked the fruit down onto the counter. "This was *supposed* to be fun. All I wanted to do was invite a few women over for a nice, simple dinner party, see if I could help them make friends, find a connection. Buy some bread, make a green salad, roast a chicken, and boom! Dinner is served.

"But *nooo*. Calvin said that wasn't *festive* enough. 'Bake some homemade breadsticks,' he says. 'Roast some butternut squash and fennel for the salad. Throw in some pomegranate seeds for color and a citrus vinaigrette for flavor. And why not duck à l'orange?' he says. 'If you're going to the trouble to roast a chicken, you might as well make a duck. It's not that much more complicated,' he says."

"Is it?"

"I bought a five-pound duck. So far, I think it's given off six pounds of grease."

Just then, as if to underscore my point, the smoke alarm emitted an unrelenting, ear-piercing screech. Pris sprang into action, snatching a dish towel from the counter and flapping it through the air like a flag of surrender, trying to clear the smoke. At the same time, I shoved my hand into a mitt and opened the door to the oven, releasing a choking cloud of greasy, duck-scented smoke.

Pris gave up flapping the towel and ran to the back door, opening and closing it over and over. I took the bird out of the oven, eyes watering from the sting of smoke, ears ringing from the wail of the alarm, and plopped the roasting pan onto the counter before taking up Pris's abandoned dish towel and flapping it as hard and fast as I could. When the air finally cleared and the alarm ceased squealing, I inspected the duck.

"Uh . . . is the skin supposed to be that black?" Pris asked.

"What do you think?"

I stabbed a meat thermometer into the fleshy part of the bird with enough force to kill it a second time, then tilted my head backward and shouted at the ceiling in a voice I hoped was loud enough to be heard in Manhattan. "Calvin, I hope your next cake falls flat! I hope your meringue separates and your pie crusts have soggy bottoms!"

"Maybe you can salvage it," Pris said hopefully. "What if you took the skin off and sliced the meat from the bones?"

I removed the thermometer and looked at the gauge. "One hundred and thirty degrees. How can a bird that has been in the oven *that* long and has skin the color of coal be almost raw inside? How?"

Pris stood by, waiting patiently while I piled more curses on Calvin's head. "Really," she said when I finished. "What *are* you going to serve for dinner?"

"Well, not this. We'd all end up in the hospital with ptomaine." I picked up the roasting pan, carried it across the kitchen, and tipped the contents unceremoniously into the trash can.

"You still got the salad though, right? That looks really good." Pris peered into the big bowl of greens topped with a mixture of roasted butternut squash, fennel, and candied pecans. I wasn't sure if it looked "really good" or not; maybe it would after I tossed in the pomegranate arils. But at least it was edible, which was more than you could say for the rest of the meal. "What about the bread-sticks?" Pris asked. "Did you make those yet?"

"Just the dough," I said, pointing to a counter covered with an avalanche of flour and a beachfront of broken eggshells, where the mound of uncooked dough sat resting under a tea towel.

"Okay, so you've got bread and salad. That's a start," Pris said in a deliberately encouraging tone. "What can we serve for the main course?"

"No clue. But I know for sure what the appetizer will be."

I opened the refrigerator door and pulled out a bottle of chilled pinot grigio.

"*THIS IS AMAZING*," Caroline declared, chewing and talking at the same time.

Felicia bit into her last slice and declared it delicious. "I never thought about putting bacon and egg on a pizza before."

"Can I have the recipe?" Polly asked, taking a bite and stretching out her slice so the glob of smoked gouda became a cheesy string.

"You'll have to ask the chef," I said, tipping my wineglass toward Pris. "My only contribution was a kitchen that looks like a combat zone and an emotional meltdown."

I reached for the wine bottle, our third of the evening, and topped up my glass with what was left inside. Fortunately, there were two more bottles in the refrigerator. When it came to the menu, Calvin was worse than useless, but he had convinced me to buy plenty of wine. That part, at least, had been a good call.

"Stop," Pris said. "You made the salad *and* the dough; that was the hard part. All I did was roll out a crust, toss on some toppings, and put it in the oven."

"The salad is really good too," Caroline said, spearing pieces of lettuce, squash, pecan, and pomegranate in turn. Caroline didn't eat much, I'd noticed, but every mouthful was a carefully composed work of art.

"Who's ready for dessert?" I asked, eyeing the pecan bars Polly had brought.

Much to my disappointment, everyone swore they were too full to eat another bite and preferred to let dinner settle. But I was having a good time; everybody was.

Felicia settled back into her chair with a contented sigh.

"This is just so nice," she said. "Reminds me of when Beau and I were first married. Beebee, Sissy, and the other women in the neighborhood used to get together at each other's houses almost every week. My, but we had fun!"

She took a ladylike sip of wine, pushed her glasses up on her nose, and leaned closer to the table. I could tell by the look on her face that there was a story coming on, so I leaned in too. Felicia always had the best stories.

"One time," she said, "way back when Foster was still a baby, *Southern Living* ran a how-to on magnolia-leaf Christmas wreaths and I got it into my head that *all* of us needed to make one." She swept her arm wide. "Well. We'd have had to denude every tree on the street to get enough leaves for everybody, but I got an idea of where to get some. Late one night, Beebee, Sissy, and I hopped in the car and started driving around. We found a median strip on the highway planted all over with hee-*uge* magnolias."

Felicia dropped her voice to a stage whisper.

"Do you know that Sissy drove the car right onto the median strip? Right over the curb!" The whisper melted into peals of laughter. "We piled out and started snipping leaves as quick as we could. Two minutes later, a state patrolman shows up." Felicia clapped her hand to her chest. "I thought for sure we were all going to be arrested!"

I put down my glass and propped my chin on my hand. It wasn't hard to imagine Felicia taking part in this caper. But Beebee? That was harder to picture. It was also kind of wonderful. Beebee hadn't always been a fat old widow woman who did little besides knit and eat pralines. She'd had friends, and adventures, and a life.

"Sissy was the brave one," Felicia continued, after taking another sip. "She explained about the wreaths, except she made it sound like we were on the decorations committee for some charity ball. When she was finished, that big old police officer frowns and crosses his arms over his chest, and says, 'So you ladies thought it would be a good idea to park in the middle of the highway and steal state property?'

"And Sissy blinks those big blue eyes of her and says, 'Well, sir. Maybe not our *best* idea.'"

Felicia's timing was perfect. Her flutey laughter was infectious. The sound of it rang through the high ceilings and halls and was echoed by everyone else's merriment, circling on itself again and again, like a chorus sung in the round.

"Well, sir. Maybe not our *best* idea," Caroline hooted.

"Not our *best*," I parroted, grinning because I knew that a catchphrase shared by an earlier generation had been resurrected. From now on, if one of the women in this room did something dumb, somebody would say, "Not our *best* idea," and everyone would howl.

Felicia, still smiling, dabbed at the corners of her eyes. "Oh, I loved those girls. They were like sisters to me; we were that close. Of course, that was a long time ago. So many dear old friends have moved away. Or passed away." She lifted her glass a couple of inches, saluting the departed. "And the few who are left here have so many health problems or . . . other problems."

Felicia's smile melted into reverie. I was sure she was thinking about how Sissy had tottered into Beau's party wearing two different shoes, having completely forgotten it was a surprise party.

"Sometimes I feel like the last sister standing," she said softly.

I didn't know what to say to that. Nobody did. Just as the mood was about to cross the line from quiet to too quiet, Caroline pushed her chair back and looked toward me.

"Hey, Celia, how about a tour?"

"Oh, my word!" Felicia's eyes went wide. "I had *no* idea that Beebee had this much yarn. And it really was like this when you opened the door?"

"Yes, ma'am. Seems this was the one room Calpurnia thought was worth taking care of. It's my oasis of sanity."

"Celia," Polly said, shaking her head and giving me a crooked smile, "why didn't you say something before I made you buy that yarn?"

"You didn't *make* me buy it. I wanted it. And the needles. Really."

"Uh-huh. Sure you did. Have you used them?"

I winced. "Well . . . I had an issue with extra stitches. And dropped ones. Clearly, I haven't inherited Beebee's knitting gene."

Polly put her hands on her hips. "You're not seriously going to let all this beautiful yarn go to waste, are you? What about making something for the baby? A blanket? It'll be fun. Come to think of it," she said, looking around at the group, "anybody else want to learn to knit?"

"Not with my arthritis," Felicia said. "But I wish I'd learned to quilt when I had the chance. My mother left so many quilt blocks when she passed. I always told myself that I'd finish them some-day, but I'd never be able to hold a needle now."

"You could quilt by machine," Polly said. "I can teach you."

"I don't have a sewing machine."

"Celia does," Pris volunteered. "We found an old Singer Feath-erweight under the back stairs last week. It still runs. I was going to put it up on Craigslist . . ." Pris looked a question at me.

"I'd love for you to have it, Felicia."

"Would you?" Felicia seemed genuinely pleased. "Well, that would be lovely. But Polly, don't you think it's a little late for me to learn to quilt?"

"Absolutely not," Polly replied. "And if it involves yarn, fabric, thread, or any kind of fiber, I can teach it."

Pris's eyebrows popped up. "What about embroidery? I'd love to embroider some of my thrift shop finds."

"Embroidery too," Polly said.

Pris let out a little squeal. "Think about the blogs I could post—embroidered jeans, jackets, skirts. I'll pick up tons of new followers!"

Polly turned to face Caroline. "What about you?"

The question seemed to alarm her. "I'm the least crafty person on the planet. Seriously." She rolled up her sleeve. "See this scar? That's what happens when I get near a hot glue gun."

"No glue guns in my classes, I promise," Polly said. "Come on, Caroline. There must be some craft you'd like to try."

"I'll come and hang out. But crafting just isn't my thing." Caro-line sounded pretty definite and Polly didn't push the issue.

"Okay, what about everybody else?" Polly asked, looking right at me. "Are you in?"

Was I?

Thinking that knitting something for Peaches might jinx the adoption was ridiculous, utterly illogical. But it lurked in the back of my mind just the same. I might not have inherited the crafty gene, but the family bent toward superstition had definitely been passed on. And it wasn't like I had a whole lot of time on my hands.

But I liked having these women in my home. Their presence felt like a down payment on the life I longed to have, one filled with laughter and creativity and friends. I wanted and needed that. I think they did too.

Felicia, with a mind more supple than her arthritic hands, needed new challenges and friends to fill the gaps left by those who had gone away or gone before. Polly needed support during the uncertain launch of her shaky business venture and a way to share her gifts with others. Pris, still trying to figure out how to be a grown-up, needed the influence and acceptance of older women who cared about her. Caroline was in the market for new best friends, but what else did she need? There must be something, because even stronger than my superstitions and the sense that bringing these women together was Good and Right, was a sudden and powerful intuition that every person who passed through my door was absolutely supposed to be there. Don't ask me how I knew. I just did.

"Sure. I'm in," I said. "Do Monday nights work for everybody?"

Four heads bobbed.

"This is going to be fun," Felicia said, pushing her big red glasses up higher on the bridge of her nose. "But shouldn't we invite Happy too?"

Pris, whose eyes were already starting to look a little glassy, took a large swallow from her wineglass. "Forget it," she said. "She'll never come. She doesn't trust women. Well, she doesn't really trust anybody, not anymore."

"Why not?"

"Because of what happened to her in Savannah." Before I could ask for clarification, Pris, who was clearly a little buzzed (as was I) volunteered the rest. "Momma and Daddy had this group of friends from the club, the Masons, the Chastains, and the Thatchers. They got together all the time, took vacations together—New York, Miami, Bermuda, even a cruise through the Panama Canal. But four years ago, about two months before they were set to leave for a long weekend in Memphis, Daddy had a heart attack and died."

Everybody except Polly already knew this, but we murmured condolences just the same. Pris went on with her story. "Birdie Mason came through the reception line after the funeral and hugged Momma and said they were sure going to miss her. Momma thought she was just talking about how they hadn't seen each other since Daddy's death, and said she'd missed them too and was looking forward to getting away to Memphis.

"Then Birdie said, 'Oh, Happy. It's just a group for couples. I'm sure you understand,' and walked right out the door. After ten years, they dropped her like a hot potato." The fire from Pris's eyes could have started a blaze.

"Oh, wait," she said, after pausing to take another drink. "I almost forgot. Candie and Dwayne Chastain didn't walk *right* out. They stuck around almost until the end of the reception and ate about five pounds of boiled shrimp. *Then* they dropped her like a hot potato. Can you believe it?"

I couldn't. Judging from the shocked silence, neither could anyone else. What kind of people dump a friend, especially after her husband has just died? The kind who'd never been friends to begin with, that's what kind. Suddenly, a whole lot of things about the seemingly misnamed Helen "Happy" Browder made sense. No wonder she was such a miserable individual. I had no reason to like Happy, but I've never been able to stand by and watch people get shafted, especially after my third glass of wine.

"That's outrageous!" Felicia exclaimed.

"Oh, your poor mom," Caroline murmured.

"That settles it," I said, smacking my leg. "Happy has *got* to join the group."

Even Polly, who had never even met Happy and, unlike the rest of us, wasn't even the tiniest bit intoxicated, agreed. "We should include her."

"She'll never come," Pris slurred. "Not in a million years."

"We can ask, can't we?" I took a fortifying sip from my wine-glass and rocketed out of Beebee's pink chair. "Come on, y'all."

Five minutes later, we were standing on Happy's front steps. Pris, who was bringing up the rear and still carrying the now-empty wine bottle, said, "Are you sure this is a good idea?"

"A very good idea," I assured her. "Maybe even our *best* idea."

I poked the doorbell with my index finger.

Nothing happened.

I poked it again. And again. The porch light snapped on. Happy was dressed in a green sateen kimono and had about an inch of cold cream on her face.

"Well? What do you all want?" she demanded.

Chapter Twenty-Six

Lorne knelt on the ground next to the front steps, tape measure in hand. I leaned down to get a better look as he stretched it out next to the bottom riser. "See? Seven and three-quarters inches. Exactly." He looked up at Brett, daring him to deny the evidence.

"But the others measure eight." Brett ticked a red mark onto his clipboard.

Lorne climbed to his feet. "No," he said, his voice tone low and menacingly deliberate. "They're all seven and three-quarters. I measured them. And even if they weren't, the building code makes allowances for variances for historic properties."

"Nineteen twenty isn't exactly historic," Brett countered, puffing to show he wasn't impressed. "Not in Charleston. Anyway, you rebuilt the steps, so now they have to comply with current building standards."

"I only rebuilt them because *you* said I had to." Lorne took a personal-space-invading step toward the young inspector, getting up into his face. "There was nothing wrong with the steps before and there's nothing wrong with them now."

"I can't sign off on them until every tread is the same height."

Brett Fitzwaller, the mid-twenties, pencil-necked, clipboard-toting, power-drunk building inspector, was the bane of my existence. He never approved anything on the first go-round and had that smirking sort of face that, according to Lorne, was begging for a punch.

I didn't disagree with him but a man on probation couldn't afford to get involved in fisticuffs and I couldn't afford to lose my contractor. That was why I'd started making sure that I was standing by when the inspector came around, so I could step between him and Lorne if the need arose.

"I'm just doing my job," Brett said, and looked in my direction. "You should be happy that I'm looking out for your interests. Nobody's going to let you adopt a baby if your house isn't safe, are they, Miss Fairchild?"

I stared at him for a second, processing what he'd just said. "How do you know I'm trying to adopt a baby?" Though Brett showed up to make my life miserable a couple of times a week, I'd never shared anything about my personal life or the reasons behind the renovation with him. I popped my eyebrows at Lorne, wondering if he'd said anything, but Lorne shook his head.

"Who told you about that?" I asked.

The odious inspector swallowed and his ping-pong ball–sized Adam's apple bobbed up and down. "Uh. Not sure." He looked down, suddenly deeply intent on his clipboard. "Somebody must have said something sometime, I guess. People are always talking. You know how it is." He ripped a copy of the red-marked inspection report off his clipboard, smirking as he handed it to Lorne. "Y'all have a nice day now. See you next time."

"How long will it take to redo them?" I asked Lorne after Brett got in his car.

"Couple of hours," Lorne said. "I don't have to rebuild the whole thing, just pry up and replace those treads."

"Okay, so. Could be worse, right?"

I smiled, but Lorne was not in the mood to be encouraged. He hooked a thumb in his belt, lip curling as he watched Brett's car drive off.

"Celia," he muttered, "the minute I finish my probation, I'm going to find that guy and clock him." He made a fist and mimed a short, sharp punch.

"I'll help you. The *minute* you finish probation. And how long is that? About eight months?"

Lorne grinned. "Something like that."

"Right. Well, in the meantime, maybe we'd just better get back to work."

"Yes, ma'am." Lorne touched his fingertips to his forehead and snapped a small salute before picking up his claw hammer. "Whatever you say, boss."

I'D GOTTEN SO used to the ring of hammers and the whine of saws that they were almost white noise to me by now and I barely heard them. But the previous night's overindulgence had left me with a pounding headache that got worse with every swing of Lorne's hammer.

I was not having a good morning.

Storming the castle to invite Happy to the crafting club had been a mistake. After she answered the door, a simple "thanks but no thanks" would have sufficed. Instead, Happy got mad, told Pris to get inside, and the rest of us to clear off her property and never come back, me in particular.

So much for a beautiful day in the neighborhood.

In retrospect, I could almost see her point. It was late and she was already in bed. The bell rang (several times) and Happy opened the door to find a clutch of semi-inebriated women, her own daughter among them, babbling on about some scathingly brilliant but not particularly well-defined idea for a crafting club and insisting that she *had* to take part in it.

It was the in-person equivalent of drunk dialing and definitely not our *best* idea. But why be so nasty? If the same thing had happened to me, I'd have thought it was funny. Happy had no sense of humor, so maybe it was just as well that she wouldn't be joining the group. But I felt bad for Pris. "I worry about that child," Felicia said when we left. So did I.

Losing a parent is terrible at any age, but Pris was so young when her father died. In a sense, she lost her mother too. From what Pris said, I understood that Happy was never the same after that. On top of everything else, they'd torn up stakes and moved to Charleston. Yes, Pris went off to college soon after, but still, it couldn't have been easy. Yet until the wine had loosened her tongue, she'd never really talked to me about her father's death.

Oh, she had plenty to say on all sort of subjects. She was bright and insightful and consistently cheerful, maybe too cheerful. Everybody wants approval, especially when they're young. But I sometimes felt that Pris was working so hard not to disappoint anybody, taking the responsibility for everyone's happiness upon her own young shoulders. I knew all about that.

A driver drifted into oncoming traffic and nothing was ever the same. Suddenly it was just me and Sterling in a shiny new apartment that looked and smelled as sterile as an operating room, five miles from Harleston Village and a world away from everything I'd known. My mother and grandmother were gone, I'd been forbidden to see Calpurnia, and Sterling spent his days going through the motions of teaching, parenting, and living, and his nights drinking in the subconscious but ultimately successful attempt at speeding his own death.

And me? I tried to prop everything up by being a bright, cheerful, perfect daughter in hopes that my father would someday notice I was there and remember he still had something to live for. It didn't work.

Sterling's slow swan dive into depression and alcohol was painful to witness. After I went away to college, I didn't have to. I still feel guilty for saying it was a relief, but it's true. It was the same with Calpurnia and going to New York.

If Calpurnia *had* opened the door that day, would I have stayed here? Moved in? Tried to save her and maybe lost what was left of me in the process? Probably. Dotty as she was, I wonder if Calpurnia might have realized that too. Maybe that's why she didn't open the door. Maybe she was trying to rescue me.

Or maybe she was just crazy.

When the bell rang in the afternoon, I thought my new refrigerator was being delivered. I ran downstairs as quick as I could, expecting to see burly men in overalls. Instead, I found Happy standing on my porch.

She was scowling, which didn't surprise me, but also looked somewhat unkempt, which did. Whenever I'd seen Happy before, I'd been reminded of those models in the Talbots clothing catalogs: trim, tidy, well-preserved women who favored tasteful jewelry and pumps that matched their purses—Southerners all, I was sure. Today Happy looked like a cover model for *Dissipation Monthly*.

She only wore one earring. Her wrinkled cotton blouse had been buttoned incorrectly; the collar was off-kilter and the tail of the right side hung three inches below the left. Her carefully coiffured chignon had mysteriously migrated from the back of her head to a spot just behind her left ear. Until that moment, I hadn't realized that Happy wore a switch. The way she swayed on her feet told me that happy hour had started several hours ahead of schedule.

Happy was in much rougher shape than we'd been the previous evening, but I was in no position to judge, so I opened the door wide and tried to look surprised but pleased.

"Well, hello, Happy!"

"Where's Pris?" Her voice wasn't exactly a snarl but it was close.

"She's mailing some packages. Do you want to come inside and wait for her?"

"You tell her to come home," she slurred. "I've made up my mind. I don't want her working for you anymore."

"I think Pris might have something to say about that, don't you? She's an adult. You don't get to say where she can and can't work."

"Leave my daughter alone." This time she was in full snarl. She stabbed a finger in my direction. "Quit putting ideas into her head."

"Excuse me? What kind of ideas do you think I'm putting into Pris's head?"

"Ideas!" she cried, flapping her arms over her head as if she were swatting away a swarm of flies. "Do you know how hard it's been for me to put her through school? All alone with no husband and no help? We had *nothing* when Peter died. Nothing! That's why I made her study business. She needs to graduate and get a real job. But you! You keep filling her head with this blogging nonsense."

"That's not true. Pris was excited about her blog way before she met me," I said. "I've given her a few pointers, but honestly, she doesn't need my advice. She's doubled her audience in the last month alone. That's all her."

"You can't make a living writing about old clothes!"

"Maybe. Maybe not," I said evenly. "But if anybody can make a living writing about old clothes, it'll be Pris. Happy, if you and I were in our early twenties, we'd be taking our fashion cues from her. Her aesthetic might be different but she definitely inherited your sense of style. She's an entrepreneur, like you. She sees opportunities that other people miss and isn't afraid to go after them. You should be proud of her."

I was still smiling, hoping to break through and be heard. But Happy wasn't listening. She stabbed the air again, hissing at me through bared teeth.

"Do *not* tell me how to raise my daughter."

Too much alcohol can make you do some dumb things, like inviting a woman who hates the world in general and you in particular to hang out at your house and knit stuff. It can also be a powerful truth serum. Happy shook her head so hard that I thought her hair switch might fall off.

"She's over here all the time. Day and night. She likes you better than me. I am her mother but she likes *you* better."

"Oh, stop. That's ridiculous." I was beginning to lose patience. "Have you asked yourself why she's spending so much time here? Pris is smart and energetic and full of ideas, but she's also trying to figure out who she is. Don't you remember what it was like to be her age? The anxiety and uncertainty? Pris needs connection and affirmation, an older woman to tell her it's okay to believe in herself. She needs you, Happy. But you're not available, so she comes here."

"Oh, shut up," Happy slurred. "What do you know about it?"

"Loneliness? Everything. So does Pris." By then, I could hardly look at her. I lifted my face skyward, trying to muster the will to hold my tongue. I failed. "You're not the *only* one suffering, you know! If you could take a day off from wallowing in your own grief, you might think about that. *You're* her mother. Start acting like it!"

I was out of line. I admit that. I was projecting my feelings about Sterling onto Happy, which wasn't fair. The situational similarities were undeniable and my observations weren't wrong, but my approach was. I realized that almost immediately and was about to apologize but I didn't have a chance.

Happy made a fist and then swept back her arm like a pitcher winding up to throw a curveball. Lucky for me, whatever she was drinking made her slow, so I had plenty of time to duck. The wine had affected her balance as well as her timing. After slugging empty air, Happy spun around like a dizzy ballerina and tumbled backward. If Lorne hadn't heard the commotion and arrived when he did, she would have fallen off the piazza and down the stairs.

"Whoa!" he yelped in surprise, then caught her under the arms from behind. Happy hung there like a limp rag doll for a moment, then scuttled her feet back beneath her body and pushed herself to a stand. The switch had fallen forward and was flopping against her ear. Happy slapped at it as if she were swatting a bug and squared her shoulders.

"You okay there, Happy?" Lorne asked.

She glowered at Lorne and me in turn. Her eyes narrowed and her lips twisted as if she were trying to think up something really cutting to say. Apparently, she came up short.

"You!" she spat, then stomped down the stairs.

She swung the front gate so hard that it clanged against the wrought iron fence, then marched down the sidewalk and took a hard right into her driveway. Hedges blocked the view of the front door but we heard it slam.

Lorne looked at me and grinned. "Guess I'm not the only one who felt like throwing a punch today."

I DIDN'T SHARE *all* the details of Happy's visit when Pris returned from the post office. But I did say she should take the afternoon off and go check on her mother.

At three o'clock, a robot called to say that the delivery of my new refrigerator had been rescheduled to a six-hour window two days hence. When I pressed one to express my annoyance, I was informed that my call was very important and the wait time to speak to a human would be seventeen minutes.

At four o'clock, I opened the door of a previously blocked closet and a crate filled with cheap glass vases crashed to the floor, smashing them into ten zillion pieces.

At five o'clock, the doorbell rang again.

"If you're here to make my life miserable," I shouted as I trotted down the staircase, "you're too late! Go away!"

"Bad day?" Trey asked when I opened the door.

"Bad. But I'm sure it could have been worse. Or maybe not." I stepped back and swung the door wide. Trey stepped into the foyer. "So have you decided to quit being mad at me? Because I wasn't kidding before; if you're here to make my life miserable—"

Trey frowned, giving a pretty good impression of someone who was perplexed, or pretending to be. "I'm not mad at you."

"Oh, please." I rolled my eyes. "Lorne puts his arm around my shoulders at Beau's birthday. You do an about-face, leave the party, and don't return my phone calls because . . ." I spread my hands and made a "feel free to fill in the blank" face.

Trey shook his head, still looking perplexed. "Because I got an urgent text from a client and had to leave."

"Okay, fine," I said, though I wasn't really buying it. I'd seen the look on his face when he left. "Then what about my phone calls? I left you a voicemail."

"My cell froze up and locked me out; it was a huge pain. I got a new one but all my data and messages were wiped out. Celia. I'm not mad at you. My phone died and I've been busy. That's it."

"Good. Because there's nothing going on between me and Lorne, you know. I'm not interested in him. I'm not interested in *anybody*," I said, wanting to make my position absolutely clear. "No offense."

"Honestly, Celia. I was just involved with a client. I didn't notice that Lorne had his arm around you, and if I had, it wouldn't have made any difference to me."

"It wouldn't?"

A surprising nugget of disappointment appeared out of nowhere and lodged somewhere near my breastbone.

"Why would it?" He shrugged. "You're entitled to see, or not see, anybody you want. Makes no difference to me."

He looked and sounded entirely convincing. The nugget swelled into a lump.

"*Exactly*. But I'm not. Seeing him," I clarified. "Or anybody."

Trey nodded. "Okay. Sorry I didn't get your message. What were you calling about?"

"Oh. Nothing. I just wanted to make sure we were okay. Because I thought you looked kind of upset when you left."

"I was not. I assure you."

"Well, good." I bobbed my head, feeling suddenly awkward and kind of dumb for having misread the signal. "So," I said after too long a pause (the nugget was dividing my focus), "what's up? Just in the neighborhood?"

"I heard some news and I thought I should tell you in person."

"Good news or bad news?" I asked with a wince, steeling myself for the bad.

Trey took a breath. "Well. Guess that depends on how you look at it. Maybe we should sit down."

Chapter Twenty-Seven

*H*is name was Robert Jordan Covington. Everybody called him RJ." I pushed the photograph across the table so Trey could take a look.

Calpurnia was wearing a pink watered-silk evening gown with white roses pinned to the bodice. RJ was looking very handsome in his Citadel dress uniform, white trousers with a knife-edged crease and a close-fitted blue jacket with tails and three rows of brass buttons. It was hard to say which of them was the better dressed. I couldn't blame Calpurnia for falling for him.

Trey tapped his thumb on the edge of his coffee cup as he studied the picture. "How did you find out his name?"

"I made friends with a research librarian at the Citadel. There was a picture in the yearbook that's basically identical to the group shot I found in Auntie Cal's treasure box." I pulled out the second photo that showed Calpurnia in her pink gown, three other girls in evening dresses, one holding a glass of punch, and half a dozen handsome young cadets, all smiling for the camera, probably following an instruction to say *cheese*. "This was taken at the graduation formal in late May of 1971. RJ joined the Marines, was sent to Vietnam, was killed in a firefight a few weeks later."

I handed him the third photograph, the Polaroid shot showing Calpurnia standing near the brick arch, wearing the too-hot-for Charleston coat, and pointed to a stamp on the white border of the snapshot that read, "Jan 72." I'd also found a stub for a train ticket from Atlanta to Detroit in Calpurnia's things, dated October 14, 1971, and a return ticket for March eleventh.

Trey tapped his thumb on his coffee cup a few more times. "So you think that Calpurnia got involved with this cadet—"

"RJ," I prompted.

"RJ," Trey repeated. "But he was killed in Vietnam, so Calpurnia went off to have the baby in Detroit and then gave it up for adoption?"

"Or somewhere in the Midwest," I said. "I can't think of any other reason she'd travel to Michigan in winter."

"Well, the timing is right," Trey said, shuffling through the pictures again. "Edward Hunter was born in Ann Arbor, Michigan, on March third, nineteen seventy-two. The birth certificate lists Calpurnia as the mother but the father as unknown. The adoption was finalized almost immediately, but I didn't find much else in the way of a paper trail. The interesting part is that Mr. Hunter lives right here in Charleston. Must have been a private adoption, maybe even someone the family knew."

"But they shipped Calpurnia up north to have the baby so nobody would know," I said. "Unwed motherhood was such a stigma back then. Girls told everybody they were going visit a maiden aunt or take a grand tour of Europe but went to maternity homes instead. Poor Auntie Cal."

I fell silent, picturing Calpurnia sitting alone in the seat of a southbound train less than ten days after giving birth, her arms empty, her breasts swollen and tender with milk for a child she would never be able to see again or speak of again, not even to me. For the first time, I thought I understood why Auntie Cal had fought so hard to keep hold of me.

The waitress brought a plate of warm-from-the-oven banana bread with chocolate-hazelnut cream cheese to the table, then refilled our coffee mugs. When Trey had said we should pick a neutral place to meet my newly discovered cousin, I'd suggested Miller's All Day.

"Do you want to order?" the server asked.

"Thank you, ma'am, but we're still waiting for someone," Trey said. "This'll hold us over for now."

"No rush," she said, and went to check on her other tables.

I glanced at my phone to check the time. "Maybe he changed his mind."

"He's not late. We were early. It's thirty seconds past nine."

Trey took a chunk of banana bread and slathered the cream cheese stuff the way only Polly and professional athletes or those with a testosterone-fueled metabolism can, thoughtlessly and without the least twinge of guilt.

"Don't you want some?" he asked. I shook my head and he popped his eyebrows. "Are you feeling okay?"

I looked at the picture on the top of the stack, the one of RJ and Calpurnia at the dance, maybe the only picture they'd ever had a chance to take together.

"Does he look like his father?" I asked. "Did you see any re-semblance?"

"I don't know. We've only talked on the phone. After you gave me permission to get in touch, I called to tell him he had a cousin and asked if he wanted to meet you. He said yes and agreed to meet for breakfast. That's about it."

"Did he sound nervous?" I asked, leaning forward. "Because *I'm* nervous."

Trey swallowed the bread. "Celia, you don't have to do this, you know. If I hadn't been sending up flares while searching for you, chances are you'd never have known you had a cousin. As far as the state of South Carolina is concerned, you're not even family. That's why the house went to you, because according to state law, you're the closest relative. Adopted children have no inheritance claims on the birth family. You're under no obligation here, Celia."

I wasn't really listening; I was too anxious/excited/curious about meeting my cousin. Assuming he hadn't changed his mind about meeting me.

"It's three minutes after."

"He'll be here," Trey assured me.

I craned my neck, looking around the restaurant and toward the front door, looking for . . . ? I had no idea. "How's he going to know us? I mean, if you've never seen him and he's never seen you? Maybe he's already here. Or maybe he came and left."

"It'll be fine. I told him I'd be wearing an ugly black suit."

"*That's* your plan?"

"You see anybody else in here wearing a black suit?"

I did not. Because no Charlestonian would think of wearing a black suit in early July when the humidity averaged eighty percent.

"Your suit's not *that* ugly."

"Since when?"

"Well"—I broke off small piece of bread—"it's starting to grow on me. You've got a kind of Johnny Cash, Man-in-Black vibe going. All you need is a guitar and some Ray-Bans."

I checked the time on my phone again. "Where *is* he?"

"Let's talk about something else." Trey folded his hands together and placed his arms on the table with a kind of calling the meeting to order deliberateness.

"Like what?"

"Like you. I've always wondered: your family all lived together until you were . . . ?"

"Twelve."

"Then you and your father moved out and you never saw Calpurnia again." I nodded. I'd told him that part when we first met. "Why? Because she was behind the wheel when your mother was killed? Did he blame Calpurnia for her death?"

"He did. But that wasn't the reason he wouldn't let me see her again."

"Then what was?"

I wrapped my hands tight around the ceramic curve of my coffee mug and stared down at the mocha-colored pool inside the rim.

"Because Calpurnia kidnapped me."

"Excuse me?"

I knew he'd heard me. He just didn't believe it. I spoke louder so he'd know I wasn't kidding.

"Aunt Calpurnia kidnapped me. We disappeared for nine days." I lifted my head.

"They were the greatest nine days of my life."

Chapter Twenty-Eight

Twenty-five years before

Mrs. Christiansen, the school secretary, escorted me to the foyer and peered through the glass double doors toward the driveway, where Calpurnia's silver sedan sat idling.

"Do you have everything, Celia? Books? Jacket? Lunchbox?"

Mrs. Christiansen was kind but tenderhearted. If I started to cry, I knew she'd cry too and I'd have to endure another round of hugs and sympathy before I could get to my aunt and find out why I'd been summoned from class on a Friday morning. And so, instead of crying, I nodded and looped the straps of my backpack in the crook of my left arm, ready to make my escape.

Mrs. Christiansen placed her hands on either side of my face. "Poor little thing. First your momma and granny and now this." She sighed. "You take care of yourself, Celia. You hear?"

"Yes, ma'am," I said, then wriggled loose and ran out the door, the heavy backpack whacking my leg with every step.

Calpurnia climbed out of the car, coming around to the passenger side to meet me. I flung myself into her arms and let the tears flow.

"Hush now, sugar. Everything's going to be fine."

"What's wrong? Is Daddy okay?"

She bent over me, talking into my hair, her breath warm and scented with cinnamon. "Yes, honey. He's fine. Just get in the car."

"But is he—"

"Get in the car, Celia Louise."

Every child knows that when an adult uses your middle name, they're really saying, "Do not even *think* of arguing with me," so I flung my backpack onto the front seat and climbed in after it. Auntie Cal looked back toward Mrs. Christiansen, who was watching from the door, smiled weakly and sadly, and then got behind the wheel.

"What happened?" I asked. "The principal said it was a family emergency."

Calpurnia pulled out of the parking lot and into the traffic. "Well, it's not *exactly* an emergency," she explained. "Your daddy got called away on important business. There's a big writers' conference in New York City and the main speaker came down with the shingles, so they asked Sterling to fill in at the last minute.

"Since he's going to be gone all week, having a grand time in the big city, I thought that you and I deserved a little getaway too. We're going on a road trip, sugar! Just you and me. Doesn't that sound wonderful?"

I glared at her, frowning. "But you *said* there was an emergency. Why would you tell my principal a lie?"

What I really wanted to know was why she'd lied to me.

I'd been through it all before, just five months previously, the seemingly normal day that is interrupted by a somber-faced adult who tells you to get your things and follow them but won't tell you why, then delivers you to another adult who is higher on the food chain, who tells you there's been an emergency but won't provide details, the walk, the wait, the pounding heart, until you're finally handed off to your family and told the terrible truth.

I was only just getting past all that; so were the kids in my grade. Being introverted, unpopular, and twelve is even more miserable when your classmates either look through you because they don't know what to say, whisper about you behind your back, or pretend to like you because they feel sorry for you. Until recently, the only person who treated me like she always had was Polly. I just wanted for things to be normal again. Finally, it was starting to happen.

Earlier that week, Andy Green, whom I had been praying on my knees would notice me, begged the teacher to put me in his history project group. I knew he only wanted me because he planned to foist most of the work off on me. Still. It was a start. Maybe, if I did his homework, Andy would start liking me for real.

How could she put me through that again? The old Calpurnia wouldn't have. But this new, post-accident Calpurnia was different, erratic and unpredictable. She got flustered easily, left pots to boil dry on the stove, cried over little things, like not being able to open a jar of pickles, even after I ran the lid under hot water and opened it myself. This Calpurnia got into fights with my father too, and he with her.

The police had clearly determined that the other driver was at fault, but none of that mattered to Sterling. Some people experience grief as anger, even rage, and need someone to blame. My father was one of them. Every evening, he would go into his office and drink behind closed doors. After I was in bed, the fights would begin.

Sterling always said that people who had to raise their voices to make a point usually didn't have one, so at first, this new turn was shocking. I would climb out of bed in the dark, grab one of my stuffed animals from the bed, then clutch it close when I cracked open my bedroom door and leaned in, trying to hear what they were saying.

After a while, I realized I was better off not knowing. I learned to sleep on my side with one ear pressed against the mattress and my pillow covering the other to block out the sound of once-familiar voices made unrecognizable by rage. Had I been listening the night before, I would have known that Sterling told Calpurnia he'd had enough, that the two of us were moving out, and that he didn't want me spending time with her. "After that, she just went crazy," Sterling told me later. "But I never imagined she'd try to kidnap you."

Things had been crazy for a long time. That's why I couldn't say what I meant, because I couldn't predict how she'd react anymore.

"You shouldn't tell lies to the school," I said. "Especially not about emergencies. You'll get me in trouble."

"Well. It wasn't *really* a lie," Calpurnia explained. "After all we've been through these last months, I believe a little getaway is absolutely necessary to our mental and physical well-being. It's a Fun Emergency. But principals don't usually understand that sort of thing.

"So, yes," she said, bobbing her head a little in concession of my point, "I stretched the truth just a teeny bit. But it wasn't really a lie, sugar. More of a fib. Besides, your spring vacation is next week. You're just leaving a little early."

When she put it that way, it kind of made sense. Also, I was happy to see her smiling again, and a road trip did sound kind of wonderful. Maybe it was what we needed to put things right again.

"Aren't we going home to pack?" I asked when she nosed the car onto the highway.

"Already took care of that," Calpurnia said breezily. "Our suitcases are in the trunk and I've got a picnic basket full of snacks in the back seat. You want a praline? Get one for me too, sugar."

I unbuckled my seat belt briefly to retrieve our sweets, then settled in for the drive. Calpurnia's sedan was practically new, a replacement by the insurance company after the old one had been declared a total loss in the accident, and it still had traces of that rubbery new-car smell. I finished my praline, licked the sugar off my fingers, then fiddled with the radio until I found a song I liked and hummed along, trying to decide which Hanson brother was the cutest, thinking I was lucky to be missing the end-of-week math test.

"Where are we going?" I asked when the song ended.

"On an adventure."

"I know, but *where?*"

"First stop is Savannah. I have some business to attend to. We can get some lunch too. And after that? It's a *surprise*."

Calpurnia turned her head in my direction and beamed, looking and sounding like the old Calpurnia. Suddenly I felt bathed in pure, unadulterated love and instantly forgave her everything, the way only children can. Anywhere she wanted to go was fine with me—Savannah, Ecuador, the dark side of the moon.

"You and I are going to have the time of our lives. Trust me," she said.

I did trust her. I always had.

In Savannah, we ate drive-thru fried chicken sandwiches, then went to a used-car dealership on a seedy strip of highway. Calpurnia said she might be a while, so I dug the latest Redwall novel out of my backpack and became happily engrossed in the adventures of Matthias the mouse, while Calpurnia went inside the office. She emerged forty minutes later with the keys to a blue 1987

Chevy Cavalier and a wad of cash, which she quickly stowed in her purse.

"Why would you want this old thing?" I asked when she asked me to move the suitcases to the Cavalier. "It's all scratched. Your other car was brand-new."

"I know, but the mileage was terrible. Besides, this one's a convertible. If you're going on a road trip, a convertible is absolutely *required*." She opened the trunk. "Didn't you ever see *Thelma and Louise*?"

I had. It was the greatest of all girlfriend road trip movies with a poetic but disturbingly tragic end. But when Calpurnia slammed the trunk and beamed at me again, I forgot all about convertibles plummeting off cliffs.

"Ready?"

"Yes, ma'am."

"Wonderful. The adventure begins!"

FOR A CHILD as sheltered as I had been, who had journeyed only in books because the ailments of her mother and grandmother made family travel almost impossible, it really was an adventure.

Our first stop was Waycross, Georgia.

We took a boat ride on the murky, mysterious waters of the Okefenokee Swamp, through trees shawled with Spanish moss. It was strange and beautiful and unlike anything I'd ever seen in my life. Gray-green garlands brushed my face and shoulders. I pushed them aside again and again, as if parting an infinite series of proscenium curtains, imagining myself entering a time portal to an exotic, prehistoric land. It truly did seem like another world.

Turtles sunned themselves on waterlogged tree trunks. Water lilies bloomed yellow and abundant in brackish ponds. Alligators lazed on boggy banks and slipped beneath the blackened waters if we came too close. Cranes waded through fields of swamp grass searching for frogs. Osprey called from the treetops, summoning potential mates in high-pitched whistles that raised the hair on the back of my arms. It was peculiar and mystifying and just spooky enough to be thrilling, the perfect beginning to a grand adventure.

Next we rode a steam train on a two-mile track through the swamp. It was anticlimactic after the boat ride. We posed for a picture with Old Roy, a taxidermied alligator almost thirteen feet in length. I bent down and stuck my head in his open mouth while Calpurnia put her hands on each side of her face and bulged out her eyes, miming a panicked scream as the photographer snapped the picture, then requested four dollars for a copy. Calpurnia peeled off the bills and put the snapshot in her purse.

When the sun dipped lower, we checked into a tourist cabin, Calpurnia paying cash for one night in advance. We had apples, pimento cheese on crackers, bottles of lukewarm sweet tea, and more pralines for dinner, then changed into warmer clothes before getting back into the car for another destination Calpurnia refused to disclose.

"Wait and see," she said. "Sometimes it's good not to know what comes next."

What came next was a return to the Okefenokee and a magical, nighttime hike through a state park. We were surrounded by strange cheeps and growls and rustlings. When the path narrowed, I imagined the trees were leaning closer to whisper secrets. I turned my flashlight toward the swamp and saw spots of orange flame floating on the water; the watchful eyes of alligators. When we came to a clearing, Calpurnia said, "Look up!" in a voice breathless with awe.

Before or since, I have never seen so many stars.

The next morning, we rose before the sun—to beat the traffic, Calpurnia explained. We left the room key dangling from the doorknob and drove slowly out of the parking lot without headlights. Calpurnia said we were being polite, careful not to wake the other guests. I never thought to question it.

"Where to now?" I asked when we hit the road and picked up speed.

"Wait and see," she said.

It was the same every day. We left our motel before dawn without checking out, traveled to the next destination—I never knew where until we arrived—taking circuitous routes on country roads through microscopic towns until we got to wherever Calpurnia had decided we were going. And I was fine with it. We'd talk or sing along with the radio; "Girls Just Want to Have Fun" was a favorite. Sometimes I would read, or take out a notebook and scribble a story. I wrote "Letticia Phoenicia: Jungle Guide" the morning after our dark-of-night hike in the swamp, also a love letter to Andy Green that I tore up later.

Once, after I begged and begged and begged, Calpurnia pulled to the shoulder of a particularly straight and desolate stretch of road, traded seats with me, and let me drive for almost a mile. I felt so powerful, and so scared. It was the first time that I understood that the two are often linked. I begged her to let me try one of her cigarettes too, but there she drew the line.

Beyond the sights, the sounds, the adventure, what I loved most about those nine days was the feeling that Calpurnia and I were becoming something we'd never been before: equals.

Caring for Momma and Beebee had left the boundaries of her world as limited as mine. Apart from a St. Philip's choir tour to Memphis and Nashville when I was nine, I don't recall Calpurnia ever traveling farther than Savannah. For all I know, that journey to Michigan might have been the longest trip she'd ever taken. Our odyssey was just as thrilling for her as it was for me, maybe more so. She oohed and aahed at every unfamiliar vista, squealed with delight at every new experience. I had never seen her so happy. This was a new Calpurnia, a better one. I loved her and always had. But for the first and only time, we were friends.

We went to Panama City, Florida, and made the rounds of the tourist attractions—the "Believe It or Not" museum, Zoo World, window-shopping on the pier. We took a long walk along the beach, and when the sun started to sink, we sat down at the base of a dune and watched the tide go out. Calpurnia lit a cigarette, inhaled deeply, and said, "Nothing ever stays the same, Celia. Not even the sea." It was one of the few times I remember seeing her sad on that trip.

We went to St. Augustine and saw the lighthouse and a seventeenth-century Spanish fort. We went to Daytona Beach to watch the surfers and have lunch on the pier. I tossed fries over the railing and watched birds swoop down to catch them.

We went to the Kennedy Space Center in Cape Canaveral, and of course, we went to Disney World. Calpurnia was even more excited than I was. We rode every single ride, some more than once. But I drew the line when Calpurnia wanted to ride Pirates of the Caribbean a fourth time. It was a long, exhausting day and so much fun.

I wanted to call Sterling and tell him about everything we'd done, but Calpurnia said it was too late. When I made a similar request the next day, Calpurnia said he would be in meetings all day. That was the first time I recall thinking something wasn't quite right, but I didn't dwell on it.

In Miami we ate fried plantains and got a manicure, both firsts for me, then took a sunset cruise of Millionaires' Row. We leaned on the railing, picking out which houses we'd want to live in if we ever got to be rich and famous. "But you know," Calpurnia said, after I'd decided on a ridiculously huge mansion with pale-pink stucco walls and Corinthian columns, "the real worth of a house depends on the people who live inside. The rest is just furniture."

As far as I can at this moment, I have forgiven Calpurnia, and myself. The need for forgiveness, I have discovered, comes in waves, like tides and memory and anger. I still don't understand how the woman who taught me most of what mattered journeyed from wisdom to madness. But I do remember what came next, the hundred-mile highway that traced the coastline, then hopscotched across the sea to islands and atolls, kissing the crests of waves, leading to the end of the road at the end of the world.

Calpurnia drove us to the precipice. But I sent us over the cliff.

Chapter Twenty-Nine

I stopped to catch my breath, propped my elbow onto the table, and wedged the edge of my thumbnail into the crevice between my front teeth. The server walked past with coffeepot in hand, gave us a glance, and correctly ascertained that the time was not right for interruption. I went on with the story.

"I just assumed we'd head home after leaving Miami. But we got on the highway, heading south. I asked Calpurnia where we were going and got the usual answer, "Wait and see," but that day I pushed back. Finally she told me we were going to Key West to see Hemingway's house, populated by scores of six-toed cats.

"She almost had me there," I said, smiling a little. "A colony of cats with six toes sounded pretty interesting, but spring break was almost over and I was worried about getting back. 'Don't worry,' she told me, 'transportation has already been arranged.' I asked her what she meant but she wouldn't give me a straight answer, just smiled and gave me the old 'Wait and see.'

"We got to Key West, had lunch, saw Hemingway's house, and petted some six-toed cats. Then we checked into another motel, one-night cash in advance, as usual. Calpurnia said she had some errands to run and would be back in a couple of hours. She told me to stay in the room. I locked the door, watched some TV, and ate the last praline. It was dried out by then and so grainy that I ended up spitting it into the wastebasket."

I lifted my cup and took another sip, swishing coffee around in my mouth, welcoming its bitterness, remembering that sensation of chewing sickly sweet sand and the return of the feeling that something wasn't right.

"I decided to call Sterling but the phone in our room didn't work. And then, for some reason, I decided to look inside Auntie Cal's suitcase. I don't know what I expected to find . . ."

No, I didn't. But I can still recall sitting cross-legged on the bed in my shorts, the way the blue chenille bedspread felt on my bare legs, the sick, clenching sensation in my stomach as I stared at Calpurnia's suitcase. I didn't know what I would find inside, but the grown-up part of me knew I'd find something and that it probably wouldn't be good.

"At first it seemed like the usual—clothes, cosmetics, hair rollers. But when I picked up the cigarette carton, I noticed it was bulging on one side. When I dumped the packs onto the bed, two blue booklets fell out."

I paused, bit my lower lip. "Passports. One for Calpurnia and one for me."

Trey had been perfectly silent this whole time, barely moving a muscle, letting his coffee go cold. Now he pursed his lips and let out a soft, low whistle.

"What did you do?"

I'd never told anyone the whole story, not even Sterling. I had started to once, but when I began talking about our adventures, the swamp and the beach and boat and Disney, how exciting it all had been, Sterling started to scream at me. "Do you know what it was like? Do you know what I went through? I thought you were gone forever, I thought you were dead! Do you have any idea?"

I was just a kid; I couldn't understand what he'd gone through. But I understood that what I'd felt during my time with Calpurnia, joy and excitement and wonder, was wrong and that I shouldn't talk about it. So I never had, not to my father, not to Polly, not to my therapist, and definitely not to my ex-husband.

But now, for reasons that were hard to pin down, I wanted Trey to know my story, to know *me*. I'd gone this far, let him come closer than anybody ever had. But it was hard to talk about what happened next, impossible when looking him in the face. I lowered my eyes, stared at my hands, and answered his question.

"I went to the motel office, asked the guy at the desk if I could use the phone. He was cranky—I don't think he liked kids—and said that the office phone was only for emergencies. He leaned over the desk so he was right up in my face and practically growled at me. 'Is this an *emergency*?'

"I thought about it for a minute and said it might be. I told him that my name was Celia Louise Fairchild and I needed to call my dad because my aunt might be trying to kidnap me.

"The next thing I knew there were police cars, and sirens, and . . ."

I stopped there, pressed a fist to my lips and turned my face away, blinking back tears. A hand covered mine.

"Celia. Celia, you didn't do anything wrong. You were twelve years old. What else could you have done?"

I nodded dumbly because, of course, he was right.

In that moment, I had only had two options: ask that man to call my father, or do nothing and follow Calpurnia up the gangplank and onto the ship the following morning, a ship that would sail across the sea without a stop to the Canary Islands and then

Lisbon, Portugal. The tickets Calpurnia was carrying when the police searched her said that was where we were to disembark.

What was her plan after that? I don't know. I never got to ask her.

Calpurnia returned to the motel two hours later. In that time, she'd sold the car for cash, bought the tickets, a bottle of sunscreen, and a giant bag of gummy bears: leave it to Cal to remember the important things. There were police cars everywhere. She had to know what was going to happen, but she didn't tell the taxi driver to turn around or keep going. She stepped out of the cab and asked the police if I was all right. They arrested her on the spot.

I was inside the motel room with two police officers and a social worker. There was a lot of noise, so I looked out the window, saw them putting her in handcuffs, and ran out the door, screaming for them to let her go and that I was sorry, that I didn't mean it, that I'd just been joking. The social worker tried to calm me down. I bit her hand as hard as I could and then one of the cops picked me up, tossed me over his shoulder like a sack of meal, and carried me back to the motel room. Two others put Aunt Calpurnia in a squad car and drove away.

That was the last time I saw her.

For months, Sterling barely let me out of his sight. He took me to school and picked me up every day, altering his teaching schedule so he could. Charleston is such a small town; the last thing Sterling wanted was the publicity of a trial. He brokered a deal to drop the charges in exchange for a restraining order. If Calpurnia got within a thousand feet of me, she could be arrested and the charges reinstated.

Sterling told me that if I tried to get in contact, Calpurnia would be sent to jail for years, and I believed him. I rode my bike back to Harleston Village once, when I was about fourteen. Felicia was out in her garden, watering some plants, and I was afraid she'd recognize me and call the police, so I pedaled away as fast as I could and didn't go back until after Sterling died. By then it was too late.

"Anyway." I didn't have to say more. Trey knew the rest of it. I picked up my coffee mug and took a big gulp. It was cold but I was thirsty. "Do you know that you're the only person I've ever told that story to? Guess you look trustworthy or something."

"Must be the suit."

It really wasn't funny but I gave him fifty bonus points anyway, for helping relieve the tension. I'd revealed so much, more than I'd planned on, and still didn't understand why. Maybe it was the suit. Maybe it was him. There was so much I didn't know about him but one thing I was sure of: Trey Holcomb was a good man, a man you could trust your secrets to.

"Well. Looks like my cousin is a no-show. Should we go ahead and order?" I asked, forcing a smile and shifting gears. "I'm buying. No arguments. You should at least get a free meal out of this rabbit chase."

"How do you know I'm not billing you?"

"Are you?"

"No." Trey smiled and took the last piece of bread.

Trey ordered biscuits and gravy with tomato jam. I considered the waffles but chose grits again: the daily special was sausage, roasted red and green peppers, fresh grilled corn, snow peas, and green onions over smoked gouda cheese grits. When the food arrived, I pulled out my phone and took a picture of my plate to text to Calvin later. I was looking at the screen, fiddling with the lighting, when I heard a familiar voice.

"Hey, Celia."

"Well, hey, Teddy!" I raised my hand so he could smack it.

Since we'd bonded over ice cream, Teddy and I always exchanged high fives. "How are you today?"

"Late," he said. "Missed my bus and had to wait half an hour for the next one."

"Again? Well, that stinks."

For all that he was late, Teddy didn't seem to be in a hurry to go anywhere. I didn't want to blow him off, but things were getting a little awkward, so I smiled and gestured toward Trey.

"Teddy, let me introduce you to a friend of mine—"

"Hey, Mr. Holcomb. Sorry I'm late."

I blinked a couple of times. "Oh. You've already met?"

"No." Teddy shrugged. "I just figured. He said he'd be wearing an ugly black suit and that's about the ugliest suit I ever saw. It's too bad my momma's not here. She could have fixed it for you, made it fit right. She was a seamstress when she was alive, sewed dresses for ladies all over Charleston. Now she's an angel."

Teddy paused for a moment, then frowned.

"Sorry. I shouldn't have said that. Didn't mean to hurt your feelings, Mr. Holcomb. Your suit's not that bad. Anyway, it's clean."

Trey smiled and extended his hand. "You never have to apologize for telling the truth, Teddy. It's nice to meet you."

"Nice to meet you too. I was so happy when you called me." His frown was suddenly displaced by a sincere and radiant smile. Teddy swiveled his head in my direction. "And I am so, *so* happy we're going to be cousins, Celia. I am. It's been lonely with no family."

Chapter Thirty

Calvin was dumbstruck. As far as I could recall, this was a first.

"Are you serious?" he asked after an uncharacteristically long silence. "You mean the Teddy you told me about before? The big guy from the coffee shop who makes great mochas and told you to take more breaks? *He's* Calpurnia's baby?"

"And my cousin," I said. "Yes."

"Really. Wow," Calvin murmured. "That's just . . ."

"Unexpected. I know."

When Teddy told me how happy he was to know we were cousins, it took a second for the truth to sink in for me as well. Talk about something I never saw coming. But once my brain got done processing the information, I agreed with him. It was lonely without any family and I was glad to have a cousin, especially one I liked as much as Teddy.

"And sad," Calvin said. "The kid getting killed in the war, Calpurnia left all alone and having to give up her baby. Do you think he knew she was pregnant?"

"Don't know. I didn't find any letters between them. Maybe it was just a fling and she decided not to tell him? Or maybe she did and he didn't care or didn't respond? Or maybe he was the love of her life, and they were planning to get married but RJ was killed before they could arrange for a wedding."

Though there wasn't any way for me to know for sure, I hoped it had been like that. Calpurnia's life had been so hard, I hated to think of her being rejected in love on top of everything else. I would never know how RJ felt about Calpurnia or the prospect of unintended fatherhood. But I felt certain that he truly had been the love of her life and that losing him had broken her heart. Why else would such a pretty, young woman never have married, or even dated?

"RJ was from Alabama but it seems he had family in Charleston," I said. "Teddy was adopted by Eloise and Clinton Hunter. She was a dressmaker and he worked at an auto body repair shop. They were an older couple and had never had children of their own. I did a little online research; Eloise seems to have been RJ's aunt."

"So you think the two families might have gotten together and arranged for a private adoption?"

"It all fits," I said. "Back then, they would have wanted to keep things quiet. Calpurnia wouldn't have had much choice except to give up the baby, especially after RJ was killed. If he was adopted by a Charleston family, maybe she thought she'd be able to keep in touch with him."

"Did she?" Calvin asked.

"I showed Teddy some pictures but he says he doesn't ever remember meeting her."

"Well, that's an amazing story," Calvin said. "But poor Calpurnia."

"I know. I wish Calpurnia had told me what happened. Teddy is such a sweetheart, but I feel sorry for him. It's been rough since his mother died. He's just not happy in the group home. He has to take two buses to work or just about anyplace else. Also, there's almost no outdoor space. Teddy loves to garden and—"

"Celia Fairchild," Calvin interrupted. "Please, tell me you're not thinking what I think you're thinking."

I didn't say anything.

"No," Calvin said, correctly interpreting my silence. "No, no, no, no. You cannot seriously be thinking about inviting your cousin to move in with you. You hardly know him."

"That's not true," I countered. "I see him almost every day at the coffee shop. And after that day I ran into him and we went out for ice cream, I really feel like we've gotten to be friends."

"I'm sure you have. But that doesn't mean you should be roommates. Look, Celia, I love your compassion. I'm sure Teddy is just as nice as you say he is, and it's sweet that you're worried about him. But I worry about *you*. What about the birth mother? She might not be that keen on placing her baby in a home with some strange man."

"He's not a strange man," I protested. "He's family."

"I know," Calvin said gently. "But that doesn't change the fact that you know almost nothing about him. You can't rescue the whole world, cupcake. What if helping Teddy means that you won't be able to adopt Peaches?"

Calvin wasn't asking me anything that I hadn't already asked myself fifty times since leaving the restaurant. When I didn't respond, Calvin said, "Promise me you'll really think it through before you do anything, okay?"

THAT WAS AN easy promise to keep. For the next couple of days, it was impossible to do much besides think it through. There was so much to think about.

In the ideal scenario, the birth mother might actually like the idea of seeing the baby placed into a home that came complete with an on-site uncle. It was possible. But it was also possible that offering a home to Teddy might jeopardize the chances of my being able to adopt Peaches. Was I really prepared to take that risk?

But Teddy *was* family and I knew in my bones that this is what Calpurnia would have wanted. Possibly even what she'd been trying to tell me all along?

Charleston was a small town, but not that small. What were the chances of our meeting the way we had, of my just happening to choose the shop where he worked as my regular coffee shop? There were a dozen places closer to the house but, for some reason, I'd decided that Bitty and Beau's was the right one for me.

Could that have been a coincidence? Maybe. But what about finding the pictures? And the fact that, on the very day I'd gone to my aunt's grave with a picture of Calpurnia and the father of her child, I'd left the churchyard, rounded a corner, and literally run into my cousin? Was that a coincidence too? And what about the dream?

I'd assumed that the bearded man in the shadows was Trey Holcomb, but couldn't it just as easily have been Teddy? In the dream, Calpurnia held the baby in her arms out to me. Couldn't she have been pointing me to her baby just as much as to mine?

It was only a dream, a strange one. And I still wasn't sure I knew exactly what it meant, if anything. The whole thing could have been a result of my subconscious brain trying to sort through the confusing confluence of desire and circumstance that had become my life since returning to Charleston. It was possible that the dreams were just dreams. It was also possible that being thrust into Teddy's orbit even before knowing we were related *was* a coincidence, however unlikely. There was no way to know for sure.

But one thing I did know. No matter what the law said about the nonexistent inheritance rights of adopted children, my aunt would not have wanted her son to be unhappy or lack a proper home. Teddy was Calpurnia's son; he had just as much right to live here as I did.

No matter how much you think or consider the consequences or try to justify going another direction, some things are impossible to ignore. That's what I tried to explain, when I opened my journal that night.

Dear Peaches,

    When you know in your heart that something is right, that's what you have to do, even if other people think it's a mistake, even if it means losing something you've wanted very, very much for a very long time.

    There is something that I am thinking about doing— No, that's not quite it. There is something I know that I have to do, because I know that it's right. Following through on it might mean that I won't get to be your mother. I hope not, but it's possible. But if I did anything else, I wouldn't deserve to be.

Teddy was a grown man. He could make his own choices, say yes, or no, or that he'd have to think about it. But there was no question for me. I knew what I had to do.

First thing the next morning, I got into my wallet and pulled a scrap of paper with a phone number that had been printed in a slow and careful hand, then punched the numbers into my phone.

"Teddy? Hey, it's cousin Celia. I hope it's not too early to call. There's something I wanted to discuss with you . . ."

Chapter Thirty-One

*I*t had been a busy and very interesting week. I'd hosted the first dinner party in my half-restored house, been accosted by an inebriated neighbor, learned that Calpurnia had given birth to a love child, met my cousin, invited him to share my house, and worked out the details of his move. Now I was getting ready for craft night with my new friends.

Polly showed up first and brought a suitcase the size of a steamer trunk.

"Are you planning to move in?" I asked when I opened the door. "Because, I have to tell you, the rooms are filling up fast."

Polly shot me a look, then bent down and placed both hands on her thighs and panted like a dog on a hot day. "Stairs," she gasped. "Heavy."

"Here, let me help."

The suitcase had wheels, so rolling it through the front hall was a piece of cake. Hauling it up the stairs to Beebee's yarn cave was a different story. I had to turn around backward, grip the strap with both hands, and drag it up one step at a time, thumping and bumping on every tread.

"Polly, what's in here?"

"Stuff from Sheepish. I know you've got tons of yarn already, but I thought people might want different colors or weights."

"This is yarn?"

"Not *just* yarn," she said, sounding a little defensive. "Instruction books, patterns, scissors, rulers, needles, and fabric. I want to make sure that everybody has whatever they need for all the different kinds of projects. And well . . ." She looked a little hesitant as we reached the top step. "I was thinking that they might see some things they want to buy. The clearance sale hasn't been going very well."

"Good idea."

I was absolutely sincere: it was a good idea. But Polly still looked embarrassed, as if I might be thinking she was taking advantage of my hospitality to make a profit. But if the others started new craft projects, they'd probably need some supplies, so why not buy them from Polly? At forty percent off, it wasn't like she'd be making much money off the deal. What was there to be embarrassed about?

The doorbell rang. Polly ran downstairs to answer it while I dragged the suitcase into the yarn cave and started unloading the contents onto one of the two eight-foot tables I'd set up inside. Pris had helped me move my stuff across the hall into my new bedroom earlier that morning. I really wasn't kidding when I told Polly we were starting to run out of rooms.

The small room next to mine had yet to be cleaned out, but I planned to turn it into the nursery. Teddy would take my parents' old room and the room next door, which had once been Sterling's office. It would make a nice sitting room and I thought he might appreciate having a little private space. Lorne had yet to put a door between the two rooms, creating a suite, but we were on schedule for Teddy to move in early the following week.

I heard the sound of feet running up the staircase and knew Pris was in the house; she never walked anywhere if she could help it and had been looking forward to tonight. But when she bounced into the room and saw the suitcase, the smile froze on her face. "We're supposed to be bringing stuff out, not in. Remember?"

"Polly thought we might need more supplies."

"More yarn?" she asked skeptically. I pulled out several skeins of variegated yarn in shades of turquoise, aquamarine, and blue with just a touch of pink and piled them on the table. "On the other hand . . . that is pretty." Pris picked up a skein and squashed it between her fingers. "Oooh. Feel this. What do you think it's made of?"

"Cashmere," Polly said as she came through the door. Pris dropped the skein as if she'd been holding a hot coal. "I know, I know. But it's not as expensive as you'd think. You'd only need two skeins to make a scarf and I'll sell them to you at cost."

"Okay," Pris said after thinking it over. "But can I still learn embroidery?"

"Absolutely. No problem," Polly assured her. "I brought a booklet to show you the basic stitches and a little linen sampler. It'll be good practice and you can make it into a pillow when you're done. I brought you some threads too; perle cotton is the best for embroidery."

The pastel collection of threads nested inside the creamy white box looked like those luscious little macarons sold in French patisseries and were just as irresistible. Pris gasped in delight the second she saw them. Polly and I exchanged a grin, knowing she'd made a sale. While the transaction was being completed, Felicia entered the room, toting an old, slightly battered Dillard's shopping bag. Caroline followed, carrying a paper plate covered with tinfoil.

"Key lime bars," Caroline explained. "I'm only here to hang out, so I thought maybe I should bring something."

She uncovered the plate and passed it around. The bars were a beautiful pale green, similar to the walls in my newly painted bedroom, cut into perfect two-inch squares, and decorated with snowcaps of whipped cream dusted with bright-green flecks of lime zest. They were gorgeous. Even Calvin would have been impressed.

Polly, who never could resist a sweet and, as far as I remembered, had never tried, took a bite and groaned with happiness.

"Heaven!" she exclaimed. "Can I have one more?"

"Take as many as you want," Caroline said, looking pleased as she brought the plate back to Polly. "Baking is kind of my hobby."

"Well, if everything you bake is as good as this, it could be your profession," Polly said as she bit into the second bar. "But Caroline, are you sure you don't want to give crafts a try? I brought a bunch of different project samples and books. I'm sure there's something here you'd like to make."

"Thanks, but crafts just aren't my thing. No offense, but I've never really seen the point in— Uh-oh. Hang on."

Caroline put the cookie plate down and moved toward the table where I'd been piling Polly's stock as if she'd been captured by some sort of invisible magnetic force field. She plucked a funny-looking white creature with a long snout and a tangle of white yarn curls and floppy ears from the table and stared into its black yarn eyes.

"Well, hello, lovebug. Who are you?"

Polly grinned. "Cute, right? It's crocheting. I can teach you to make one just like her, or one that's a little different. The pattern book has tons of variations."

"You honestly think I could do this?" Caroline asked, still staring into the creature's face. Polly assured her she could, and Caroline turned the animal toward me. "Is that not the most darling thing you've ever seen in your life?"

"Absolutely," I replied. "What is it?"

"A poodle," Caroline said, sounding offended. "Look at the ears."

"If you say so. Dogs have never really been my thing."

"Okay, Polly, you got me," Caroline admitted. "I have no idea what I will do with a crocheted dog, but I absolutely have to make one. So how do I start?"

"Just flip through the pattern book and choose a breed," Polly said. "I'll help you get started, but tonight is mostly about helping everybody pick a project. Felicia," Polly said, "are those your mother's quilt blocks?"

"Yes." Felicia hefted the bag onto the table and started pulling out blocks. "I'd love to finish at least one quilt for Foster and another for Beau and myself. But where do I even begin?"

There must have been at least fifty blocks inside the bag, maybe more, of different sizes, patterns, and colors. They were beautiful. I don't know a lot about quilting but it was clear that Felicia's mother had put a lot of work into making them. It was nice to think that her efforts would finally come to good use. It was nice too to see the change that had overcome Polly in the last few minutes.

When we'd been unpacking the suitcase, Polly had seemed tentative and uncertain, almost apologetic about the idea of selling her wares to the others. Now she was in her element. Commerce might not have come easily to Polly, but she was a natural-born teacher. Her confidence in her skills and her ability to pass them on to others made her students feel confident as well.

"How about a sampler quilt?" Polly said, after looking through the blocks. "You could choose six of your mother's blocks, make six new ones yourself, and then pull it all together with a neutral-colored sashing."

Felicia appeared intrigued but not entirely convinced. "I like the idea of collaboration but . . . Mother did such lovely work. I'd hate to take away from that."

"Trust me," Polly said. "I can help you to make some simple blocks that will complement your mother's work beautifully. Pick out your six favorites. I'll come back and help you after I get Pris and Celia started on their knitting."

"I'm good," Pris said, waving a skein of her gorgeous cashmere yarn. "All I need is a scarf pattern. An easy one."

"I've already got something in mind," Polly replied. "And for Celia . . ."

Polly pulled out a sheet of paper with a drawing of a color-blocked knitted blanket that looked like a puzzle, with sharp triangles of lemon yellow, dandelion, sapphire, eggshell blue, cream, and light gray, drawn with a colored pencil.

"What do you think?"

Before Polly arrived, I had made up my mind to tell her that I wanted to make a scarf too, something for myself. The chances of the birth mother choosing me were as slim as ever, and knitting something for Peaches just seemed too risky, like I might be tempting fate. But as soon as I saw the drawing, my resolve started to waver.

The colors were vibrant, fun, and cheerful, good for a boy or a girl. For all that I called her Peaches, I didn't actually know the baby's sex, so hedging my bets made sense. Plus, it was just so incredibly cute. The practical part of my brain said I should wait. The impractical part was racked by an overwhelming, instinctual urge to make something for the baby I hoped to have. Maybe that's what women mean when they talk about nesting.

I bit my lip, vacillating, looking for an out, but not very strenuously. "You don't think this would be too hard for a beginner?"

"No," Polly assured me. "It's all done in the garter stitch, which is as easy as it gets. You will have to do some decreases along the way and pick up stitches on the bias, but don't worry, I can teach you that. You got this, girl."

Bias? Pick up stitches? I had no clue what she was talking about but Polly sounded confident and the blanket was so, so cute.

"Where'd you get the pattern?"

"I designed it myself," Polly said, and then smiled. "Just for you."

Well, that clinched it. How could I say no?

I told Polly that I wanted to buy yarn from her, but she absolutely refused to sell me any. "You already have a ton of fingering-weight yarn on hand," she said. "This will help use it up. I created the design around colors you already have."

She had a point: I'd already inherited more yarn than I could use in a lifetime, enough so I could almost have opened a shop of my own, at least a small one. I would have been happy to buy a little more, just to help Polly out, but she wouldn't hear of it. And when I said I wanted to pay her for the pattern, she rolled her eyes, and demurred in that ever-so-genteel, ever-so-Polly fashion.

"Shut up. I am not taking your money."

"You put a lot of work into the design. Why can't you just—"

"Because it's a gift. I made it for you." Before I could launch into a counterargument, Polly planted her hands on her hips and cut me off. "Celia. Do you want to fight? Or do you want to knit?"

"Beginners usually start out knitting either way too loose or way too tight. Celia, you're falling into the way too tight category. Relax!" she commanded. "You look like you're wearing your shoulders for earrings. Try to loosen up."

I put the needles down, shook out my hands, and groaned. "My fingers keep cramping up."

"That's because you're holding the needles too tight. Hang on a sec." Polly leaned over me, pried my fingers from their death grip, and rearranged my yarn. "Don't clutch. Just let the yarn drape over and through your fingers. Relax!"

"I'm trying! You *said* this would be easy. Liar."

"Oh, quit whining. I never said it was easy, I just said it wasn't too hard for you. And it's not. You'll get the hang of it. Don't be so nervous, this part is just for practice, so you're knitting in the right gauge. We'll start the blanket next time. All I want you to do this week is cast on and knit a piece that's four inches square. Don't worry if you have to rip it out and do it over a few times. Practice makes progress."

"Practice makes progress," I muttered in a nasally and wholly inaccurate imitation of her voice, which was way more cigarette smoke and gravel than nasal and nag.

"I heard that!" Polly chirped.

As I sat there, grumbling and struggling, the knots in my shoulders were almost as tight as the stitches on my knitting needles. But after a few minutes of struggle, it occurred to me that knitting a blanket, or crafting anything by hand, was actually hard and that was what made it special. I hadn't expected that something as seemingly simple as knitting could stir up so many emotions or make me feel so connected to other women, and not just those in the room.

For generation upon generation, expectant mothers had chosen yarn, fabric, and thread, wielded needles and hooks, to create lovely things for children they hoped to have. Crafting was an act of faith as well as love. Sometimes those hopes were dashed. But they did it just the same, and now I was one of them. The thought was so big and so beautiful that I dipped my head low over my knitting and frowned, pretending I'd dropped a stitch, and quickly swiped away a tear.

It was a good night, unexpectedly good, and it got unexpectedly better. Just as we were wrapping up, I heard footsteps on the stairwell and looked up to see Happy standing in the doorway, looking tired but sober, and clutching a crumpled paper grocery bag.

"I . . . I hope it's okay that I let myself in," she said, and clutched the bag a little closer to her chest. "I was just wondering, is it too late to join you?"

AFTER EVERYBODY LEFT, I helped Polly repack the suitcase and carry it down the stairs to the front door. She'd made a few sales that night, so it was lighter, but not a lot lighter.

"Thank you for this," Polly said, bobbing her head and then pressing her lips together, as if she was afraid to say more.

"Are you kidding? All I did was make iced tea and open the door; you're the one who did the work. What are you thanking me for?"

"Because it was fun. And because you gave me a chance to do what I love. I'm still a good teacher. Even if I am a bad businesswoman." Polly paused, swallowed hard, and forced a smile. "I went over the books again this weekend and . . . It's just no use. I'm closing the store at the end of the month. July thirty-first will be my last day in business."

"Oh, Polly."

Sheepish was her dream. She'd put everything into making it come true—sweat, money, and hope. My heart broke for her.

"It's no big deal," she said, even as her smile became brittle. "Could have been worse. At least I had my shot, you know? At least I tried. Some people never do."

I blinked back tears. Polly's smile flattened to a line.

"Stop. Do not look at me like that." She pointed a finger directly at my nose. "Celia, if you make me cry, I swear I will never, *ever* forgive you. Do you hear me?"

"Oh. Polly."

I couldn't help myself. Neither could she. When I opened my arms, Polly fell forward and cried on my shoulder, and I cried with her. Sometimes, the only thing that makes life bearable is not having to bear it alone.

Chapter Thirty-Two

*H*ang on."

I lowered my end of the dresser back down to the floor, then bent down to put my hands on my knees and sucked in several big breaths.

"You okay?" Pris asked.

"Just gimme a second."

I took a couple more breaths and straightened up. "Lorne took Red and Slip to help move Teddy and left us here to get the room ready because he didn't think I'd be strong enough to lift furniture. So what are we doing?"

"Lifting furniture," Pris said at the same time that I did.

"This thing is *heavy*. Maybe we should just leave it here."

"In the middle of the room? That'd be an interesting design choice."

"You think?" I bent down to grab the bottom of the dresser. "Okay, let's do this. Ready? One. Two. Three."

"Use your knees!" Pris cautioned, just as a twinge in my back gave me the same reminder. I held my breath and shuffled across the floor, following Pris's lead, who was making this look annoyingly easy, until we reached the wall.

"Great. Looks good." At that point, I honestly didn't care how it looked, but I was the boss so I felt like I should be encouraging. "Now we just need to make the bed."

"Sit down and rest for a minute," Pris said. "I've got this."

I sank into a nearby chair, feeling bad about leaving the bed-making to Pris, but not bad enough to actually get up and help. "How's your mom doing?" I asked.

Pris grabbed the edge of a sheet and unfurled it with a snap of her wrist. The field of crisp white cotton hovered in the air for a moment before floating down onto the bed. "Better. We finally have something to talk about besides my wardrobe choices and career prospects. Guess what? She knows how to embroider but never told me. Yesterday, she showed me how to make French knots. I'm stitching a sunflower on the pocket of a jacket and want to use them for the middle part, you know, the seeds."

I nodded because, yes indeed, I understood about sunflowers and seeds. Pris jabbered on. She was in a very chatty mood.

"I never knew she'd kept all Dad's old dress shirts. After he died, she was preoccupied with the funeral, and the lawyers, and the estate, and then moving here, starting her business, and hardly ever talked about him. I thought maybe it was because she didn't love him, didn't really care. Now I'm wondering if it was because she cared too much."

Pris picked up a pillow and stuffed it in a case. Guilt overcame exhaustion, so I stood up and helped with the second pillow. "Some people find it really hard to let themselves be sad or grieve."

"I guess. It was a big deal, though, her coming over and joining the group. No idea what changed her mind but whatever it was, I'm glad."

"Did she decide what kind of quilt she's going to make from your dad's shirts?"

"Not yet," Pris said. "She's still thinking about patterns. But it's nice, you know? She has all the shirts out on the dining room table. Sometimes I walk past and see her just sitting there, looking through the pattern book, and smiling. She told me a story about one of the shirts, how they went to some party and she tripped and spilled red wine on his shirt, and instead of getting mad, Dad asked her to dance."

I fluffed the pillow and dropped it on the bed. "That's a great story."

"Dad was like that," Pris said. "Didn't sweat the little stuff. But he wasn't much of a businessman. Now that I'm older, I understand how much strain that put on Mom after he died. But I'm glad she's starting to remember that there was good stuff about him too. Anyway," she said, putting her arms to her sides, "I just want to thank you for making that happen."

"Happy's the one making it happen," I said, "and it's very brave of her."

"Well, thank you anyway. And listen, Celia." Her gaze flitted from mine. Her cheeks colored and she bit her lower lip. "About the other day, when she got so hammered and came over here. I'm really, really sorry about that."

"Don't be. It wasn't your fault."

"I know, but—"

I made a chopping motion with my hand, cutting her off mid-apology. "Pris, something I wish I'd learned a lot earlier in life is that it's not my job to ask forgiveness for other people's bad behavior. Did I ever tell you when I finally decided to divorce my husband?"

Pris shook her head as she stuffed a pillow into a case.

This was not a story I enjoyed relating but I felt like I had to, for Pris's sake. Sharing a personal story, even if it's embarrassing—and maybe especially if it's embarrassing—is sometimes the best way to make a lesson stick. There are lots of advice columns out there, but the reason so many people loved reading Dear Calpurnia was that she was willing to be vulnerable. Writing behind the veil of Calpurnia's persona was one thing, but being willing to open up like that in real life is a lot harder, and more uncomfortable. For Pris's sake, I would. She was my real-life friend. For friends, you go the extra mile, even at the risk of looking dumb.

"One day, Felix Glassman, the husband of yet another woman Steve was sleeping with, showed up on my doorstep with pictures of his wife and my husband. Basically, they were trying to reenact scenes from the *Kama Sutra*."

I made a retching sound that wasn't entirely for effect. Thinking about those photos still made my stomach churn. Pris hugged the pillow to her chest and looked appropriately horrified.

"That's awful. You must have been so humiliated."

I shrugged. "Actually, I was almost getting used to it by then. But I felt embarrassed and guilty and somehow responsible for all the pain and humiliation that Steve had caused poor Felix Glassman. So I started to apologize. But before I got very far, Mr. Glassman looked at me and said, 'I'm sorry, were *you* shtupping my wife?'

"Felix was right. An apology by proxy is meaningless. I couldn't make amends for something Steve did. The person who needed to be sorry was Steve, and he wasn't."

The doorbell rang. The lesson ended. Hopefully, it would stick.

"They're here!" Pris grabbed the duvet and quickly spread it out on top of the bed. Lorne's voice boomed up from the foyer, asking if anybody was home.

"We'll be right down!" I called.

I gave the pillows a final fluff and headed for the bedroom door, only to be met by the commotion of excited male voices, shouting something about bugs and pebbles, and the pounding of feet—more feet, as it turned out, than I had been expecting. Eight more, to be precise.

At the top of the stairs, I was greeted by a din of barking. Two dogs bounded up the staircase at something approaching Ludicrous Speed, coming straight for me. There wasn't time to get out of the way so I braced for impact.

It was no good.

Before my brain had time to really process what was happening, I was bowled over by an avalanche of jumping, writhing, wiggling, licking, joyfully barking puppy flesh. It wasn't frightening so much as disorienting, like finding myself thrown into a washing machine with a pack of huskies and put on spin cycle. There were, in fact, only two dogs and both were fairly small. But it felt like more at the time, a lot more.

"You okay there, Celia?"

I caught sight of Lorne's extended hand through the flurry of lolling tongues and fluffy ears and grabbed hold. He pulled me into a sitting position, extracting me from the dog pile. The pounding of size-thirteen feet on the stairway, a sound that would soon become familiar, announced Teddy's arrival on the scene.

"Bug! Pebbles! Why did you run off like that? I told you to wait so I could bring Cousin Celia down to meet you first. Bad dogs!"

The dogs, two spaniels with reddish-tan patches on white coats, sporting long ears with waves of curls, and black shoe-button noses, sat down on their furry behinds. Their tails thumped the floor slowly, tentatively, and in unison. Staring at Teddy with a mixture of guilt and confusion, their enormous chocolate-brown eyes said that they might be really, really, *really* sorry, if only they could figure out what they'd done wrong.

While I was lying at the bottom of the dog pile, blinded by fur and fending off sloppy advances, I'd thought they might be mastiffs or Saint Bernards or some other huge breed, golden retrievers at the least. But no. They were spaniels and petite ones at that. I'd met cats that were bigger.

"Bug," Teddy admonished, "tell Cousin Celia you're sorry. You too, Pebbles."

The larger of the two, Bug, whose protruding eyes earned him his name, scooted close to me with drooping, shamed shoulders and started to gently lick my hand in what I supposed was a doggish apology. His littermate, Pebbles, moved toward me too. I wiped my hand on my jeans and gave her a quick pat on the head before she could lick me too. "You really didn't need to do that," I told Bug. Lorne pulled me to my feet.

"I'm okay," I said, addressing everyone, including the dogs. Their tails thumped harder and quicker as if they actually understood they'd been forgiven. The smaller one, Pebbles, actually looked like she was smiling. Pris, who had been watching from the sidelines, crouched down and started scratching the dogs' ears, looking in their eyes and cooing. I wiped my hands on my pants again, wicking away the last traces of dog spit. Lorne, who seemed to be enjoying himself no end, cleared his throat.

"Well. Guess Red and I'll start unloading the truck."

"Right," Teddy said, making a move to follow. "I'll come help."

"Hang on a minute, Teddy," I said.

Lorne beat a hasty retreat and Teddy turned toward me. The expression on his face was almost as sheepish as the dogs' had been a moment before.

"So, Teddy. Bug and Pebbles: these are your dogs?"

"Uh-huh. Didn't I tell you about them?" I shook my head and he scratched his. "Gee. Guess I forgot."

I crossed my arms over my chest but said nothing.

Teddy sighed. "You're right; I didn't forget. I just didn't tell you."

"Teddy, if we're going to share a house, then we've got to be honest with each other, okay?"

"But I was afraid you wouldn't let me bring them," he said. "They didn't allow dogs at the group home, so I had to give them to Mr. Menzies, one of my old neighbors. When I told him that my cousin was going to let me live with her, in a real house with a garden and a fence, he said I could have them back. They're real good dogs," Teddy assured me. "Most of the time. They just got excited because we're so happy to be here. Do you like dogs?"

Teddy looked at me with a heartbreakingly hopeful expression. I considered my options.

"Absolutely. Love 'em."

"Me too!" Teddy whistled and the dogs swiveled toward him, eyes bright, ears perked. "Come on, guys. Let's go help unload the truck."

Teddy clomped back down the stairs and the dogs pranced after him, tails swishing like furry flags.

"Hey, Teddy?" He stopped in mid descent and turned toward me. "I'm really glad you're here."

That *wasn't* a lie. For all my worries about how inviting Teddy to move in might impact the adoption, worries that still hadn't completely dissipated, it felt right to have him there, like he'd always belonged. While helping him unpack later that afternoon, I realized how true that was.

"Teddy," I asked, after opening one especially large box, "what *is* all this?"

Teddy, who was busy shelving his considerable collection of CDs, glanced in my direction. "Sweaters."

I laughed. "Yeah, I can see that. But how many sweaters do you need? There must be fifty in here!"

Teddy shook his head and corrected me. "Only forty-seven. It's not all sweaters; there's some hats in there too, and a scarf."

"Okay," I said, still grinning. "But that still seems like a lot. Where did you get all these? Was your mother a knitter?"

"No," Teddy replied, as he unwrapped a speaker and put it on the shelf next to a very old-school CD player. "Momma sewed clothes. She didn't knit. But a box with a sweater and a note would show up every year on my birthday. Well, not this year," he said, pausing and looking a little puzzled by this, before going on. "But I don't know where they came from."

"A note? From who?"

"Don't know." Teddy shrugged. "Said the same thing every year—'Happy Birthday, Dear Teddy. Sending you some sugar.' That's all. Here," he said, then walked over to the box, reached into the neck of the topmost sweater, and pulled out a note that had been written on a typewriter, an Olivetti typewriter with a wonky *y*:

Sending *y*ou some sugar . . .

Suddenly I understood. The yarn cave wasn't my grandmother's. It belonged to Calpurnia. Perhaps the idea had started with Beebee. Perhaps, after Calpurnia gave up the baby and returned home, Beebee had taught her depressed daughter to knit, offering her an outlet for her grief and a way to stay in contact with her son. Or perhaps she'd taught herself? Maybe that was why, though no one else in the family ever locked their bedroom doors, Calpurnia sometimes did. Maybe she was locked in with her memories and secrets, knitting something special for Teddy. Maybe, when Sterling moved out and took me with him, and she was left all alone, she had created a small haven of sanity for herself in the midst of madness.

So many maybes.

When it came to Teddy, there were so many questions that would go unanswered, but one thing was sure: Calpurnia had never forgotten her son, never stopped loving him. Later, when the time was right, I would explain it to Teddy. There was no need for secrets now and I was sure that knowing the truth, knowing that she had always cared, would make him happy.

But I couldn't speak of it just yet. Instead, I placed some of the sweaters carefully in the bottom drawer of Teddy's dresser and made a silent promise to myself and my aunt: no matter what happened, I would always love Teddy. Just like Calpurnia had.

Chapter Thirty-Three

I woke up to find myself clinging to the edge of the mattress like a mountain climber taking refuge on the ledge of a treacherous crevasse. Another inch and I'd have plummeted into the void.

"How can a fourteen-pound dog take up eighty percent of a queen-sized bed?" I scooted backward, pushing my backside against the warm, seemingly immovable lump that lay behind me until I gained enough space to turn over. Pebbles opened one eye and thumped her tail, then uncurled her body and got to her feet, yawning and stretching briefly before moving toward the pillow to lick my nose.

"I'm serious: you really don't have to do that." How many times did I have to tell her?

For reasons that were unclear to me, Pebbles had decided that my bed was the place she absolutely *had* to sleep every night. And for reasons that were even less clear to me, I allowed it. But what else could I do? She was so desperately cute.

Cuteness, I had concluded, was a dog's natural protection. Like camouflage for lizards or venom for snakes, irresistible cuteness was what dogs used to keep dangerous predators, such as irritated humans, from killing them.

I raised my arms over my head and stretched, feeling a satisfying ache in my shoulder blades. Pris and I had cleared the last of the boxes downstairs the day before, including two that had been filled with old cast-iron cookware. Most were so pitted or cracked that they weren't good for anything but the dumpster, but a few were in good condition. After some online research, Pris said she thought they'd bring in somewhere between one hundred fifty and two hundred dollars. That was good news, as was the fact that those skillets were the last pieces of merchandise to be salvaged from Calpurnia's hoard. Yes, I'd probably held on to more than was strictly sensible—Marie Kondo wouldn't have given me a gold star—but the house was habitable at last and the hoard was gone. Later that afternoon, the dumpster would be gone too. We'd have a smaller one to accommodate debris from the ongoing construction, but the big behemoth that had been filled and emptied and refilled countless times in the previous six weeks would be gone by lunchtime, which meant we could finally start working on the garden. Teddy was eager to begin.

I sat up in bed. Pebbles took this as a sign that the day had commenced, which could only mean that Exciting Things were about to happen, like Breakfast and a Morning Wee. She started bouncing and wriggling with an enthusiasm that was disproportionate and slightly alarming. Pebbles was full-grown and house-trained, I knew that, but all that bouncing and wriggling made me worry that she might take her Morning Wee a little early. I climbed out of bed and scooped up the pup, tucking her under my left arm.

"Teddy, are you up?"

His voice boomed through the stairwell from the ground floor. "Uh-huh. I'm supposed to open this morning."

I walked to the banister and looked over the edge. Teddy was standing there, wearing his Bitty and Beau's uniform. Bug was standing at his feet, gazing up at Teddy's face with obvious adoration.

"Made some cinnamon toast," he said. "You want some?"

"Maybe later, thanks. Could you take Pebbles out before you leave? I think she needs to go."

"Sure thing."

I walked to the top of the staircase and put Pebbles down. Teddy whistled and patted his leg. The dog flung herself from the landing, bounded down the stairs, then leapt into the air and Teddy's outstretched arms.

Jumping into people's arms was Pebbles's party trick. She did it all the time, often with no warning. It was kind of impressive, but only if the human she flung herself at understood their role in the performance. The first time she tried it with me, I was unprepared. Rather than open my arms to catch her, I put them in front of my face to shield myself from the incoming furry projectile. Pebbles bounced off my chest and onto the floor, where she looked up at me with a mixture of disappointment and disgust. I felt so bad about it that I gave her half my scrambled eggs at breakfast.

That was two weeks ago. Teddy had settled in now and so had the dogs. We were used to each other, so much so that I sometimes wondered how I'd ever lived here alone. It was a big house, meant to be filled with family. Now, once again, it was.

"My shift ends at one," Teddy reported. "You sure they're taking the dumpster away today? I want to start cutting back some of those hedges."

"Should be gone by the time you get home. That's what Lorne said."

"Good," Teddy said. "If we're going to have a baby, we need a garden."

I kept telling Teddy not to get his hopes up, that there were three families who wanted this baby, but he was excited about being an uncle. Sensible caution aside, I couldn't help but smile when he referred to Peaches as "our" baby.

Teddy grabbed two leashes from the entry table and opened the door. I told him good-bye and turned back toward my room to get dressed.

"Hey," he said, looking up at me, "what are you going to do today?"

"You mean after I get dressed and eat a piece of cinnamon toast?"

"Uh-huh."

I shook my head. "Absolutely no idea."

KNOWING THAT THE kitchen was next on the renovation schedule and that I might not have access to the stove for much longer, I skipped the cinnamon toast and made myself a cheese omelet, trying to ignore the pleading eyes of the two dogs who sat hopefully at my feet while I cooked.

"The scrambled eggs were a guilt offering," I told Pebbles. "It's not something that's going to happen on a regular basis."

Pebbles blinked pathetically. I took a pinch of shredded cheddar from the bowl and tossed it to the floor, then repeated the procedure so Bug could get a bite. They inhaled the cheese, then sat down sweetly, blinking again. "That's *all*," I said, pointing my spatula toward each dog in turn. "I'm serious this time."

"You sure? Smells pretty good." Lorne came into the kitchen and headed toward the coffeepot. By this time, we were all used to each other. Lorne and the rest of the crew wandered in and out at will, popping in for coffee or a snack, or just to say hello. I liked that. The house made more sense with more people.

"Hey, Lorne. I can make you some breakfast if you want. I want to use up the eggs before you and the guys start tearing my kitchen apart."

"Nope, I'm good. Just need a warmup." He poured coffee into a green thermal mug. "And to tell you that, unfortunately, I won't be able to tear up your kitchen today. There has been a delay." He lifted the mug to his lips, giving me a meaningful look over the rim of the cup. I felt my jaw set.

"Let me guess, Mr. Fitzwaller paid us a visit. What is it this time?"

"He doesn't think the plan for the kitchen remodel meets code."

"Of *course* it meets code!" I shouted, tossing my hands in the air to express my disgust. Bug sat up straighter and licked his chops, hoping more cheese was forthcoming. "The people at the building department already approved it!"

"Yes, indeed," Lorne said, sarcasm made clear by his exaggeratedly polite tone. "And I pointed that out to young Fitzwaller. However, he is of the opinion that they were wrong and insists the plan go back for a second review. Until it does and is approved—again—I can't get to work in here." Lorne made a growling noise as he slurped his coffee.

"I know we were joking about seeing if Slip knew anybody who could cure our inspector problem, but I'm starting to think it might not be such a bad idea. Just kidding," he said, holding up a hand. "But seriously, Celia, this guy is way more trouble than he's worth. He's costing me time and you money."

Both were important, money as well as time. The home visit was less than a month away, but the money part was an even more immediate concern.

"What now?"

"After all the fuss about the electrical panel, Fitzwaller has decided that the new one isn't sufficient to carry the load. He says we have to install a subpanel." Lorne hooked his thumb into his belt loop and shook his head. "Was there some kind of ancient feud between the Fitzwallers and the Fairchilds? Because I'll tell you, Celia, I have never come up against a guy like this."

I turned the flame off on the burner and took the pan from the stove. I wasn't hungry anymore. "What's a subpanel going to cost? And how long will it take to install?"

"Don't know," Lorne said. "I put a call in to Tony. It won't be as much as the big panel but, Celia, we don't need it! The new panel is plenty big. I swear, Fitzwaller is deliberately jerking us around and I don't know why."

"Well, should we lodge a complaint? Take it up with the city?"

Lorne sighed. "Up until now, I didn't want to make waves: that kind of thing can backfire on you. But . . ." He paused to think it over. "I think we have to. I don't know what else to do."

"Maybe you could call Trey?" I suggested. "Ask him for help?" But when Lorne broke my gaze, I knew that the task would fall to me.

I hadn't *exactly* been avoiding Trey since that day in the restaurant; we'd talked on the phone a couple of times. But I'd made sure to keep the conversations short, businesslike, and to the point, and resolved to avoid face-to-face meetings with him unless absolutely necessary. I had good reason.

In the two months and then some since I'd returned to Charleston, I'd seen Trey Holcomb, what—seven? Maybe eight times?

And yet, on two of those occasions, for reasons beyond understanding, I had opened my mouth and impulsively spewed out extensive details of my private life, including the strange story of my strange family that I'd never told *anyone* else. What was it about Trey? Why did my social veneer disappear in his presence?

That was embarrassing enough, even a little humiliating. But the thing that truly bothered me was that Trey never returned the favor, never offered up a hostage of his own, not even after I'd freely and openly handed over mine, and more than once. When Calvin first explained the principles of the whole trading hostages thing to me, he said that exchanging hopes, secrets, fears, and failings, things you wouldn't have wanted to share with the world at large, was a way to get to know someone very well, very quickly. But as I now understood, it was also a way to grow a relationship, to develop trust. Love and trust go hand in hand. As I'd learned too well from Steve and the long line of heartbreakers who had come before him, you can't have one without the other.

For all that was good about him—intelligence, competence, devotion to justice, and amazing eyes—Trey Holcomb obviously had trust issues. Even if I hadn't already picked up on that during our exchanges, or lack thereof, and taken note that he refused to talk about his own past even after I'd told him everything about mine, not even when I'd pressed him, the fact that his own brother didn't even feel comfortable calling to ask for his help was a huge red flag. I liked Trey, a lot. In the right circumstances, I was certain we could be friends, maybe even more than friends. But the circumstances weren't right and, for once in my life, I had resolved to take my own good advice and avoid seeing or talking to him unless I absolutely had to.

Now I did have to. We needed help.

"It's okay, Lorne. I can call him."

"Thanks, Celia," he said, looking relieved. "I'd do it myself but, you know how it is, Trey and me . . ." He looked away, poured a little more coffee into a mug that was still fairly full, and changed the subject. "We'll get started on the dining room drywall today. I planned on doing it all at once, after the kitchen, but I don't want the guys just standing around. Don't worry, Celia. We'll get it done, one way or another."

"I know you will. Thanks, Lorne."

He touched his fingers to his forehead, gave me a little salute, and picked up his coffee mug. "Well, I'll get back to it. What are you up to today?"

THE ANSWER, AS it turned out, was a whole lot of worrying.

The afternoon before, Pris and I had grabbed the handle of a rusty, cracked, and incredibly heavy cast-iron Dutch oven, the last item from the last box of junk, counted off one-two-three, swung it over the side of the dumpster, and then smacked our hands in double high fives before going into the house to celebrate with White Claw seltzers and red velvet cupcakes from Sweet Lulu's Bakery. We were almost giddy with joy. I told Pris to take the next day off with pay as a reward. The house was transformed. But transformation, as any used-to-be advice columnist can tell you, is a process.

We'd done so much—replaced the roof, and the exterior steps (several times), and the rotted columns on the piazza; rebuilt the chimney; and rewired the entire house. But there was still so much left to do. It was the unexpected stuff that really made me anxious, the stuff you couldn't plan for. Hardly a day had passed when Lorne hadn't called out, "Hey, Celia. Can you come here a sec? There's something I need to show you."

The thing was never something you'd *want* to see, a hilarious meme or adorable cat video. No, it was always something rotted or broken or incorrectly installed, which was going to mean more delays and more money. Now when Lorne called out, "Can you come here a sec?" I called back, "Now what?"

Dealing with Brett Fitzwaller's whims and overly zealous interpretation of the building code only made it harder. I did call Trey right away and he said he'd look into it, but there wasn't much more I could do. And *that*, I realized sometime during my fourth lap through the house, was the thing that made me so nervous.

Lorne looked away from the sheet of drywall he was hammering and said, "Is there something I can *do* for you, Celia?"

I took the hint and went upstairs. Pacing through the bedrooms wasn't helping either. I needed something to *do*. Finally, I went to the yarn cave and got my knitting out of the basket.

We'd only had two more crafting sessions since that first gathering. I'd had so much fun talking with the others and checking out their projects that I hadn't finished more than a couple of inches on mine. For me, talking while knitting was a lot like trying to rub my stomach and pat my head: I couldn't do both at once. Knitting required my complete attention.

That turned out to be a good thing.

I sat down in Beebee's squashy old pink chair, stuck my tongue out the side of my mouth and my needle into the first stitch of the next row, and started to knit, slowly, pausing every couple of minutes to take a deep breath and consciously drop my shoulders so my stitches didn't get too tight. It wasn't relaxing but it *was* absorbing. Pretty soon, I forgot about the money and the *now what*s and the *what if*s. I gave all my attention and mental energy to sliding the needle through the back of the stitch, wrapping the yarn around the tip and pulling it through the loop, then sliding it from the left needle to the right.

After about fifteen minutes, my tongue slid back into my mouth of its own accord. After twenty, I was able to keep my shoulders down and my stitches loose without the breathing breaks. Half an hour in, muscle memory took over and my fingers found their rhythm. I didn't have to think about it anymore, didn't have to repeat the steps in my mind, which meant my mind was free to wander, and remember.

Something about seeing those two inches of knitting grow to four, then six, then eight, helped remind me of all that had happened in the last month and a half, the seemingly insurmountable obstacles I'd faced and, surprisingly, overcome, one by one by one. I don't recall having many truly meaningful conversations with my mother, but now I remembered something she often said. "If God wants you to be somewhere or do something, He'll supply everything you need at the moment you need it, and not one moment before. Never forget, Celia, God is in the business of Just-in-Time Inventory."

I hadn't thought about that in a long time. I hadn't thought about God in a long time either. We weren't really on speaking terms anymore. Though he remained a member of the congregation until he died, Sterling and I stopped going to St. Philip's after the kidnapping. Sterling didn't want to risk running into Calpurnia, and after everything that had happened, I didn't feel like running into God. But as I sat there, knitting and thinking and remembering, I could just about believe that Somebody was trying to send me a message, if only to tell me that my mother had been right. Every time I thought I'd reached the end of my rope, I'd reached out in desperation and found just one more handhold.

When my marriage ended, the door to motherhood opened. When I lost my courage, hope, or sense of humor, Calvin renewed them. When I lost my job and livelihood, suddenly there was a house and Trey, a champion to fight my battles and keep the wolf from the door. It was all there when I needed it, but not a moment before. And it wasn't always about me. So often, the solution to problems I'd never foreseen came in the form of people who needed me just as much as I needed them.

I desperately needed a contractor and suddenly, there was Lorne, who desperately needed a second chance. I longed for a family connection and along came Teddy, who needed the exact same thing. I needed friends, practical help, encouragement, and a sense of belonging, and there was Felicia, Pris, Caroline, Polly, and even Happy, each of whom came with her own set of needs and gaps that the rest of us helped to fill, each in our own way.

I'd never really had women friends before, not close ones. I'd had acquaintances and colleagues but not real girlfriends. Calvin was my best friend and always would be, but I had never had a wide circle of female friends. I hadn't known I needed them. Now, only a month after that first dinner, I couldn't imagine my life without these women. Did they feel the same? I thought so. I hoped so.

Ostensibly, we were getting together to make stuff, but what we were really creating was a safe space, a space where we could be real with each other. When I say it like that, it sounds like some big touchy-feely group therapy session, but it was different from that, easier and more organic. We weren't *trying* to be known or heard or understood; we just were.

The Sunday before, Teddy had invited me to go to church with him. It wasn't like anything I'd ever experienced before, much different from the quiet, orderly services I'd attended as a child at St. Philip's, with everyone murmuring prewritten prayers in unison. Everyone seemed so excited to be there. Whenever someone new came through the door, the faces of those who'd entered previously lit up with joyous recognition, and they gathered around the newcomer for greetings, embraces, and backslaps, as if seven months had passed since their last meeting instead of only seven days, and Sunday was the day they looked forward to all week long. The service was the definition of spontaneous. Whenever anyone, whether pastor or parishioner, shared some insight or observation, be it large or small, the congregation would nod, murmur, or amen, or sometimes just lift a hand, as if to be counted present. It took a little getting used to but I liked the feeling that they were simply there for one another, listening with empathy, affirming with compassion, wholly available to the moment and each another.

That was how I felt about my new friends. We were really still getting to know each other, but the more I did know, the more I wanted to know. Monday was now my favorite day of the week. Was Someone trying to tell me something? It seemed possible. At least so far.

But . . . what now? What next? What if?

I picked up another ball of yarn, looped it around the needle, changing the color from sapphire to dandelion. There was only this moment, this day, this room, this stitch, these thoughts. I worked there in silence, looping the yarn and pulling it through again, and again, and again, adding inch after inch to the blanket meant to wrap the child my heart was so ready to love.

Calm fell over me like a soft mist and I tied a mental knot in my memory, to remind myself about just-in-time inventory and the futility of worry and the seemingly contradictory truth that sometimes the freedom to be yourself can only be found by tethering yourself to others.

I needed to write it all down, for Peaches. Someday she would need to know what it had taken me so long to learn.

Chapter Thirty-Four

*O*h, look! Another pot holder! Just what I needed." Polly lifted my offering from the wrapping paper and held it aloft so the others could see before putting it down on her lap and wiping tears from both eyes.

"You people are ridiculous."

Today was Polly's last day in business. Happy had suggested we move the weekly crafting get-together from my house to Sheepish so everyone could help pack what was left of Polly's considerable inventory. After a little resistance, Polly gratefully accepted our help. She didn't know that we'd decided to turn the packing party into a surprise party.

Pris and I had done a little sleuthing, identified ten of Polly's most loyal customers, and invited them to the party. When Polly looked up from the register a few minutes before she was due to lock the shop door for the last time and saw fifteen friends parading through the door, toting platters of food and presents, she burst into tears. They were a good kind of tears, the tears that come from soldiering on for a long time and suddenly realizing you're not alone. But the tears she shed while opening the gifts were the *best* kind, the kind that underscore the uncontrollable laughter that bubbles out when people you like *get* you so thoroughly.

"Let me guess," she said, as she swiped her eyes and pointed to the remaining pile of wrapped gifts, *"all* pot holders?"

Yep. All pot holders.

Quilted pot holders, knitted pot holders, crocheted pot holders, and even one with little lazy daisies and vines and a lopsided bumble bee, embroidered by Pris. As time was short and some of us were still crafting novices, pot holders were the only thing I could think of that could be finished before the party. Polly might not have been a financial genius, but as a craft teacher, she was a huge success. Hopefully, receiving handmade gifts from her students and friends would remind her of that.

"Well, I love them *all,*" Polly declared after opening the last one. "Now if only I knew how to cook."

"I can teach you." Vera, whose pink, green, and white quilted pot holder was an intricately folded pineapple block, and who had brought an insanely delicious hot artichoke-and-collard cheese dip, waved her hand. "Come on over anytime, Polly. I'll teach you everything I know about southern cooking."

"Sounds good," Polly said. "But I think having a real job is going to cut into my playtime."

"You found a job already?" Drucie, whose white pot holder knitted with a blue teacup and green saucer made my purple stockinette-stitched pot holder look sad by comparison, filled a cup with punch and brought it to Polly. "Doing what?"

"Property manager for an apartment complex in North Charleston," Polly said. "I'll collect rent, keep track of maintenance orders, and show property. The pay isn't amazing but it comes with a free two-bedroom apartment. I'm going to sleep on a pullout sofa in the living room and use the bedrooms to store the inventory until I can figure out what to do with it. Hopefully, it'll all fit," Polly said, casting a doubtful glance around the overcrowded shop.

"Sounds like a good opportunity," Drucie said. "Have you ever done anything like that before?"

Polly sipped her punch and shook her head. "Not even close. But they needed somebody right away, so when I said I could start Monday, they offered me the job. Speaking of which . . ." Polly put down her cup, slapped her hands on her thighs, and got to her feet. "I've got to turn in the keys to the shop on Sunday before starting work on Monday. Anybody feel like packing a box?"

"Way ahead of you." Pris entered the room, carrying an armful of flattened cardboard containers out of the back room and then going around the circle, passing out boxes, packing tape, and slips of paper to each guest.

"Here's the drill," she said. "If everybody packs at least five boxes before they go home tonight, it'll be a huge help. It's a tight space so try to stay within the area I've listed on your assignment cards. For example, Caroline, you're going to pack all the quilting pattern books from M to Z, listed by author, and all the crochet books."

Caroline clapped her hands together. "Perfect!"

"*No* reading," Pris cautioned, stabbing a finger in Caroline's direction and then waving it from left to right to make it clear she was talking to everyone. "Just packing. Otherwise we'll never get out of here."

Caroline leaned over and whispered into Happy's ear. "What was her major again? World Domination?"

"With a minor in Intimidation," Happy muttered. "I fully expect her to be named dictator of a medium-sized country before she's thirty."

I snarfed out a laugh, unable to keep from snorting. Caroline dug an elbow into my ribs.

"Did you have a question?" Pris was staring at me, her arms crossed over her chest.

"No, ma'am." I pressed my lips together to stifle another laugh. Pris shot me a "don't make me separate you" glance before continuing to outline the guidelines.

"When you've finished packing, taping, and clearly labeling your box with the black marker I gave you, raise your hand over your head." She lifted her arm high to demonstrate. "I'll carry your box to the staging area by the front door."

Darling Pris. She was like the bossy baby sister I'd never had. Sometimes I felt like smacking her in the head to remind her who was in charge, but I loved her anyway. Without Pris, I might never have finished sorting through Calpurnia's hoard. Or if I had, it wouldn't have been nearly as much fun.

Pris finished her instructions. I went to my battle station, carrying my box to a display rack of crafting needles near the front of the shop. According to the instructions which Pris had emphasized with italics and underlines, when packing I should take care *not to mix knitting needles with crochet needles!* The exclamation point was possibly a little overdone but still . . . good to know.

Polly, who was supposed to be boxing up all the alpaca yarn, snuck over when Pris wasn't looking and sat down next to me on the floor. "Hey, Celia," she said, leaning closer. "Is Pris still working for you? Because if she's done, I was thinking about asking her to do some work for me. She seems pretty organized, and I could use some help dealing with this mess."

"Definitely talk to her," I said. "The clean out is done, so she's not doing much for me anymore. She's a hard worker and super smart. I bet you she'll have ideas about how to help you liquidate some of this inventory."

"That would be great," Polly said, looking around at the quickly growing piles of boxes. "It's so incredible of everybody to pitch in and help but . . . I'm feeling kind of overwhelmed. What am I going to do with all this?"

I smiled. "Well, I wasn't going to tell you this until later, but I've asked Lorne to come over here on Friday to move all the boxes and display units over to your new apartment. Teddy's got the day off, so he's going to help too."

"Celia . . ." Polly's lips flattened into a line. "I can't let you do that."

"The guys will be doing the heavy lifting. My only job is to supply the pizza."

"No," Polly said, giving her head a hard shake, like a golden retriever coming up out of a stream. "I'll buy the pizza. It's the least I can do."

I shot her a look. "Do you know how much pizza those guys can *eat*? Teddy can polish off two large pepperonis all by himself." Polly didn't smile. I dropped my teasing tone and locked my eyes onto hers. "Let me help. I want to."

Polly looked down at her lap. I leaned closer, until my hair fell forward, veiling my face, and our foreheads were practically touching. The room, the boxes, the hum of voices melted into the background. For a moment it was just me and Polly, trading confidences like nine-year-old girls telling stories in a blanket fort after curfew.

"Oh, Celia," she whispered. "I feel like such a failure."

"You're *not* a failure," I said. "It was a bad location, that's all. Starting your own business from scratch is really tough. I read an article somewhere that most successful entrepreneurs have at least three businesses failures in their past."

"Really? Is that true?"

Was it? I couldn't honestly remember reading any such article but it sounded like it ought to be true, and Polly looked miserable, so I just nodded my head. "Look at all you've learned," I reminded her. "That won't be wasted. You'll do better next time."

"Next time?" Polly let out a derisive little laugh. "Don't think so. The biggest lesson I've learned is that I've learned my lesson: self-employment is not for me. Do you know when my last day off was?"

"The day before you opened the shop?"

"Bingo," Polly replied. "Celia, those men should be working on your house, not helping me move. Why should this be your problem? I'm glad we're friends again, but until last month, we hadn't spoken for twenty years."

I tilted my head to one side and pushed my hair away from my eyes. I wanted to see her eyes. "And that was a terrible mistake. I should never have let it happen."

"Neither should I," Polly said.

"Good." I smiled. "Now that we've cleared that up, let's start making up for lost time."

Chapter Thirty-Five

My jeans already looked like a Jackson Pollock painting, so when Calvin's name popped up on my cell phone screen, I just swiped my hands on my pant legs, leaving peachy-tangerine streaks on the denim canvas, and took the call.

"Hey! Haven't talked to you for days. I was starting to think you'd fallen into a black hole."

"More like a stand mixer." Calvin yawned. "Pulled my first all-nighter since college but *The Ultimate Encyclopedia of Baking* is finally a wrap. And only a month past the deadline."

"Calvin, that's awesome! Congratulations. You must feel really proud."

"I swear, Celia, I thought the zuger kirschtorte would be the death of me. Maybe I'll feel proud later, after I sleep a week or two. Right now, I'm just relieved. How're things with you, gum-drop?"

I set my brush down on the edge of the paint can and took a seat on the floor, crossing my legs. "Frazzled. Three days until the home visit and it feels like I've already painted a mile-wide path to the moon and back. I really miss Pris. And there's still so much to do. But Polly has the day off, so she's coming over to help in the afternoon."

"What about Teddy? Can't he help?"

"Have you ever tried to paint with two dogs underfoot? Besides, he's busy with the garden. The planters have been weeded, the hedges hacked into submission, and the trees are in the process of being pruned. It's starting to look like a proper Charleston garden. All we need now are flowers. Teddy said he'll plant some annuals after his shift on Saturday."

"The more I get to know Teddy, the more I like him."

"Me too. This house makes more sense when there are people in it. And dogs," I said.

"I thought you said dogs were invasive."

"I know, but they're also kind of cute. Pebbles invented this game where she takes the edge of the toilet paper into her teeth, then unrolls it to see how far she can go before it tears. On Tuesday she got it all the way to the front door."

"Adorable. Had you considered closing the bathroom door?"

Calvin has never been a dog person. I understood. Up until recently, neither was I. But there are dogs and then there are dogs . . .

"Don't be a grump. Wait until I tell you what Bug—"

"Uh . . . Celia? Do you have a sec?"

I twisted my neck and rolled onto my side. Lorne was standing in the doorway with a look on his face that I'd seen before; it never spelled good news. When I sat up and looked out the window, I saw Brett Fitzwaller climb into his car and drive off. He never spelled good news either.

"Calvin? Let me call you back later." I ended the call. "How bad is it?" I asked.

"Bad." Lorne pulled a sheet of yellow carbon paper out of his pocket and started reading. "The electrical outlet in the powder room is five inches too close to the faucet. The dryer vent is six inches too long. He wants two smoke alarms in the attic instead of one and an additional alarm in the foyer. And," he said, letting his hand and the yellow sheet flop to his side, "he says the openings between the second-floor railings are three-sixteenths of an inch too wide."

"Are they?"

"Not by my ruler. Our inspector makes his calculations according to the Brettric system, measurements calibrated on the level of misery that he wishes to inflict on any given day." Lorne shook his head in disgust. "Have you heard anything back from Trey?"

"He wrote a complaint to the head of the building department but hasn't heard anything so far." I ran my fingers through my hair, trying to process what Lorne had just told me and figure out how to deal with it. "Look, let's just focus on finishing the paint and tilework now and wait until after the home visit to deal with the railing. I doubt that Anne Dowling is going to notice three-sixteenths of an inch one way or the other, but a floor with no tile is pretty obvious. If the cosmetics are good, she probably won't notice the rest. And if she does, we'll say it's a work in progress."

"Yeah." Lorne paused and made a sucking sound with his teeth. "But there's more. Red and Slip tried to buy some weed from an undercover cop. So they're back in jail. And it gets worse." Worse than having no crew? Lorne gave me a pained look. "The windows aren't up to code."

I blinked in disbelief. "How is that possible? We didn't replace any windows. They've been there for over one hundred years."

"Exactly!" Lorne chopped the air with his hand. "These windows should be grandfathered in! Fitzwaller never said a word about the windows before. But today, out of the blue, he says that every single bedroom window has to open and to be big enough to climb through."

I knew Lorne was just the messenger but I started arguing with him anyway, throwing my hands out in exasperation, saying how insane and unfair it was to just spring this on us at the last minute. I probably would have said a lot more than that, some of it pretty colorful, but he interrupted me with news that was, astonishingly, even worse than what he'd already told me.

"He says you have to move out."

"What! You can't be serious."

Lorne nodded to let me know he was. "Fitzwaller said he's revoking the occupancy permit until all the bedroom windows are replaced."

"But . . ." I threw out my hands again. "Half the houses on this block don't have bedroom windows that open. Is he going to evict everybody?"

"If they have to get a building permit, he just might," Lorne said grimly. "Oh, and he posted a placard on the front door, saying that the house doesn't meet the fire code."

"He can't do that!" I cried. "Anne Dowling is coming for the home visit on Monday. She's never going to recommend giving a baby to a family that's living in a firetrap!" I started pacing the room. "Well, this is just . . . This is just . . ."

"Crazy," Lorne said. "I know."

I stopped pacing. "How long would it take to replace the windows?"

"By myself? Every minute of the next three days and probably more. The bigger problem is even getting them. Could take a couple of weeks for an order to come in."

"We don't *have* a couple of weeks. Anne Dowling is coming on

Monday," I said. "Her visit is the whole reason we're doing this. Did you tell Brett that?"

"About fifty times. I pleaded with him, Celia. I'd have offered him a bribe if I thought it would do any good, but this guy . . ." He shook his head and puffed his disgust. "There's no way I can get it done before Monday, not without my crew."

The doorbell rang. I hollered for whoever it was to come in. Polly appeared a moment later, wearing beat-up tennis shoes, cargo pants with a rip in one knee, a black T-shirt that said "Crafting is cheaper than therapy," and a blue bandana over her hair.

"My painting outfit," she said, spreading out her hands and turning around in a circle. "*Très chic*, yes?"

"Very," I said, without really looking at her.

Polly frowned. "What's up? You look like you just had a visit from the IRS."

"Brett Fitzwaller," I said. "It's basically the same thing."

Polly tilted her head to one side. "You know Brett Fitzwaller?"

"Unfortunately, yes. He's our building inspector."

"Skinny, mid-twenties, bad skin, bad hair, bad attitude Brett Fitzwaller?" Polly asked.

"That's him. The universe couldn't be cruel enough to have made two," I said. "How do you know him?"

"He's one of my tenants and a real pain," Polly replied, twisting her lips in disgust. "Always parking in other people's spots. Leaves his trash bags on the ground next to the dumpster but never actually puts them inside. Plays his music loud at all hours. Last week I got a call from one of his neighbors at two a.m., wanting me to do something about the noise. I'd evict him if I could, but"—she shrugged—"there's nothing I can do. His uncle owns the building and signs my paychecks.

"Who's his uncle?"

"Cabot James."

The hair stood up on my arms. "Hang on. Brett Fitzwaller is Cabot James's nephew?"

"Uh-huh. He's a big developer," Polly said. "Owns my complex and a whole bunch of other properties in Charleston. Do you know him?"

I didn't answer her, just looked at Lorne.

"We need to call your brother," I said. "Right now."

"I CHECKED IT out and you're right," Trey said. "Brett Fitzwaller is definitely Cabot James's nephew. He was hired as a building inspector very recently and with very little experience in the field. He worked for Cabot Corporation for about nine months but that's it. Before that he was taking classes for a construction electrician certificate but he only finished one semester."

"Wow," I said. "I called you, what? Maybe half an hour ago? And you already found out all this? You're an amazing researcher."

"I read his Facebook page," Trey said.

"Oh. But how can they hire somebody to be a building inspector if they don't have any experience? Isn't there a certification process or something?"

"Yes, but Fitzwaller might have been offered the job on the condition that he had to pass his certification within a year. The same thing happens with law students. Firms hire recent graduates anticipating that they'll pass the bar later. What's strange is that they'd have him doing inspections by himself right away. Normally they'd pair him up with an experienced inspector for a few months."

"So there is something fishy going on here."

"Not necessarily," Trey cautioned. "If they were short-staffed, they might have handed him a clipboard and turned him loose.

It's not inconceivable during a building boom. But the really interesting thing about all this is the timing. Fitzwaller took the job only a week after you say you turned down Cabot's offer and he threatened you."

"I'm not *saying* anything," I said, a little annoyed that Trey always insisted on acting like a lawyer. Whose side was he on? "I rejected Cabot's offer to buy the house, then he got furious and threatened me, said that I didn't know who I was up against and that I'd be sorry. I'm not making this up, Trey. It *happened*."

"I believe you," Trey said. "But were there any witnesses? Did anybody else hear your conversation?"

I pressed my lips together and closed my eyes, picturing the coffee shop, trying to remember where we'd been sitting that day and if anyone had been sitting nearby. My eyes flew open.

"Teddy!" I cried. "This was back before I knew that we were related but Teddy was working that day. He must have heard us; Cabot got really loud at the end. He's at work right now but I'll ask him about it as soon as he gets home."

"Good. There's more work to do, but if Teddy remembers Cabot threatening you, I think we could make a pretty convincing case for conflict of interest."

"Great!"

"Not that great. It'll take weeks and probably more like months before we could get any kind of a ruling. And by then—"

"Anne Dowling will have come and gone and decided that Peaches will be better off with somebody else."

I closed my eyes and rubbed at the pounding in my forehead. I had worked so long and battled so hard to get to this moment. I'd fought against the sense of worthlessness that clung to me in the wake of my failed marriage and powerlessness in the face of nefarious plans of a greedy man who robbed me of my livelihood and sense of self. I'd fought grief, loneliness, displacement as well as a score of smaller, more common skirmishes—shortages of money, time, confidence, and courage. I'd fought all that and more, in hopes of having a chance at happiness. I'd risked everything on my chance. And lost.

"Well. I guess that's—" I was trying to say that was that, to throw in the towel and admit defeat, but I couldn't get the words out. Not without crying. And what good was that going to do?

"Celia? You still there?"

I coughed to clear the tears from the back of my throat, then swallowed hard. "Yes. Still here."

"Is Lorne with you?"

I glanced toward Lorne, who had been standing in the doorway with his arms crossed over his chest, listening in to my side of the conversation. "He's right here."

"Put him on the phone."

I pressed the phone to my chest. "He wants to talk to you."

"Me?" Lorne mouthed the word. His expression of disbelief was understandable; according to Lorne, they hadn't spoken since the day Lorne was sentenced.

I held out the phone. Lorne took it and put the receiver to his ear. "Hey, brother. What's up?"

Chapter Thirty-Six

*Y*ou'll get better leverage if you hold it closer to the top."

Trey came up behind me and moved my hands higher on the pry bar, bracing his feet on either side of me before counting to three and helping me shove the tool into a small crack under the sill, then stood back.

"Now just press down as hard as you can. It'll pop right up."

The sill didn't exactly "pop right up" but the nails started to separate from the wall, creating a bigger opening. I shoved the bar farther beneath the window sill and pushed again, leaning onto the bar as hard as I could. On the third try, I heard a groan and a crack. The entire ledge of the windowsill did, indeed, "pop off." I stepped back to appreciate my handiwork.

"Okay, *that* was extremely satisfying."

"Demolition always is. Best anger management tool known to man."

"I feel so powerful. Can I do it again?"

"Be my guest."

I slammed the bar as hard as I could against the window frame but aimed a little too high and ended up splintering the wood. A chunk of it flew across the room, landing on the wood floor with a clatter.

"Oops! Here. Maybe you should take over," I said, holding the pry bar out to Trey. He waved off the offering.

"Doesn't matter if it breaks; it's all going in the dumpster anyway. Don't worry. You've got this."

He took a step back and crossed his arms over his chest to watch, leaving me on my own. This time I wedged instead of slammed, then leaned my weight onto the bar. Once again, the frame popped off. It was even more satisfying than it had been the first time, because I'd done it completely on my own.

"Good job," Trey said. "Now all we have to do is remove the rest of the old woodwork and then do the same in the other rooms. I don't want to take out the windows until Lorne and Polly get back from the hardware store. Hopefully they'll have enough in stock. If they do, it'll probably be a real mishmash of styles and sizes."

I didn't know exactly what had transpired between the brothers after Trey asked me to put Lorne on the phone, but obviously, some kind of truce had been declared. The next thing I knew, Trey was standing on my front porch wearing faded jeans, a plaid shirt, and a tool belt, and the brothers were actually talking. However, not with any warmth, nor with any acknowledgment of the fact that they hadn't spoken in years.

This seemed really weird to me. I mean, when estranged women decide to call a truce and cooperate for some larger cause, the work cannot possibly proceed without some acknowledgment of the wrongs suffered and inflicted, followed by apologies and possibly a few tears. Depending on the timing and circumstances, there might be an exchange of gifts, possibly a themed brunch with floral arrangements and thank-you notes. The air would be cleared, fences mended, and everybody would move on.

Not so with the Holcomb brothers. Their means of dealing with the elephant in the room was, apparently, to pretend it wasn't there. They didn't shake hands or even really say hello. Instead, they launched immediately into a discussion about what had to be done and the fastest way to make it happen. Five minutes after Trey arrived, he and I were heading upstairs to start the demolition and Lorne was on his way to the hardware store to buy any windows he could lay his hands on.

"I'm not worried about the windows matching," I said. "As long as it satisfies the inspector and gets the placard off the door before Monday afternoon, I'm good. But do you really think we can get it done before then?"

"Well . . ." A noncommittal shifting of shoulders relayed Trey's doubt. "There's a lot to be done and not many hands to do it. But win or lose, I refuse to go down without a fight."

I smiled. "I knew I liked you. So, where did you learn all this stuff? Construction, I mean?"

"My dad was a contractor. Lorne and I worked with him every summer from eighth grade on." Trey picked up the pry bar, wedged it beneath the remaining frame, and popped it off in one piece, then kicked it out of the way and glanced in my direction. "You seem surprised."

"I am, kind of. I just figured that Lorne was the brawn and you were the brains in the family. But I have to say," I moved my hand through the air with a waving motion that took his working man's ensemble in from head to toe, "this is a *much* better look on you. You should dress like this all the time, even in court."

"Yeah?" He let out a laugh. "I know some judges who'd disagree with you. Also, metal detectors don't really like tool belts. But hey, thanks for the advice."

"You're welcome," I said. "It's kind of my specialty. Of course, in my experience, free advice is usually worth exactly what you paid for it."

"Which is why God invented lawyers. And billable hours."

Trey chucked a hunk of wood toward the can with a flicking motion of his wrist, as if he were dunking a basketball, and grinned when he hit the target, clearly pleased with himself. Watching him, I grinned too. He seemed so different today, more relaxed. From the first moment we'd met he'd shown himself to be that rarest of creatures, a genuinely good man. He went out of his way to help me and, from what I could tell, just about everybody else who came across his path, a champion of underdogs, a man who really did refuse to go down without a fight. I appreciated that and respected him for it. At the same time, I always knew Trey was holding a piece of himself back, and that bothered me.

But today was different. He seemed a lot more open and willing to talk—at least at first.

"When did you stop working for your dad?"

"The summer after college, when I decided to go to law school."

"Do you ever miss it? Working with your hands?"

"Sometimes," he said. "It feels good to get to the end of a long day and know you actually created something people can touch and see and use. But if I had it to do all over again, I'd still pick the law. Justice isn't always meted out as impartially as it could be, but the law is the closest thing we've got to an equal playing field."

I started gathering the demolished bits of wood and putting them into the trash can one at a time, taking care to avoid bent nails. "So you went off to law school. But what happened to Lorne? Did he stay on with your dad?"

"For a while."

Trey bent down and started gathering up big armfuls of boards and throwing them into the can, making me feel like a slacker even as I wondered about the date of his most recent tetanus shot. "The company went under. Holcomb Construction was in business almost forty-seven years. My grandpa founded it and then, when he died, my dad took over."

"After so many years? I'm so sorry. What happened?"

Trey looked past my shoulder, then sniffed and pulled on his nose before putting a hand on one hip, right above his tool belt, and just like that, the door was shut. I could tell by the look on his face the conversation was closed and the wall was up.

"Yeah. Think I'll start on the next room," he said, still looking past me. "It'd be good if we can have most of the frames removed before Lorne and Teddy get back. Do you mind finishing the cleanup?"

"Trey? Hey, hang on a second! I wasn't trying to—"

But Trey was already halfway out of the room and my apology was cut off by the sound of the doorbell.

"You want to get that?" Trey asked without turning around.

His gruff tone and the question itself, a dismissal that reminded me much too much of Steve, who had raised passive aggression to an art form, annoyed me. No. I did *not* want to get that. I wanted to find out what had happened to his dad's company, among other things. Why did he get to know all my secrets but refuse to tell me his? It wasn't just unfair, it was disproportionate! I thought about chasing him down and saying so, but then the bell rang again. I ran downstairs to answer the door.

"Hey, Pris!" She was standing on the porch holding a six-pack of kombucha in one hand and a bottle of white wine in the other. "I thought you were working for Polly today."

"Polly called and told me what happened with the inspector," she said, "so I called Mom, Felicia, and Caroline. Everybody's coming over to help as soon as they can but Mom had to finish up a presentation for a new client and Felicia was at the dentist. Caroline went to Harris Teeter to pick up some provisions, but she should be here any minute." She put the bottles down on the hall table. "What do you want me to do?"

"Do you know anything about demolition?"

"No. But it sounds like something I'd be really good at."

Chapter Thirty-Seven

Lorne and Trey were in another room, installing the frame around the final window, when the call came in. But the ring of the hammer and whine of the Skilsaw were still so loud that I had to press my phone to my ear to hear what Anne was saying. Keeping my voice calm, conveying pleasant surprise instead of panic, required a supreme effort.

"Yes, that's just fine. Uh-huh. No problem at all. See you soon. Bye."

The room wasn't exactly spinning when I hung up, but my pulse was racing and I felt light-headed. I took in a big breath and let it out with a whoosh, and murmured an expletive. Pris stopped painting in mid-stroke.

"That wasn't the inspector, was it?" she asked, looking anxious. "He's not supposed to be here until noon."

"Worse," I said. "It was Anne Dowling. And the Cavanaughs."

"Who are the Cavanaughs?"

"The birth mother's family—Becca Cavanaugh and her parents. Anne never said anything about *all* of them coming. But they are. I mean, they did. They're here."

Pris put down her paintbrush. "What? You mean like *here* here? In Charleston? You said Anne wasn't landing until three."

"They got on an earlier flight. They should be here in about half an hour." I pressed my hand over my mouth, trying to think what I should do next, apart from panic. Then I realized that panic was the only reasonable response. I ran out the door into the center hall, circling past the doors, and started yelling.

"Code blue! Code blue!"

Hammers stopped hammering. Saws stopped sawing. Heads popped out of various rooms where work was still being done. Everyone was looking at me like I'd lost my mind, which I kind of had.

"Code blue!" I shouted again.

"Code blue?" Caroline emerged from the bathroom, where she had been installing the last of the tile. "What's that supposed to mean?"

"Don't you watch television? Code blue! It means there's an emergency! The Cavanaughs are coming!"

Caroline looked at me blankly. Pris showed up to provide translation.

"It's the lawyer, and the birth mother, *and* her parents. They landed early and are driving in from the airport. We've got less than half an hour to clean up and clear out." She clapped her hands. "Hurry people! Code blue!"

Did you ever see one of those movie scenes where a hungover heroine who's engaged to the wrong guy and can't quite remember what did or didn't happen the night before sits bolt upright in bed, spots the sleeping, only semi-clothed form of the guy she should be with but isn't, only to realize that there was a power outage during the night so her alarm didn't go off and her fiancé will be showing up in five minutes?

The next twenty-five minutes were basically that.

The only thing that could have made it worse was if the dogs had been there, running around in circles and yapping. Fortunately, I'd sent Teddy off to buy breakfast pastry for the crew, so it could have been worse. But not a lot worse.

Pris took charge, shouting instructions, telling everybody to roll up the tarps, close up the paint cans, and for heaven's sake be careful not to spill paint on the floor! But nobody was really listening; they were too busy.

Heath, who had taken the day off work to help with the push to the finish line, started ripping miles of painter's tape off still semi-wet woodwork, rolling it up into balls the size of blue basketballs. Happy pitched in to help Caroline lay the last four bathroom tiles, then took my handheld hair dryer to the floor in an attempt to dry the mortar. Felicia took charge of cleaning up the kitchen, throwing out a weekend's worth of empty pizza and donut boxes, takeout Thai cartons, Coke cans, and paper plates, then moved on to the rest of the house, frantically wiping down furniture covered with construction dust, vacuuming floors, and fluffing sofa pillows. Lorne and Trey hammered the last bit of woodwork around the last window in the nursery and slapped on a coat of paint in record time. Polly and I worked as a team to take down ladders and scaffolds and cart them and the tools downstairs to Lorne's truck, until Pris pushed us aside.

"Polly, go help Celia get changed," she said. "Caroline and I can finish this."

"Okay. What do you want her to wear?"

"I'd planned on the blue dress with the white cardigan and the huarache sandals. Teddy was going to pick it up from the dry cleaners but he's not back." Pris bit her lip and looked me up and down. "Go with the white pants and the green flowered blouse instead. They're in the closet."

Pris grabbed the ladder Polly had been holding and started toward the stairs, shouting her final instructions up the stairwell as she carted it off to the truck. "And the wedge sandals with the cork heels and the tan belt. And earrings. Just gold posts. We're going for a suburban mom look."

"Got it!" Polly grabbed me by the elbow and started steering me toward the bedroom. "What about her hair?"

"Scrunchie and a ponytail. There's no time to wash it."

"But there's paint in it. How am I supposed to get it out?"

"I don't know. Think of something. They'll be here any minute!"

We made it, but barely.

Twenty-five minutes after I'd called the "code blue," Felicia was shooing everybody out the door and herding the women over to her house, leaving me alone to greet Anne Dowling and the Cavanaughs.

"Call us the *second* they leave," Felicia instructed, then gave me a quick hug before scurrying off with the others. Trey, Lorne, and Heath were right behind her, carrying one last load of equipment to the truck. When that was done, Heath jogged across the street to his house, turning to give me a big thumbs-up before going inside and closing the door. Lorne and Trey jumped into the pickup and drove off, tires spinning.

Seconds later, a silver sedan that looked like rental cars always do—nondescript and sporting out-of-state plates—approached from the opposite direction. I smoothed my hair with my hand and caught a whiff of paint thinner and perfume. Polly had brushed both through the paint-splashed strands, thinner to remove the paint and perfume to cover the smell. It didn't work but there was nothing to do about it now.

I took a deep breath and gave myself a little pep talk. "The house is ready and so are you. Everything is going to be fine. You've got this."

Just as I was about to paste on a smile and come down from the piazza to greet my guests, I heard a dull but insistent tapping sound. I glanced to the right and saw Felicia, Polly, and the others standing at Felicia's dining room window. Caroline knocked on the window and mouthed something and Pris motioned with her hand.

At first, I thought they were just trying to be encouraging and gave them a big thumbs-up. Then all six of them started waving their hands and pointing, their eyes panicked and their lips twisting silently. It was like the world's most frustrating game of charades. The more they pointed and flapped and gestured, the less clue I had about what they were trying to tell me.

Was there lipstick on my teeth? Toilet paper on my shoe? Had I sat in paint? Was the porch about to collapse? I had no clue.

The rental car pulled up in front of the house and a flash of red caught my eye. I reached out, ripped the fire hazard placard off the front door just as Anne and the Cavanaughs climbed out of the car. I crumpled the placard into a ball, shoved it in my pocket, and descended the steps to meet them.

"Welcome," I said, as I opened the gate. "Did you have any trouble with the directions? Downtown Charleston can be tricky if you're not from here; streets just start and end for no good reason. I'm Celia, by the way." I laughed nervously, realizing I'd been babbling, and reached out to shake Anne Dowling's hand.

Even if I hadn't recognized her from her photo on the law firm's website, Anne would have been easy to spot. She wore a black suit, just like Trey did when he was lawyering. But unlike Trey's,

Anne's suit actually fit and looked good. The fabric was fine and obviously expensive. She'd accessorized it with pearl earrings, a circle pin with emeralds and diamonds, and a black leather briefcase with a Kate Spade logo.

She looked like a lawyer, all right. A very high-priced one. One glance at Mr. and Mrs. Cavanaugh told me they could well afford the services of Anne Dowling, and just about anything else they wanted. It never occurred to me that the Cavanaughs would be well off, but in retrospect, I guess it should have. If you can afford to hire a private lawyer to handle every aspect of a private adoption and fly around the country to check out potential parents, you're probably not hurting for cash. The Cavanaughs certainly weren't.

Their clothing was understated but expensive, devoid of designer labels or trendy designs, simple pieces that were never quite in or out of style, a look favored by old families with old money, one I'd come to recognize during my years in New York. Their manner was restrained and their fifty-something bodies were tanned and taut in a way that spoke of personal trainers and winters in Bermuda.

I realize now that I'd bought in to a stereotype, but when I'd thought about the families of unwed mothers, I'd pictured people a little more down on their luck. On the other hand, luck is about a lot more than money.

Becca, a quiet, green-eyed girl with corkscrews of black hair cascading past her shoulders and a peapod bulge under a lightweight gray cashmere maternity top, gave every appearance of being just as well-heeled as her parents, but the look in her eyes told me she felt sad and far from fortunate. Maybe that's why I took her hand first and covered it with both of mine before greeting her parents.

"Becca, I'm so glad to meet you. So glad you're here," I said, turning back to her.

"Thanks."

She smiled shyly and looked around, her eyes coming to rest on the crape myrtle in the far corner of the garden, which, after a very slow start, had obligingly come into full bloom the previous week.

"What's the tree? I've never seen anything quite like it."

"Crape myrtle. Very common here in Charleston."

"It's pretty."

"It was looking a little sad until recently. It had some kind of powdery mildew. But my cousin Teddy pruned it and sprayed it with some organic something or other. Neem oil? I don't remember for sure but it must have been good, whatever it was. The tree perked right up. Teddy's a wonderful gardener, which is lucky for me *and* the garden. So far, I've managed to kill every houseplant that has ever had the misfortune of coming into my possession."

I made a cringing face and Becca smiled; it was as if she'd suddenly forgotten to be sad.

"I want to study horticulture and landscape design in college. I was accepted to Penn State for the fall semester, but . . ." She cast her eyes down and placed a protective palm on the peapod. "Guess that'll have to wait for a while."

Anne Dowling took a step forward. "Maybe we should go inside. It's awfully warm out here."

"Good idea. This humidity takes a little getting used to. Come on inside. I've got a big pitcher of cold sweet tea inside—something else that's very common in Charleston," I said as Becca fell in step beside me. "I bet there are all kinds of things you'd like to ask me."

Becca smiled shyly. "Well, I kind of feel like I know you already. I used to read your column. Once I even—"

Mrs. Cavanaugh suddenly appeared at my side. "Miss Fairchild, you're very kind. But I think it might be better if you just showed us the house and we skipped the tea. We have to catch a flight to Chicago this afternoon, so there's really no time to linger."

The two women exchanged a look that was hard to read. Mrs. Cavanaugh fixed her eyes on her daughter, but Becca was the one to break the gaze first, looking away and then down. When she lifted her eyes, the sadness was back.

I didn't know these people, this family. I couldn't imagine what the last few months had been like for any of them. Mrs. Cavanaugh might have been just as sad as Becca but more skilled at masking it. It couldn't be easy, giving up a grandchild. I couldn't imagine how she could, or why. It wasn't because she lacked the means to feed another mouth, that was clear. So maybe Becca was the one driving this train? She was young and bright and obviously had big plans for the future, plans that might not include a baby. It made sense. She could have opted for an abortion but decided not to. Or perhaps she had wanted an abortion but her mother had pressured her not to. Maybe that explained the tension between them.

Over the years, I'd gotten used to thinking I had the answers, reading a few lines of a letter and supposing I understood what the writer had done in the past and should do in the future. If there was anything I'd learned since digging into my family's past, exploding the myths of who my people were and what they'd been through, it's that I don't have a crystal ball into other people's lives. I did not and could not know what these women had been through, nor could I understand the events and influences that had brought them to this moment and my doorstep.

And so I fought back the urge to step between them, to wrap my arms around young Becca, shepherd her into my house, and lock the door.

"Of course," I said, stepping ahead and leading the way. "Let's start with the nursery."

Chapter Thirty-Eight

Felicia clucked her tongue and filled my glass.

"How do you know that? You *don't* know that," she said, and clucked again. "You told us yourself that she hardly said a thing."

"She barely spoke." I shoved another benne wafer into my mouth and washed it down with a swig of iced tea that I wished was wine. "The only comment she made was that the nursery seemed small—"

"Nonsense!" Felicia said, and plunked another plate of cookies onto the table to replace the one I'd nearly emptied. "There's room for a crib, dresser, changing table, and rocking chair with plenty of room for toys besides. How much space does one baby need? And it's right next to your bedroom, so you'll be able to hear her if she cries during the night."

"That's what I told her."

"And what did she say?"

"Hmm."

"Hmm?" Felicia's eyes went wide behind her red glasses. "That's all? Just hmm?"

I sighed. "*Hmm* seems to be very big with Mrs. Cavanaugh.

However, she also took the trouble to point out that the windows in the bedrooms were all different sizes and styles and that my hair smelled like paint thinner."

Polly sucked air in through her teeth. It was the kind of sound you make when somebody falls down right in front of you and you just know it's going to end up leaving a bruise. "Sorry. I thought that cologne I sprayed on you would cover up the smell."

"It's not your fault," I said. "And it's not like my hair was the thing that pushed me over the edge. Becca's mom just flat out did not like me, not from the first minute."

"Oh, that's ridiculous," Felicia said, flapping her hand.

"I know," I said. "Usually people take ten or fifteen minutes to decide they hate my guts." I stuffed another cookie in my mouth, then got up from the kitchen table and opened the refrigerator. There wasn't any wine inside. Felicia, perhaps reading the disappointed droop of my shoulders, took a bottle of bourbon out of a cupboard and glugged a little into my iced tea. I sat down and covered my face with my hands. "All that work. For nothing."

Pris placed a hand on my shoulder. "Don't say that. You don't know what's going to happen. What about Mr. Cavanaugh? And Becca? How did they seem?"

"He was quiet. She was quiet." I shrugged. "Everybody was quiet except Anne. She asked a lot of questions about the house, so I played up the history, the fact that the Fairchilds have lived in Charleston forever, possibly intimating that I have greater social connections than is actually the case. Then she asked about my nonexistent book. I told her it was coming along just fine."

"Well. It's not a *total* lie," Pris reasoned. "You're always writing in your journal."

I shot her a look and took a sip of the now-fortified tea. It didn't seem necessary to explain the difference between writing a book and scribbling in a journal. Even if it had been necessary, the mere mention of all those letters to an unborn child I would now never get to meet, let alone mother, would open the floodgates to a deluge of tears.

"So the girl didn't say anything at all?" Polly said, looking a little pained.

"No, she talked a little. She's just kind of quiet. I showed her the blanket I'm knitting for Peaches and she liked that a lot. She was also very intrigued with the hidden yarn cave story."

"It *is* a good story," Polly said. "Did you tell her about Teddy and finding the pictures hidden in the floor? Calpurnia, and the hoarding, and how you've killed yourself to sort through the generations of junk and restore this place?"

I shook my head. "Too much information, especially with her parents standing there. They didn't seem like people who would appreciate the whole crazy hoarding aunt sending messages from beyond the grave angle."

"Yankees," Polly muttered.

I've never been a fan of cataloging people into geography-based personality types, but Polly had a point. Anyone with a drop of southern blood would have eaten that story up with a knife and fork. Down here, we take pride in our crazy relatives. But Mr. and Mrs. Cavanaugh were most definitely not from down here.

"Becca liked the garden too," I said. "I told her about what a mess it had been before Teddy started working on it, how he'd cleaned out the weeds and trimmed back the trees. She was curious about him, asked a couple of questions before her parents came upstairs."

"That seems like a good sign," Happy said.

"I thought so too. Until Teddy actually showed up. *With* the dogs." I dropped my head to the table and groaned.

"Oh, no," Felicia murmured, putting her hand to her mouth. "They didn't."

Head still down, staring at the tabletop, I gave an exaggerated nod. "They did. They jumped all over everybody, barking and going crazy. Teddy was yelling at them to knock it off even while he was introducing himself, saying how much he loved babies and that he had been adopted and it was fine, so Becca shouldn't feel bad about giving up the baby because he'd turned out okay and had a good job and was so excited about being an uncle, and then asked her did she like coffee because Bitty and Beau's has the best lattes in Charleston and if she ever came in, he'd give her one on the house."

"Oh, no," Felicia said again.

"Oh, *yes*," I said and picked up my head. "All of a sudden, he turns into a chatterbox. Honestly, it wouldn't have been that bad if not for the dogs. The only time I saw Becca truly smile was when Teddy started talking to her. But while Teddy is spilling his guts to Becca, Pebbles decides to do her party trick and jump right into Mrs. Cavanaugh's arms. She wasn't expecting it so, of course, instead of catching the dog, she threw out her hands to shield herself, then lost her balance, and fell backward onto the nursery windowsill, and . . ."

I waved my hand over my head with a dramatic flourish, prodding them to fill in the blank. They did and almost in unison.

"It was still wet? No!"

"Yes! Mrs. Cavanaugh fell backward into *wet* paint. When she got up, there was a big white streak across her derriere." I thumped my forehead onto the table.

"It's over. I'm doomed. Doomed." Felicia squeezed my shoulder.

"When are you supposed to hear back?" Priscilla asked.

"Anne didn't give me a definite date," I said. "Maybe next week?"

"Okay, well. You'll know when you know, right? Until then—"

"I'll sit home, waiting for the phone to ring. And drinking tea." I took the stopper out of the bourbon bottle and added a little more to my glass.

"Bad plan," Polly said. "Trust me on this. I haven't spent four years going to AA meetings for nothing."

"Don't be so gloomy. The lawyer liked you," Caroline said in a clarifying sort of tone. "That should help.

"That's right," Happy added encouragingly. "You said before that you thought she was on your side."

"Before today, I thought she was. Now I'm not so sure. Even if I'm wrong, it doesn't matter. Mrs. Cavanaugh is obviously the one who makes the decisions, and she hates me."

"Stop," Caroline said. "You don't know that."

Except I did.

Chapter Thirty-Nine

*N*ine days had passed since the home visit. Still no call.

My friends meant well. They had done their best to buoy my spirits, to distract me by working on our projects, calling, or dropping by to check on me, and just generally to help me hold it together.

And it helped. For a while.

But now it was time to face reality, because spending my nights lying awake and the days staring into space, and launching into panic attacks every time the phone rang was not working for me. Or anybody else. Teddy was anxious. Even the dogs were upset. Pebbles had stopped eating and refused to leave my side.

Knowing that my chance for happiness had passed me by was terrible, but the *not* knowing, the waiting, was even worse. I just couldn't do it anymore.

"I just don't know what I should do next," I told Calvin, while glancing at an advert for an online master's program on my laptop. "I'd always planned to go back to the city if things didn't work out. But now Teddy's part of the equation. I can't just say,

'Hey, sorry but things didn't work out like I'd hoped, so you're on your own.' He loves it here.

"Maybe I should just let him have the house? He could keep on living here, I'd go back to New York and come visit sometimes. But . . . what would I be going back *to*? My career is at a standstill. I don't have a job. And apart from you and Simon, I don't have any real connections there. I guess I could freelance. Or maybe I should go back to school?"

"Know what I think you should do?" Calvin asked.

"What?"

"Make an appointment with an audiologist. Because clearly, you are losing your hearing." He let out a growl. "Celia, for the fiftieth time: You. Don't. Know. *What* is going to happen! So quit pretending you do!"

I stretched out my arm, holding the phone as far from my body as possible, but could still hear every word of Calvin's tirade. It went on for quite a while. "Are you done now?" I asked when he finally took a breath.

"Are you?"

"Calvin, look. I know you're just trying to help and I appreciate that. I do. But there's no point in my—" The familiar beep interrupted my explanation. I pulled the phone from my ear, glanced at the screen, and felt my stomach knot and my pulse gallop. "Calvin, I've got to hang up. Anne Dowling is calling."

"She is? Oh, honey! Be sure to—"

The phone beeped again. I hung up on Calvin, took a deep breath, said a fervent and to-the-point prayer, "*Please*, God," and tapped the red button.

"Hello?"

"Hi, Celia. It's Anne Dowling. Is this a good time to talk?"

Chapter Forty

*W*ho was I kidding?

I honestly thought I'd prepared myself for Anne's call, but as soon as we hung up, I completely fell apart. You can think through the outcomes and mentally rehearse your responses, but some things in life you simply cannot prepare for, no matter how hard you try.

There'd been enough tears for one day and I needed time to process, so I let Calvin's call go to voicemail three times. I didn't want to talk to him until I felt sure I'd be able to hold it together. The fourth time he rang, I took a big breath, promised myself out loud that I was not going to cry, and shattered that promise the second I said hello.

"Oh, cupcake. Oh, honey. I am so, so, *so* sorry." I gulped in a couple of big, ragged breaths and tried to pull myself together, but the catch I heard in Calvin's voice launched me into another round of sobbing. "Listen to me," he said when my weeping subsided enough so I actually could listen. "I know this is hard. But it's going to be okay. You've got to believe me. I'm going to catch the next plane to Charleston."

"No, Calvin," I rasped, fighting to catch my breath. "You don't have to do that."

"Don't try to be brave," he said. "I'm coming down there. No arguments."

I wiped my eyes with my sleeve. "No, no. You don't understand."

"Celia, I know you don't want to be a—"

"Calvin, shut up! It's not what you think. Anne called to say that Becca picked me to take her baby." There was a moment of silence. I think he was just as shocked as I'd been. "Calvin, Peaches is mine! I'm going to be a mother!"

After that, both of us were completely wrecked. We cried and laughed and cheered and talked over each other and cried and laughed some more.

"See?" he said. "The Cavanaughs liked you after all. You always think you can read everybody's mind but you can't."

"Oh, no," I countered. "I was absolutely right about Mister and Missus. They couldn't stand me, especially Mrs. Cavanaugh. And they absolutely loathed Teddy."

"What? Who could loathe Teddy? Was it the thing with the dog?"

"Nope," I said. "Guess again."

A couple of beats passed before the answer dawned on him.

"It's because he's developmentally disabled? You've got to be kidding."

"I'm not. Peaches doesn't know how lucky she is not to be getting those two for grandparents."

"But then how come they picked you to get the baby?"

"*They* didn't," I explained. "It was all Becca. She turned out to be tougher than I thought. There was quite a battle; that's why it took so long for Anne to get back to me. Anne probably shared a little more than she should have," I said, "but Becca used to read Dear Calpurnia and had been leaning toward me from the beginning. She really liked the house and the garden, and Teddy, and even the dogs. Apparently, she'd always wanted a dog but her parents said no. In fact, sounds like Becca didn't get much that she truly wanted."

"Poor little rich girl?"

"Something like that," I said. "Becca was raised by nannies and shipped off to boarding school when she was fourteen. She wants something different for her baby, a real home and family, a neighborhood where people know each other. Anne said she was very impressed that so many friends and neighbors had pitched in to help with the house.

"Oh! And she loved that I was already knitting a blanket for Peaches and that my girlfriends come over for crafting parties every week. She told her parents that's what she wanted for her baby, to be raised in a place where people take care of each other."

"Well," said Calvin, "her parents might be narrow-minded jerks, but Becca is one very smart cookie. Peaches is going to be a genius. And *you*, Miss Thang, are going to be a mommy."

"I am!"

"I know!"

Calvin hooted and cheered again, then immediately switched gears. "We need to start making plans, cupcake. So much to do! How does 'Lullaby of Broadway' strike you as a baby shower theme? Or maybe 'Broadway Baby'?

"Calvin, it's still August. The baby isn't due until mid-November. Do we really need to worry about this now?"

"Are you kidding? Pulling off a really good baby shower takes months of planning. I won't have my honorary niece welcomed to the world with stale cupcakes and grocery-store flower arrangements. We've got to get on this *now*."

I wanted to laugh but Calvin was dead serious. Clearly, baby shower planning would be our primary topic of conversation over the next several weeks. However, at that moment, we were mercifully interrupted.

"Calvin, somebody's at the door. I've got to run."

"Fine, but give some thought to the theme. How do you feel about omelet stations?"

The bell rang again.

"Calvin. I'm hanging up now."

"Fine," he huffed. "But we're not done with this."

"I'm sure we're not."

I ended the call. The bell rang a third time. Somebody was very persistent.

"Coming!" I called, and jogged out to the foyer, smiling and thinking about Calvin. But my smile fled when I opened the door and saw the look on Pris's face.

"What's wrong? You and Happy aren't fighting again, are you?"

She shook her head. "It's Polly. She didn't want me to say anything because she's afraid you'll think it's your fault."

"What will I think's my fault?" I said. "Come on in and tell me what happened."

Pris stepped across the threshold and pulled her blue crocheted beanie off her head, smoothing a hand over her braids. "Trey must have gotten somebody's attention at City Hall. The local news says that an investigation is being launched into corruption in the building department. I don't know exactly how it went down but the report said that a nephew of developer Cabot James had been hired with almost no experience. Brett was fired this morning.

"Somebody must have told Cabot James that Polly had tipped Trey off about Brett being his nephew, because he fired her. Which means she's lost her job and her apartment. And James says she has to be out by Monday morning or else. Polly didn't want me to say anything but I *had* to."

Pris looked at me with pleading eyes. "Celia, she's got nowhere to go."

Chapter Forty-One

Lorne hopped out of the rental truck, grinning when he saw Polly coming down the piazza steps behind me.

"Polly, darlin', we have *got* to stop meeting like this," he said.

She smiled. "Hey, Lorne. Thanks for doing this. I really owe you one."

"Yes, you do." He propped a booted foot onto the curb and gave an exaggerated nod. "You do realize that in some indigenous cultures, moving a lady twice within two months is practically an engagement, don't you?"

"Never heard of that one," Polly said.

"Well, neither did I. But it sounds about right to me." He winked at her and swiped his brow with the back of his hand. "Dang, but it's hot today!"

Lorne stretched out his arms and peeled off the sweat-stained chambray shirt he'd worn over his sleeveless white undershirt revealing broad shoulders and muscled biceps. I rolled my eyes. If he tried just a little harder, could he be even more obvious? Obvious or not, it seemed to be working. Polly's cheeks were bright pink and I didn't think it was because of the heat.

"I'll just run and get the iced tea out of the fridge," Polly said, and trotted off toward the house.

"Hurry back, darlin'!" Lorne planted his hands on his hips, which made his shoulders look even broader.

I stood there, shaking my head.

"What?" Lorne asked.

"Do you have to flirt with every single woman who crosses your path?"

"Just the cute ones," he said. "Hey, it's not like you didn't have your chance, Boss Lady."

"Knock it off," I said, smiling. He was such a kid; how could I be mad at him? "And quit calling me Boss Lady. You volunteered for this, remember?"

"That's because I'm such a nice guy." He pounded the side of the truck with the flat of his hand. "Ted-O! Let's unload this beast!"

Teddy climbed out of the truck. Bug and Pebbles, who had been lounging on the piazza to escape the searing August heat, jumped to their feet, ran down the steps, and flung themselves at Teddy, barking and wiggling and basically losing their minds.

"Sorry," Teddy said, catching Pebbles in his arms. "But I've got to change and get over to the coffee shop. My shift starts at noon."

"That's right," Lorne said. "I forgot. Don't worry about it, Ted-O. Trey's coming over to give me a hand after church. Should be here any minute. But thanks for your help, big guy."

Lorne clapped Teddy on the back. Teddy gave him a high five and headed toward the house with Pebbles still in his arms and Bug trotting along at his heels.

"Does Trey go to church every Sunday?" I asked. "I saw him once, over at St. Philip's. But that was on a Monday. There was an older man with him, maybe your grandfather?"

Lorne's grin faded. "That's our dad. He had a stroke a while back. He lives in a retirement home now but Trey takes him to church whenever he wants, which is at least a couple times a week."

I would have liked to know more, but if there was anything I'd learned in the previous months, it was that trying to pry information from a Holcomb, especially if it involved family, was a pointless exercise. Just in case I hadn't gotten the hint, Lorne thumped the side of the truck to signal a change of topic, then walked to the back and yanked the handles on the door. It rolled up like a window shade. The truck's interior was stacked floor to ceiling with boxes and furniture.

"Where d'ya want it, Boss?"

"Well . . ." I pulled an apologetic face.

Lorne's shoulders drooped. "No," he said, frowning and shaking his head. "Not the attic."

"I've got nowhere else to put her," I said, spreading my hands. "Once the baby comes, I'll only have one bedroom upstairs and I need to save that for guests. Calvin's coming down for the baby shower.

"Come on, Lorne. Polly's got nowhere else to go and she needs some space to spread out. If she hadn't ratted out Cabot James, Brett would still be our inspector and *I'd* be the one with no place to live."

Lorne groaned and hinged his head back, as if he was too tired to carry its weight. "She'd better be here for a while," he said at last, lifting his head and stabbing the air with his finger. "Because I am *not* moving this stuff again."

"That's up to Polly. But I told her she can stay as long as she wants."

Lorne growled, then sighed, then shrugged, working his way

from frustration to resignation. "All right. I guess, one flight of stairs one way or the other doesn't make that much difference. But we're still putting the shop inventory and displays into the ground-floor storage, right?"

When I didn't respond, Lorne set his jaw and shook his head.

"Uh-uh, Celia. No way."

A car door slammed, signaling Trey's arrival. It was ninety-six degrees out and ninety-seven percent humidity, but he was still wearing a black suit. "Church clothes," he said when I arched my eyebrows. "I've got shorts and a T-shirt in the car." He peered into the back of the truck and frowned. "I thought Pris sold the inventory."

"Some of it," Lorne said. "But there's still a whole lotta boxes here. And guess where Celia wants us to take it?"

"What do you want me to do!" I shouted, throwing out my hands. "The humidity is terrible on the ground floor, the walls are practically dripping. Polly invested her life savings in the store inventory. We can't put it down there and just hope it won't mildew."

"The attic," Lorne said, crossing his arms over his chest and looking at his brother. "She wants us to cart all this stuff up three flights of stairs to the attic."

"Ah." Trey put his hands on his hips and popped his lips three times. Apparently, this is the noise all Holcombs make when they're thinking.

"Who wants tea? Hope y'all like it sweet. I made sandwiches too." Polly trotted down the steps with a tray of food but paused when she got to the gate. Her eyes shifted from Lorne's face, to Trey's, to mine. "Oh. You told them. Sorry, guys, but the storage area is just so—"

"Wait a second. What's over there?" Trey asked.

I looked in the direction he was pointing. "My great-grandfather's haberdashery shop. But it's been empty for close to a hundred years. Teddy's using it as a garden shed. His tools are in there plus about a zillion terra-cotta pots, all the ones from Calpurnia's collection that weren't broken."

Trey grabbed a glass of tea from Polly's tray and drained it by half.

"Huh. Let's take a look."

THE WINDOWS HAD been painted over decades before and there was only one working light. When I tugged the grubby string that served as a switch, the unshaded glare from the bulb made the dust motes and spiderwebs glow and threw sharp shadows against the rough plastered walls.

"It's dirty," Polly said, turning in a slow circle as she took in the jumble of rakes, shovels, hoses, pots, and pruning shears. "And buggy. But it's dry. Do you think Teddy would mind if I moved his tools to the ground-floor storage? The humidity wouldn't be an issue for this," she said, gesturing toward the jumble. "But if I cleaned it up a little, this would be a perfect spot to store my stuff."

"Or . . . maybe sell it?" I offered.

Polly started shaking her head, but I jumped in before she could actually say anything, spreading my arms wide to encompass the room. "Polly, look at all this space! It's perfect for retail. Why? Because that's what it was built for!

"Think about it: it's right on the street, has a nice little back room for an office and extra storage. The showroom is big enough to hold all your inventory with room left over to hold classes. You've got room for at least three tables in that back corner by the window. More importantly, you've already got all the inventory, a business license, and a small customer base. Why not just reopen the store here?"

Polly didn't quite say "Doh," but the look on her face said the objections ought to be obvious, even to me. "Well, first off," she said, "this place is a hundred-year-old ruin. It's filthy and dark and infested with spiders, has one working light fixture, and all kinds of issues we probably can't see—termites, or a bad roof, or I don't know what all. It's probably five minutes from completely falling down around our ears."

Lorne hooked a thumb into his belt loop and craned his neck, examining the ceiling and walls. "Looks to me like it's plaster over cinderblock, so no termites and no mold. The roof might be another story; I'd have to check. It'd take some work to bring it up to code but . . . it's doable."

"*If* I had the money. Or the inclination. Which I don't," Polly insisted. "Why are we even talking about this? I'm a terrible businessperson, remember? I had my shot and I blew it."

"You are *not* a terrible businessperson," I countered. "You had a terrible location and you were inexperienced, but look at all you learned. You've got nothing to lose by trying again. This was your *dream*, remember? Now you've got a second chance at it. And I can offer you an amazing rate on the rent—free."

Polly crossed her arms over her chest and set her mouth into a line.

"Okay, okay," I said. "Don't be so stubborn. How about free for a year? You'll know if this can work by then. If it does, you can start paying me. If it doesn't, you'll close the shop and be no worse off than you are right now."

"But a year older and a failure twice over." Polly sighed and closed her eyes momentarily. "Celia, look. I appreciate what you're trying to do here. I do. But even if this could work, there's the whole issue of zoning. Things have changed since your great-grandfather was selling suits in the nineteen twenties; this is a residential area now."

Trey was doing that thing he does, standing back and being Switzerland. I knew he hadn't missed a thing and had opinions, but unlike pretty much every man I'd ever encountered in my life, he wouldn't offer them unless asked, which . . . was kind of nice. He also seemed to understand what I was thinking even before I said anything, which was also nice. And kind of surprising.

"The zoning is mixed-use, isn't it?" I said, turning toward him. "Happy has her design showroom in her carriage house, and the Queen Street Grocery is doing business just a couple blocks away."

"But the grocery store is grandfathered in," Trey said. "They've been in business since nineteen twenty-two."

"So? Fairchild's Fine Haberdashers did business here until nineteen twenty-six. Doesn't that count?"

"Possibly." Trey turned toward Polly. "Do you want me to look into it?"

Polly closed her eyes again, pressed her fingers against her forehead, and groaned. "This is. So. Crazy. There are about two hundred reasons why this is a bad idea. But if you want to look into it . . ." She paused. "Fine. Knock yourself out."

Lorne cleared his throat and Polly's eyes popped open.

"What?" she barked.

"Nothing," Lorne said, lifting his hands to prove his innocence and shooting me a what-got-into-her look. "I was just wondering what you put on the sandwiches. Because if you used mayonnaise, we'd better eat before the sun gets to them."

Trey and I exchanged grins. Leave it to Lorne to get to the heart of things.

Dear Peaches,

> *It takes guts to take a chance on a dream. Doing it again after failing the first time takes not only superhuman courage but a willful suspension of logic.*
>
> *But here's the thing; hardly anybody grabs hold of their dreams on the first go-round. Even when you fail and fall, even if it doesn't make sense, you've got to keep going.*
>
> *Maybe especially then . . .*

Chapter Forty-Two

*B*ritney Spears was wailing so loudly that I could hear her the second I got out of the car and started unloading the groceries, trying to carry all eight bags in one trip.

When Calvin said he'd booked a rental car to use during his visit to Charleston, I'd told him it wasn't necessary. Downtown Charleston is almost as walkable as New York and it's just as easy to hire a Lyft here as it is in Manhattan. Also, Calvin is a notoriously bad driver. I went to a food show in Edison with him once and barely escaped with my life. The other turnpike drivers were responsible, even sedate by comparison, which, if you've ever driven in Jersey, is saying something. So, I was understandably concerned about unleashing Calvin on the unsuspecting motorists of South Carolina. But my worries were unfounded because, as it turned out, I was the one who ended up doing all the driving. Calvin was just in charge of making lists.

Fewer than twenty people were coming to the shower; so why did we need eight pounds of bacon, ten dozen eggs, three pounds of lox, and six dozen bagels in assorted flavors? Not to mention a balloon arch, red carpet, custom-printed invitations that looked like theater tickets, and a karaoke machine? The theme was "Broadway Baby," but if Calvin honestly thought that people were going to grab a mic and sing show tunes tomorrow, we needed more champagne. Three cases wouldn't be nearly enough.

I carted the groceries up the steps and rang the bell. Nobody answered, so I twisted sideways, arms loaded with bags, then crouched low and pushed the door handle down with my elbow before bumping the door open with my hip. My grip on the bags was precarious, so I trotted into the kitchen as quickly as I could. Before I could get to the counter, four blood oranges tumbled from the top of a bag. The whole load was starting to slip.

"Hey! Could I get a little help here?"

Calvin stood at the kitchen sink, shaking his shoulders and pulling the cord of the salad spinner in time with the bass beat, throwing back his head and howling that he wasn't *that* innocent as the chorus came around. When I shouted again, louder this time, he stopped mid-wail and sprang into action, catching the bottom bag just before it hit the floor. I stumbled toward the counter and put the bags down with a thud.

"Watch it!" Calvin barked. "You'll crack the eggs!"

I told Alexa to turn down the music and gave Calvin a glance that, had he been a houseplant, would have withered him instantly. "Do you know how many stores I had to visit to find ten dozen organic, pasture-raised eggs? Five. What kind of egg could possibly be worth two hours of searching and seven dollars a dozen?"

"The organic, pasture-raised kind." Calvin pulled egg cartons from the bags and opened them one at a time, searching for cracks. "Were you able to find everything else? Crabmeat? Gruyère? Tuscan kale?"

"I got kale. It didn't come with a passport." I sniffed the air. "What smells so good?"

Calvin closed the last egg carton. "Two possibilities. Either the peach turnovers I just put in the oven, or the lingering scent of the scrumptious hummingbird cupcakes that Teddy made and is now decorating with exceptional skill and artistry. Try one."

Calvin broke a piece off an unfrosted cupcake and popped it into my mouth. He was right, they were scrumptious. Mary Berry would have been proud.

Teddy stood at the island with Bug and Pebbles sitting at his feet, alert and attentive, clearly hoping he'd drop something. I walked to the other side of the island and spotted two trays of the finished product, cupcakes iced with a snowy swirls of cream cheese frosting, each topped with a perfectly proportioned peach rosebud. Teddy's hands were steady and his eyes intent as he carefully piped a perfect little rosebud onto a metal disc, then used a metal spatula to place it on a cupcake.

"Whew!" he said. "Last one."

"Teddy, they're gorgeous. Where'd you learn to do this?"

"Momma made birthday cakes for all the kids in the neighborhood. I used her hummingbird cake recipe. It has pineapple, bananas, toasted pecans, and extra coconut."

"The man knows his pastry," Calvin said, dipping his head in homage. "Teddy, next time I have to edit a baking book, think I could hire you to test recipes?"

"I don't know. Depends on how much you're paying," Teddy said without a trace of irony, then slipped his plain black apron over his head and laid it on the counter. "I've got to walk the dogs and change my clothes. I'm going to the movies with Gloria Jean and Wayne. You going to be all right here?"

"No worries," Calvin said. "I've got this. Celia can help me."

Calvin turned his attention back to the groceries. Teddy slipped a hand into the pocket of his jeans. The dogs hopped to their feet, tails thumping, hoping for a treat. Instead, Teddy pulled out a plastic packet and pressed it into my hand.

"What's this?" I asked.

"Earplugs," he whispered. "I like Calvin. But his taste in music?" Teddy shuddered. "Try to get him into Billie Eilish or even Lady Gaga. Somebody cool."

I pocketed the plugs. "Calvin really, really likes Britney."

"Yeah, I *know*," Teddy said, giving an enormous eye roll before grabbing two leashes and making his exit, the dogs padding along in his wake.

Calvin was using my apron—yellow cotton with blue butterflies and flowering vines—so I put on Teddy's plain black one, then washed my hands.

"Scullery maid, reporting for duty, Chef," I said, touching two fingers to my forehead. "What do you want me to do?"

"I'm promoting you to sous-chef. Why don't you finish washing the salad greens and then massage the kale? I'll grate the cheese."

"Massage the kale?"

"You know," Calvin said, in a tone that suggested I was being deliberately obtuse, "with olive oil and salt? So it'll be tender?"

I did not know but Calvin explained the procedure, then unwrapped the Gruyère. I took his place at the sink and put the earplugs on the counter where they'd be easy to reach, just in case. Calvin likes his music loud, but today he left Britney in the background, and for a while, we worked without saying anything.

Sometimes I save up funny phrases or observations just especially, because making Calvin laugh feels a little like winning a prize. But the real test of friendship, I think, is when you *don't* need to impress each other, when occupying the same space without saying a word is the place you most want to be.

I finished washing the greens, then poured a few glugs of olive oil and a sprinkle of salt onto the kale, thinking how happy I was that Calvin had come down to visit and how much fun the baby shower was going to be. Calvin worked the cheese grater, pausing only to pull the turnovers from the oven when the timer went off, thinking whatever he was thinking, until the Gruyère was shredded into a fluffy mountain and the kitchen smelled like a fondue shop. When that was done, he took a pitcher of tea from the tightly crammed refrigerator, filled two glasses, handed one to me, and said something I wasn't expecting.

"I'm proud of you."

"You are? Why?" I was doing a pretty good job massaging the kale but this hardly seemed reason for praise.

"Because." When I looked at him blankly, Calvin swept his arm wide, nearly sloshing tea over the rim of the glass. "Because *this*. When I left you here five months ago, I wasn't sure you were going to make it. But you did. The house looks great, you look great, your friends are great—Polly, Teddy, and all the others. You fit here, Celia. You've got a life now. A real life."

"And a baby on the way." I paused. "Sometimes I still can't believe it."

"I know," he said. "But that's not what I mean. Remember when you first told me about the baby? You said you were going to transform yourself, become a better person. And you did. No, I mean it," he said, talking over me when I tried to brush off his praise. "Remember when you got back in touch with me after Steve walked out? You were a hot mess."

"Who isn't after a divorce?"

"But there was more to it than that," he said, shaking his head. "I'll never forget the day we met, when you sat down next to me at the coffee shop. There you were, you and your drawl, trying to be all cosmopolitan and street smart. One minute you were talking about the new exhibit at the Guggenheim and the next minute you launched into a detailed and weirdly earnest discussion of why *It's a Wonderful Life* was the greatest movie ever made. And I sat there thinking to myself, 'This woman is a total nutcase and I absolutely *adore* her.'

"But the thing that really got to me was when you started talking about your readers. You wrote back to every single person who wrote to you, whether their letter got published or not. Who *does* that?" he asked, his expression a combination of disbelief and admiration. "I know you'll hate this, cupcake. But, deep down, you're really kind of a Crusader."

"Stop. I am not."

"That's a *good* thing," he countered. "There's room in your heart for everybody, Celia. Even strangers. But Steve was one of those people who can't share the spotlight. He had to have *all* of you: all your attention, all your love."

Yes, he did. Which was pretty stupid, considering he never loved me to begin with. Calvin looked at me intently, like he was trying to read my thoughts. His next sentence just about convinced me he could.

"Someday, Celia Fairchild, somebody's going to come along who'll love you the way you deserve to be loved. He won't be perfect but he'll be caring, and steady, and loyal, smart enough to know how fabulous you are, secure enough to share you with the world, and absolutely crazy about you. And if you're lucky," Calvin said, lifting his bushy eyebrows, "he'll *even* be straight."

"Well, there's a thought."

I laughed and went back to massaging the kale. Calvin just stood there, slurping tea and staring at me until I couldn't stand it anymore.

"What!" I finally barked, shaking my hands, flinging off shreds of slimy, well-salted kale, and wiping my oily hands onto Teddy's apron. "Why do you keep looking at me like that?"

Calvin clicked his tongue against his teeth a couple of times and smiled. "I read your memoir."

"My what?"

"Your journal," he clarified. "I read it."

"Calvin! Nobody is supposed to read that. It's private!"

He slurped some more tea and shrugged. "Then don't leave it lying around where nosy houseguests can find it. You know what a snoop I am, Celia."

Yes. Yes, I did.

So maybe a part of me had wanted him to see it?

"It's fabulous," Calvin said with an earnestness that made me feel simultaneously pleased and uneasy. "You're a good writer, Celia, even better than I realized. I'm serious. It takes guts to be that vulnerable, to open the door to the past, sort through the crap, and plant your stake in the ground saying, *This* is what's worth holding on to.

"That's why I'm proud of you," he said. "Not that you've been transformed, but that you're more yourself than you ever were. You're still the Celia who has a heart for everybody, the total nutcase I'll always, always adore."

I looked away for a moment. I had to. "Calvin LaGuardia, if you make me cry, I'll never forgive you," I rasped, meaning something else.

"I know," Calvin replied, understanding perfectly, as best friends always do.

Chapter Forty-Three

*S*tanding under an arch of silver balloons in front of a lighted marquee sign reading "A Star Is Born" that hung on the fireplace, and wearing a short skirt of pink tulle and an upcycled denim jacket with hand-embroidered cactus flowers on the yoke, Pris looked even cuter than usual.

When the *Frozen* song started, she lifted her champagne glass high above her head, moved the microphone closer to her mouth, screwed her eyes shut and threw back her head, wailing about not caring what they said, and the storm raging, and the cold never bothering her anyway.

The crowd went wild, whooping and shouting and "Amen, Sister"-ing. It was almost like going to church with Teddy.

"You go, girl!" Caroline hollered, punching the air with her fist.

Polly leapt to her feet. "Yes, ma'am! That's what *I'm* talkin' about!"

Even Mr. Laurens, who surprised me and everybody else by actually responding to the invitation I'd issued purely from politeness, and even brought a gift, a onesie emblazoned with the University of South Carolina logo on the front and the words "Future

Tailgater" written on the back in Gamecock red, clapped his approval before biting into his third cupcake.

Clearly, I'd been wrong about the karaoke. People were *really* into it.

After a sumptuous brunch and the opening of gifts, Calvin had kicked off the festivities by singing a duet with Simon, who had arrived early that morning, flying in between natural disasters. Their campy version of "Anything You Can Do, I Can Do Better" had everybody laughing.

After that, everybody wanted a turn.

Lorne, who really did have a good voice, tossed show tunes and the whole "Broadway Baby" theme to the curb, singing "God Bless the Broken Road," flirting with Polly the whole time. Beau, who was sporting a peacock-feather bow tie and turquoise-colored pants, sang a duet with Felicia, "Ah, yes, I remember it well," that made everybody tear up. Next, Caroline hopped to her feet, grabbed Happy's hand, and dragged her up to sing "I Could Have Danced All Night." Caroline's choreography was excellent, and what they lacked in pitch they made up for in enthusiasm.

Yes, a certain amount of inhibition-lowering champagne consumption had been required to get people to this point, but I thought there might be more to it. Almost everybody in the room had played a part in making the adoption possible. It was our house, our baby, our party. And in another few weeks, when I brought Peaches home, these people would be her family. I think that's why everybody was so ready to celebrate, including me.

Pris put her champagne glass down on the mantel and reached for Happy's hand, pulling her onstage and slinging her arm over her mom's shoulder. Happy belted out the *Frozen* song's chorus and then beckoned to Felicia, who hopped to her feet and then reached out to Caroline and Polly. They bounced and bopped and circled around the mic like a sixties girl group, urging each other to let it go. Polly saw me standing in the back and gestured for me to come up and join them.

Lucky for me, and for those who would have been forced to hear me sing, the doorbell rang just at that moment. I spread out my hands, pretended to look sad about missing out on the fun, and trotted off to answer it.

Getting from the living room to the foyer required stepping over piles of crumpled wrapping paper and discarded ribbons, and turning sideways to get past the small mountain of baby presents that included a combination baby carriage/car seat from Calvin and Simon, a Bitty and Beau's Teddy bear from Teddy, a wooden rocking horse that Lorne had built himself, a diaper bag that Polly had sewn and filled with supplies, a crocheted toy pug dog and set of board books from Caroline and Heath, a handmade quilted play-mat and electronic baby monitor from Felicia and Beau, a vintage cradle that Pris and Happy had stripped, repainted, and stenciled themselves, and a diaper cake from Dana Alton, not to mention a whole wardrobe of baby clothes from the other neighbors.

I had a zillion thank-you notes to write, but Peaches would be well supplied, which was kind of a relief since the remodeling budget had gobbled up the baby budget and then some. I'd handed the last of the invoices and files off to Trey just a couple of days previously, so he could review everything before I wrote Lorne his final check. Things were tight, but Teddy and Polly had insisted on paying rent. That would help a little. And maybe I'd find some freelance work somewhere. I'd figure it out, one way or another. For the moment, we were fine.

The only thing Peaches *didn't* have yet was a blanket knitted by her mother. Between helping Polly get settled into the attic apartment, taking Calvin sightseeing around Charleston, and preparing for the baby shower, there hadn't been much time for knitting. But Peaches wasn't due for a month. I'd get it done in time to bring her home from the hospital in her new, mom-made blanket.

Trey was late, so I supposed the doorbell was announcing his arrival. But I opened the door and found Anne Dowling. "Anne! You came after all!" I threw my arms out and gave her a squeeze. "I thought you were at some legal conference."

"I was," she said. "But after sitting through a five-hour work session to write questions for the next bar exam, I remembered hanging out in a conference room with a bunch of lawyers is the opposite of fun and hopped a plane to Charleston. Hope you don't mind that I'm late. I come bearing gifts, just in case." She thrust a gift-wrapped box into my hands. "It's a silver baby cup. You can engrave it later, after you pick a name."

"Oh, Anne. How sweet. Thank you."

"You know I was rooting for you from day one, don't you?" I had suspected this but it was nice to know for sure. "You're going to be terrific mom, Celia. Becca made the right choice."

"How's she doing?"

The closer we got the due date, the more I found myself thinking about Becca. What was she feeling right now? I was sure she was ready to get on with her life and studies, but this had to be an emotional time. I'd picked up a pen to write a couple of times but after thank you, thank you, thank you, what was there to say? For once in my life, I couldn't summon the right words. Hopefully I'd be able to see her after the birth. If I could see her face, I felt sure the words would come.

"I haven't talked to Becca lately," Anne said, "but her mom texted to say they'd bought her a condo just off campus. Sounds like, I guess, everything's on track for her to start classes in January."

"I'm glad. How about some champagne? You're just in time for karaoke."

Anne gave her head a solemn and very lawyerly sort of shake. "Oh, no. No, no, no, no. I do not sing. Not under any circumstances. But if there's any food left . . ." She sniffed the air, looking hungry and hopeful.

"Tons. I highly recommend the crab and Gruyère frittata. Come on," I said, as I began escorting Anne to the dining room, "let's get you a plate."

The doorbell rang again. From where I stood, the only thing I could see through the beveled glass was an arm and shoulder, but I'd have recognized that shoulder anywhere. "Anne, could you excuse me for just a minute?"

"No worries. I'll just follow the smell of bacon."

Anne headed to the dining room and I opened the door.

"Hey! I was starting to worry that something had happened. It wouldn't have been a party without you," I said sincerely.

It wasn't that Trey was exactly a party animal; I couldn't imagine any amount of champagne that would have convinced him to pick up the karaoke mic. But none of this would be happening without him, so he *had* to come. Trey's arrival felt like a cherry on the cake of an already perfect day.

"Is Lorne here?"

"Sure. Everybody's here." I frowned. The expression on Trey's face made me feel like the cake might be about to fall. "What's wrong?"

A fresh round of whooping and applause floated out of the living room. I heard the tinkle of a piano and the twang of a banjo and knew what was coming next. After two months of working with Lorne, I knew the opening bars to every single Rascal Flatts song. Lorne launched into "My Wish," sounding eerily like Gary LeVox.

Trey pushed past me and set off toward the living room, jaw set and eyes front, stride so long and pace so brisk that I couldn't keep up. I got there just in time to see him grab Lorne by the collar and swing back his arm like a pitcher winding up for a fastball.

There was a dull crack as Trey's fist connected with Lorne's jaw, followed by gasps and squeals. People jumped out of chairs and scrambled to get out of the way. The microphone arced through the air and hit the ground with an amplified *thunk* and an earsplitting screech of feedback. Lorne tumbled backward and hit the ground hard, then lay on the floor, cursing and holding his jaw.

"What the hell was *that* for?"

He sat up and opened his mouth wide a couple of times, testing his jaw, then planted a palm flat on the floor as if to get up. But when Trey took a step closer and clenched his fist again, Lorne seemed to think better of it and stayed put.

"You *know* what it's for!" Trey shouted. "And if you think I'm going to defend you this time . . . You'd better find a lawyer, brother, and quick. After I call your probation officer and the police, you're going back where you belong."

Lorne lifted his hands. "Hey, I don't know what you think I did, but—"

Trey glared down at his brother. "How did I talk myself into believing you could change? If you'd steal from your own father, you'd steal from anybody, including Celia."

His father? That broken old man I'd seen shuffling next to Trey at St. Philip's that day, the man who'd once owned his construction company, who'd taught his boys to build, and had a stroke, and lost his business . . . The crimes Lorne had committed had been against his own dad? And Trey had defended him anyway?

No wonder they hadn't wanted to talk about it. I was far from understanding everything that had happened between these men, but the truth of what I did understand broke over me like an icy wave, especially when I heard Trey's accusation that his brother was at it again. How was that possible?

I thought about everything Lorne and I had been through these last few weeks, the work, sweat, time, and dedication he'd put into the job—so much more than either of us had counted on—the battles we'd fought, the setbacks we'd suffered and overcome. I just couldn't believe that Lorne would steal from me!

But then, when I looked at Lorne's face, I knew I *couldn't* believe it. Maybe I didn't know who Lorne had been before prison, but I knew who he was now. That man would never steal from me. It simply wasn't possible.

"Get up," Trey commanded.

Lorne's eyes sparked as he scrambled to his feet. Trey tore off his jacket and crouched down. The brothers started circling each other with locked gazes and clenched fists, looking for an opening. I pushed my way through the crush of bodies and thrust myself between them, a split second after Lorne threw a punch and Trey ducked.

"Stop it! Both of you!"

Trey tensed his arms and resumed his stance, eyes trained on his brother even as he talked to me. "Celia, get out of the way. He's got this coming. I've seen the invoices. It's just like last time."

Invoices?

Then I remembered—the initial estimates, the materials that weren't in stock, and blown budgets when we had to substitute or change course, the files I'd sent over to Trey with the invoices

Lorne had asked me to hold back, not because he was trying to cheat me but because he knew Trey didn't trust him.

"Trey, listen to me. You've got it all wrong. Lorne didn't—"

"Doesn't matter," Lorne said, shaking his head and glaring at Trey. "This was always going to happen. Do what he says, Celia. Get out of the way."

"No! This is *my* house, and my party! And I'm not—"

Lorne flinched and drew back his fist. Trey bobbed and then lunged for him. Before he could make contact, I did some lunging of my own, swinging my arm out and slapping Trey as hard as I could. The sharp crack of my hand against his face was so loud that it startled me. Trey looked surprised too. He unclenched his fists and dropped his arms limply to his sides.

"Get out!" I shouted. "If you two testosterone-crazed idiots want to beat each other's brains out, then go right ahead. But do it someplace else!"

When neither brother budged, Teddy stepped forward, spreading his feet and planting his hands on his hips so he looked even bigger than he already was. "You heard her, Trey. This is *our* house. You need to leave."

Polly came up from behind and placed her hand on my shoulder. "Lorne, that goes for you too."

Lorne opened his mouth as if he was about to argue his innocence. But when Polly crossed her arms over her chest, he looked at Trey and jerked his head toward the door. "Come on, Trey."

Trey scanned the faces of the onlookers as if he'd just noticed they were there, then licked his lower lip. He had the good grace to look embarrassed, but when he tried to speak, I lifted a hand to stop him.

"I don't want to hear it. This was a really good day and you ruined it."

"I was just trying to look out for you."

"Trey Holcomb, when I need someone to look out for me, *if* I need someone to look out for me, then I'll ask. Until then . . ." I pointed my finger toward the door.

Trey and Lorne started to walk out at the same moment that Anne walked in. She was clutching her cell phone in her hand and looking anxious.

"Celia? I just got a text from the Cavanaughs," she said. "Becca's gone into labor."

Chapter Forty-Four

*I*t was late September, but just after midnight the clouds rolled in, the sky crackled and cracked and rumbled, and the heavens split open to pour down the kind of deluge that usually comes in the hot, humid days of August.

It seemed portentous, that thunderstorm, a meteorological sign. But as I had learned so well in the previous months, signs can be good or bad or simply evidence of an overactive imagination. With the rain coming down in buckets, the wheels of the semitruck in front of us throwing curtains of water onto the windshield, and the wipers unable to keep up, I was too busy trying to keep us on the road to contemplate what kind of sign this might be.

Even without stops, the drive from Charleston to Philadelphia usually takes eleven hours. We'd done it in ten, stopping once for gas and coffee, once when I simply could not hold it any longer, and twice more when we pulled to the side of the road to change drivers. Anne had suggested we fly but there weren't any flights until the morning and I just couldn't wait that long. The three of us piled into Calvin's rental car—Calvin, Anne, and me—and drove straight through and pedal down.

Thanks more to Google Maps than the efforts of the over-worked windshield wipers, I pulled off the highway at the right exit, then reached over and gave Calvin a nudge. He startled and then blinked a few times.

"Are we there?" he yawned.

"Almost. Wake Anne up, will you?"

Calvin reached across the back seat and tapped Anne on the shoulder. She stirred and stretched, asked the same question as Calvin, got the same answer. We pulled into the hospital parking lot.

Anne had a pocket umbrella in her bag but I couldn't wait that long. The others had slept during the trip. I'd closed my eyes and tried my best, counted backwards from one hundred and all that, but sleep wouldn't come. My brain was on spin cycle and my body was pumping adrenaline. Now that I'd been released from automotive purgatory, all that energy finally had somewhere to go.

I sprinted across the parking lot, pelted by rain, and hurdled across puddles, sometimes clearing them and sometimes not. By the time I got to the door, my hair was dripping, my pants were wet from hem to knees, and I was out of breath.

I ran up to the reception desk and bent over and clapped my palms to my legs, wheezing and sucking air. The man behind the reception desk looked concerned. But when I gasped, "Maternity?" he grinned and pointed to a bank of elevators.

"Seventh floor. Turn left after you get off."

"Thanks," I panted. "Two more coming. Big man, peach sweater. Short lady, wrinkled suit."

"I'll tell them. Good luck!"

A trip up seven floors in the world's slowest elevator left me plenty of time to think. Thousands of babies are born every day, hundreds of thousands, almost all of them without incident. There was every reason to believe Peaches would be among them. But she was more than a month early. Was it too soon? Was she big enough? Were her lungs developed enough?

The elevator stopped at the third floor, which, apparently, was the location of the hospital cafeteria. Half a dozen people wearing scrubs got on. The night shift was taking their sweet time getting back to work. Two got off on floor four, one at floor five. Two more got off at six. Finally, the doors opened. Calvin and Anne were standing there, talking with a tall gray-haired woman in a white lab coat.

"Where've you been?" Calvin asked.

I glared at him. Anne introduced me to the gray-haired woman, Dr. Gould.

"Becca's doing great," the doctor told me. "She's fully effaced and five centimeters dilated. The baby is fine. Heart rate is strong. Everything looks good."

"Ten hours of labor and she's only halfway dilated? Doesn't that seem like a long time?"

"Not for a first-time mother," the doctor said. "It's probably going to be a while yet. You might want to find a hotel and get some sleep. We can call you when Becca's getting close to delivery."

I shook my head. "No, I'd rather stay here."

The doctor smiled. "Somehow I thought you'd say that. We've got a waiting room with comfy chairs and bad coffee. But maybe you want to come to the birthing suite and say hello to Becca?"

Anne glanced at me. "Becca's mom and dad are in there." I

took the hint. The Cavanaughs didn't like me any more now than they had before. Best to avoid a face-to-face meeting. "I'll be fine in the waiting room. I could use some bad coffee."

"Somebody will come find you as soon as the baby's born." The doctor laid her hand on my arm. "Don't worry, Mom. We're going to take good care of your baby."

My throat felt thick.

It was the first time anyone had ever called me Mom.

ANNE CHECKED INTO a hotel. After some arguing, I convinced Calvin to do the same but refused to join him. "There's no point," I told him. "I'm not going to be able to sleep anyway."

For a long time I didn't. But even adrenaline rushes don't last forever. In the middle of a dream that I can't really remember, something involving Teddy and a baby squirrel, I felt a hand gently shaking my shoulder.

"Mrs. Fairchild?"

I opened my eyes, blinked, pushed myself up off the vinyl sofa. A dark-skinned young man in green scrubs was looking at me.

"It's Miss—Miss Fairchild."

"Dr. Gould asked me to come find you. Would you like to see your daughter?"

I jumped up, ran a hand over my messy hair, grabbed my purse. "Yes. Thanks. Is she—"

He smiled. "She's absolutely perfect."

Oh, yes. Yes, she was.

Ten toes. Ten fingers that gripped tight when I placed one of mine in her palm. A full head of black hair as fine and fluffy as down. Little rosebud lips that opened wide to reveal a tiny pink tongue when she yawned.

Most miraculous of all were the two slate-blue eyes that opened and blinked and gazed in mine when I leaned close and whispered, "Hello, little girl. I'm Celia. I'm your mommy."

The nurse smiled down at us.

"What do you think, Mom?"

It took me a moment to know what to say. I'd never felt anything like this before.

"That this is the person I've spent my whole life waiting for."

Chapter Forty-Five

"*C*alvin, hurry! I don't want to be late."

Calvin shifted one of the huge Target shopping bags to his other hand, balancing out his load, but quickened his pace not at all. "Calm down. You said you'd be here at ten. It's five minutes past. You think they're going to give the baby to somebody else if you're a few minutes late?"

Well . . . no. At least highly unlikely. But today was my first full day as a mom and I wanted to get it right. Being anything less than one hundred percent on time felt like stepping off on the wrong foot.

So did the fact that I'd had to delay picking Peaches up by an hour because I'd forgotten to bring the car seat from Charleston. Calvin and I had been standing outside the doors of Target fifteen minutes before opening, waiting to buy a car seat, formula, disposable diapers, and a baby blanket, since I hadn't finished knitting mine. Yes, she had been born early, and yes, the race to Philadelphia had been a little frantic. And of course it would all work out. But having to go out and buy things at the

last minute was making me feel unprepared and a little over-
whelmed at the prospect of being responsible for an entire tiny
human.

This was not the way I had envisioned starting out.

"I'm pretty sure that's the way every new mother feels," Calvin
said when I shared all this with him.

"You think?"

"Absolutely. I think it's just part of the deal."

This was oddly comforting.

"Okay. Well . . . good."

We went straight from the lobby to the seventh floor; the elevator didn't stop once, which seemed like a good sign. Anne was
standing there when the doors opened. At first, I thought it was
a coincidence, that we'd just happened to arrive at the same time.
But something about the look on her face gave me the feeling that
she had news and that it probably wasn't good. And when the
Cavanaughs came marching down the corridor to the elevator,
she with red-rimmed eyes, he with a glowering gaze, the feeling
grew.

I lifted my arm to stop the elevator door from closing and stood
aside. The Cavanaughs swept by me without making eye contact.
But just before the doors closed, Mrs. Cavanaugh glanced up to
glare at me with wet, angry eyes.

"This whole thing is *your* fault."

The doors closed and the Cavanaughs disappeared. I exchanged
anxious looks with Calvin, then looked to Anne.

"What's going on? Did something . . ." I paused, afraid to say
what I was thinking. "Is Peaches—"

"She's fine," Anne assured me. "Absolutely fine." I closed my
eyes and let out the breath I'd been holding. "But . . . something
has happened."

Anne paused. Her eyes flitted away from mine.

"Becca wants to talk to you."

LYING IN THE hospital bed, wearing a shapeless, oversized cotton gown, Becca seemed even smaller and more vulnerable than she had the first time we'd met, but somehow older. Maybe she was tired. She pushed a remote control to raise the head of the bed into a sitting position.

I said hello, asked how she was doing, got the expected answer, and pulled up a chair. My heart was thrumming. Though I was filled with dreadful anticipation of the reason she wanted to see me, I could never have imagined what she was about to say.

"I know we never met until I visited you in Charleston," she said. "But when I found out I was pregnant, you were the very first person I told."

Becca paused, perhaps waiting for me to put two and two together. It just didn't register, and when I frowned, she went on. "I sent an email to you, to Dear Calpurnia. I told you that I was a high school senior, that I'd gone to a party, drank too much, slept with a boy I barely knew, and got pregnant. I said I hadn't told my parents yet but was pretty sure they'd want me to get an abortion and that I didn't think I could go through with that. I also said I didn't think I was ready to be a mother and asked you what I should do. I signed my name No Good Choice."

Becca's eyes started to fill. She cast her gaze to the ceiling and pressed her lips together for a moment before continuing with her story. "Honestly, I didn't really expect you to answer. But a couple days later, you did."

Becca had been holding a piece of copy paper with deep creases and frayed edges in her hands. Now she unfolded the paper and started to read.

Dear No Good Choice,

When I was a little older than you, my father died and suddenly I was alone in the world. I was very sad, also very afraid. I didn't think I was ready to be an adult. In some ways, I was right. Hardly anybody crosses the threshold to adulthood with confidence. Those few who do probably shouldn't.

But sooner or later, ready or not, everybody gets to the place you're standing now, the moment where they have to decide. Are you going to move ahead, make your own decision, and be responsible for your own choices? Or retreat to childhood and let others do it for you?

The fact that you're struggling with this decision tells me that you're probably more grown-up than you think you are. It also tells me that you're stronger than you know, strong enough to make this choice independent of the influence and pressure of other people, and strong enough to survive whatever comes next.

You asked me what you should do. I can't tell you that. No one can, including your parents. But if you calm yourself and search your heart (and only yours), I know you'll find the right choice. Once you do, don't let anyone or anything sway you from it.

Nothing about what comes next will be easy. But you're strong and you're capable. You can do this, sweet girl. I have faith in you.

This is hard, but you do have choices. And while it might not feel that way right now, someday, maybe even years from now, you'll look back and see that, ultimately, the right choice was also the good choice.

Sending you some sugar,
Calpurnia

Becca folded my letter back along the well-worn creases and wiped the corners of her eyes.

"When I told my mom I was pregnant, she was totally calm and super understanding, at least at first. Mom is a big believer in a woman's right to choose. Well . . ." Becca gave a small, sad shrug. "As long as the choice doesn't include her daughter becoming an unwed mother. She kept saying, 'Why would you put yourself, put us, through that? A quick procedure and it's over and done with and you go on with your life. It'll be like it never happened.'"

Becca gave her head a hard shake. "But I knew it wouldn't be like that, not for me. I don't know about other people, but for me, having the baby was the right choice, the only choice. That's what I told my parents."

She paused and let out a breath.

"They were so, *so* mad. They said I was going to ruin my life. They said I was being stupid and selfish. They even accused me of getting pregnant on purpose, trying to get their attention." She let out a bitter laugh. "Please. Like I hadn't given up on that years ago."

Becca lowered her eyes, looking at her hands and the letter that was still clutched in her fingers. "Whenever they told me I was being dumb and self-centered, whenever they made me doubt myself, I would read what you wrote, the part about me being strong and capable and you having faith in me."

She looked up. Tears spilled over onto her cheeks. By that time, I was crying too.

"It was like you were right there with me, Celia, cheering me on. You gave me courage to make my choice and stick with it."

"I'm glad," I said hoarsely.

I was. But I knew what was coming. It felt like my heart was about to crack. Becca swiped away tears with the back of her hand.

"When Anne said that one of the 'Dear Birth Mother' letters was from you, I just . . . I couldn't believe it. It felt like a sign, you know? Like confirmation that I was doing the right thing."

I mirrored her nod. But as I knew only too well, signs don't always mean what you think they do.

"My parents wanted to go with one of the other families," Becca said, "because they had more money. I said that I'd meet them, just to make Mom and Dad happy, but I was sure you would be a good mother. And then, after I met you, saw your house, your neighborhood, your cousin and his crazy dogs . . ." She smiled momentarily. "I knew it was true. You would be an amazing mom, Celia. The best.

"But then . . . After last night, after I saw the baby, and held her . . . I just . . ." Becca's voice was shaking. She paused, tried to catch her breath, to find words, failed, and sobbed, covering her face with her hands. "I'm sorry, Celia. I'm so, so sorry. I thought I could do it. I know it's not fair but . . . I can't," she gasped. "I just can't."

I don't remember standing up. But somehow, there I was, standing by the bed, wrapping my arms around the girl's bowed, shaking shoulders, saying the only thing there was to say.

"I know, Becca. I know."

CALVIN WAS WAITING for me.

His eyes were red and puffy, so I knew he'd already guessed what had happened, and that was a relief. I didn't want to say it out loud, to explain that Becca was keeping her baby, and that Peaches wouldn't be coming home with me, and that the last six months of my life had been a waste of time, money, and dreams, a heartbreaking and cosmically cruel joke.

Calvin opened his arms. I stumbled forward and practically fell into his embrace. If Calvin hadn't been supporting me, I might have melted like candle wax, slipped slowly to the floor, and never gotten up again.

I'd never felt so tired, so defeated, so hopeless.

That morning, and the one before that, and the one before that, in a succession that seemed like it stretched back further than my remembering, the only thing that had gotten me up in the morning and through the days was the hope of *this* day, the day I would carry my daughter home in my arms.

And now?

"What am I going to do, Calvin? I don't know what to do."

He pushed me back just a little, shifting my weight from his chest to my own feet, and looked into my eyes. "What do you *want* to do, cupcake?"

The answer came quickly.

"Let's get out of here. I want to go home."

Chapter Forty-Six

Polly tapped on my bedroom door.

"Hey, you decent?"

If by decent she meant dressed, the answer was yes, sort of. Pulling on leggings under the sleep shirt you'd never bothered to change out of that morning counts as being dressed, doesn't it? At least technically?

"Sorry I didn't get to say good-bye to Calvin," she said after I waved her in, "but first day at the new job and all." She shrugged. "Did he get home okay?"

I nodded. "He texted me a couple of hours ago. He was in a cab, heading back to his apartment."

"That's good," Polly said. "It was nice of him to drive you all the way home and then hang around to cheer you up."

After leaving the hospital, I told Calvin to drop me off and I'd catch the next flight to Charleston. It would only have taken him a couple of hours to drive back to New York, but he insisted on coming back to Charleston with me and staying on for over a week, cooking and hovering and, as Polly said, trying to cheer me up. He meant well, everybody did, including Polly, so I now scooted myself into a sitting position in the middle of my bed and tried to pretend that I didn't want her to go back upstairs and leave me alone.

"How was work?" I asked.

"Thrilling!" she said, clapping her hands together with feigned enthusiasm. "I rang up about a zillion chicken sandwiches, put new rolls of toilet paper in all the bathroom stalls, and mopped up no less than three spilled Coca-Colas. All in all, a red-letter first day in the exciting fast-food industry!"

She chuckled. "It's okay for now. It'll pay some bills until I find something better or until we find out if I'll be able to reopen the shop. Have you heard anything from Trey about the zoning?"

I shook my head. I hadn't heard from Trey or Lorne since the baby shower. Not too surprising given that I'd banished them from the party, and probably just as well. I wasn't in the mood to see Trey. I wasn't in the mood to see anybody, but Polly sat down on the edge of the bed just the same.

"So?" she asked cheerfully. "What did you do today? I mean, after Calvin left."

The more interesting question would have been what had I not done. A partial list included not showering, not putting on real clothes, not making the bed, and not really even getting out of bed. But I was pretty sure Polly could tell that by looking at me, so I spread out my hands and shrugged my shoulders to indicate the obvious.

Polly kicked off her shoes, twisted sideways, and sat on the bed, crossing her legs under her body so she was facing me. The look on her face told me she was about to launch into A Serious Discussion. I closed my eyes for a moment. I was not in the mood for this.

"Celia. I know that losing Peaches was devastating. And I know you're depressed. But really, girl . . ." She cast her gaze around the room, taking in the rumpled bedclothes, the drawn shades, the untouched yogurt parfait that Calvin had made for my breakfast and left on my nightstand before saying good-bye. "How much longer are you going to go on like this?"

"I don't know." I looked at my lap and bunched the edge of the sleep shirt into my fist. "I'm trying, Polly. I really am."

"No. You're not." I looked up. Polly's expression twisted into the kind of frown that comes when disappointment turns to anger. "You're *not* trying, Celia. You're wallowing. And I'm getting worn out with worry from watching you do it. *Everybody* is," she said, leaning closer than felt comfortable before launching into her list.

"Calvin flew home feeling like a failure because he couldn't cheer up his best friend. Teddy is moping around the house like a whipped pup and the pups are doing the same because they can't figure out what's wrong with him. Felicia's so distracted that she burned her hand, taking a tray of benne wafers that you wouldn't eat out of the oven. Caroline decided not to go to that conference in Williamsburg with Heath because she'd feel guilty having a good time while you're so miserable. Pris and Happy are bickering again. And I haven't slept in days because I've been lying awake, trying to figure out how to tell you to quit feeling so damned sorry for yourself!

"The plan was to do it diplomatically. But obviously *that* didn't work out," Polly said, sounding almost as frustrated with herself as she was with me. She got to her feet and started to pace across the room. "Look, Celia. I know this is hard and a huge disappointment. But you've got to get up and go on with your life! You can't hide up here forever, acting like somebody died."

"You don't understand," I said, and turned my face to the wall, not from despair but from bitterness and anger. Polly had never even wanted a child; she'd told me so herself. So how could she possibly understand what I was feeling? To have everything I'd ever longed for, to have held her in my arms, believing she was mine, to have loved her and then lost her— No, Polly didn't understand. No one could. "It's like she did die."

"No. It's *not*."

Polly stopped pacing. The adamant tone in her voice drew my attention, and I turned toward her again, expecting to see an angry face, hear angry words, and prepared to answer with some of my own. But instead of anger I saw desperation, heard the pleading voice of a frightened friend, and felt the edge of my own anger soften.

"Don't you see, Celia? Because you wrote that letter and helped Becca to be strong and stand up to her parents, Peaches is very much alive and very much loved. Because of you, Peaches *didn't* die." She paused, looking at me with sadness and sympathy. "But your dream did. And I know what that feels like."

She was talking about having to close the shop, of course. She was trying to help, I knew that, but it wasn't the same. Peaches wasn't a dream, she was *the* dream, my chance for happiness.

"And Sheepish was mine," Polly said, after I finished speaking. "I put everything I had into it—all my money, all my hopes and dreams. I'll never forget how I felt the first time I unlocked the door and turned the open sign face out. For the first time, I felt like I doing something important with my life, sharing what I loved most with the world, spreading a little joy. I know it was only a little shop, a small dream. But it was mine," she said, her voice dropping to a whisper, her eyes glassy with memory. "When it failed, I felt like I'd failed too, blown the only chance I had at getting the only thing I wanted.

"But *you're* the one who told me I couldn't give up," she said, refocusing her gaze and sounding less sympathetic than she had a moment before. "You're the reason I'm putting myself out there again. You're the reason I took a dead-end job that'll be easy to quit if Trey does manage to get me that zoning variance.

"'Try again,' Polly said, shifting her voice into a nasally twang that was meant to imitate mine. "'You've got nothing to lose by taking a second chance.' Nothing but getting my hopes and heart broken again," Polly said, tossing me a glare and planting a fist on her hip. "I'm not saying you're wrong, but why are the rules different for you than the rest of us?"

"They're not," I insisted. "But this is different, don't you see?" Of course she did. The fact that she was pretending like she didn't was starting to tick me off. "You can always open another craft shop. But I'm not going to get another baby."

"How do you know that?"

"Oh, come *on*, Polly! Because I do, okay?" I scooted toward the headboard, putting as much distance between us as possible, and hugged a pillow to my chest to keep from throwing it at her.

"Do you have any idea how many 'Dear Birth Mother' letters I sent out the first time?" I asked before answering my own question. "Sixty-seven. Do you know how many birth mothers responded? One. Becca. And that was only because she found out that I was Dear Calpurnia. Well, I'm not Dear Calpurnia anymore. Now I'm just me, just Celia Fairchild, a single woman with a big house, no job, and no prospects. There won't be a second chance." I paused. "And maybe that's just as well. Because I don't think I could go through it again, Polly. I really don't."

I looked away and pressed my hand to my mouth. Polly bent down, ducking her head low so I had no choice but to look into her eyes.

"I'm sorry," she said softly. "I didn't mean it like that. I know you're hurting. But there's something I have to tell you and I don't want you to take it the wrong way." She took in a big breath and let it out. "You know I love you, Celia Fairchild. But I swear, you are just about the *dumbest* smart person I've ever met."

I swiped my eyes and frowned. I'm not sure what I'd expected her to say but it definitely wasn't that.

"I mean it," Polly said, rightly reading my confused expression. "I don't understand how somebody who has such good insights into other people can be so incredibly clueless about herself. Do you ever go back and read some of your old columns? Because maybe you should. I found a bunch on the Internet this week and . . ." She shook her head and popped her brows. "Damn, girl! There was some really good stuff there."

"That was Calpurnia," I said, shaking off Polly's undeserved praise. "I just wrote down what she would have said."

Polly pursed her lips and moved her head from side to side. "Nope. Not buying it. I knew Calpurnia too, remember? She was a wonderful woman who loved you and gave you a good start in life—well, until she lost her mind. But you hadn't seen her since you were twelve years old," Polly reasoned. "After that, you were on your own.

"Calpurnia's name was in the title," she went on, "but what came after that was all you. Your voice, your experience, and especially your compassion. That's the reason all those people were willing to share their problems and secrets with you, because they knew you cared.

"And that's just who you are, 'Just Celia,'" she said, smiling and making air quotes with her fingers. "Just a good, honest, open woman who cares about everybody. I know because I see it every day. You can't help yourself from helping, Celia. That's why everybody's crazy about you. Including me." Polly sat down next to me, shoulder to shoulder, with her back against the headboard and her knees pulled to her chest.

"You handed out a whole lot of good advice in your columns, Just Celia. Maybe it's time you tried following some of it." She leaned hard to one side, bumping into me purposely and hard enough that I had to put out my hand to keep my balance.

"You think?" I asked, smiling a little. "Starting with what?"

"Well. Let's see . . ." Polly paused, made a sucking sound with her teeth. "I seem to recall a letter you wrote to somebody called Heartbroken in Hoboken, advising him to look at what he'd gained instead of all he'd lost. Basically, you told him to count his blessings. But you said it more eloquently than that."

Did I?

Over the years, I've written thousands of letters. I doubt that any of them contained anything the recipients didn't already know deep down; the only sense I've ever had to offer is the common variety. But I do care. Maybe caring is eloquent enough.

"You did good, Celia. For Peaches and Becca, for Teddy, for Pris, for me, for all of us. And you did good for you too." My forehead creased as I tried to make sense of this last. Polly smiled.

"Don't you see? You started out fixing up a house but ended up creating a home filled with people you love and who love you right back. No, you don't have a baby. Maybe you never will. But you *do* have a family."

Polly searched my eyes with her own. "Isn't that what you always wanted? Wasn't that your dream all along?"

Chapter Forty-Seven

I'm certainly not an expert knitter. At my current rate of productivity, I doubt I ever will be. But you don't have to be an expert to understand what people see in it.

To begin with, there's the whole "maker" aspect of knitting, the satisfaction that comes from creating something with your own hands, not to mention the even greater satisfaction that comes from gifting that creation to somebody you care about.

When I left my room, showered, and got dressed in real clothes the next morning, I hadn't experienced that personally, at least not yet. But I understood instinctively that when your heart is too full and your thoughts too tangled to say all the things you really feel, knitting something that will let someone you love feel warm, cherished, and foremost in your thoughts says what words sometimes can't.

And for people who aren't always good at being in the moment or sitting with their own thoughts, knitting is an anchor, a gentle, centering weight. That was what I needed more than anything just then, stillness. An anchor.

I closed the door to the yarn cave, settled myself into Beebee's comfortable old pink chair, and picked up where I'd left off nearly three weeks before. The evening was blessedly cool and I had the windows open to the breeze. As I looped the yarn over my fingers and worked my needles, adding five inches of lemon-colored yarn to Peaches's puzzle blanket, I kept my mind purposely and safely empty.

But I heard the thrum of cicadas, the barking of dogs, footsteps and snippets of conversations from people walking past, laughter and music that floated from Caroline's window to mine as she and Heath practiced a rumba, and I started to hum, adding my small contribution to the larger song of the night, a song called belonging.

I grafted another color into the blanket, robin's-egg blue, feeling calm, safe, and thoughtful. I thought about my mother and father, about Beebee and Calpurnia, about Teddy and me, and all those who'd come before, the people who shared my blood and had lived inside these walls. I thought about Pris, Felicia, Caroline, Happy, and Polly and all the things she'd said. She was right. They were part of it too, this place of belonging, this family I had longed for, this dream fulfilled.

And as I finished knitting the blue and brought in the sapphire yarn, the final color, I thought about the baby and Becca. I let the tears flow one final time for dreams lost, and let them subside and be replaced by love and prayers, good wishes and future hopes, growing my heart row by row, binding off bitterness stitch by stitch until the work was done and only a single stitch was left on the needle.

The work was done.

I brushed my fingers across the blanket, enjoying its softness, admiring the uniformity of the stitching and the way the colors came together, each separate hue making all the others so much more beautiful. I thought about that last remaining stitch and how the whole thing had begun with exactly that, just one simple stitch.

I thought about beginnings and endings, and the number of times I'd begun the work, only to fumble the row or drop a stitch, and been forced to unravel the work and begin again. And with a suddenness that surprised me, I thought about Trey.

A door slammed downstairs. Teddy and Polly were back. I heard voices, the padding of paws, footsteps on the stairs. Teddy stuck his head into the room.

"We picked up some pizza for dinner—pepperoni and buffalo chicken. You want some?"

"Sounds good. I'll be down in a few minutes. I'm almost finished here."

Teddy smiled and pointed to the blanket draped across my lap. "Hey! That turned out good, didn't it?"

"Yes," I said. "I think so too."

Teddy went downstairs. I cut the yarn and wove in the ends, placed the blanket inside a big box that was already filled with the baby shower presents I no longer needed, and found a pen and paper.

Dear Becca and Ella,

Anne sent word that you'd found an apartment and she passed on your new address. I thought the baby clothes and equipment might come in handy. Well . . . maybe not so much the USC onesie, but a baby needs something to spit up on, right?

You've been on my mind lately. I've been wondering how things are going. Becca, are you getting any sleep? Ella, are you trying your best to let her? (By the way, Becca, you did great picking out a name. The right name is important. She looks exactly like an Ella.)

Along with the clothes, toys, supplies, and the blanket I knit myself, I'm sending so much love and so much hope that you're well and happy, and always will be. I know you've got this, Becca. But if you ever need anything, I hope you know that you can call on me. As I've recently been reminded, whether you're born into it or make it yourself, everybody needs family.

Everything I wrote to you as Calpurnia was and is true. You've made the right choice, the good choice.

Sincerely,
Celia

Chapter Forty-Eight

"Oh. Hey, Celia. Is Polly home?"

"She just left for work."

Trey couldn't have been all that surprised when I answered the door; it was my house. When I took a second look, I realized his features weren't registering surprise but something closer to discomfort, the kind of expression people get when thrust into a situation they know they'll have to deal with eventually but had been hoping to avoid.

Only the day before, much to my own surprise, I'd found myself thinking about him, imagining what I might do or say if, by some strange chance, he did show up at my doorstep. Now he was here and it was awkward, also a little scary. Being vulnerable, opening the door to admit feelings you've tried to hide, is always scary. It didn't look like I was the only one who felt that way.

Trey shuffled his feet and shoved his fists so deep into his jacket pockets, it was a wonder the seams didn't rip, which might have been an improvement, or at least an incentive to buy a new suit. "Right. Well. I was just in the neighborhood and hoped she might be home. I've got good news. The city ruled that your great-grandfather's old shop is . . . uh . . . grandfathered. You know. I mean for zoning purposes."

I didn't say anything. It wasn't that I enjoyed watching him twist in the wind exactly. But until that moment, I'd never seen Trey look anything less than sure of himself. It was kind of endearing. He cleared his throat. "Anyway . . . If Polly is still interested in reopening Sheepish in your great-grandfather's old shop, she can."

"Thanks. That's great, Trey."

"Yeah. I thought she'd be excited. So. Just wanted to stop by. You know, to tell her." He bobbed his head with a kind of okay-that's-all movement. He turned to leave and I felt something sink inside me. But then, as he reached the edge of the piazza, his head lifted and his shoulders squared. The person who turned around to face me was old Trey, the man who is always sure of himself, or at least sure of what he wants to say.

"Sorry. That was a lie."

"The part about the zoning?" I asked.

"No," he said. "That's a done deal. They're mailing the permits. I meant the part about me wanting to tell Polly face to face. The truth is, I came here because I was hoping I'd find you home and we could talk."

"About what happened at the shower?"

He nodded. "Yes. Among other things. But let's start with that." Trey took a breath, like a swimmer bracing himself for the plunge into frigid water.

"I was way out of line," he said, "on all kinds of levels. I ruined your party and I'm sorry. There really isn't an excuse for how I acted but . . . I thought this might help you understand." He reached into his pocket, took out a piece of paper, and held it out to me.

A note? He was handing me a note? I glanced down at the paper, then up at him, frowning.

"Just read it," Trey said, flapping his hand as I unfolded the paper.

Dear Celia,

Please excuse my brother for acting like an idiot. It wasn't all his fault because it had to happen eventually. But I'm really sorry it happened during your party. So is Trey.

Sincerely,
Lorne

I looked up at him. "You brought me an excuse note? From your brother?" Even with my hand pressed to my mouth, I couldn't quite cover my smile. "Does this mean that you and Lorne are talking again?"

"It's an ongoing discussion," Trey said. "There's a lot to talk about."

Over the last weeks, I'd drawn a broad outline of the events that caused the break between Trey and Lorne. And when brotherly tensions boiled over and the fistfight broke out, I'd been able to color in the rest of the details. But this was the first time Trey had voluntarily shared the story with me. As he talked, I started to realize what a leap he was taking by doing so, a leap of trust.

"Dad's business was already shaky," Trey said. "He'd under-bid on a big construction project and lost a lot of money, so the company might have gone under even if Lorne hadn't embezzled the money to feed his drug habit. And Dad was a lifelong smoker, a two-pack-a-day man, so it's possible he'd have had the stroke anyway, but I still blamed Lorne for everything. I defended him in court, but only because somebody had to. And I *never* forgave him."

As Trey shook his head, the pain in his eyes told me that he was almost as disappointed with himself as he'd been with his brother. "I've always said that I thought everybody deserves a second chance. After you kicked us out, I realized I meant everybody but Lorne. I was so ready to believe the worst about him. And I was furious with him but . . ." He paused and ducked his head.

"Well, the truth is, a part of me was almost happy when I thought Lorne was at it again," he said. "I felt justified about being so mad and never giving him that second chance. My own brother . . ."

Trey was talking more to himself than to me at that point, but I wanted to tell him I understood how it feels when people you love let you down, how hard it can be to forgive, and how much I admired him for doing it and for facing his own faults too. Before I could say anything, Trey came to himself again, looking a little embarrassed.

"Anyway, I'm sorry."

I smiled. "Apology accepted."

Trey reached into an inside pocket of his jacket, pulled out a flat rectangular-shaped packet. "This is for you," he said. "Peace offering."

When he prodded me to go ahead and open it, I ripped the paper off the package, smiling at what I found inside. It was a collector's edition of *The Santa Clause*, the original as well as the two sequels, on Blu-ray.

"I hope you don't already have them," he said.

I did but not all on one disc and not with bonus footage.

"Thanks. I'd have forgiven you anyway, but this is great. Really great."

I paused and took a breath, remembered sitting up in my yarn cave the night before, thinking about Trey and that single stitch and how just about every good, big thing starts with one good, small thing.

"Do you want to come over and watch them with me? Maybe this weekend?"

Trey shook his head. The hopeful knot that had formed in my middle fell to the bottom of my stomach with a disappointed thump.

"Lorne and I have plans this weekend. Dad always loved fishing before his stroke. We're going in together to book a charter boat, take Dad out, and see if we can hook a few mackerel, maybe some tarpon if we're lucky."

"Oh, I'm glad," I said sincerely.

"But I was thinking about something else we might do next weekend, I mean, if you don't have plans." Trey reached into yet another pocket and pulled out two tickets. "It's a reunion concert," he explained. "Lorne said you love Rascal Flatts."

Very funny, Lorne.

Given some time, I suspected I could learn to love Rascal Flatts. Now that he'd started to trust me, I suspected it might take even less time to learn to love Trey Holcomb. I was halfway there already and that was even before he pressed his lips together, like he was trying to decide how much more he should say, then made up his mind to take the chance.

"The thing is," Trey said, "I kind of gave up on dating a few years back. What with the bankruptcy, and my dad getting sick, all the stuff with Lorne, and trying to keep my practice going, there hasn't been much time for anything else. Besides, I went out with a lot of nice women before but none who made me think about wanting to do more than date. So really," he said with a shrug, "what was the point?"

"But you . . . ," he said softly, his voice turning husky as his brandy-brown eyes locked onto mine. "Celia, I've never met anyone quite like you. But . . . the more I know about you, the more I want to know, and the more I want you to know me too. I guess what I'm trying to say is, for the first time in a long time, you made me think about wanting more."

The way he was looking at me, the words he was saying, took my breath away for a moment. Before I could catch it again, Trey shifted into another gear, his words tumbling out as he clarified his position. "It's sudden, I know. And I get that this is a lot to put out there all at once. I'll understand if you say no or would rather take it slow, but I just thought this might be a good way to start. Or not. So . . . what do you think? Is it a date?"

There it was again, that hopeful, vulnerable, less-sure version of himself, which, I decided, was not only endearing but really devastatingly cute.

"Well," I said. "Possibly. I do have some conditions."

Trey's eyebrows arched. "And they are?"

"First, that I take you shopping for new suits. Actually, forget suits," I said, waving my hand. "How about sport jackets? And more jeans for the weekend. You look really good in jeans—"

"Thank you for noticing—"

"And the second condition," I said, talking over him, "is that you kiss me."

For a second, Trey looked surprised; then the corners of his mouth twitched into a smile. "I see. Any particular order in which these conditions should be met?"

I shook my head. "Gentleman's choice. Whatever seems most urgent to you."

Trey took a step toward me. "Well, in that case . . ."

He lowered his head slowly, until his lips met mine. I closed my eyes, wrapped my arms around his neck, and pressed closer, sinking into his embrace, realizing I'd wanted to for a long, long time.

Oh, yeah. I could definitely *learn to love Rascal Flatts.*

Chapter Forty-Nine

*A*fter changing out of my interview outfit and looking through the mail, I trotted across the garden toward the shop, following the sound of hammering and the smell of paint. Polly, carrying an empty cardboard box, came out the back door just as I was about to come in.

"Hey! How was the interview?" I shook my head and Polly frowned. "Oh, I'm sorry."

"It's okay," I said. "Technical writing probably isn't my cup of tea anyway."

This was true. I really wasn't that disappointed not to have gotten the job, but at some point, I needed to figure out what really was my cup of tea. It was getting a little discouraging.

This was the second time one of my interviews had ended with the interviewer pulling out a copy of one of my old columns and asking for my autograph. I never had a chance. The HR manager wasn't seriously considering me for the job; she just wanted to meet Dear Calpurnia. Without thinking, I'd started to sign my real name, and the woman had actually let out a nervous giggle and asked if I would sign as Calpurnia instead. The whole thing had been a waste of time.

"However," I said, reaching into my pocket for the picture Becca had just sent, "in better news . . ." Ella, wearing a robin's-egg blue headband with an enormous bow, was lying on her knitted puzzle blanket, looking insanely cute.

"Aww . . ." Polly clapped her hand to her heart. "What a sweetie. How can she already be two months old?"

"I know, right? She's getting so big. Becca says she's already starting to hold her head up. Clearly, she's very advanced."

"Clearly," Polly said. "But we knew that."

I tucked the picture into my pocket. "So? How's it going in there? When I left, Happy was bossing everybody around, Trey and Lorne were arguing about light fixture placement, and Bug had knocked over a can of paint."

"The paint's been cleaned up," Polly said, "the guys worked everything out, and Happy is still bossing everybody. Things are looking pretty good. Come take a look."

Polly tossed the empty box to one side and went back inside the shop. I followed her, pushing aside a piece of plastic tarp that was hanging across the door.

"Oh, my . . ." My mouth dropped open like I was one of those homeowners on the decorating shows who are astounded by the Big Reveal. "I can't believe it. This is amazing!"

It really was.

Though we both knew it would be a stretch, when Polly and I had talked about a date for reopening the shop, I'd encouraged her to aim for the Friday after Thanksgiving. Opening at the official kickoff of the Christmas shopping season would help get the business onto a solid footing quickly.

When I'd peeked in earlier that morning, I'd had serious doubts that the shop would be ready for the scheduled grand opening party. But an incredible transformation had taken place during my absence. Light poured in through the once grimy, painted-over display window and onto the freshly painted white walls, making the whole space look bright, clean, inviting, and even bigger than it already was. There was still plenty to do in the forty-eight hours, especially since we'd be taking a break to celebrate Thanksgiving, but with everyone bustling about and pitching in, it looked like Sheepish would open for business on schedule.

Beau, looking dapper as always in a black-and-white-checkered waistcoat and red bow tie, unloaded boxes and handed yarn off to Felicia, who was filling floor-to-ceiling cubbies with a rainbow of soft, colorful skeins that practically begged to be touched. Caroline was stocking display towers with pattern and instruction books, pausing to look at each one before assigning it to the correct category—knitting, crocheting, quilting, sewing, or miscellaneous. Heath stood on a chair, hanging a blue-and-coral patchwork quilt on the wall, a sample for the first class Polly planned to teach in the new shop. Teddy unloaded more boxes, arranging a small but carefully curated collection of bright, modern cotton fabric on shelves. Bug and Pebbles lay on the floor nearby, paws tucked under their chins, following Teddy's every move with their big brown eyes. Trey stood on a ladder in the center of the room, hanging a circa 1960s crystal chandelier unearthed from Calpurnia's hoard that hadn't found an eBay buyer but looked totally perfect in the space.

I looked up and smiled at him as I walked by. He smiled back, pursed his lips into an air-kiss meant just for me, then popped his eyebrows up and down and gave me a look, the look that said he couldn't wait until we were alone, and that always gave me the same giddy, fluttery, shuddery, roller-coaster-drop sensation that came over me the first time we kissed. I kept waiting for it to wear off, but so far, it hadn't. I was starting to think that it never would, which was wonderful.

I touched my fingers to my lips, tossed Trey's kiss back to him, and went to the front of the shop to see how things were progressing there.

Happy, looking sharp but casual in a crisp white blouse over a pair of black cigarette pants, was in her element, cheerfully barking orders to Lorne and the recently paroled Slip about where to place groupings of cushy, chintz-covered armchairs and pillow-strewn benches. The mismatched mélange of shabby chic, thrift shop furnishings brought the space together in a cozy, comfortable, inviting jumble that shouldn't have looked good together but somehow did.

"Can you believe it?" Polly asked, coming up behind me and beaming as she looked around the room. "When I dreamed about opening my own shop, this is exactly what I had in mind—something modern and open but still homey. I mean, look at that." Polly pointed to an overstuffed armchair upholstered in sage-green toile. "Doesn't it just make you want to curl up and knit something? Happy, I don't know how to thank you. I'd never have been able to pull this together myself."

"It looks fantastic," I said. "Happy, you've got wonderful taste."

Seeing that the rest of our crafting crew had gathered by the front window, Felicia and Caroline left their workstations and joined the party.

"I can't believe the difference," Felicia said, looking around the room and pushing her glittery red glasses, the ones she reserves for special occasions, up the bridge of her nose so she could see better. "Every single thing in this place looks like it was absolutely meant to be here. Happy, sugar," she declared, "it's absolutely *perfect*."

"You've got a gift," Caroline said, nodding her agreement as she looked toward Happy. "You really do."

"Oh, well." Happy flapped her hand to dismiss their praise but looked more than a little pleased. "It's coming along. Lots to do yet, but we're getting there."

"I wish we had some champagne," Polly said. "Not that I would have any, but still, if we did, I'd raise a toast to Happy. To everybody. It's not going to be like last time, is it?" she asked, looking at me with a grin that was anxious and excited all at once, as if she might explode from pure happiness.

"It's not going to be like last time," I assured her. "Sheepish is going to be a big success. I'm sure of it."

"So am I," Polly said. "And I've got all of you to thank for it."

"How about sweet tea?" Caroline said, pointing to a pitcher that was sitting on a nearby table. "Can't we toast with that?"

"In Charleston? Absolutely," Felicia ruled, bobbing her head so the rhinestones in her glasses glinted in the sunlight that poured through the front window, casting a sparkling rainbow against the freshly painted white wall. "Come on, ladies. Everybody get a glass."

We filled plastic cups to the brim with cold, sweet tea and stood in a circle.

"To you," Polly said, raising her glass.

"To *us*," I corrected.

"To us," everyone chorused, then drained their glasses.

Polly was looking a little weepy, so I threw my arm over her shoulders, then rocked sideways, bumping her body with mine and throwing her off balance.

"Hey," she said, pretending to be annoyed.

"Hey," I said, and stuck out my tongue, making Polly laugh.

Happy put down her glass and clapped her hands together to get everybody's attention. "Okay, that's enough now. No more time for female bonding," she said. "Still got lots of work to do."

Happy made a shooing motion, fluttering both her hands. Polly tossed me a look that said what I was already thinking, that Happy and Pris were from the same end of the gene pool, the efficient but bossy end.

"What do you want me to do?" I asked, after Happy had finished issuing marching orders to the others. "Stock shelves? Paint walls?"

Happy frowned, considering my question. "It's so crowded in here already," she said, glancing at her wristwatch. "I don't suppose you'd be willing to pick Pris up from the airport, would you? I was planning to pick her up myself but . . ." She leaned closer and lowered her voice. "I really should stay here and supervise. These boys just don't seem to have *any* instincts about balance and spatial relationship."

Lorne, who had been shuffling backwards as he and Slip carried a heavy antique table to the front of the shop, put down his end and glared at Happy, then looked to me.

"Bring back some food," he commanded.

Chapter Fifty

Pris's flight wouldn't land for over an hour, and since Lorne's patience seemed to be dropping in direct correlation to his blood sugar, I decided to go inside and make sandwiches before I left. Pebbles and Bug, who either understood the word *food* or were able to read minds, followed me back to the house and into the kitchen, and took up stations near the refrigerator. I pulled out packets of ham, turkey, roast beef, and various types of cheese, trying to remember who had asked for what kind of meat, who wanted extra mayonnaise or none at all, and whether both Lorne and Slip had asked for Swiss cheese, or just Slip.

"Celia?"

"In the kitchen!" I called out, tucking a jar of mustard on top of the load of deli goods, anchoring it under my chin before carrying my burden to the counter, nearly tripping over Bug in the process. "Lorne? You've still got time to change your sandwich order," I said, as I heard the sound of approaching footsteps. "But tell the others that they'd better—"

I looked up and gasped.

"Calvin?"

"Hey, cupcake!"

"Calvin! You're here!" I squealed with excitement and ran to throw my arms around him, knocking two slices of bread to the floor, which were immediately gobbled by Bug and Pebbles. "Everybody will be so excited that you made it to the opening! But why didn't you let me know you were coming? I'd have picked you up at the airport."

"I wanted it to be a surprise," Calvin said, loosening his grip and pushing me back just far enough so I could see his eyes. "There's someone I want you to meet."

Calvin looked over his shoulder. "Come on back, Janie!"

A tall and stunningly beautiful woman with dark skin, enormous brown eyes, and a mass of tightly woven, silvery gray cornrowed braids that fell to the middle of her back walked into the kitchen and extended her hand. "Hello, Celia. I'm Jane Gardiner-Todd. I can't tell you how much I've been looking forward to meeting you."

She was? Why? I took Jane's hand but looked to Calvin.

"Janie and I go way back," he explained. "She was a pastry chef at a restaurant I worked in when I first moved to New York. Then she wised up, left the food world, and went back to school, eventually landing a job as an editor at Flagler and Beckwith."

My eyebrows popped. Flagler and Beckwith was a publishing house in New York, small but well respected. I swallowed to quiet the flutter in my chest. Jane's gaze was calm and steady, but the smile in her eyes told me she'd picked up on the flutter. Reading the questions in mine, she got right to the point.

"A couple of months ago," Jane said, "the publisher gave me my own imprint. That gives me a great deal of autonomy when it

comes to signing authors and making deals. Right now, I'm looking for female writers who have a strong, intimate voice and a
unique perspective on the feminine experience. I plan to publish
only three or four books a year." She paused. "Celia, I wanted to
talk to you about the possibility of including your book in that first
group."

I opened my mouth, then closed it again, trying to make sense of
what she was saying. But it *didn't* make sense. "My book? But . . .
I don't have a book."

"Yes, you do," Calvin said. "Your journal, the letters you wrote
to Peaches."

My jaw went slack. How could Jane Gardiner-Todd, an editor
from New York, have possibly read my journal? It was upstairs,
stashed away in my nightstand drawer. I hadn't written anything
in it since just before the baby shower. I hadn't read it since then either. I planned to, someday, when I felt a little less raw. But not yet.

Seeing the question in my eyes, Calvin twisted his lips and
squirmed, drawing his shoulders up toward his ears, looking simultaneously guilty and proud of himself. "It's just possible that
when I was down here last, I *might* have borrowed your journal,
made a copy, and sent it to Janie."

"Without asking my permission? Calvin! Why would you do
that?"

"Because you were never going to," Calvin retorted, tossing out
his hands. "It's a terrific book, Celia. People should read it."

Calvin flashed what I supposed he thought was a winning
smile, but I wasn't impressed. In the first place, he'd taken my
journal without permission and shared my private thoughts with a
stranger. And in the second place, he was out of his mind.

"You can't be serious," I said. "It's just a bunch of letters to a
baby that's not even mine. I might as well have been writing to an

imaginary friend. In a way, that's exactly what I was doing. It's *not* a book," I insisted.

"You're right," Jane said. "It's not a book yet. But I think it could be."

I could see just by looking at her that Jane was a serious person, calm and deliberate when choosing words, but also straightforward, the kind of woman who never pulled her punch. "Celia, what's going on here—me reading the manuscript of a book that hasn't even been submitted to me directly and then speaking to the author in person?" Jane shook her head. "That's not the way publishing works. In any given week, I send out scores of rejection letters, often to very talented writers. And I *never* read unsolicited manuscripts."

Jane wasn't telling me anything I didn't already know. During my early days in New York, between failing as a journalist and starting my blog, I'd thought I might try my hand at novel writing. I think every editor in New York turned me down, some politely and some not. My foray into fiction was spectacularly unsuccessful, even worse than my short-lived journalism career.

"I wouldn't have read your manuscript either," Jane continued, casting a glance in Calvin's direction, "but our mutual friend can be very persistent, pushy, and, if he wants to be, incredibly annoying."

I nodded, knowing exactly what she was talking about. Calvin clucked his tongue and shot us both a look, pretending to be offended.

"The only reason I agreed to take a look at your manuscript was to get Calvin off my back," Jane said. "I told him I'd only read the first ten pages and made him swear that if it didn't grab me by then, he'd quit bugging me." A slow smile spread across Jane's face. "Celia, you had me by page three. After that, I couldn't put it down. And since I'm from Charleston originally, and was coming down anyway to spend Thanksgiving with my sister, I told Calvin I'd like to meet you.

"But this isn't usual, Celia. Editors don't just show up on doorsteps, dangling publishing deals. And I'm not doing so now," she said, tilting her head slightly forward and gazing down her nose toward me, like an assistant principal who was letting a delinquent sophomore know that you only get one opportunity for a second chance. "But I do think it'd be worth your time and mine to have a talk.

"As a journal," Jane continued, "it's a delight. As a book, it needs work. But if you were willing to put in the effort, I think it could be something really special. I did feel like you were holding back at times, but those moments when you really let yourself be vulnerable were incredibly brave, and that's the kind of writing that can change lives. The structure, the whole memoir-meets-life-coaching in a letter format is, well . . ." She paused and narrowed her eyes, like she was trying to solve a math problem in her head. "It's tricky. But it's also unique and very intimate. I think we can tweak it a little, tighten things up, work on the pacing . . ." Jane's voice trailed off for a moment before she came back to herself and turned her honest, no-nonsense eyes back toward me.

"Celia, let me be clear, I am not offering you a book deal, at least right now. I am inviting you to revise it and submit to me for a second read. Then," she said, lifting her shoulders a little, "we'll see. But the raw material is there. If you're willing to put in the work, I think you have a chance to create something special, a book that readers will cherish and that we could both be proud of."

Jane looked toward me, waiting for a response, but I wasn't sure what to say. A part of me was tempted; I can't say that I wasn't feeling it. A few years ago, I'd have jumped at a chance like that, even if, as Jane made clear, it was *only* a chance. But my writing career seemed like something that had happened a long time ago in a galaxy far, far away. Now I couldn't even get a job as a technical writer. Did I really want to get my hopes up, only to suffer still another rejection? The answer was no. Even so, the flutter was there, faint but unmistakably present.

"I don't know, Jane. I'm not sure that I'm that kind of writer. I'm just a columnist. Or was."

"Talent is talent, no matter the format," Jane countered. "And you've got it. I was a huge fan of Dear Calpurnia, used to read it on the subway every morning."

The fluttering stopped, replaced by a disappointing dose of reality. Suddenly everything made sense: Jane was looking to trade on the name of someone I used to be. It was the autograph-seeking HR manager all over again.

"Jane, it was nice to meet you," I said, putting out my hand. "I'm sure you're a fantastic editor, but I'm sorry. I just can't do it."

Jane frowned. She probably wasn't used to getting turned down. "Celia, I understand that this has come out of the blue. But if I didn't believe you were up to the task, I wouldn't be talking to you."

"No, it's not that," I said. "I really *can't* do it."

"Why not?"

"Because I signed away the rights to my pen name. I'm not allowed to publish anything as Dear Calpurnia now," I said. "Not columns, not books. Nothing."

Jane's frown of confusion dissolved to a smile. "Celia, the only thing I care about is your talent. I don't care what name you write under."

"So, you're serious," I said flatly, not quite believing she could be. "It doesn't matter if the name Dear Calpurnia would appear on the cover. You would want me to write—"

"As yourself," Jane said. "As Celia Fairchild."

"Just Celia?"

Jane nodded and the flutter returned. I looked toward Calvin, who was wearing his what-did-I-tell-you face, then back to Jane.

"Okay," I said at last, more to myself than anyone else. "Okay. That, I can do."

Chapter Fifty-One

I stayed at my desk until long past midnight, writing feverishly, savoring the clarity of thought that emerges when houses are still and voices fall silent, and woke well past ten, roused by the scents of cinnamon and baking apples.

"Why didn't somebody wake me up?" I asked when I got to the kitchen and saw Calvin, Teddy, and Pris, all wearing aprons, all hard at work on Thanksgiving dinner. "I said I was going to help."

"Absolutely not," Calvin said, pointing the baster at me and shaking his head. "Pris already told me all about the duck fiasco. You're not coming within fifty feet of this turkey, or anything else."

When Calvin turned his attention back to the turkey, shoveling a small mountain of stuffing into the cavity of the enormous bird, I glared at Pris, who was peeling potatoes. She didn't come to my defense or deny her treachery, but she did have the good grace to look embarrassed.

"It's okay, Celia. You were tired and we've got this. Felicia and Beau are bringing homemade rolls and ambrosia salad when they come. Caroline and Heath are bringing a green salad and home-made cranberry sauce. Polly and Lorne are finishing up a few last-minute things in the shop. Trey is going to pick up his dad, buy a couple of bags of ice on the way, and be here by one. As far as the rest of it," Pris said, making a motion with the potato peeler, "everything's covered. Calvin's in charge of the turkey, I'm on potatoes and the green-bean casserole, and Teddy is baking the pies."

"Apple's all done, pumpkin just went into the oven," Teddy reported as he rolled out a circle of pastry. "Pecan and sweet potato are next."

"But you've got to let me do something," I protested. "It's *my* kitchen."

"Yeah, but it's our dinner," Calvin said. "And Thanksgiving only comes once a year. I'm not taking any chances."

"Fine," I huffed. "I'll be in charge of setting the table."

Pris shook her head. "Mom already did it, when she brought over the flower arrangements."

"Wait till you see them," Calvin enthused. "Chrysanthemums, yarrow, thistle, and dahlias the size of dinner plates. They're fabulous!"

I planted my hands on my hips, silently vowing I would never sleep late again. "Well, this is ridiculous. There must be *something* I can do to help."

Teddy looked up from his pastry. "Would you take Pebbles for a walk? Bug is sleeping but Pebbles is getting under my feet and making me crazy."

"I'm on it," I said, and grabbed a leash from the hook.

A dog gives you a reason for being wherever you are, but I didn't need an excuse to visit the churchyard at St. Philip's. In the wee hours of the morning, after putting down my pen and climbing into bed, I'd made up my mind to return. There were things to be said.

Fall in Charleston is different from fall in New York. The sky is blue and clear instead of gray. The air is cool rather than crisp, chilly enough for a sweater but soft as a caress, especially when the breeze picks up, rattling the heart-shaped leaves of the redbud trees, sprinkling a shower of yellow gold to guide your footsteps, like a flower girl at an autumn wedding.

The ground over Calpurnia's grave has settled now. The grass is even with the earth, a dense, spongy carpet of green with no patches of threadbare brown or sign of seed. But just to the right of the headstone, perhaps a foot away from the white marble cross, I spotted a bare circle of soil, recently disturbed. Teddy had planted a tuber there a few weeks before. In the spring, if all goes well, a bright-pink peony will bloom to soften the hard edges of marble and let people who pass by know that the woman resting beneath the ground was remembered well, and loved.

"Well. It's just something I wanted to do," Teddy said, shrugging off praise when I told him that was kind. "I wanted to tell her thank you for never forgetting, and for bringing me home."

I took the flowers I'd brought with me—mums and thistles and yarrow that I'd plucked from the two massive arrangements Happy had left on the table—then placed them in the cone-shaped vase at the foot of the grave and added my thanks. I thanked Calpurnia for bringing me up, for never forgetting, for bringing me home. I promised her I would always live well, always remember, always take care of my family, those I was bound to by blood and those I had gathered by choice. And I said I would return willingly, and often. "After all, Auntie Cal, all the best people are here."

I made a kiss-kiss noise to let Pebbles know it was time to move on. She wagged her tail and led the way, kept to the path as if she already knew where I wanted to go, and then lay down on the ground when we arrived, muzzle resting on her paws, watching and waiting patiently as I placed three more bunches of flowers at three more graves.

Standing before my father's headstone, it was harder to know what to say, hard even to know what to think, but I believe that in time I will, and that peace will come. Love is complicated. Restoration takes time.

As I turned away and walked toward home, the breeze troubled the redbud branches. The stalwart old trees of Charleston released showers of golden-yellow hearts that fell upon me like a benediction, and I knew that my restoration had begun.

Acknowledgments

With heartfelt thanks to . . .

Lucia Macro, my editor at William Morrow, for having the imagination to see what Celia could be, for insights that made Celia's story better, and for treating a stressed-out writer in the midst of assorted family crises with regard and humanity.

Liza Dawson, my literary agent, who brings the best out of me, never pulls punches, and gets so up in my face (in a good way) that it has become impossible to conceive of writing without her.

Asanté Simons, assistant editor at William Morrow, for keeping the wheels turning, and the process on track, and the writer on time (more or less).

Elizabeth and John Walsh, my sister and brother-in-law, for copyediting and beta reading above and beyond the call of duty, and extreme valor in enduring writerly mood swings, failures of courage, and generalized venting.

Brad, my husband, who hates it when I thank him but is just going to have to suck it up and deal because I wouldn't be able to do this (or anything meaningful) without his faith, love, unflagging support, and occasional well-intentioned nagging.

Faithful Readers, who are always in my thoughts as I write, and are the reason I continue to do this work I love.

About the author

2 Meet Marie Bostwick

About the book

4 Letter to the Reader
9 Reading Group Guide

Insights,
Interviews
& More . . .

Meet Marie Bostwick

Deanna Leach

MARIE BOSTWICK is a *New York Times* and *USA Today* bestselling author of heartwarming fiction for women. When not writing, she enjoys quilting, reading, cooking, spending time with family and friends, and especially playing with her grandkids. Marie travels extensively, speaking at libraries, bookstores, quilt guilds, and quilt shows.

Marie's latest endeavor is Fiercely Marie, a lifestyle blog that encourages women to live every minute and love every moment.

Marie lives in Oregon with Brad, her husband of thirty-seven years, and a beautiful but moderately spoiled Cavalier King Charles Spaniel. ∾

Letter to the Reader

Dear Reader,

The first seeds of this book were planted in my brain more than three years ago. I thought it would be fun to write a novel about an advice columnist who has insight into everybody's problems but her own, and to set the story in one of my very favorite cities, Charleston, South Carolina. "Fun" was the operative word. I would write myself a fluffy little rom-com and set it in a beautiful, historic city with fabulous food. Clearly, lots of research (and delicious meals) would be required. Fun, right?

During many moments, writing Celia's story was fun. And I did get to return to Charleston, spending hours and hours walking in what I believe to be the loveliest city in America, learning more about Celia's world, and eating a *lot* of amazing food. (If you come to see me during my book tour, ask about the night I ate two dinners back to back. Don't judge. It was research!)

But I never could have imagined what this book would become, the ways it tapped into my own experience, forcing me to pour more of myself into the story than I'd bargained for. It wasn't easy, but I believe it made Celia's story richer, and better, and more real. I hope you agree.

Writing is a labor, there's no doubt about it. After sixteen books, I keep thinking it will get easier, but it hasn't happened yet. Fortunately for me, it's a labor of love. I continue to be thankful and amazed that I am lucky enough to make my living as an artist.

As difficult as writing a novel can be, helping a novel find an audience is even harder. And, try as I might, no matter how hard I've worked or how much I believe in the book, it's not something I can do alone—I need the help of faithful, enthusiastic booklovers like you.

If you enjoyed *The Restoration of Celia Fairchild*, please help Celia find her audience by spreading the word about this book. How? Tell your friends and family! Write an online review! Propose it to your book club! Invite me to speak at your library, book festival, community event, quilt show, or craft guild! (More details about that below . . .) Word of mouth from passionate readers is the best form of advertising and the greatest compliment that any author can receive. Thank you in advance for your support. It means so much.

I do love hearing from readers. I read every note personally and do ▶

Letter to the Reader *(continued)*

my best to make sure each one receives a response. If you have a moment, drop me an email at marie@mariebostwick.com or by regular mail. My mailing address is:

Marie Bostwick
18160 Cottonwood Road
PMB 118
Bend, Oregon 97707

If you're curious about my world and daily goings-on, you can find me on Facebook at www.facebook.com/mariebostwick, and on Twitter, Pinterest, and Instagram by searching @mariebostwick. Social media is the easiest, fastest way for me to stay in touch with readers on a regular basis.

And, of course, I very much hope you'll take some time to visit my website, www.mariebostwick.com.

While you're there you can find out about my other novels (sixteen and counting!), sign up for my monthly newsletter, check my appearance calendar, and download free recipes and quilt patterns created exclusively for my readers. As I write this, there are nine free quilt patterns available on my website, companion patterns to my earlier books, most of them designed by my dear friend, Deb Tucker, Creative Kingpin at www.Studio180Design.net.

And though this is still a project in progress, I am hoping to offer a free knitting pattern, based on the blanket Celia made in the book, by the time of release. I suspect some of Calvin's recipes may be available as well. Or perhaps Caroline's Key Lime Bars? We shall see. Check my website for details. (Please note, ALL patterns and recipes are for your personal use only and may not be copied to share with others or published by *any* means, either print, electronic, or mediums yet to be invented.)

And I've got two other suggestions for things you should do when visiting www.mariebostwick.com.

First, check out my lifestyle blog, Fiercely Marie, for posts, recipes, craft projects, and other ideas to help you "live every minute and love every moment." You might even sign up for the weekly blog newsletter so you never miss a post.

Second, I make personal appearances year-round, speaking at libraries, bookstores, quilt guilds and craft shows, book festivals, and community events across the country. If you're interested in inviting me to speak in your area, you can find more information in the Press Kit section of my website, make a booking inquiry by sending an email to christie@authorsunbound.com, ▶

Letter to the Reader *(continued)*

or check out my speaker's profile at www .authorsunbound.com/marie-bostwick.

The longer I live, the more cognizant I am of the finite nature of time and how quickly it passes. I am honored and deeply grateful that you've chosen to spend some of your precious time reading *The Restoration of Celia Fairchild*.

You are the reason I get to do this work I love. Thank you for making it all possible.

Blessings,
Marie

Reading Group Guide

1. Celia says that her fans "don't want me; they want the show. They want Calpurnia." In what ways do you ever feel like an imposter in your own life, showing the people around you the "someone else" they want you to be?

2. At one point we're told that "*love* is maybe the most overused word in the English language, the second most overused being *hate*." Do you believe this is true? Why or why not?

3. At the beginning of the novel, Celia seems to have a love-hate relationship with Charleston, her hometown. Discuss the ways you feel about the town in which you grew up.

4. Celia decides that "the antidote to chaos is routine." Discuss times that routine has become important in your life. When does "routine" become a rut you can't get out of?

5. Celia's aunt Calpurnia made her feel loved and important. Was there someone growing up— not your parents—who made you feel this way? ▶

6. Celia blames herself for the rift with Calpurnia, but of course it's not her fault. What do you think Calpurnia's plans were? What do you think made her behave the way she did? How did the kidnapping tie into Calpurnia's issues as a hoarder?

7. Against all common sense, Celia gives Lorne Holcomb a second chance. Do you feel we give people enough second chances in life? When does it become more important to not give someone those chances?

8. In what ways does Celia's drive for a child tie into her childhood?

9. Celia has the family she was born with and the family she creates around her. Discuss the concept of family. Are our blood ties truly "thicker" than our friendships? Do you feel you have a second family in addition to your relatives? Can the family you create be healthier than the family you were born with?

10. In what ways is Celia "restored" as the book progresses? ∽

Discover great authors, exclusive offers, and more at hc.com.